Also by Meir Shalev

FICTION

The Loves of Judith

A Pigeon and a Boy

Fontanelle

Alone in the Desert

But a Few Days

Esau

The Blue Mountain

NONFICTION

*My Russian Grandmother and
Her American Vacuum Cleaner*

*Beginnings: Reflections on
the Bible's Intriguing Firsts*

Elements of Conjuration

Mainly About Love

The Bible for Now

CHILDREN'S BOOKS

Roni and Nomi and the Bear Yaacov

Aunt Michal

The Tractor in the Sandbox

How the Neanderthal Discovered the Kebab

A Louse Named Thelma

My Father Always Embarrasses Me

Zohar's Dimples

A Lion in the Night

TWO SHE-BEARS

TWO SHE-BEARS

··

MEIR SHALEV

TRANSLATED FROM THE HEBREW BY

Stuart Schoffman

SCHOCKEN BOOKS

New York

Translation copyright © 2016 by Meir Shalev

All rights reserved. Published in the United States by Schocken Books, a division of Penguin Random House LLC, New York, and distributed in Canada by Random House of Canada, a division of Penguin Random House Canada Limited, Toronto. Originally published in Israel as *Shtayim Dubim* by Am Oved Publishers Ltd., Tel Aviv, in 2013. Copyright © 2013 by Am Oved Publishers Ltd., Tel Aviv.

Schocken Books and colophon are registered trademarks of Penguin Random House LLC.

Library of Congress Cataloging-in-Publication Data
Names: Shalev, Meir, author. Schoffman, Stuart, translator.
Title: Two she-bears : a novel / Meir Shalev ;
translated from the Hebrew by Stuart Schoffman.
Other titles: Shetayim dubim. English.
Description: New York : Schocken Books, 2016.
Identifiers: LCCN 2016001663. ISBN 978-0-8052-4329-1
(hardcover : alk. paper). ISBN 978-0-8052-4330-7 (ebook).
ISBN 978-0-8052-4330-7 (export edition).
Classification: LCC PJ5054.S384 S5413 2016. DDC 892.43/6—dc23.
LC record available at lccn.loc.gov/2016001663.

www.schocken.com

Jacket images: (top) *Jewish Refugee, Vienna* by David Jagger (detail), Nottingham City Museums and Galleries/Bridgeman Images; (middle) Tree © CSA/iStock; (bottom) *A Jewish Bride* by Isidor Kaufmann (detail), private collection, photo © Christie's Images/Bridgeman Images; (background) Kevin Clogstoun/Getty Images
Jacket design by Janet Hansen

Printed in the United States of America
First Edition

2 4 6 8 9 7 5 3 1

FOR AVRAHAM YAVIN

With love and thanks

TWO SHE-BEARS

ONE

....

THE TELEPHONE CALL

The cell phone rang. The tall, beefy guy peered at the screen and said to the woman across the table: "Gotta take this. Be right back."

He went outside, trying to suck in his potbelly. He wasn't accustomed to it, and it kept surprising him: images in the mirror, pressure on his belt, the reaction of his partner as he moved atop her body.

"Hello?"

The familiar voice replied, "I counted nine rings. You made me wait."

"Sorry. I was in a restaurant and came outside."

"We have a problem."

"I hear you."

"I will explain it to you intelligently and carefully, and you will attempt to respond the same way."

"Okay."

"You remember the nature walk we took?"

"This morning?"

"What did I just say? Intelligently and carefully. No times, no dates, no hours."

"Sorry."

"It was a nice walk."

Silence.

"You didn't hear what I said? It was a nice walk."

"I heard you."

"You didn't respond."

"You wanted intelligent and careful. Whaddya want?"

"What kind of language is that? Say: 'What sort of response?'"

"Okay."

"'Okay' is not enough. Say what I said."

The young man contracted his belly and released it at once. "What sort of response?"

"You could have said whether you agree or disagree with what I said."

"About what?"

"About our nature walk."

"I agree. It was a very nice nature walk."

"You should have answered immediately. Twice you made me wait. First the ringing and now the response."

"Sorry."

"Don't you ever make me wait."

"Okay."

"Do you remember where we relaxed at the end of the walk?"

"Sure do. In the wadi under the big carob tree."

"What did I say? Intelligently and carefully. No times, no places, no names."

"I didn't say names."

"You said 'carob,' no?"

The young man gently made a fist with his right hand and studied it. It was wrapped in a white bandage, and only his fingertips protruded. His eyes, small and close together, shut for a moment and opened, as from pain that recurs when its origin is recalled.

I visualize him in my mind. He stands outside the restaurant, considers his boots, lifts his left leg a little, rubs the shiny square boot tip on the right leg of his pants.

And I hear his interlocutor continue: "If you had only said 'carob'— that's one thing. Only 'big'—not so terrible. But 'the big carob,' noun and adjective and the definite article—this is serving it up on a plate.

Bon appétit, please eat. Not just any tree: a carob. Not just any carob, a big carob. And just not any big carob: the big carob in the wadi. This is a wording that limits the possibilities. This is why language was invented, so things will be clear. But for us, clear is very bad. Do you understand?"

"Yes. I'm sorry."

"Enough apologizing. Just pay attention."

"Okay."

"Good. Now the point. The point is we forgot something there."

"The gas gizmo you made us tea on?"

"More important."

"The sugar spoon?"

"Would we be having a conversation like this about a spoon? Think back and remember. For once use your brain properly. Even a small brain can achieve results if operated correctly. And when you do remember what it is, don't say it. Just say: 'I know what you are talking about.'"

"I'm thinking."

Silence.

"Again you're making me wait."

Silence.

"I remember. I know what you are talking about."

"So go there, look for it, find it, and bring it to me."

"How urgent?"

"If someone else finds it before us, it will be very bad."

"I'm outta here in half a minute. Go looking with the flashlight."

"A lost cause. That's what you are. A lost cause. 'I will go and look.' Say it: 'I will go and look.' I want for once to hear you speak properly."

"I will go and look."

"And don't make me mad anymore."

"Sorry."

"And don't go there now with a flashlight. It's dark now. Someone could see the light from far away. Go very early tomorrow."

"First thing in the morning."

"At dawn. And don't park in the usual place. Find another spot, continue on foot, get there at first light, and start looking."

"Okay."

"How's your hand?"

"Okay."

"It hurts?"

"Less."

"You put on a bandage?"

"Why would I?"

"So you shouldn't get rabies."

"Okay."

"And let out your belly already. I can feel it without even seeing you. Go on, send your girlfriend home and go to sleep. You have to get up early tomorrow. She doesn't need to know what time you leave."

TWO

....

GETTING ORGANIZED

1

How harsh the revenge would be, and how simple it was to prepare. The avenger's wife, standing behind him, saw and understood every detail, which reminded her of preparations for a hike, like the ones they had made together years before. Vigorously shaking out the backpack, which was glad to emerge from storage. Checking the laces on hiking boots that had all but abandoned hope. Roll call of buttons on the work shirt.

She also saw the differences: instead of the delicacies he took along to please her on those hikes of theirs, he now took a modest amount of simple food—slices of bread, hard-boiled eggs, unpeeled cucumbers, a container of sour cream. The word "ascetic" came quickly to mind.

And she noticed other details: He peeled the eggs here, in the kitchen of their home, lest telltale bits of shell be left in the field, revealing human presence. He paid no heed to the salami, a constant companion on those hikes, which yearned to come along. Its aroma would likely attract dogs, and after the dog its owner would likely appear. He's making the Turkish coffee here at home, she observed, and pouring it into the old thermos. A campfire, a gas cooker, fresh coffee boiling, would be seen and heard and smelled from a distance.

And she remembered: Back then, on those hikes, he'd cook up the coffee on his tiny, meticulous fires. He boiled, stirred, and poured, served her with the gestures of a flirty waiter. They had a little coffee-pot, with a long funny handle, which came with them on every hike. But now this too—Where is it? she suddenly wondered, twelve years since last seen—didn't go into the pack.

She knew: Something big and terrible was about to happen. Revenge would be taken, blood would be redeemed, someone would die, maybe more than one. Nevertheless a smile dawned on her face, as if in sympathy with the coffeepot: Sooty and snubbed, he's not taking you along? No big deal. He's doing the same to me. Like David in the Bible leaving two hundred men behind as he unsheathed his sword, boiling with vengeance, to confront Nabal.

She drew a bit closer. Did he sense her? Did he still have that eerie ability to sense what was going on behind his back? Whether he did or not, he did not turn around, did not look at her. She came closer, keenly and pleasantly aware of the two-centimeter difference in their height, and smiled inside: There is no other husband in the moshava who is shorter than his wife, and surely no other who loves her for it.

Once, before the disaster that befell them, when they still walked together in the street—What a beautiful couple, everyone said—he would lean his head on her shoulder, in a role reversal that embarrassed people who watched them, but pleased and amused her. "It's very important," he kept saying back then, "to make your lover laugh." In their Ten Commandments, which he wrote out and hung on the bedroom wall, the Third, Fourth, and Ninth were identical: "Entertain thy wife."

Where'd he get that? she wondered when she first saw the words, and again now, in retrospect. Several years ago, on a particularly bad morning, she tore the commandments from the wall, ripped them up, and threw them in the trash. He did not write her new ones, and she did not forget the old ones—they still hang on the walls of her heart.

His back got so broad, she said to herself now.

On those hikes of theirs, they always walked side by side, but when the road narrowed to a path, she slowed down, so he could go first. She would look at his back, thin and boyish, and he would turn around and say to her, "Why're you walking behind me? You lead."

"I don't know where."

"Go with the trail, it'll take you."

"It's not marked."

"It is marked, but not by trail signs. It's marked by footprints, trampled grass, stones moved from their normal place, shiny patches on the rocks. You just have to look and see. And it's also marked by its own logic, that's the most important thing. Trails have logic. If you comprehend it, you find the trail."

"I'm on vacation today. I have no will to comprehend and no head for logic. You do the comprehending and I'll enjoy the scenery."

"Not a chance. I'll walk behind you and look at your butt. It's much more beautiful and I also deserve enjoyment."

Though he was her husband, she gave him a look that mothers give to their adolescent sons: a look of puzzlement, hope, anxiety diluted by amusement and curiosity. She never had an adolescent son, and ever since the disaster she has known she won't have one. But for many years she has been a teacher at the local high school and she knows the look that mothers give their young sons and she now gives her husband.

I feel fluttering inside. Have I any more sons in my body? Is there hope for me?

The beautiful biblical words tug the womb and the heart: "Could I have a husband tonight and bear sons?" A husband? My man? You?

2

They had done a lot of hiking. At first the two of them alone, later on with their son. First when he floated and tossed in her belly, later on wrapped in a homemade snuggly, dozing on her shoulder and breast, then in a baby carrier improvised by his father at the workshop of his army reserve unit. He stitched it together and bore it on his back, on this very back that now faced her.

Her tearful eyes were flooded with pictures. The son, a tiny cavalryman, riding on his father's back. The father galloping, neighing like a horse, the mother hurrying after them: "Be careful! Please. He's scared. He'll fall. Be careful!"

But her prophecy did not come to pass. True, the child was frightened, but he enjoyed his fright, as children do. He laughed. He grew. Stood on his feet. Took his first steps. Fell as babies fall and got up again. His parents' agility was apparent even then—in his step, his stance, his stumbles, his smile.

In the beginning they hiked with him nearby, in the scrubland of poppies and chrysanthemums east of the moshava and the patches of pink flax on the hill beyond the avocado grove. Later to the little pond, hidden from the world, where they would head on a hot summer's day and where her older brother had taught her to swim and dive when she was a girl. And when the son began to walk confidently they also took him to Grandpa Ze'ev's wadi, which is what they called the wadi where his big carob tree stood—Grandpa's big carob, to be precise.

There, in that wadi, she and her brother had hiked with their grandfather when they were children. There he taught them to identify wildflowers, to locate and gather their seeds. Under that carob tree he told them a story that later on she would write down for her son: the story about the prehistoric man who lived in the nearby cave, the one with the deep pit, where sometimes a wandering sheep or goat would fall in, and afterward there'd be an awful stench.

And from that wadi she would later hike with her husband to the gullies beyond, climbing and descending—"We hauled ass north," he would say in his army slang—and go where they would not see another soul. They loved to make love outdoors and had their favorite secret places. And from there onward and upward to the top of the hill where they could see down the other side, which for them was a pleasantly familiar view, and for their son a strange and distant and inviting and wonderful world: Come closer, touch and smell, come and fill the cabinet of your memory.

And then the two of them, just the father and son, began to take hikes without her. "Hikes for guys," he would say, and one day he even added: "Girls not invited."

That's what he said, and I just laughed. I didn't imagine what was coming. I never had that famous intuition, the foreknowledge attributed to women, especially to mothers. Even on the day of the disaster itself I didn't sense a thing.

Hikes for guys. Just the two of them together. The little guy has to learn from the big guy all the nonsense that a father has to teach his son—how to light a campfire, to know which leaves could be used for tea, to walk barefoot on the ground—and girls were likely to get nervous: "What if he steps on broken glass?" And "What if there's a snake?" And "Even Grandpa Ze'ev always walks in his work boots."

"If a snake shows up we'll deal with it, right, Neta?"—that's what we called him, our son, who grew up complaining: "They laugh at me in kindergarten. Why did you give me a girl's name?"

"Laugh back at them."

And how to find the North Star and drive the old pickup truck—Neta on his father's lap, his three-, four-, five-, and six-year-old hands gripping the wheel with excitement—and how to tie a hitch knot, and improve night vision by looking to the side, and to identify and recognize everything the ear hears and the finger feels and the nose smells and the eye sees: "This is a porcupine quill, and this is a snakeskin, feel how delicate and thin it is. Touch it, Neta, don't be afraid, it's just his skin, he's not here, he shed his skin and slithered away. And even if he were here—I'm here, protecting you.

"You hear that, Neta? Listen carefully—that's the cawing of a jaybird and that's the trilling of a falcon and that's the wailing of a curlew and that's the chirping of a finch and that's the tsk-tsking of a robin redbreast. Every year a redbreast like that comes to our yard, always to the same tree. We planted the tree, that's true, but in his opinion it's his tree. Now smell: this yellow flower is called inula. Your mother thinks it stinks. Smell it and tell me what you think. It's like camphor, not bad. Close your eyes. You should smell things with your eyes closed. Just with your nose. You can remember smells better than what you see and what you hear. This smell is inula, this is common rue, this is the mastic tree, this is thyme, and, best of all—sage. Sage is our friend. If you can remember all the names, I'll tell Grandpa Ze'ev and he'll be really happy. Maybe he'll take you to the big carob tree in his wadi and the cave next to it, and he'll also teach you the names of plants and tell you about the caveman that once lived there and make a wooden club for

you too, in case a bad dog might come or a poisonous snake or a bad
person. And when you get a little bigger, he'll teach you to shoot his old
Mauser and hit the bull's-eye.

"And these are the tracks of a hyena, it looks like a big dog, with a
low butt and high shoulders. Look, Neta: the footprints of the front legs
are bigger than the footprints of the back legs. What are you laughing
about? Daddy said 'butt'? You say 'butt' too. We'll say it together: Butt.
Butt. Butt. Butt.

"And here's another thing, really interesting: this stone. Every stone
in the field has an upper side and a lower side, the side of the earth and
darkness and the side of the sun and light. You see? The underside is
smooth. There's only a little dirt on it and a bit of spiderweb. And the
top, the sunlight side, is rough. Touch it, feel this. This is called lichen.
If a stone has lichen on the bottom it means that somebody turned it
upside down. Somebody picked it up and didn't put it back the right
way."

"Nature looks like one big mess," he told her more than once, "but
it's not. Everything in nature is in its place." And she smiled to herself
as she remembered, because that's what he would say when they were
making love: "What a mess in this bed! One leg there, one leg here, and
this little friend, what's he doing here? Let's put him in place. Here.
Much better when everything's organized."

"So come, Neta, let's put the stone back in its place. Here, the way
it was. You see these little sprouts? How here they're totally white and
only their tips are green? They sprouted underneath, crawled sideways
to escape, and only when they got into the light did they become green.
Everything white was under the stone, and everything green was outside. And that tells us one more thing—that it was moved recently. This
is interesting, right, Neta? We're like police detectives."

"Hikes for guys," he told her. He looked at their son, their son looked
at him, and the two of them—like generous winners—at her. Who could
top a pair of guys like this, a father and son, smiling at each other, sharing secrets and schemes? Hikes for guys on hills in the south, hikes for
guys in the big cornfields north of the moshava, where they picked fresh
ears of the sweet corn she loved so much.

"We'll roast them for Mommy on the fire. Come here, I'll show you how."

"I brought you this, Mommy, is it yummy?"

"Eat, just for you."

I ate. I enjoyed. I got angry.

And hikes for guys along the rocks on the seashore, and over the rocks behind the Crusader fortress, where at Hanukkah time the cyclamen are already in bloom. "Lookee here, what a miracle," Grandpa Ze'ev told me when he was alive and I was a girl. "These flowers are blooming, and their green leaves haven't even pushed through the dirt. This only happens here, by us. So close to the village and nobody knows. Just you and me."

And a hike for guys in the desert, for the first and last time, twelve years ago exactly, the hike after which they never hiked again, not the guys alone or me with them—and to tell the truth, we never did anything together again. Twelve years have passed, which for me seem like a hundred.

3

I see him getting ready to go. I know him and don't know him. I again take note of the changes in him. Were it not for the disaster that caused them I could happily smile inside. Despite the time gone by and everything that happened, I still look young, as I see reflected in the mirror and the eyes of my students and their parents, the misty gaze of men and women in the street. And he, you, my man—that's what I called you then—became a different man, you lost your looks.

I know: It can't just be dismissed as aging. Aging is slow, always preserving some youthful features, which is gratifying at first and, later—when it's clear that they linger only to remind us and taunt us—is annoying. Whereas in your case the change is complete, like an insect's metamorphosis.

And I look at him and again count the ways: His smile is erased. His fire, his eternal flame, is extinguished. His golden skin, the delight of my fingers and eyes, has paled and chilled and lost its luster. His good smell, the myrrh of early manhood, has evaporated. His body—once the body of a youth—became thick and clumsy. He didn't get fat and weak; he actually got stronger. His arms, once shapely and nimble, became the heavy arms of a bear with a fearsome hug.

My man, my first husband, golden and lean, has disappeared. A second husband—white and thick and different—has taken his place. His thickness is pure power. His whiteness is the whiteness of death. The eye of the sun does not tan him, and human eyes are averted.

I remember: One day he cut himself, and blood flowed from his finger. He didn't even look at me when I bandaged it, but I was filled with joy: He's alive. His blood is as red as ever. If only I could, I would have taken that second white and strange husband and cut him open, birthing my other husband from inside him.

4

I looked at him, all set to go: I was confident that he had prepared thoroughly and happy for the small details that had returned to his mind and his hands. He put the food into two plastic containers that he took from the kitchen cupboard. He tucked the containers in his pack along with two bottles of water and did something, strange and new, that he'd never done before on those hikes of ours—he wrote down on a slip of paper all the items he was taking. Like a grocery list: "6 slices of bread," "2 cucumbers," "3 granola bars," "1 sour cream," "2 hard-boiled eggs." Also "2 plastic containers," "thermos," "spoon," "2 water bottles," "backpack," "toilet paper," "this note," and "pen."

He stuck the note and pen in his pocket, then surprised me with one more thing: he took our thick little bath mat and walked out of the house, taking it and the backpack to the plant nursery.

I followed him: the wife knowing the events to come, the mother imagining them, the granddaughter happily anticipating—Come, bring it on, breathe life into our dry bones—and watching and remembering every detail. From the tool rack in the nursery he took items not taken on an ordinary hike: pruning shears, a sinister Japanese folding handsaw, a roll of green duct tape.

The slow, purposeful pace of his activity suddenly quickened. More items were added to the list and the backpack—a spool of cord, a pocket-knife, and, of course, the constant friend: the small pickax used for uprooting the bulbs of wildflowers, which in his hands, I knew, was likely to be a terrible weapon. All these he wrote down on the slip of paper, adding "car keys" to the list. He pocketed the keys, went out to the pickup truck in the carport, and put the pack on the backseat.

Now he returned to the tool rack, took down the big scissors, and cut the bath mat into two equal pieces. He bored holes along their edges and attached pieces of the cord and placed them near the knapsack. From a pile in the corner of the carport he pulled a faded-green tarpaulin with metal-rimmed holes along the sides and slipped pieces of cord through them too and fastened them with knots. He put the canvas tarp in the back of the pickup and threw in a leaf rake and small broom; he rinsed out and cleaned the portable sprayer, filled it with water, pumped the compressor, sprayed some water on the ground, and then released the pressure valve, opened the tank, poured plastic glue into the water, closed and shook it, and compressed it again, put it in the back of the pickup truck, and added it to his list, along with "tarp," "rake," "broom," and "sheep-shoes." What sheep-shoes are and why one wears them I discovered only the next day, when he returned from the place he had gone and from the deed he had gone there to do.

Now he turned to the old storeroom in the yard, a small wooden shed, a vestige of the early days of Grandpa Ze'ev and Grandma Ruth in the village, and emerged after a few minutes with a bundle in his hand: something long, rolled up in an old blanket with faded flower embroidery and tied with rope, like a corpse in a shroud bound at the ankles and neck.

He laid the bundle on the floor by the backseat of the pickup, wrote down "rope," "blanket," and "*the* rifle," the definite article. He bent down and locked the front wheel hubs manually the way guys do on trips for guys in treacherous off-road terrain, then sat down in the driver's seat and shoved a hand in his shirt pocket, suddenly recalling the pack of cigarettes that had sat there for years, which he tossed with perfect aim into the trash bin.

I was thrilled: something in the movement of his hand reminded me of his old agility.

I said, "Eitan."

He did what he hadn't done for twelve years: he looked into my eyes.

I asked, "Eitan, where are you going?"

He didn't answer.

"Don't worry. I won't tell anybody."

Silence.

"You want me to come with you? Do you remember how to drive? You haven't driven in twelve years."

Silence. Ignition.

He remembers, of course he remembers, I reassured myself. A man like him would not forget. Not how to drive, how to walk on the trail. Not camouflage, ambush, sharpshooting.

"Eitan," I said again.

Again he looked at me.

"I know where you're going. I know what you're going to do. Just know that I'm with you in this but be careful. Please."

The pickup moved forward, exited the gate of the nursery.

"And come back on time," I called out. "You hear me? We have a funeral tomorrow."

He drove off. Not to the right, to the main road, but left, into the fields.

5

I imagine: He got on the road a few kilometers later and met up with the wadi around sunset. He didn't turn on the pickup's headlights, kept driving slowly for another few hundred meters, up to the parallel wadi. Here he downshifted twice, and without braking or signaling he turned right onto a short dirt road that led to a pumping station at the edge of the gully. Without stopping, he expertly downshifted the sticks to second low gear and inched the pickup forward as slowly as possible, so as not to make noise or spray pebbles or leave deep tire tracks.

I imagine: A few dozen meters before the pumping station he swung behind a stand of oak trees and came to a halt with a gentle pull on the hand brake. He switched the interior light to the off position, opened the door, extended his legs, and keeping his feet in the air he wrapped the pieces of bath mat around his boots. He tightened the cords in a diagonal pattern and stepped out of the vehicle in his covered footgear. He hung the knapsack and the spray gun on the branch of an oak, and the rifle—concealed in its blanket like a snake—on an adjacent branch, picked up some stones, and positioned them around the pickup truck, which he covered with the tarp till it vanished underneath.

As the sunlight waned he hastened his activity. He tied the tarp to the stones he had arranged, sprayed it with diluted glue, scattered fistfuls of dirt and dry leaves, which stuck to it at once. With the rake he quickly erased any trace of a moved stone, a footprint, or tire tread, then lifted an edge of the tarp and slipped the sprayer and rake under it. He stepped back a bit and checked his handiwork, then hoisted the knapsack on his shoulder, picked up the rifle wrapped in the blanket, emerged from the oak trees, and headed up the wadi.

For years he hadn't walked like this, on a narrow, dark, and rocky trail, not cleared by pickax and bulldozer or leveled by steamroller but blazed by the paws of animals and the shoes of humans and the hooves of time. But his feet instantly remembered the art of quiet, confident nighttime walking that left no imprint except upon his face: an old, inscrutable smile, slightly askew, of facial muscles that for twelve years had not smiled nor kissed nor spoken, just ate a bit and drank a bit and clenched one jaw to another.

I know the route. I've walked it more than once. After a kilometer and a half, at the third bend of the wadi, he climbed southward to the lower shelf of the ridge, lay down a moment on his belly, listened and looked, proceeded in a slow diagonal crouch, and went down the slope. He quickly arrived at the mastic tree and the oak that grew side by side a few dozen meters above a sharp turn in the adjacent wadi. The oak is taller and its branches are wider, and the mastic is typically small and thick, its aromatic branches bunched together, kissing the ground.

Here he stopped, set the rifle and knapsack on a nearby rock, turned to look at the big carob tree he knew well, which grew in the wadi below him. In the darkness the tree looked like a huge black lump, which sharpened when he looked at it sideways and blended into the night when he gazed at it directly. In a few more hours, when he will lie, rifle in hand, in the hiding place he has prepared, the sun will rise from behind him, he will see everything clearly, and the man who will come, a man whose name and face he doesn't know, but for whom he waits and whose life he intends to take, will be blinded by its rays if he looks toward him.

He undid the rope from the blanket and took out the rifle from its folds: a veteran Mauser, heavy, accurate, more than a hundred years old, fired by German soldiers and Turkish soldiers and Grandpa Ze'ev, and he himself had shot it more than once. He inserted it between branches of the mastic tree and propped it on its stock. He took the small pickax from his knapsack and put it on a rock, spread out the blanket and sat on it, untied and removed the covers from his boots and laid them on the ground.

He took off the boots, placed them on top of their covers, and rolled his socks and stuck them in the shoes to deter snakes and scorpions. He lay down on half the blanket, covered himself with the other half, reached out and felt the rifle on his left and pickax on the right, pulled over a fieldstone, placed it under his head, and took a deep breath. He had a few more hours of darkness ahead, and he hoped that tonight, perhaps, he might have a reprieve from his insomnia.

I put the little pieces together: People do not walk here at night; wild animals will not approach him. If wandering dogs do not come near, if nobody notices the pickup truck he camouflaged—everything will go as planned. The single shot he will fire in the morning is not a problem: there are hunters in the area, and there are soldiers on leave who shoot in the woods near their villages. No one will go out looking for the shooter or contact the police because of one shot—and if they do, no policeman will bother to come.

He was sure he would hear birdsong before sunrise, but to be on the safe side he fixed an hour in his mind so that the birds of his body would wake him too. Despite what was about to happen he felt at ease, a surprising, forgotten sense of well-being. It was good to know that he was about to do what was right and necessary. Good to know that he had the talent and the tools to do it well. Good to lie on the ground and feel its touch, hard and soft at the same time. To close his eyes under the dark, open sky, to breathe air that streamed from the starry heavens. And good to feel again the ability to feel what was good—I'm back, it's me, as he would say when he would surprise me with a hug from behind, when he came home, to the bed, to my flesh. That's what he always said to me: "I'm back. It's me."

I feel: his head resting on the stone pillow, his eyes canvassing the vastness of space. The sky curving above him like a woman. Soon he will touch her through closed eyelids and curtains of darkness. His body is heavy and soft as he sinks into sleep. So easily, for the first time in twelve years, unbothered by dreams.

We awoke at the appointed hour. For a few seconds we lay still. Eitan there, on the ground overlooking the carob in Grandpa Ze'ev's wadi, and I here in our house, in bed. He with eyes shut, ears sharp, listening to the familiar set of predawn sounds—Is anything different? Disrupted?—and I wait for his return, my eyes shut like his and my ears also perked: distant loudspeakers of a muezzin, joined by a chorus of wailing jackals, and then the noises nearby—the joyful screeches of the stone curlews, celebrating the end of night, followed by the jaybirds from the wadi below him and our jays from here at the plant nursery.

It's good to wake up and hear birds. To open your eyes under open, dark skies with their eastern fringe turning pale, then fiery gold. It's good to feel the tiny marvelous movement under your back. It is the earth, turning slightly on its axis, presenting a new meridian to the rosy fingers of dawn.

Another smile shone on his face. Twelve years without a smile, and suddenly—two in a single day.

We sat down at the same time. My legs feeling the chill of the floor tiles. His legs gathered beneath him on the blanket on the ground. He took a bottle of water from his pack, poured some into his hands and rinsed his eyes, shook out his socks and put them on, turned his boots upside down and shook them too, put them on, and wrapped them with the sheep-shoes he had prepared. He stepped a few yards away and pissed into a wild poterium, taking care that the stream be inaudible and its puddle unseen. He put the pillow stone back in its place, picked up the rifle, and went down to the carob tree. He examined the ground beneath it, peered into and sniffed the little cave on the bank of the wadi and the pit inside.

The sky grew lighter. Eitan returned to his hiding place and sipped a little coffee from his thermos. I got up and switched on the electric kettle, and while the water boiled I went to the bathroom. He closed the thermos and put it back in his pack, took out the toilet paper, took the rifle and pickax with him, walked about thirty meters, and dug a shallow hole. Afterward he came back, took out the small Japanese folding saw, the pruning shears, and the duct tape and headed for the mastic tree.

I made myself some tea. I drank it and looked out the window at our plant nursery. Our big mulberry tree loomed blackly behind it. Soon, when the light was better, it would be green. Eitan lifted two limbs of the mastic tree, thick branches that touched the ground. He spread them apart and crawled inside, as far as he could go. He reached up and sawed off the two branches at a downward diagonal, so the shiny wood would not attract attention or curiosity. He pulled the branches away from the tree, then returned to the empty space within the foliage and began pruning interior branches with the shears, shoving them between other branches, fashioning himself a small cell in which to hide.

A light wind arose; more birds joined in their sisters' morning choir. He cut off pieces of green duct tape and pasted them to the stumps of the sawed branches. He put the shears in his pocket, emerged from the tree, returned the saw and tape to the knapsack, and pushed it and the rifle into the hiding space. He crawled inside, spread out the blanket as much as possible, knelt down on it, and pulled toward him the two large branches he had sawed off, their leaves facing outward.

Now he sat in this tiny cell, whose walls and ceiling were leaves and branches and its floor a blanket and embroidered flowers and dirt, and he ate and drank. When he was done he scratched from his list the container of sour cream, one egg, two slices of bread, a cucumber, and one granola bar. He put the paper and pen back in his pocket and shoved the granola-bar wrapper and empty sour-cream container and spoon into a separate section of his knapsack.

Behind him the horizon was bright. He moved the barrel of the rifle closer to the edge of the foliage, looked through the gunsight. At this distance he would not need a sniper's rifle. He would do fine with the old Mauser, with its ordinary sights, its famous accuracy, and his own experience. He took out the shears and delicately snipped, one at a time, a few leaves that interfered with his line of view and put the shears back in his pack.

The sun had almost risen. He again peered through the branches at the wadi and its big carob tree. All he had left to do was wait. The waiting was hard, soporific, boring, but clearly it would not continue for long; he had waited longer in the past, had experienced situations that were far more complicated and dangerous. And indeed at 6:30 a.m. he sensed that his waiting would very soon be over. First in his gut, then his ears: a stone dislodged from its place, striking another stone and ringing out in the silence, the sliding sole of a shoe, an angry curse.

The man came into view, different from the image he had drawn in his mind: a tall, beefy fellow, his right hand in a bandage. His neck thick and strong, but his belly soft and jiggling a bit under his tight shirt. One of those people whose feet are smaller than expected and whose dark sunglasses hide their eyes more than protect them.

The man wore black pants, a bright yellow shirt, and a black leather jacket styled like a sport coat, left unbuttoned. On his feet he wore short, square-toed boots with thin leather soles, testifying to the worst kind of inexperience, a mixture of exaggerated self-confidence and sheer laziness. Eitan saw no weapon in his hand, in his belt, or under his open jacket, but over his shoulder was a small leather bag that might contain a pistol.

He looked at him from his secret hideout, cleansed his mind of hatred and malice so that his victim would not sense his existence or intention, and again reminded himself that the deed he was about to do was not an evil deed. Evil sends waves into the distance, and a person whose heart is evil can easily feel the evil heart of another. But the good and the true and the right things to do are hidden and quiet and do not give away their owner even when he is very close.

The man again slipped on rocks damp with dew, and each time he stumbled he cursed aloud. Eitan followed him with his gaze and said to himself that this was the only way to meet such a vile person—a first and last encounter, in his very last moments. He allowed him to reach the big carob, saw him bend over, explore, and examine, and he knew this was the man he was waiting for.

The man knelt down and crawled on all fours, moved stones and turned them over; Eitan knew he would not bother to return them to their places. And when he despaired of his quest—he knew he would despair—and took a cell phone from his jacket pocket—he knew he would want to report to the one who sent him—he fired the shot he had come to fire.

THREE

....

The doorbell rings.

Ruta gets up, goes to the door, opens it.

Ruta: Hello, you're Varda?

Varda: Yes, pleased to meet you.

Ruta: I'm Ruta Tavori, I'm the one you spoke to. Varda what?

Varda: Varda Canetti.

Ruta: Pleased to meet you too. Are you related to Elias Canetti?

Varda: Pardon me?

Ruta: Apparently not the same family. If you were, you would know.

Varda: Canetti is my husband's name. They're a big family. I don't know all of his relatives.

Ruta: I like him very much. No, not your husband, I'm sorry, excuse me, don't misunderstand me, I don't even know your husband. It's Canetti the author I love, actually I'm not sure, I don't know him either. It's his books that I love. Come in, we'll sit in the kitchen if you don't mind. The kitchen is my place in this house. Not that I'm such a great cook, I just love to sit in the kitchen, to write in the kitchen, to receive guests in the kitchen, to correct exams in the kitchen. To correct exams because I'm a teacher, as you probably heard from everyone you've met in our moshava, a homeroom teacher for the eleventh grade and also

I teach Bible. I talk too fast, right? So remind me what this meeting is about.

Varda: I'm writing a research study of the history of the Yishuv, and I'm interviewing people from the first families of the moshava.

Ruta: The history of the pre-State Yishuv in general or of this place in particular?

Varda: The old agricultural settlements of Baron de Rothschild. I'm meeting with people in three moshavot.

Ruta: Fine. I don't know what history of the Yishuv you'll find in the other two, but here you won't be disappointed. This moshava is no big deal, but the history is really good. So sit, make yourself comfortable. The table is big, you can write, tape the conversation, drink tea. If you stay till the evening, you'll also get something to eat. That's how it is with us in the moshava. Receiving guests properly. They wanted to establish a Jewish settlement here, and we turned out to be an Arab village. With hospitality, clans, honor, land, revenge. And after four and a half generations everyone here is related, and every family has a lemon tree in the garden, grapes and pomegranates and figs, and a big pecan tree is a must. Except that with us it's usually the breed of pomegranate called Wonderful, and with Arabs it's a sweet pomegranate. And doves on the roof and chickens in the yard. Sorry, I made a mistake before, I said "pecan," but at our house the pecan is a mulberry. And also here underneath every house is a cache of weapons, going back to the Turkish times, except we don't fire in the air at weddings.

Yes, yes, you heard right. Stockpiles of weapons. We have hunting rifles and war booty weapons, all kinds of antiques. My grandfather had an old Czech rifle, from before the days of the State. It's lucky he's dead. If he heard me calling his Mauser a Czech rifle, he'd be horrified. "There's no such thing as a Czech rifle!" he once yelled at me. "What those morons here call a Czech rifle is a Mauser, which is German."

I'm sorry, Varda, you're still standing. Sit, please, sit. Not here. Sit on this chair so you can see me from my prettier side. You still haven't told me the exact topic, the title of your research.

Varda: "Issues of Gender in the Moshavot of the Baron."

Ruta: A fine title.

Varda: I've already spoken with a few people here, older than you, and they all said that your grandfather—Ze'ev Tavori, is that correct?—that there are some very interesting stories about him.

Ruta: They're right. Also about my grandmother, by the way, but to hear them you don't need me. There are many big mouths around here, plenty of good gossipy folks who know everything about everyone else. And I also warn you in advance that I am perhaps the wrong person for your research.

Varda: Why?

Ruta: First of all, because my grandfather did not like talking about certain acts and certain periods, and I'm the same way. Not everything should be revealed. Perhaps what interests you most is what I will keep secret. Second, because at best I can provide only secondhand testimony, tell other people's stories, which means you will have to trust my memory and also the memory of whoever told me stories.

Varda: How much time can you give me?

Ruta: Today about two hours, and I've already wasted half of it for you with nonsense. But if you need more meetings, no problem. Women should help one another, and here we have a cow who wants to nurse and one who wants to suckle.

Varda: That's good of you. Not everyone has time, and even fewer have patience.

Ruta: That I do have. If somebody is finally willing to listen to me, I won't tell them no. I'll talk and I'll talk and I'll talk, a cornucopia of stories, my cup runneth over. You'll feel like you're my best friend, and I'll feel that at last I have such a friend. This wide, pretty mouth, the mouth that was made for kissing—that's what my first husband used to say—this mouth will tell stories, all right, but not everything.

Varda: I'm sorry, I didn't know.

Ruta: Didn't know what?

Varda: You said "my first husband," that you're a widow . . . maybe . . .

Ruta: You might say that I was a widow, for a certain period of time. Whatever. So you're actually a Ph.D., or still a student?

Varda: Thanks for the compliment, but I got my doctorate a number of years ago.

Ruta: The eyes of Dr. Canetti wander in space, landing upon the black stone in the wall of the Tavori family home.

Varda: Sorry? I don't understand.

Ruta: You're looking at the black stone in our wall.

Varda: Yes, it's interesting. I've never seen anything like it. A black stone in the middle of a white wall, in a living room.

Ruta: It's basalt from the Galilee, from the place where my grandfather, the same Ze'ev Tavori you're so interested in, was born and grew up. He put it in the wall so it would be seen from both sides. By us on the inside, so we would always know and feel who we were and where we came from. And by other people from the outside, so they would all know and remember whom they were dealing with.

Varda: It's a little scary.

Ruta: Yes. He was pretty scary too.

Varda: I was told he had a patch on his eye, like a pirate.

Ruta: That's right.

Varda: How did he lose his eye?

Ruta: It happened long before I was born and was less heroic than he would have wanted. No big deal, he chased after thieves in the orchard, galloping on the horse, and a branch from a tree hit him in the eye.

Varda: That's terrible.

Ruta: We got used to it. To the black eye patch on his face, and also to his black stone in the wall, and also to him in general. That stone, by the way, was sent to him by his parents and delivered by his older brother, Dov. One day he showed up here, driving a cart drawn by a magnificent ox, that's how the story always went, magnificent, no less, and besides this stone he also brought—pay attention—a rifle, a cow, a tree, and a woman. That's what his parents sent him from the Galilee, because in those days people thought and said that was what a man needed to start out. I see you are beginning to take notes, so write them down in the order I told you: rifle, cow, tree, and woman. This is important. You have no idea how many times I heard that story, and always in that order. Why not tree, woman, rifle, and cow? Or woman, cow, tree, and rifle? It's logical to think that this is about priorities, which are important and relevant to your research, but it's also a narrative decision. Every series like that creates a different music and also a different plot. In our plot the rifle is first and the woman last, and Grandma Ruth actually said that the rifle was not only the hero of this plot, it was also the one who wrote it. Who knew better than she did, having arrived in that oxcart. She was the woman who was last on the list, and in that same cart was this basalt stone.

So the rifle, we were talking about the rifle. I was old enough to see Grandpa Ze'ev shooting it. Not at people but at jaybirds. He couldn't stand that bird; I have no idea why. Once, years ago, the whole family took the rifle for target practice in the hills, and my first husband, who was a great marksman, praised the two old guys—Grandpa and his Mauser. But he has an even longer past. The rifle, I mean. It surely killed a few people in the First World War and maybe also in the Arab riots and for sure in the War of Independence and who knows when else. I once wrote a story about it, but I only show my stories to the family, and not all of them even to them.

Varda: People didn't tell me that you write.

Ruta: That's because not everyone knows. I write because there are stories that are better to write than to tell, because it's unpleasant to feel their words in the mouth. Instead of being like scorpions and centipedes on the tongue, better they should crawl on the paper and drip their venom there. There's another reason for writing—for a long time I didn't really have anyone to talk to. For that reason, by the way, I haven't shut up since you walked in. But the truth is I started with children's stories. When my son, Neta, was two years old, he was always asking me to read him books and stories. I quickly discovered that I was editing and improving them while reading and therefore realized that I could write just as well as the geniuses who wrote them, and I began to write for him myself. I wrote him a story about the magnificent ox that belonged to my grandfather and about his mulberry tree, and I wrote him a story about the caveman and the fire and about a boy who liked to wear costumes, like he did, and wanted to masquerade as the Angel of Death. And later on I also wrote for myself, all sorts of stories about our family, which are also in a certain sense about a magnificent ox and the Angel of Death and the caveman.

True stories?

Of course they're true. If I don't show them to anyone, then who is there for me to hide the truth from? From myself? In any case, you are a historian and I am a Bible teacher, so we don't need to be told that the truth isn't true, and we of all people know that over time only what is written becomes true, and what is spoken doesn't.

Once I showed a story like this to my older brother, his name is Dovik, and he got upset: "Why write those stories about us? You forgot what Grandpa Ze'ev told us. There are certain matters that should not be talked about. Certainly not written."

I said to him, "I'm not telling anyone, and I'm writing because words look different from the way they sound." And I also told him something I read somewhere, that Tolstoy and his wife would talk by writing, exchanging sentences in a notebook they had at home, left open on a table. I told him this and said that it filled me with envy: whole conversations in writing. What courage, what intimacy, not to mention the theatrics! But later I understood: maybe there are couples who speak in writing because on paper they don't have to see the other one's face, and they don't hear the shouting. Written words may be more binding, but they are also quieter. And in my case, it's true that I never corresponded that way with my husband, not the first one or the second one. But there are stories that I tell and there are stories that I write, and stories that I show and stories that I don't, and they are very different.

Dovik, as you surely figured out, was named for Uncle Dov, the older brother of Grandpa Ze'ev, the one who brought him the wagon with the rifle, the cow, the tree, and the woman. Dov was killed in the War of Independence, he stepped on a land mine, he was one of the oldest fighters and casualties of 1948, and Dovik was named for him. Grandpa Ze'ev also fought in the War of Independence, but he wasn't killed or wounded. He died at the age of ninety-two a few years ago during a hike in the Carmel mountain range. And they had another brother, called Arieh, who died in a nursing home. Have you paid attention to their names? You should write them down, because it's relevant to your research: their father gave his three sons the names of predatory animals. "We're done with all the Yankels and Shmerels and Mottels," he said. "From now on we'll have bears and wolves and lions."

FOUR

....

Varda: Forgive me for interrupting, but I ask you to return to the topic if you can, and if possible to conduct the conversation in a more focused manner.

Ruta: Focused? It seems you've really come to the wrong person. You can focus your questions all you like, but I will answer the way I want to answer. That's how it is. The history of settling the Land of Israel, with all due respect, is not only committees and disputes and values and the status of women and the attitude toward Arabs and Ben-Gurion. First and foremost, it's about stories—the loves and hates and the births and deaths and the acts of revenge—and about families, father and mother and brother and sister and bridegroom and bride and grandchildren and great-grandchildren, and not in a golden chain but in a wagon made of wood, with a rifle and a cow and a tree and a woman; that's what made history everywhere and that's what made it here.

Varda: You seem to leave me no choice.

Ruta: You came to me, not I to you.

Varda: If I remember right, you said I could record you.

Ruta: Free, on the house. Record away, and I'm sorry about my tone of voice, and I promise to try and stick more to the topic. You know what? I'll even start with personal details, to get into a practical mood. ID card, please. Here. First name, family name, identification number, you see? I introduced myself as Ruta, but my name on my ID card says "Ruth." Like my grandmother. Ruta is the name that everyone, including myself, calls me. It's a good name, user-friendly, and rhymes easily: Ruta-*smartuta,* Ruta-*mabsuta,* Ruta-*shtuta,* and once at recess in school I even heard two twelfth graders referring to me as "Ruta-*tuta.*" They thought I didn't hear them, but I stopped, at the top of the stairs near the main office, and I said to them, "I gather, children, that I am the topic of conversation, so please explain to me what 'Ruta-*tuta*' means." Did you take note of my tone, Varda? That was an imitation of myself as a teacher.

So, they looked at each other, stone-cold silence in the air, red-hot cheeks on these two clowns, and they didn't know what to answer.

"*Nu,* children, I'm waiting, because I really don't understand what 'Ruta-*tuta*' means, and I don't recall any such expression in the Bible."

Luckily for them, the bell rang, and they ran off to class, and in the afternoon, at home, I asked Dovik—my older brother Dovik, in case you forgot . . .

Varda: I didn't forget. I'm writing down all the names.

Ruta: So Dovik explained to me what *tuta* means, and as you may or may not know, it's a highly vulgar word, and he also said there was no reason to get upset, because from these boys it's a kind of compliment.

"What do you want, sister," he said, "they're high school kids exploding with hormones and they have a teacher like you, a total hottie, and at this age everything reminds them of one thing only."

That was an imitation of Dovik. It's easy to imitate Dovik because he deepens his voice on purpose and puts the emphases and pauses in the wrong places in the sentences.

"So at this age," he went on, "everything triggers only one thought for them, like in the joke about the psychiatrist who shows pictures to his patient and asks what they remind him of."

He was right. That's what they're preoccupied with, and "Ruta" and "*tuta*" are actually a nice rhyme, and they're basically nice boys, and I'm their teacher, and in truth I am not bad looking. Guilty as charged. Not a hottie, but as I once heard them saying, "She's a babe." It's funny. Their voices are still changing, but sometimes they look at me with the eyes of grown men in the street. Not quite the look the livestock trader gives a cow but still that up-and-down look, lingering where men linger: eyes, lips, then right and left from breast to breast, then downward, a penetrating X-ray of the loins, width of the pelvis, counting the eggs, measuring the legs, and returning to the eyes, but that's just to be polite, because, between you and me, eyes say nothing. Neither plus nor minus. The credit they get as windows or mirrors of the soul—that's total nonsense. Anyway, they're all the same. It makes no difference if it's someone in the street, a student, a student's father, a doctor at the clinic, or a supervisor from the Ministry of Education.

Apropos of your field of research—women also give the eye, even if they're a Ph.D. at a university. I saw you do it too when you walked in, with that gendered look I know so well, woman to woman, checking out who's stronger. There's a Hebrew expression, "A woman carries her weapons upon her"—it comes from the Talmud—in other words, she is always armed: tits at the ready, hips on autopilot, gun belt, ammo, helmet, trigger cocked. That's us: wedded to our weapons twenty-four hours a day, like punishment in basic training that will never end. Eyes, voice, looks, body. Is that gendered enough for you, what I'm saying here?

Absolutely gendered.

Absolutely gendered but not enough history of the Yishuv? I see that you're laughing. Again I went off track and lost the focus?

A little.

Soon, Varda. Not to worry, everything will work out. You won't leave the Tavori family empty-handed.

FIVE

....

Is "Ruta" an affectionate nickname? Not really and, in any case, affection is not a top commodity in this moshava. I told you my official name is Ruth, after my grandmother, and the truth is that when I was born she was still alive, and it was she who asked that I be named for her. No one objected. Everyone knew how much she had wanted a daughter and, later, a granddaughter, and those who argued that a baby should not be named after a living person also knew that she wouldn't live to a ripe old age, and she apparently knew that too.

To make a long story short, for a few years there were a grandmother and granddaughter in the Tavori family with the same name. She was called Ruth Tavori in proper Hebrew: *"Rut Tavori,"* with a dignified pause in between, like at a state ceremony. But if you say the name without a proper pause, it comes out sounding *"Ruta Vori."* Try it, Varda, say it out loud. You see? Just like Ruth the Moabite. You pronounce it formally, she's the great-grandmother of King David—but *"Rutamoaviah"* is the one who spent the night with Boaz on the threshing floor.

Whatever. Today, everyone—the students, the other teachers, women friends—calls me Ruta. I have, incidentally, no real friends, not a one, but I have no better word to describe what I do have. And every time I go to our cemetery in the moshava, which is once or twice a week, I also visit the grave of my grandmother and see my official name carved on the stone: HERE LIES RUTH TAVORI. And under that is written A WOMAN OF VALOR, A MOTHER TO HER SONS, A WIFE TO HER HUSBAND. It's like the comments written in a school report card along with the grades, no? As a wife to her husband, my grandmother got a D, but in everything else B or B plus.

Do you remember her well?

Of course I remember her well. She was the kind of woman who manufactures memories easily, including things that didn't happen, if you ask me. Back then, Dovik and I didn't yet know the whole truth about her and Grandpa, but we heard things here and there, and we knew that people both took pity on her and avoided her company— a deadly combination, in my opinion—and even as children we understood that she was a person who suffered a blow many years earlier and never got over it.

What did you mean when you said "the whole truth about her and Grandpa"?

Patience, Varda, I'm in the middle of something. We knew she was what you'd call a bit strange. More than once I heard people talking about her, saying she would cry for no reason. That, by the way, is an expression I find unacceptable. There is no such thing as crying for no reason. All crying has a reason, but people don't always know or understand, and even if they do understand, they don't always say so. Whatever. Sometimes she really did cry, so what? Who doesn't cry sometimes? And who really understands the reason? But what really drew attention to her was that she always seemed to be searching for something. Even when she opened the door of a kitchen cupboard, it looked like she was hoping to discover something more than a pot or a jar of rice.

It mostly happened when there was digging in the ground. I was a little girl, but I remember it very well. Every time they dug a foundation for a house or a trench for a water or sewage pipe or a new cesspool, she would come, just show up, and stand beside the diggers and watch. Always at the proper distance to say: I'm not interfering, but I also have no intention of leaving. Clearly she was looking for something, and the something was buried in the ground. This would also happen when they plowed the fields in late summer. She would walk behind the tractor, off to the side on the ground that hadn't yet been plowed, with the storks and crows all around her, always in one of her billowing flowered dresses and work shoes and her big straw sun hat, walking with broad, sturdy steps, not the same as her usual walk. In the sky above were two snake eagles, hungry for the goodies exposed by the plow, and on the earth below was Grandma Ruth, surrounded by strutting storks, tall and thin and ugly, and she was tall and thin and lovely, and the plow carved deep furrows and uncovered snakes and mice and lizards that the birds quickly snatched, but what she sought she did not find.

What was it? What was she looking for?

Ask the old people you interview here. Maybe they know what and why. The children thought she was just plain crazy; they would walk behind her and there'd be this strange little parade, the tractor out in front, then storks, a woman, children pointing fingers and laughing. The truth is that if this hadn't been our grandmother maybe we too would have laughed, because we as children also thought there was something not okay about her, but we didn't make a big deal about it. In those days there were not-okay people in nearly every family in the moshava, each with his own madness. Now, by the way, there aren't, and to tell you the truth, it's pretty boring. No more crazies and craziness in this moshava, and no people who follow their hearts—for love or hate or revenge.

And what's the truth?

What truth?

Was she crazy, or was she really looking for something?

The truth is someplace in between. Exactly in the middle, the place where truths love to be. When truth is unambiguous, in other words, at one extreme or another, it's boring, not only to others but to itself. But when it's between the poles, it's another thing entirely. But this you probably know even without my explanations; after all, you're a historian. But what difference does it make, really, the truth? It's possible to go looking in the dirt because you're crazy, and it's possible to look because the thing you're looking for is actually there. These things don't contradict each other—on the contrary. As for the names, I think that when it's my turn, I'll tell them to engrave "Ruta-*tuta*" on my tombstone and not "Ruth" from my ID card. Ruta is a good name for a gravestone. There's something alive in it, mischievous, it'll be a refreshing contribution to the not-so-hot milieu of the cemetery. Besides, Ruth is the name of someone who is really okay, with that long *u* that purses the lips and *t* that seals the syllable decisively, or else the name of someone like my grandmother, who was not at all okay but maintained her pose of okayness with a series of unforgettable impersonations of everything that would be written on her gravestone: woman of valor, mother to her sons, good wife to her husband. Maybe I inherited her gift for impersonation, what's your opinion?

I have no opinion or knowledge regarding that.

One might think . . . who wasn't a woman of valor in the history of the Yishuv? You hear that, Grandma Ruth? You were a woman of valor even if you cried for no reason. And you were a good wife to your husband, even if he didn't deserve it. And you were a mother to your sons, even if they ran away from your home at the first opportunity. Excuse me, I have to drink a little water. To protect my throat. I am a teacher. My throat is a tool of my trade. I need it to teach, to talk, to fight back, to cry and laugh, to tell you tales.

It's good, water. And I say this as someone who likes alcohol. I drink water and I hear myself sigh with great pleasure and relief. So, Varda, have I started to deliver the goods? I've told you a little about women and the history of early settlement. As you may or may not know, history in the Bible is inseparable from genealogy, all those long lists of people who begat and begat and begat, this one begat that one who begat that one who begat that one, because that is what's really important and not all the Zionist slogans about coming to the Land of Israel and founding a village and forming committees and plowing the first furrow—what's really important are names, births, deaths.

Whatever. Let's drop that for now. What a couple they were, Grandpa Ze'ev and Grandma Ruth. How she slept with another man, how he took revenge on her—and her early death, which is how she took revenge in return. She had the nerve to die before he did, without asking permission or telling him in advance, and this is not something that a woman is allowed to do to a man, surely not to this man in this family.

Twice in her life she dealt him a fait accompli. The first time when she cheated on him and the second time when she died on him. She had clearly learned a lesson, because she didn't give him a second chance to punish her as he had done before. What punishment can be given someone whose death is the crime? What can you do to them? At most you can forget them, but nobody could do that to her, least of all he. Anyway, my throat is really starting to hurt. We'll stop here. You see, this is another good reason to write instead of speak.

SIX

....

MURDER AND SUICIDE

1

In the year 1930 three farmers committed suicide here at the moshava. That is what was written in the records of the committee and also what was concluded by the British police sergeant who came here after each suicide. He examined and investigated, and apart from their natural suspicion of any visit from the authorities, those who watched him were puzzled, for his hair was black, but his arms and face were densely dotted with freckles.

That, then, was how it was written down and how it was determined in the investigation, but contrary to the chronicles of our committee and the conclusions of the British policeman, the people of the moshava knew that only two of the suicides had actually taken their own lives, whereas the third suicide had been murdered. The whole moshava knew—people say so even today—they knew but covered it up and kept quiet. The committee fully supported this—Let the British investigate to their heart's content, we will not hand anyone over to the foreign regime. And the British policeman, lazily and indifferently, let the natives commit suicide to their hearts' content; it was all the same to him and the Empire that sent him here.

And the killer also made his contribution to the suicide version. Although he did what he did in a tempest of jealousy and rage, he acted with forethought and planning: he shot his victim as suicides shoot themselves, in the mouth. He carefully arranged the proper angle and made sure to remove the dead man's right boot and sock—only a few seconds after the shot he could feel the foot getting cold—so that it would be clear to all that the trigger was pulled by his big toe and not by the finger of somebody else.

The whole community knew, they knew and kept silent. Knew that the suicide was murdered, knew who killed him and why, but our dirty laundry we wash at home, not outside, and even today we do not tell outsiders the story.

Many years have gone by. The killer died. His wife—"It was all her fault," people still say, here in the moshava—died before he did. Their two sons left the moshava, and one of them is already dead, and today only the killer's grandson and granddaughter and their families live here on the family's land. And because it's inconvenient to tell a story whose characters are named "the killer" and "the killed" and "the killer's wife," whose fault it all was—the time has come to speak their names: the killed was called Nahum Natan, the killer was Ze'ev Tavori, and his wife was Ruth.

Ze'ev Tavori was a large man, quick to anger, strong as an ox, and equally stubborn. He grew up in one of the moshavot in the Lower Galilee with two brothers—Dov, the elder, and Arieh, the younger—and a taciturn and hardworking mother and a father who wanted to make all his sons into men worthy of his name. At age five they could gallop on a horse, at nine they herded oxen and milked cows, by age twelve their father had taught them to shoot a rifle and wield a wooden club. At fourteen, each of them could topple a tree with an ax and shoe a horse.

The man who was killed, Nahum Natan, was born in Istanbul, the only son of the eminent rabbi Eliyahu Natan. He was a mild-mannered young man, gentle and refined, very different from his murderer. Nor did he in any way resemble the two farmers who took their own lives here that same year. He was a bachelor and lived alone, whereas they were older men with families. One killed himself because he was drowning in debt and the other because of an incurable illness. Whereas Nahum, in the embellished version of his death, did it because he could not endure, given his personality and background, the workload and atmosphere of the moshava. There were even those who tacked the epithet "pampered" on him after his death.

The Natan family had produced many rabbis and scholars, and Nahum's father, Rabbi Eliyahu Natan, was the greatest of them all. An exalted Torah scholar was he, and his official title of Hacham truly befitted a man so wise.

Had Natan followed in his path, he would have remained in Istanbul and become a rabbi as well. But the halutzim, the pioneers who came through Istanbul on their way from Eastern Europe to the Land of Israel, filled him with longing and wonder. And the pioneer girls, with their uncovered braids, thickly layered on their heads, often golden braids, a rare sight in his city, and their eyes—some of those blue eyes gazed at him, and amazed and aroused him.

Word quickly spread that at his home a hungry halutz could get a bowl of soup with rice, beans, leeks, onions, and meat bones. The pots of soup were filled and emptied, the blue-eyed gazes deepened, conversation ensued, golden braids were braided, bright ideas flashed like lightning, ripped the darkness, electrified and freshened the air, which had been stagnant for many years. Nahum Natan was seduced by Zionism, and aspired, so he informed his father, to make aliyah to Eretz Yisrael and work its land.

Rabbi Eliyahu Natan was alarmed. He implored his son not to halt his Torah studies and certainly not to become a farmer. Not to leave the "Tent of Jacob" and go to the "Desert of Ishmael" and the "Field of Esau." But Nahum's heart yearned for faraway places, and he sometimes felt it fluttering in his rib cage like a migratory bird eager to fly. He insisted and requested and explained and made excuses and in the end he convinced his father to let him join a group of halutzim heading for Eretz Yisrael and to give him his blessing as he set out on his journey.

The father, a good and tender man, agreed with a heavy heart. He thought of the patriarch Jacob, when he sent Joseph wearing a coat of many colors to join his sheepherding brothers, not sensing or imagining the enormous calamity that would befall his son and him. "From the pasture to the pit": the words rattled inside him, but his mind could not comprehend them, not in their full meaning. He feared disease, robbery, heresy, even death, but not murder, certainly not at the hands of a fellow Jew.

His heart was heavy, but he did not withdraw his agreement. He imposed only one condition on his son: that he not join any of the various socialist factions or workers' associations or one of the kibbutzim, which lacked synagogues and ritual baths and kosher butchers, and where the male pioneers, it was said, frolicked freely with the women—but go instead to one of Baron Rothschild's moshavot, to an established community where he would find a synagogue and a ritual slaughterer, and strap on his phylacteries for daily prayer and observe the Sabbath and dietary laws.

The son agreed, and the father surprised him with a gift: a pair of excellent boots, suitable for working the land.

"My size exactly!" declared Nahum Natan as he tried them on, took a few steps, and smiled the smile of a child. "So comfortable, and the shoemaker didn't even measure my feet."

Rabbi Eliyahu Natan smiled a fatherly smile and did not reveal that one night, when Nahum was sleeping soundly, he had brought the cobbler to their home, and without the young man's knowledge the two had bared his feet. The father held a large candle in his hand, and the shoemaker traced the son's feet on a piece of cardboard and measured the circumference of his ankles and calves and the distance from his ankles to his knees, one leg at a time, for the feet, as everyone knows, are different from each other.

This scene—the lad in bed, eyes closed, shadows dancing on the walls as measurements are taken—aroused such strong emotion and anxiety in Rabbi Natan that he fled to another room to cry and calm down and returned only after washing his face. But now, as his son, Nahum, put on the boots with such delight, he relaxed and hugged him until he was again filled with fear, and more than he feared for his son's future he was afraid of his own fear, and again felt his tears welling and again went to the other room to weep and wash.

2

Nahum Natan said goodbye to his father, his neighbors, his teachers, and his students and sailed by ship to Jaffa and from Jaffa went to the Mikveh Yisrael Agricultural School. There he learned planting and plowing, grafting and pruning, and became acquainted with the pickax and the scythe. There he also became friends with his future murderer, namely Ze'ev Tavori, who came from the Galilee.

The two were very different. Ze'ev was powerful and fearless and accustomed to working hard in the fields, and Nahum was soft and gentle and a dreamer of dreams. And nevertheless they became friends. Nahum was happy that Ze'ev—"He rides raising dust, like a Janissary," he wrote his father, "swinging a staff like an Anatolian shepherd and plowing straight furrows like a German engineer"—regarded him as a friend, and Ze'ev looked at Nahum as a delicate little brother. He learned new words from him and helped him when the need arose.

At the end of their studies the two parted ways for a while. Nahum went to Jerusalem at his father's request, stayed there a few months, worked for a farmer in the settlement of Motza outside the city, and learned to grow grapes. Ze'ev did not return to his family's home in the Galilee. He wandered about the country, plowing and quarrying, planting and standing guard. His muscles and experience served him well, and so did what he learned from his parents, who had taught him the value of hard work. Everywhere he went he readily found employment, but nowhere did he make friends. In his view, the farmers of the moshavot of the Judean Hills were soft and coddled, like the crumbly reddish soil of their orchards and vineyards, so different from the basalt farmers of the moshavot of his native Galilee.

"We grew watermelon, cattle, and olives, and the neighbors were Arabs, who were either good friends or total enemies, and the toys their children got on their birthdays were a horse and a stick," he told his grandchildren many years later. "Whereas in moshavot like this one," he teased, "they danced minuets and sipped wine and chatted in French with the Baron's officials."

He also kept his distance from the halutzim, the pioneers who'd enchanted Nahum in Istanbul. They seemed to Ze'ev, born in Pales-

tine and accustomed to its ways, to be both eccentric and fearful, as
evidenced by their body language and manner of speech and their long-
winded debates and strange enthusiasms. In addition, their propensity
for intimate conversation and endless hora dancing seemed pointless
to him. "They talk like they dance," he wrote at the time to his father,
"everything in circles. They never get anywhere."

For a while he was involved with Hashomer, the Jewish self-defense
group of the Yishuv, but discovered they were overly fond of fancy mustaches and belligerent chatter and ostentatious horse racing, and quit.
He found himself sitting during lunch breaks with the Arab workers,
whose language he spoke and whose customs he knew and whose food
he loved, and even though his parents had always told him, "They're
the enemy!" it was with them that he felt most comfortable.

Once a fortnight he wrote three letters. One to his parents, the second to the daughter of the neighbors in the moshava where he was born
and raised, a girl named Ruth Blum, and the third to his schoolmate
Nahum. Writing was hard for him, and the length of his letters was
determined by the paper he wrote on: long if he found a full sheet and
short if a small slip. He would tell them where he was and what he was
doing, and to Ruth Blum he added a word or two of affection or longing,
and signed all his letters with same four words: "I am Ze'ev. Shalom."

For a while he worked in Zichron Yaakov, where he heard about a plan
to establish a new moshava. He informed his parents and a few friends,
among them Nahum Natan. They got organized, borrowed money, and
bought land in the new place. The parcel of Ze'ev Tavori was adjacent
to that of Nahum Natan, and nearby was the home of another young
man, Yitzhak Maslina by name, son of a Hasidic family that had come
from Russia in the mid–nineteenth century, before the First Aliyah, and
settled in Tiberias. Yitzhak Maslina was already married, to a woman
named Rosa, and Ze'ev had known him a long time: before his marriage
to Rosa, Yitzhak had worked in her father's store, where Ze'ev's father
would buy tools and seeds.

They planted trees and vineyards, and built houses, and in that year,
1930, the same year that three of our farmers committed suicide, Ze'ev
at age twenty-three married Ruth Blum, who was then nineteen and, a

few months after the wedding, displayed a pleasantly bulging belly of early pregnancy.

3

Those years have passed, those people have died, but the stories live on and reinforce one another. A few of them are told here in public, at anniversaries of our moshava's founding, in renovated versions. A few were published in various studies and books, and a few rustle underground and suddenly peek out and wink: *We're still here.* Or cry for help—*Let us be known*—and then disappear. So we have such stories as "Stealing the Ransom Money" and "Robbing the Jerusalem Money Changer" and "The Little City Girl Who Drowned in the Ancient Aqueduct," which are still told in public. While the tales of "The Moshava Boy Whose Eye Was Plucked Out" and "The Moshava Boy and the Prostitute from Tiberias" are only whispered.

The story about the suicide of Nahum Natan—"The Rabbi's Son and the Neighbor's Wife"—is told to no one, of course, and certainly not to the general public. But when it occasionally floats to the surface in conversations among family and neighbors—each of them adding or subtracting—it becomes clear that nobody remembers the exact place or date when he killed himself or was murdered, but they argue over the type of rifle barrel in his mouth, if it was a British Enfield or a Russian Mosin-Nagant or a German Mauser, and since his bones were removed from our cemetery many years ago and there is no mark or memorial of him here, there are also those who argue over whether he was Nahum Natan or Natan Nahum, or maybe had a different name.

But all agree that he died in the autumn, on the night of the first rain of the season. This is important, because our area gets an abundance of rain. Some rainfalls are so torrential that they dig new channels in the earth, and the first rain of autumn 1930 was so strong that between its thunder and lightning and the shuttered windows, no one noticed or heard the rifle shot, except for three people: Ze'ev Tavori, who fired it; Nahum Natan, into whose mouth it was fired; and Yitzhak Maslina, whose wife, Rosa—I still remember her, Rosa Maslina, with teeth like a rabbit and legs like a gazelle—demanded that he go outside and clean the rain gutters, which he'd kept postponing despite her insistent nagging, because the rainwater had now started leaking into the bedroom.

Yitzhak Maslina leaned a ladder against the wall of his house and climbed up, and when he placed his right foot on the fourth rung, he thought he heard screams near the fence of his yard. He glanced in that direction and saw nothing, got down from the ladder, and approached with caution, lifting his storm lantern upward and to the right so he could see what was going on.

The lantern did not light up the darkness, but when Yitzhak reached the fence a mighty diagonal bolt of lightning slashed the sky from east to west, and by its light he could see two men standing in the field, facing each other, as two bluish silhouettes. The smaller of the two cried out twice "No!" and when he noticed the figure of Maslina, also bluish, he shouted, "Help, he's going to kill me!"

Maslina immediately recognized the voice, the voice of his bachelor neighbor, Nahum Natan, and even called to him, "Nahum, Nahum . . . ," but the only reply he heard was a terrible roar. The bigger of the two men roared and punched the smaller one with his fist, first in the left temple, and as the man fell, he added a blow to the chest. Nahum Natan collapsed and lay on the ground, and the lightning illuminated the man who punched him, bending over and holding a long object. Maslina supposed this was a stick and that the man intended to beat Nahum with it, but when the shot was fired he understood it was a rifle, and he too shouted a great shout and lay facedown in the mud. He feared that the shooter—presumably a bandit, for the truth did not occur to him— had noticed the light of the lantern he carried and would now shoot him too.

And the shooter indeed saw him. At first as a silhouette in the open doorway, then as a quivering light, moving forward and stopping, and now the silhouette dropping to the ground and the light going out. He removed the boot from the right foot of the dead man and called out: "Come here, Yitzhak, come here now!"

Maslina recognized that voice too and was shocked. It was the voice of Ze'ev Tavori, his other neighbor. He rose and opened the gate and approached, his steps growing smaller as he drew closer, and because his eyes did not want to meet Ze'ev's eyes he averted them downward.

Lightning bolts flashed, one after another. Yitzhak saw the corpse and was terrified. The bullet had shattered the dead man's skull, and what was left intact was covered with blood and rainwater, brain and mud, almost beyond recognition. But his boots were the uniquely excellent boots of Nahum Natan, famous throughout the moshava.

Ze'ev Tavori asked him what he was doing outdoors at such a late hour on a stormy night.

Yitzhak Maslina spoke the truth, that rainwater had leaked into his house and he had gone out to clear a blocked gutter.

"And why did you come over here?"

"I heard shouting," said Maslina, "and I wanted to see what was going on."

"And what did you see?"

"I didn't see anything."

"You are mistaken," said Ze'ev Tavori, "you saw a great deal. And if you don't remember what you saw, I'll remind you. You saw a suicide. You saw our unfortunate neighbor Nahum Natan shoot himself in the mouth."

"But where did he get the rifle? Whose rifle is that?" asked Maslina.

"It's my Mauser. The rifle that my brother Dov brought me from the Galilee in the same wagon as the cow and the tree and Ruth."

Ze'ev Tavori spoke all this in remarkable detail with complete calm, adding, "Nahum stole it from my house, and I woke up and ran after him, and you saw me running after him and also heard me shouting for him to stop, but I was too late. Straightaway he put the rifle in his mouth and shot himself. Now do you remember what you saw?"

Maslina did not answer, and Tavori bent down and positioned the dead man's big toe against the trigger of the rifle.

"Here," he said, "like this. Look and learn, maybe one day you too will want to kill yourself."

Yitzhak Maslina opened his mouth wide with shock, perhaps even intending to say that he had seen something else entirely, but Ze'ev Tavori was ahead of him. He picked up the rifle with one hand, extended it toward Yitzhak's neck, right under his chin, lifting it so that Yitzhak's eyes could not escape his stare.

"'According to two witnesses shall a matter stand,'" he said. "If we testify together, you will receive a gift of a cow like my cow, a Dutch cow, pregnant by a prize Dutch bull. But if you tell a different story, you will also kill yourself, the same way. Three people have already killed themselves here; there will be one more."

Yitzhak wanted to say that there had been only two suicides, but his body was wiser than his brain: he froze and kept quiet.

And now a brief and necessary explanation: When Yitzhak Maslina was a boy in Tiberias, he worked each summer, as mentioned above, at a shop belonging to the father of Rosa, the girl who would become his wife. First he worked as a porter and a delivery boy and then cleaning and stock sorting, and eventually accounting as well, but he was mainly engaged in thinking about Rosa, his employer's daughter.

In Tiberias, Rosa was known as Toothy Rosa because when her baby teeth fell out they were replaced in the front of her mouth by a pair of incisors so huge she could not close her jaws, giving her a slightly ridiculous facial expression. But when she got older people started talking about "Rosa's teeth" and also "the rest of Rosa," because apart from the teeth she became a lovely, graceful young woman with long legs and a fine blossoming body.

Once, when Yitzhak Maslina walked into her father's storage room, Toothy Rosa was up on a ladder and asked him to bring her a package from the floor. When he raised the package he also raised his eyes and saw a few inches of her thighs. Whenever he saw her thereafter, that picture came to mind, and always, even many years later, when she was his wife and he could no longer bear her voice or her presence or her teeth, he would feel the same longing for "the rest of Rosa." It was enough to recall that day and that ladder and the mystery of her thighs hovering above him.

But let me return to the accounts he managed back then for her father, for these too he had not forgotten. Even now, all those years after he handled them, he still excelled at calculating profit and loss quickly and precisely and immediately understood the meaning of Ze'ev Tavori's words, and the chilling touch of the rifle barrel under his chin enhanced his talent for calculation.

He backed off and said, "Suicide is a bad thing in every respect, a cow is a very good thing, and a pregnant Dutch cow is even better."

"You can also have his boots," said Ze'ev Tavori, "because they are too small for me."

"But what will I say? That I took them off the dead man?"

"Absolutely. You took them so that a thief would not come and steal them. You took them with you for safekeeping. That's what you say to them now, and later we'll see what to do with them."

Yitzhak Maslina hesitated, but excellent work boots were nothing to sneeze at. He bent over quickly and tried to remove the left boot from the foot of the murdered man. But the boot refused to be removed, and for a moment it seemed to him that the dead man was pulling away his foot, and he recoiled with fright.

Tavori chuckled and Maslina tugged and finally fell on his rear end in the mud with the boot in his hand, and the murderer chuckled again and said to him, "Now run to Kipnis and tell him everything you saw and that I am standing here in the rain guarding the body."

Kipnis was the chairman of our committee, a tall, sharp man with a wicked sense of humor.

"At this hour? People are sleeping now."

"When a man commits suicide you're allowed to wake the chairman of the committee at any hour," said Ze'ev Tavori, and prodded him: "Run, run already! Run and tell him what you saw and I will stay here with this wretched carcass."

"And we'll both say it was suicide?" Yitzhak Maslina again asked, seeking confirmation.

"Obviously suicide," said Tavori. He pointed with the rifle barrel at the exploded head of the dead man and again turned it toward Maslina, bringing it very close to his forehead. "Doing what he did to me, what was that if not suicide?"

4

Everyone thinks now and then about suicide, and some even ponder the best way to do it and wonder what heartbroken relatives and shocked friends will say. In general, there's something appealing and intriguing and contagious about suicide, and sometimes the thought arises not only out of pain and despair and distress but a desire to punish somebody else or to arouse pity and attract attention or perhaps out of temporary boredom or weakness. Therefore the members of the committee decided to tell the British police sergeant that Nahum Natan was a soft, weak man who lived alone and could not deal with the hard labor and the loneliness, and because he had no one close to him to share his troubles with, no wife and no children to take care of, he was influenced by what the two previous suicides had done, and did the same.

This version of events was also written in the telegram sent to Nahum's father, Rabbi Eliyahu of Istanbul, dealing him a devastating blow. Not only had he lost his only son, but he was a distinguished rabbi, and the news of the suicide gave rise to theories and whispers in his congregation. He wrote a Hebrew eulogy for his son, titling it "My Son Was Devoured by a Beast," as Jacob mourned Joseph, suggesting that Nahum had not taken his own life but was murdered, for there are also wild beasts who walk on two legs, and one of these had eaten him. But in the text of his eulogy, the rabbi made use of linguistic allusions to hint that the suicide story was plausible.

In any case, the rabbi quickly sailed from Istanbul to Haifa, accompanied by his loyal beadle—a strong silent man in an old suit and soft red shoes like a baby's, with huge hands, a strong chin, and a curly blue-black beard as square as that of an Assyrian king. Awaiting them at the Haifa port was a driver who took them to the moshava. The secretary of the committee, as well as its chairman, the aforementioned Kipnis, welcomed them and took them into the meeting room. Waiting at the table were the treasurer and the principal of the district school, and Ze'ev Tavori and Yitzhak Maslina were also present, sitting on a bench by the wall.

"These are the two witnesses," indicated the chairman of the committee, after the greetings and consolations. "Neighbors of Nahum, may his memory be a blessing. The Honorable Rabbi may ask them questions."

The rabbi asked and the witnesses testified. The neighbor began by speaking the truth about the rain and the gutter and the leakage and the ladder, and the killer began with a lie, that he heard someone that night in his house, a creaking door, intruding footsteps. "A thief caught in the act, Honorable Rabbi," he said, employing a phrase from the Torah. "He was in my house and left." When he rose to get his rifle, said Tavori, he was shocked to find it missing and rushed outside and saw a figure running away in the rain, carrying a riflelike object, and ran after him.

Both of them mentioned the tremendous diagonal lightning, and both emphasized that by its light they had seen what happened next: the fleeing figure halted in the field, beyond the fence of Yitzhak Maslina, and before they understood what the thief was about to do, the shot rang out, and when they hurried there, "I from my yard and Yitzhak from his yard, we saw that it was your son, Nahum, of blessed memory, Your Eminence," and Ze'ev Tavori, to the rabbi's great dismay, even added the Arabic words "Allah have mercy," and said that because of the darkness and the rain "and the gunshot, forgive me, that blew off his head," he recognized him at first by his boots, which were unique boots familiar to everyone in the moshava, the right one lying in the mud and the left one on his foot.

"The boots which I have given him," moaned the rabbi, bursting into tears, "for him to walk his new path and work the land." And the muscular beadle, who had till now not spoken a word, suddenly asked where those boots were, had someone taken them?

Maslina did not miss a beat. "The boots are at my house," he said, looking first at Tavori and then at the rabbi. "We ran right away to get the chairman of the committee, Your Eminence, Mr. Kipnis, who is sitting here, and the chairman called the police, and I feared that in all the commotion someone would steal them. Boots like those you don't see every day, especially not around here."

The rabbi said he would like to see them. Maslina hurried home and fetched them. The rabbi looked at them silently. He choked up, his eyes welling with tears, and finally managed to say, " 'Know now.' "

"Know what?" asked the committee secretary fearfully.

" 'Know now whether it is thy son's coat or not,' " said the rabbi, and pointed: "It is still stained with blood."

"It won't come out." Ze'ev Tavori chuckled. "Blood never comes out in leather, Your Eminence. My father once smashed a thief's head with a club, and the bastard's blood is still on the belly strap of his saddle."

The bereaved father gave him a look, as if wondering, From what stinking pond did this vulgarian slither? He then turned to Yitzhak Maslina and said, "These are boots for agriculture, not for city folk. You take them. I think they are your size."

"I already tried them on," Yitzhak quickly said, surprising himself no less than his interlocutor, "and they fit me perfectly."

Silence prevailed. Yitzhak realized he had said something awful. Felt that his body suddenly wanted to expand, to overwhelm his contemptible soul, to speak the truth, to tell Rabbi Eliyahu Natan how his son had died. But Ze'ev Tavori sensed all this too. He looked sideways at his neighbor and remarked, "Beautiful boots. You can wear them to the pasture with your new cow."

Maslina sank again into his seat. "Thank you, Honored Rabbi," he said. "Every time I put on these boots I will remember your son, may he rest in peace."

The bereaved father asked a few more questions. They bore no sign of suspicion or disbelief. He did not express the possibility that his son was murdered, nor did he inquire whether anything in his behavior had indicated suffering or despair, as if not wanting to hear the typical answers. Who can know his hidden thoughts? Did he imagine the terrible magnitude of the straight-faced lies he was told?

5

After the conversation and the testimonies, the rabbi and his beadle were taken to the cemetery. In those early days only a few graves had been dug there, and on the grave of Nahum Natan there was merely a simple wooden marker. The rabbi climbed out of the carriage and nearly collapsed, and the beadle, as if accustomed to this, quickly took him in his huge arms, clasped him to his chest, and carried him to the grave, his legs dangling in the air, and, because there was no chair or bench, did something not seen here before or since: he got down on all fours like a dog, and the rabbi sat on his broad back like a man on a bench, placed his hands on his knees, and looked at the grave of his son.

The astonished escorts went to wait outside the fence, sensing that the rabbi wanted to sit there alone. After a few minutes the beadle raised one hand from the ground, gave his nose a quick, strong scratch, and replaced it without shifting his position. After a quarter of an hour the rabbi got up, and so did the beadle, brushing bits of dirt from his knees. They left the cemetery, and the chairman of the committee invited them to lunch at his home.

"Everything is prepared and our home is strictly kosher," he declared, and the secretary suddenly smiled and said that Mrs. Kipnis was a marvelous cook, and added: "This is a great honor for us. Too bad it's because of such a great tragedy."

The rabbi accepted the invitation. Despite his anguish he needed to eat, but lost his appetite and failed to enjoy his meal. He ate sparingly and with good manners, watching the others at the table and thinking about Joseph's brothers, eating and drinking beside the pit into which they had cast him. His face expressed no suspicion, just guilt—every parent feels guilty over the death of a son or daughter—and sadness.

He ended his meal with two small cups of very sweet hot tea and finally mustered the courage to ask to see his son's house. The little group left the house of the chairman of the committee and accompanied him. The chairman unlocked the door with a key he had brought, the rabbi entered and walked around the vacant house—two rooms, a pantry, a kitchen with a big porch facing the yard—examining the few clothes in the closet and the books on the shelf, folios of Talmud and prayer books for Sabbath and High Holy Days, alongside books about agriculture.

"He had just planted a vineyard," said the secretary, "and planned to build a henhouse."

" 'Planted a vineyard and hath not yet used the fruit thereof,' " murmured the rabbi. He looked at the narrow single bed and loudly wept. "Not yet a father, nor yet did he know a woman."

This was the first time the rabbi had wept since he arrived at the moshava. The beadle quickly went and stood close beside him, as if offering his body to lean on, and Ze'ev Tavori, who had entered the house uninvited, angrily thought to himself, He knew, the dog. He knew, all right. But his lips were sealed, and his face was blank.

Then the rabbi asked everyone to withdraw. He stayed in the house alone, and no one knows what he did there, but apparently he looked out the bedroom window and saw something, because he left the house at once and rushed to the fence between the yard and the neighbor's yard, where a tall young woman was standing.

The young woman's eyes met the eyes of the rabbi. She covered her mouth with her hand. The rabbi trembled as he looked at her. Though tall and broad-shouldered, she was also slim, and though she was slim, his heart and her eyes told him she was pregnant, and his heart filled with vague longing, which arises at times in the heart of a man who sees a pregnant woman, even if he is an elderly rabbi and she is young and foreign.

Ze'ev Tavori, who stood beside the chairman of the committee together with Yitzhak Maslina and the secretary and the beadle, strode toward her and grumbled, "Get inside, Ruth!" And the rabbi understood at once that this was his wife, and that between the two there was no love, but fear on her part and suspicion and jealousy on his.

The woman called Ruth was about to do what her husband told her, but the rabbi said, "Come here, please," because he wished to see her walking, either to support his hunch or dispel it.

She drew near, and the rabbi said to her, "May it be a boy," and he did not know what she was feeling, that it would be a girl, and did not imagine what she knew, that this would be his granddaughter, the daughter of his son who was killed by her husband.

"Get in the house, Ruth," Ze'ev said again. "Now!"

He suddenly felt dizzy. She went back into her house and closed the door behind her, and Ze'ev opened and closed his fists until the dizziness passed.

The chairman of the committee asked if the Honorable Rabbi wished to put his son's house and parcel of land up for sale, and the muscular beadle said not to burden the rabbi with such questions but to direct them to him and that he would let them know soon. The chairman asked if the rabbi would like to erect a gravestone, and the beadle said that for the time being the rabbi would make do with the simple marker that was there, because in the near future he would move his son's bones to the Mount of Olives in Jerusalem, to the family plot where his mother and father were buried and his elder brother, and there he would erect a permanent stone.

"And there I buried Nahum's mother," said the rabbi, adding that when his time came he too would be buried there.

He gestured to the beadle. Everyone could tell he intended to deliver words of farewell.

"'I shall go to him, but he shall not return to me,'" he began, but the words, though they came from his mouth and left his body, offered him no relief. Nothing lightened the terrible weight of agony and guilt, the "if" and the "if only" that tormented him like whips and scorpions. Again he faltered, almost collapsed, and the beadle again wrapped his arms around him and carried him to the car.

The driver rushed to the front of the car and turned the ignition crank, put on his cap, and got in his seat. The visit was over. The children from the area, who had waited for hours for this very moment, shouted joyfully and clapped their hands. The car drove off, vanishing in the distance as the children chased it, and reappeared after three years that seemed like only a day: same driver, same cap on his head, and the very same passengers, the rabbi and the beadle, the former of short stature and teary eyes, the other with the rock-solid body and blue-blackness of his square beard and the red shoes, the span of his shoulders, his strong embracing arms.

In that year, a new synagogue was built in our moshava, to replace the shack used for prayers in the early years, and Rabbi Eliyahu Natan had brought with him a Torah scroll in memory of his son, Nahum, to assure the ascent of his immortal soul. The Torah was too heavy for the elderly, grieving rabbi to lift, and the beadle carried it just as he had carried the rabbi himself, hugging it to his chest like a baby.

The people of the moshava were delighted by this precious and important donation, and happier still about its meaning, for if the rabbi had suspected that one of them had harmed his son, he would not be revisiting the place and certainly not bearing such a gift.

Rabbi Eliyahu Natan brought the Torah scroll into the synagogue with joy and sorrow, prayer and tears, and then asked to see his son's house once more. In the meanwhile it had been sold to another man, who received him with respect and invited him in, but the rabbi said that going inside would be hard on him and he only wanted to meet the buyer, about whom he had heard through the beadle who arranged the sale, and to wish him success and well-being.

As he walked from his son's house to the home of the chairman of the committee, the rabbi tried to remember the name of the witness who took his son's boots and wondered if he had worn them as he had permitted him to do. Even as he searched his memory, he saw a faraway figure in the field, and as he wondered who it was, his feet already knew and began to lead him to that person. When he drew closer he saw that this was the same woman, just as he thought, the young woman he had seen on his earlier visit in the yard adjacent to his son's home, and whose face had not strayed from his memory and indeed inhabited his dreams.

He now saw that she was carrying a baby boy, about a year old, in her arms. It had been three years ago that he had seen her pregnant, and he wondered, Where is the child who was then in her womb?

The woman stood beside a farmer who was digging a drainage ditch at the edge of his vineyard, her eyes fixed on the shovel that pierced the ground and threw off clumps of dirt.

The digger quickly climbed out of the ditch and bowed courteously and said, "Welcome, Honorable Rabbi, all of us here are still very sorry about your son, Nahum," and came closer and said, "The poor woman. Every time someone digs the ground, she comes to watch."

He resumed his digging. And the rabbi, more emotionally than he intended, gave the woman his blessing.

She did not answer. It was clear to him that she recognized and remembered him and knew why he had come before and why now, but she gave him one short, vague look and then turned back to the ditch and the pile of earth beside it. She paid no further attention to him nor to the farmer who was digging, but only to the shovel unearthing layer after layer of soil, and to the cry that she alone heard, crying out to her from the ground.

6

The next day another vehicle arrived at the moshava, carrying members of the Sephardic burial society from Jerusalem. The chairman and secretary of the committee accompanied them to the cemetery and showed them the grave of Nahum Natan. The bereaved father had not come with them, unwilling and unable to see the bones of his son and certainly not the skull blown apart by a bullet from a rifle, nor did anyone else from the moshava come either.

The men dug, uncovered, gathered, wrapped, and raised the bones of Nahum and brought them to the Mount of Olives in Jerusalem, where he is buried to this day beside his mother, grandmother, uncle, and grandfather. His father, the eminent rabbi Eliyahu Natan, stood during the burial and looked at the small plot that awaited him too, not knowing that he would not be buried there. And it came to pass that a few years later he relocated from Istanbul to Cairo, and two decades thereafter, in fullness of years and memories, he died. In his last will and testament he again invoked the biblical Joseph and quoted his request: "You shall carry up my bones from here"—from Egypt to the Land of Israel, to the family plot in Jerusalem.

But the State of Israel had been established by then, and the cemetery on the Mount of Olives was outside its border. Rabbi Eliyahu Natan was therefore buried in Cairo, and many years later, when it was possible to bring him to the Mount of Olives, there was no one who remembered his request or anyone who would assume the expenses entailed in fulfilling it.

And his son, Nahum, is also forgotten. No one visits his grave on the Mount of Olives, and his house and land at the moshava changed hands at higher and higher prices, until it was purchased several years ago by Haim Maslina, the grandson of Yitzhak Maslina who gave false testimony and received a pair of excellent work boots and an excellent Dutch cow, pregnant by an excellent Dutch bull.

SEVEN

....

Here you are. We said four o'clock and Varda shows up at four on the dot. To see the nakedness of the moshava, to investigate and excavate. How are you? Are you hungry? Thirsty? You missed me? Just kidding. Please sit. I have an hour and a half, and then, if you like, you can come with me to a parents' meeting and see me in action. We may begin. First question.

What was the family name before Tavori?

Before Tavori we were Tversky. I'm told this is a prestigious name, but my great-grandfather wanted a Land of Israel name to replace the name of exile and changed it to Tavori. It sounds a bit like Tversky, and Mount Tavor was in the neighborhood. I love them both, the mountain and its name. The mountain is uniquely beautiful, like a breast full of milk, like a belly in the seventh month. And Tavor is a unique name, predating the Hebrew language that adopted it.

Grandpa Ze'ev, who was born and grew up nearby, told his grandchildren, Dovik and me, that for many years after he left the Galilee and came here, he missed that view of the Tavor. He'd look upward and was surprised every time—Where is it? Where'd it disappear to? I didn't grow up near the Tavor. I was born in Tel Aviv and grew up here in the moshava, but some of that stuck to me too. I kept the name Tavori even after Eitan and I got married. I hadn't told you his name? Sorry. Eitan is my husband. My first husband and also my second husband.

Interesting that they both have the same name, no?

Yes, Varda, it's very interesting. And what's even more interesting is that they're also the same person. But never mind that now. You'll understand later on. What's important is that I kept my family name. Eitan was Eitan Druckman and I stayed Ruta Tavori. It wasn't popular then like now, a woman keeping her family name. I raised many eyebrows, and not for the first time. I'm telling you, Varda, if raising eyebrows were an Olympic sport, I would bring great honor to the State of Israel. The contestants enter the stadium, each one does his thing, the number of raised eyebrows in the crowd is counted, and, as the whole moshava knew in advance: first place, Ruth—pause—Tavori, Israel! Come get the medal, national anthem, "Hatikvah," drumroll please, the blue-and-white flag is hoisted, a sea of tears and glory. I will place one hand on my chest, like the American athletes do, and a single tear will trickle down the winning cheek. I'm good at tears, I have lots of practice and it shows.

Whatever. I kept my name. I didn't want a new name, and I also can't stand the custom of married women lugging an oversize load of two family names. If you're an independent woman, do what I did: keep your family name and that's it. Eitan, by the way, didn't mind at all. The opposite. He said, I fell in love with Ruta Tavori, so I don't want any Ruth Druckman instead. And he didn't stop there. Soon enough he changed his last name to my family name. From Eitan Druckman to Eitan Tavori. At first he introduced himself as Tavori only as a joke, another one of his jokes: "Eitan Tavori, my pleasure." Then adding: "You have no idea how much pleasure." I see you're smiling, yes, he was a very funny guy back then, and I was a very good audience for his wisecracks.

To make a long story short, one day he got up and went to the Ministry of the Interior and officially changed his last name to my last name. Dovik said to him, "What's gotten into you, Eitan? Are you crazy?" But I actually liked it. I told him that I saw it as a unique sort of romance. And you know what he said? He said, "This time it's not you I'm romancing, it's Grandpa Ze'ev, he's the top Tavori around here. Not you." But to me this was downright romantic. He knew how to romance and loved to romance, but I sometimes felt that in his romantic theater I wasn't always the character who was romanced, that sometimes I was the stage on which he could mount his productions.

Birthdays, for example. In general, birthdays are of more interest to women than to men, but my first husband remembered every one of my birthdays, made it special, made an effort, invented things, and on each of those birthdays he would tack a sign on the wall: HAPPY BIRTHDAY RUTA, THERE ARE SO-AND-SO MANY—and the number would change, fifteen, fourteen, thirteen—YEARS TILL YOUR FORTIETH BIRTHDAY. And on every birthday I would laugh, God, how I used to laugh with him then, in those days, and ask, "Why are you so hung up on forty?"

"That's the age I love. The age I want you to be already."

"Forty? I still have the skin of a teenager and you want wrinkles? Gray hair is what you want? Good thing I have small tits that will always hold up."

And he insisted: "I always wanted a woman of forty, and I'm willing to wait."

"So why didn't you marry a woman of forty and be done with it?"

He laughed. "Because I wanted you. I saw in you how great you'd be when you finally got there. You were a long-term investment."

"And in the meantime? Are you suffering?"

"Suffering a lot," he said. "Suffering but looking forward with hope. Fortyward."

You get it? I'm the one who reads books and teaches Bible, and he, who barely graduated high school, my wild uneducated ignoramus, trumped me with that "fortyward" of his.

"Forty is not a nice number," I told him. "It spells only trouble: the forty days of the Flood, forty years wandering in the desert, 'forty more days and Nineveh shall be destroyed.' Besides, what will happen at age forty plus one day? Forty and a half? You won't want me anymore?"

"Don't talk nonsense. Just like it doesn't happen in one day, it doesn't disappear in one day. Just like there was something fortyish in you when I first laid eyes on you at sixteen and a half, there'll be plenty left for years thereafter."

People would say to me: "How he keeps courting you all the time, such a charming husband you have." And also—I'm imitating them— "He's so charming, it's obvious how much he loves you." I can't stand that word, "charming." You can't read a book or newspaper these days without that cliché in all its permutations. Eitan wasn't that at all; he was more like alluring, luring everyone into his net without even casting it, or maybe captivating, with all the hearts he captured that didn't want to be set free. Don't misunderstand—most of those captive hearts were men, men of all shapes and sizes, rich and poor, young and old, friends and customers, one and all in his thrall.

Whatever. Eitan also wanted, on the festive occasion of his official change from Druckman to Tavori, for me to come with him and officially change my name from Ruth to Ruta, but I didn't go. I hate bureaucracy and filling out forms, and I don't care what's written on my identity card. "You call me Ruta, and that's enough," I said, "and I also come when you call me, no?"

And what did you call him?

Did I hear correctly? Can it be that you're also not focused on the history of the Yishuv?

Tell me anyhow.

You mean a nickname? There wasn't any. I called him Eitan and introduced him as "my man." Today "man" is the politically correct alternative to "husband," but in the Bible that I teach, the most chauvinist book imaginable, the book that fit my grandfather to a tee, if he had bothered to read it—"my man" appears many times instead of "my husband." Funny. There are people here in the moshava who heard me saying "my man" and asked if I had become a feminist.

Me? Are you crazy? I just like the word for "my man," *ishi*. It's personal and sounds the same as *ishi*, meaning my *esh*, my fire, which fit Eitan well, with his bonfires that died out and cooking coals that stopped sizzling, with the glowing skin of his that grew white and pale as a result of the disaster. Can I pour you some water too? My head's a mess, my heart is destroyed, but I somehow remember to preserve my throat.

Whatever. We were in the middle of Eitan, so let's continue. Even before he formally changed his name to Tavori, we felt he was more of a Tavori than many real Tavoris. Dovik, my big brother, who discovered him and brought him to us, said, "He's just like us. It would seem that not only Grandma Ruth but also Grandpa Ze'ev got laid on the side and Eitan is his illegitimate grandson." I hope you understand, that's not my style. I don't speak like that, but I'm imitating Dovik.

So it's true that Eitan was a Tavori, one of us, but he was also very different. Like a family member who came back after many years. I remember how we had just started dating and I felt he was like the last piece of a jigsaw puzzle fitting into place. At first in spirit, later also with his body. He wasn't my first. I had a little fling in the army. A little thing in every way, if you get my drift, and, after that, with a lecturer at the university, whom I got back at by calling Quickie Dick—I see you're smiling again, that's good, you also ran into him? Which of us girls hasn't had pointless affairs like that? We all have. Even in the moshavot of the Baron. But then, our first time, mine and Eitan's, when I was filled with him, I knew this was exactly what my body had waited for and wanted to stay with.

Should I continue? Because this isn't really the sort of gender issue you are researching, and maybe inappropriate for the second conversation of two women who only just met. Yes? Thank you. I suddenly realize how complex that simple biblical phrase is, "and they shall become one flesh," and what a genius the writer was, because "one flesh" is a wonderful idiom, perhaps even better than what it describes. And if you asked me as a teacher, I would say that "one flesh" is a much better combination than "one God." It's not just a matter of style, but it's the idea: two equal one. Maybe this is why I'm a Bible teacher and not a math teacher. Because in math one plus one equals one is an error, and in the Bible it's true. That's how it should be. One flesh. Everything in its place. Organized as it should be.

It's funny. From our childhood, Dovik's and mine, Grandpa always told us how important it was to be organized, to put everything in its place: work tools and kitchen utensils, writing implements and schoolbooks, short pants and long ones, shirts and underwear, winter and summer, each in its drawer. He had a line that used to make us laugh: "Moshe, Shlomo, every man *bimkomo*," in his place. It's not only right and useful; it's also nice. And that was my feeling from the first time with Eitan—that this is what we were for each other, the place where each of us should be. The perfect fit, the fullness, joined together without a gap or barrier. In short, one flesh.

You seem shocked, Varda. Is it because I'm talking this way or because it hasn't yet happened to you? I hope it will happen; you're still young. And then you'll remember me and say, "That crazy teacher from the moshava, the one who didn't shut up and didn't contribute one useful fact to my research, I can't remember her name, but she was right." And the guy you'll be with then will say, "Who're you talking to, Vardush?" And you'll tell him, "To myself, honey"—you'll surely call him honey; girls whose guys call them Vardush call their guys honey— "to myself, honey, I'm talking to myself, I'm reporting to myself that something important is happening here." And you'll also say, "If a girl who's with a guy talks to herself out loud, it's a sign that she's relaxed and satisfied and in a good mood."

Okay, enough with that. I see I have no one to get down and dirty with. Let's go back to Eitan and how we were all happily at his mercy. He came to us the way David came to the house of King Saul. I know, because I know them both. I never stop teaching David and I never stop studying Eitan. Eitan too could be violent, even dangerous, beneath his alluring exterior, but he wasn't wickedly manipulative like David. To fling a stone into Goliath's forehead and cut off his head? No problem. Eitan would also be happy and able to do that. But to place Uriah the Hittite on the front lines of battle and leave him there to be killed—that's only David. And Eitan would not kill two hundred Philistines to collect their foreskins. Because everyone who met him, myself included, would have given him their foreskin voluntarily.

Okay, I see that you're not only grossed out, you also have no idea what I'm talking about, so let's drop it. What's important about Eitan is that we all fell in love with him, and he wasn't surprised and didn't object. He saw how goodly were Grandpa and Dovik and how pleasing was Ruta, and began the adoption process. And an interesting thing happened: it was indeed Dovik who found him and brought him to us, and it was I who married him, but the one bound to him with the thickest rope was Grandpa Ze'ev, and that happened very quickly. Dovik was jealous; I was surprised: on one hand the toughest man in the family, our black basalt rock, and on the other hand Eitan—a dancing sunbeam, a darting hornet, a butterfly in the breeze. But there was also something elemental in both of them, real, primitive, Neanderthal in the good sense of the word.

I remember: When Grandpa Ze'ev took Dovik and me to the big carob in his wadi and told us about the caveman who lived next door and the cavewoman, that's what he called her, and the fire they lit, he said that he was a simple man with a simple life, who competed with other cavemen for territory and a woman and a cave, for water and food, not for honor or God. Everything was with rocks, he declared. And really—what's simpler than a rock? They cut with a rock, peeled with a rock, cracked bones open with a rock—when necessary, picked up a rock and smashed a rival in the head. There's even a word for it, "to bash," which is more than just to break. It's to destroy. As Grandma Ruth used to say, once in a while, "I'm bashed and broken."

I'm certain, by the way, that Grandpa Ze'ev would have gotten along wonderfully with those cavemen. There are things that only men like him could fully grasp, men of his generation, who were the proverbial bereaved bear and also the lone bird upon a roof, the unmuzzled ox treading out the grain, and the deer longing for streams of water. I remember once, in one of those communal singing sessions I was roped into, a woman started singing the old song about girls with ponytails and pinafores, and another woman made a joke about boys with ponytails and mustaches, and everybody laughed, because it was true. You're also allowed to laugh, Varda. Don't hold back, that was funny.

So that's it. It took me a while to understand it. It took me a while to see how much alike they were, my grandfather and my man, and the layers they uncovered in each other. But when I understood, I understood it all: that Eitan got down to the soft layers of Grandpa Ze'ev, under his armor and flinty exterior, and Grandpa Ze'ev got down to the hard granite layers of Eitan, under his weightless, radiant wings, and maybe they also discovered a common darkness in each other. Whatever. Even though they were two generations apart, they had a friendship that all men want and few men have. That friendship is what saved Eitan after Neta died.

EIGHT

THE MAGNIFICENT OX,
THE WAGON, AND THE MULBERRY

A Story for Neta Tavori by His Mother

1

Once upon a time, in a little house in a faraway moshava, at the foot of a big mountain—lived a little boy named Grandpa Ze'ev. When he reached the age of four, Grandpa Ze'ev got a very special gift from his parents.

"Happy birthday, Grandpa Ze'ev," they said. "We brought you a small sapling of a mulberry tree. You will water it and fertilize it, and one day when it will be a big tree, you will sit in its shade and eat its fruit."

2

Grandpa Ze'ev loved his little mulberry tree very much. He didn't understand much about its shade and fruit, but he was the son of farmers and he already knew how to water and spread fertilizer.

Two years passed. Grandpa Ze'ev and his mulberry tree grew, and one day his parents sewed him a canvas bag, bought him a notebook and a pencil, and said, "The time has come to go to school, to learn arithmetic and the alphabet."

3

The next day Grandpa Ze'ev got up early, took the bag, and went to school.

On the road were many other children.

This is a new student,

And this is an older student.

This one has books tied with rope,

And that one with books in a bag.

This one rode on a donkey and that one on a bicycle.

This one went on foot and that one was carried on someone's shoulders.

Some walked slowly, some walked fast.

Some went in a group, others by themselves.

And Grandpa Ze'ev went with his mother,

And thought about his mulberry tree.

4

"Hello, first graders," said the teacher. "I am your teacher, and I will teach you addition and subtraction and reading and writing."

All the students sat and learned: letters and vowels, numbers, plus signs and minus signs, and Grandpa Ze'ev just sat and thought how much he missed his mulberry tree.

"Maybe it misses me too? Because when it's not with me, then I'm not with it."

"Maybe it's thirsty and needs to be watered?"

"Maybe it'll think that I went away, and it'll give someone else its shade and fruit?"

And "What luck that it's a tree and can't move from its place."

5

The next morning Grandpa Ze'ev said to his parents, "I don't want to go to school."

"Why, Grandpa Ze'ev?" they asked.

"Because I'm not learning. I'm just sitting in the classroom all day and missing my mulberry tree."

Mother and Dad said, "This is really not okay, Grandpa Ze'ev. It's really important to learn!"

They sat and sat and thought and thought, and finally they said, "We know what to do!"

They took a big old wagon and built four walls on it.

"What are you doing?" asked Grandpa Ze'ev.

"Soon you'll understand," they said.

And they spread a layer of good soil on the wagon floor and added some cow manure to it.

"What are you doing?" asked Grandpa Ze'ev.

"Soon you'll understand," they said.

And they took a hoe and a pitchfork and a pickax and dug a very deep hole around the mulberry tree.

"What are you doing?" asked Grandpa Ze'ev.

"Soon you'll understand," they said.

They set up a scaffold of long thick wooden beams over the mulberry tree, attached an iron pulley to it, and ran a very strong rope over the pulley.

"And now," they said, "go bring our big ox, who plows the field."

6

Grandpa Ze'ev's mother and dad held on to the rope, tying one end to the horns of the big ox and the other end to the trunk of the mulberry tree.

"Giddyap, big ox," they said, "slowly and carefully."

"What's he doing?" asked Grandpa Ze'ev.

"Soon you'll understand," said Mother and Dad and the ox and the mulberry tree.

The big ox tugged hard, the heavy rope stretched tight, the iron pulley groaned, and the mulberry tree went up in the air with a huge hunk of earth stuck to its roots.

Grandpa Ze'ev was frightened. "Go slow! Be careful! So it won't get hurt!"

"Not slow! Faster, faster!" the mulberry tree cried out. "You think this is fun for me? Hanging in the air with my roots showing?"

7

Mother and Dad told the big ox to move back a little, guided the mulberry tree down into the wagon, added dirt until its roots were all covered, and watered it until the water dripped all around the wagon, and the mulberry tree said, "Stop, enough. It's good."

"Now do you understand, Grandpa Ze'ev?" asked his mother and dad. "Tomorrow you won't have to say good-bye to your mulberry tree. You'll ride to school together in the wagon."

8

The next morning Grandpa Ze'ev hitched the big ox to the wagon, climbed up and sat inside next to the mulberry tree, took hold of the reins, said "Goodbye" to his father and mother and "Giddyap" to the big ox.

The big ox pulled out of the yard into the road.

In the road were many children, all on their way to school:

This one riding on a donkey, that one on a bicycle.

This one went on foot and that one was carried on someone's shoulders.

Some walked slowly, some walked fast,

Some went in a group, others by themselves,
And Grandpa Ze'ev rode in a wagon hitched to an ox,
with a mulberry tree planted inside.

9

When they arrived at the schoolyard Grandpa Ze'ev parked the big ox outside, went into the classroom, and sat by the window. All day long he learned songs and stories and numbers and letters, vowels and plus and minus signs, and all day long he was a very good student.

But when the teacher wasn't looking, he smiled through the window at the mulberry tree, and when the big ox closed his eyes and yawned—because oxen get bored more than any other animals—he reached out the window and petted him on the nose and whispered, "Don't fall asleep, big ox, it's very important to learn."

10

During the lunch break Grandpa Ze'ev ate pita with cheese and olives, because that's what he liked to eat.

And he gave hay to the big ox, because that's what big oxen like to eat.

And the manure that the big ox made after the meal he buried in the soil of the mulberry tree, because that's what trees like to eat.

And at the end of the school day he got into his wagon and sat under the mulberry tree and said to the big ox "Giddyap!" and went home.

11

That's what they did day after day.
Grandpa Ze'ev studied well and got a good grade,
And the mulberry grew and gave fruit and shade.

And from lots of petting and lots of hay,

The big ox grew bigger in a magnificent way.

And he wasn't just any magnificent ox—he was the most magnificent of them all.

He didn't fall asleep in class and listened to the teachers and learned all the letters and knew all the numbers.

He was Grandpa Ze'ev's ox, and Grandpa Ze'ev loved him more than all the other oxen in the world.

NINE

....

I remember: A summer evening, a messy bed, his left hand under my head, and his right hand embracing me, or the other way around, you decide which way you prefer, and I am reading him Bialik's poem "Take Me Under Your Wing." You find that funny? That was a routine of ours. Eitan had quite a few holes in his education, and I helped him fill them. I read to him, I showed him works of art, and something funny happened. Eitan, who cut all his literature classes in high school, suddenly took a shine to that Bialik poem, especially the line "And be for me a mother and a sister." It's interesting, and I tell you this as a teacher, it's interesting what turns on someone like Eitan, who was never interested in art or poetry or literature. For whatever reason it was the simple words "be for me" that he picked up with such enthusiasm.

"You mean," he said, "that was in there when they taught us Bialik in high school?"

"Yes."

"Can't be. You added it now."

Our literature lessons took place in bed, of course—"The two of us, you and me," he would say in English, "the two of us and Bialik, naked in bed." But I read him other poets too. "I like Alterman," he said, "because of the *eh* sound he uses so much—and also Yona Wallach. Her

I'd also like to meet," he said. But we were talking about Bialik and his "be for me" that Eitan fixated on and made his own and would say to me at every opportunity with different meanings; instead of "tell me," "talk to me," "hug" or "kiss" or "caress me," or "touch me"—he would say "be for me." I'm not sure that's what Bialik had in mind, but for us "be for me" meant make me feel good, in body and soul and heart. Be for me, wash me, comb my curls or tie me up, do as you wish with me. Show that you love me, that you understand my love, and explain slowly and in detail exactly what you understand, and that we have our "together," *yahdav,* not just an individual man and woman, but be for me and I will be for you, not just an imperative and in the future, but also now, in the present tense. You are now for me; I am now for you. The word "love" in Hebrew, *ahava,* is very close to Yehovah, the name of God. He said that to me one day, and it surprised me. I see in your eyes, Varda, that something is getting through the gates of gender. I am a veteran teacher, and I know that look of understanding.

I remember: One day I showed him three paintings of women. The *Mona Lisa,* Botticelli's *Venus,* the Maja by Goya. Actually four: *The Naked Maja* and *The Clothed Maja.*

He glanced at them and said, "Art doesn't interest me."

I said, "Who's talking about art, Eitan? Look at them like a man looks at a woman. Whom would you go to bed with? Whom would you go to a party with?"

About the *Mona Lisa* he said, "This one is surely considered beautiful, but she isn't radiant. She's one of those beauties who leaves you cold."

About Botticelli's *Venus:* "Her head is beautiful, but her legs are sad."

On Goya's Maja: "Sexy ugly. Butt-faced but beats the others hands down. She's the sun in sheets, shining in her bed. The naked one and the clothed one too. It's interesting which one he painted first and which next. What did he say after the first painting: 'Take your clothes off' or 'Get dressed'?"

"But all this art of yours," he concluded, "can't compare with the beauty of a Wonderful pomegranate, lying open on a white plate in the sunshine."

"You're right about the type of pomegranate," I said, "but not cut open on a white plate but pomegranate seeds in a silver cup, and not in the sun but between sun and shadow."

"Whatever you say," he said. "You know best. I'll be beautiful and quiet."

I laughed. "You just don't get whose beauty I'm talking about, ignoramus that you are."

I already told you: he didn't read much; he wasn't a man to talk to about a good book or take to a play or museum. But he had this aura, and people were drawn to him like moths to a flame, and unlike those unfortunate moths, no one was burned in his good fire. And if you ask me, Eitan's whole story is a story of fire. Light, and heat, and dying down, and cold ashes, and catching fire again. Whatever. Don't get the impression that all day long I tried to teach him poetry and art. Most of the time it was his usual nonsense. His imitations and surprises and performances. Dovik and I also like to do imitations, but we imitate people, and Eitan would also imitate animals, not just the sounds, primarily movements and facial expressions, and also inanimate objects: "I will now impersonate a desk that chicken soup was spilled on." Or "This is the face of a border collie that failed its truck-driving test."

Sometimes he would hug me and hold me close and squeeze me and inform me that he was imitating a *Clematis flammula,* a type of climbing vine that I love, with a thousand tiny white fragrant wildflowers. We, by the way, are one of the few plant nurseries in Israel that sells them. Grandpa Ze'ev brought the seeds from the Galilee, from someplace near Hurfeish, and every summer, when all the wildflowers are already dead, in the dry period between the last of the *Agrostemma* and the first squill, it's the only one that blooms. It's a little hot for it here, but somehow it manages. In the days when Neta was still alive and Eitan was still my first husband, we would drive to the Galilee to see and smell it, and I always said to it: "You sweet and beautiful and relaxed thing, you clinging clutching clematis."

He was that way too, clinging and beautiful and holding tight, telling me over and over "be for me," and I would have to guess what he wanted me to be or do for him now. And if I would guess right away, he would say, "You don't have to hit the target, Ruta; I also love it when you miss and try again."

My whole body would melt. All of me would pool to a single place. A small sea under the diaphragm and the rest of the body was dry land. I have a small anatomical anomaly: another brain, which is not inside the head but for some reason under the diaphragm.

I remember: One day he announced he had decided to set up a petting zoo. I thought he intended to bring a few little goats and bunny rabbits to divert the children of customers at the nursery, but that night I found the sign: a little note attached to a matchstick that he stuck in his belly button like a flag, with the words PETTING CORNER, 5 SHEKELS and a drawing of an arrow. Pointing guess where.

That's a very charming story, Ruta, but perhaps we can return to the topic that brought me to you?

The whole moshava heard me laughing because of that petting corner, including my sister-in-law Dalia, who doubtless doubled over with envy, and including Dovik, who pretended to be asleep but couldn't hold back and smiled. How do I know? I know. I have many ways to know. Either I see or I hear or I assume or I imagine or I remember.

That's how it goes. Once in a while voices emanate from our yard that the whole moshava can hear. Sometimes shouts, sometimes roars of rage, and there were also gunshots, sometimes weeping and shrieking, but also wailing and moans of passion and sounds of laughter. From the day Eitan arrived until the disaster, lots of laughter.

He was great not only for the family but for our plant nursery. Dovik is good with numbers and accounting and bargaining with suppliers and dealing with municipalities and regional councils, so Eitan took on the job of rustling up private customers. And an interesting thing happened: you know how a handyman puts a magnet in a drawer, so all the screws and nuts and little nails will stick to it and not get lost? That's how Eitan was with us. No sooner did he arrive than a whole little group formed around him.

You think I mean women? For God's sake, get away from gender already. I already told you: a group of men was drawn to him. Every one of them a male. Customers, neighbors, friends: a whole kindergarten of men. Women, she says . . . women are passé, Varda. What men really want are other men. That's what they lack. True friendship, real friends.

What most women have a surplus of, they have a deficit, and that deficit is the basis of everything for them.

To cut it short, Eitan set up a pair of *poikehs* under Grandpa Ze'ev's big mulberry tree, and the men began to gather round. You don't need to write down the word *poikeh*, it's a kind of heavy pot with little feet that stand in a fire. He lit a campfire, burned coals, cooked up and dished out his meat stew to customers. A wonderful period began: "The jug of beer shall not run dry nor shall the *poikeh* of beef be empty," and our customers were spending huge amounts of money just because Eitan handed them a plastic bowl and plastic spoon and let them dig into the *poikeh* for a piece of meat and a potato with gravy and a slice of white bread for dipping, and they could sit together, to eat and drink and talk and look at his eternal flame. A fire was always burning here. Because of the cooking and also because men are attracted not only to one another but to fire. Not necessarily because they're drawn to danger, but simply to fire itself. This is why the woman of the caveman tended the fire in the cave with such devotion, so he would want to return, and when he returned he would sit around it with other men who returned, sniff the embers, add twigs to the flame, keep busy with the fire and with each other, and not go out and pick fights with woolly mammoths and bears and other cavemen and do stupid things.

To make a long story short, soon enough all the supervisors of gardening and landscaping from municipalities and regional councils in the north and center of the country, who constituted most of our business and our profits, stopped inviting Dovik to their offices and started coming to us to sit and eat under the mulberry tree. And when the children—Dovik and Dalia's twins, Dafna and Dorit, and our son, Neta—got a bit older, they would come straight from kindergarten or school to the nursery instead of the house, and every school day would end the same way: Dalia would still be at work at the regional council, I would still be at my work at school, Dovik in the office of the nursery, and Eitan in the nursery itself, telling customers to wait a minute, giving each child a big ladleful from the *poikeh,* making sure they ate it all up, and sitting them down to do their homework at one of the garden tables we sell here.

I remember: If they didn't understand something, he would shout out to the whole plant nursery, "Is there someone here who finished high school? You? You have patience for kids? Sit with them a minute, please, and help them with their homework." And if they brought school friends with them, after one of Eitan's meals they didn't want to eat whatever their mothers had made for them, and soon enough we had a day-care center here. Day care for kids of forty and fifty and kids of five and six. You know what? Maybe on second thought you should write the word *poikeh* in your notebook, because if there were more *poikehs* like this in your history of the Yishuv, all that Zionism would look a lot better.

TEN

....

Ruta: Were we on for today?

Varda: No. I was at your neighbor's house, and I decided to come over and say hello.

Ruta: That's nice. It's like the joke about the bear in Alaska who says to the hunter: "You don't really keep coming here for the hunting, do you?" Maybe when you're a bit older and we become better friends, I'll tell it to you. We haven't yet gotten to the stage where I can tell you disgusting jokes. You want something to drink? Maybe instead of tea with lemon you would like some of Dovik's *limoncello*? I just now poured myself some. You caught me red-handed. Here. You like *limoncello*?

Varda: It's delicious, but I'm not much of a drinker. Certainly not at this hour.

Ruta: I'm so restless. Neta's birthday is coming up and I'm like a caged lion. Neta. Neta. My child. The child that you never ask exactly what happened to him.

Varda: I don't ask because a person should talk about things like that on her own. Not wait to be asked.

Ruta: I told you. I said his name and I said "disaster" and I said "grave" and "cemetery" and I also said "dead." I said it. All you have to do is connect the dots. I said "after Neta died." And I said I had a child who died. A boy of six. Almost six and a half to be exact. And you didn't react. Only your research is important.

Varda: I'm sorry. I didn't see it that way.

Ruta: Once I used to put it this way—"Life is over." There was the disaster, and life was over. Funny, Neta died and I said "over" about my life, his mother. But the truth is, no, it's not over, and in a certain sense it's even worse than that. Neta died, and his father, in a slightly different way, also died. He wasn't himself anymore. I lost the two of them, my man and my son, "him and his son on the same day," as it is written. Have you noticed how disasters improve the Hebrew language? They make it more beautiful and ceremonious, with those special phrases that carry heavy burdens: "too holy to touch," "too mysterious to understand," "too ancient to bear."

Dead. He did not speak and did not laugh and did not touch me even once and primarily punished himself. And you know what? He should have. He had it coming. I didn't hit him in the face with it, but he knew very well what I thought: that if there was someone to blame, it was him. And I too was to blame, for letting him take Neta on that hike. "A hike for guys," girls not invited. That's how it is with parents. Even when they're the parents of a soldier who was killed, and there's a whole list of commanders and politicians who can be blamed—even then, they blame themselves. Surely we are to blame. Always. Even if we were at work and a drunk driver went up on the sidewalk and ran over the child on the way home from school, we are to blame. And if a doctor sent him home with the wrong diagnosis, we are to blame. And even if lightning were to strike him from the sky, why did the lightning strike him and not us? After all, that's what we're there for. All the more so a father who takes his little boy on a hike and brings him back to his mother dead. There are no others to blame.

What a good boy he was, good and smart and beloved and full of love for others, but many six-year-olds are like that, and what can someone say about someone who died at that age? So many things could change. A talented boy, but not extraordinary. Maybe that was actually what was special about him, that everything with him was in moderation, properly balanced in body and soul. Already at the age of two he was steady as he moved and so bright-eyed it was almost scary, and another thing, a little hard to describe, but there's a word for it: "symmetry." Not just of right and left, also of inside and outside. No, I don't mean symmetry. I don't like symmetry. This is something else. Whatever. I feel I'm getting irritable and angry. I have a recurrent thought, it's terrible to think this way, I know, but if somebody had to die, in other words, if the Angel of Death had a quota to fill on that day, then why that particular child? There are so many other children to pick as a victim instead. And I say that not only as a proud mother but as a veteran teacher, who knows—after generations of spoiled, arrogant, stupid, noisy children who sat in my classroom year after year—I know how to identify a special child.

So that's that. Life was over. The fire went out. In two private hearts and the one shared heart. Every couple has this eternal flame, sometimes small, sometimes big, which flares up and fades down, which is sometimes too strong and sometimes needs more air and always needs to be tended and fed. And with us the disaster extinguished it with a single blow. We had been married almost seven years and knew each other a few years before that, and one already knows one's partner, his on-off switches and dials, and what he likes and what he doesn't, what makes him laugh and what makes him feel good, and also what annoys him, which can be good too because it's the flip side of boredom and routine. And suddenly—a stranger. A new husband. There are women who will tell you this is what happens in the end with every husband, but usually it happens gradually, and with me it happened overnight, all at once.

Varda: You didn't tell me how Neta died.

Ruta: It's so strange for me to hear his name spoken by another person, especially an outsider.

Varda: Do you want to tell me?

Ruta: "Do you want to tell me?" . . . Quite the therapeutic tone, all of a sudden. Not a bad imitation of you, right? No, Varda. I don't want to tell you, but I will, because I'm polite and it's only right. Neta died from a snakebite. It's weird, but I'm sometimes embarrassed to say so. As if dying in the army is honorable, and to be killed in an auto accident is part of the life people made for themselves. I mean, no society prohibits the use of cars because of the sanctity of life. Sanctity of life is bullshit. And illness is reasonable, and of course old age, but snakebite is something that must be hidden. It's a shameful, frightening death. Because who ever heard of such a thing? That here, in the twenty-first century, an animal could kill a person? Where are we, dammit? India? Africa? But every year two or three cases like these are published, and people read about them in the newspaper or see them on television and say, "Look at that, Shula, unbelievable. Somebody died from a snakebite." Who's that knocking at the door? It's me, the Angel of Death, dressed up as a snake.

You don't need to write the name Shula; it's just the generic name of a woman who reads a book while her husband is watching sports or the news and—you know what?—the editors of the papers and the husbands of the Shulas are right. It really is in the unbelievable category. To die from a snakebite? "He shall strike at your heel"? "You shall strike at his head"? What's come over you, God? We're not in the Bible anymore. Enough already with those plagues of Egypt, the vipers and snakes and all the blight and mildew and boils and leprosy of yours. We've made progress. Today you can get run over in a crosswalk, get blown up by a terrorist, overdose on drugs, be killed by friendly fire, or unfriendly fire, or in a plane crash. Why did you come down on my poor kid with your most ancient shtick? And what else are you going to take out of your arsenal for me? A lion will arise from the Jordan Valley? Two she-bears will come out of the woods and mangle children? What? A band of destroying angels? Big rocks falling from the sky? Will the earth open its giant maw and swallow me up?

A snake. You understand? A snake. And in the desert yet, in the most remote and isolated place with no way of calling for help. That's how God loves us: "As a bride you followed me in the wilderness, in a land not sown," says Jeremiah. Female not male, singular not plural. Second person singular, alone and afraid. You wanted gender? So here you are: a whole people who are one female person, hungry, tired, dependent, terrified, thirsty, dying for a shower, no cell-phone reception. Far from home, far from a road, far from love, far from a hospital, far from people—that's how God loves his spouse.

A hike for guys, with all their dumb army slang for loading gear, locking down, navigating, zeroing in. Orienting with a map, so he could take our son without getting lost, straight to the place and time of the snake.

This cannot be denied or changed. He took him there. Not I. Girls not invited, he told me, and smiled that smile of his, and Neta looked at him and gave me the same exact smile. Did I stand a chance? A hike for guys. Just the two of them alone. You and he.

Varda: You can stop here, Ruta, you don't need to say it all at once.

Ruta: But I'm also to blame. I could have said: No, don't go. I could have objected: No, I won't allow it. But as opposed to what they say about mothers and motherhood, I didn't feel the famous feeling that something was about to happen. And by the way, even at the moment that it happened I didn't feel that something had happened, as better mothers than I am, or better liars, feel. Nothing. I sat at home fully relaxed and then went to sleep with no problem. After all, Eitan is the most responsible and organized guy there is. He never forgot a detail, and on that hike everything was organized like clockwork, the list of equipment and checking the vehicle and planning the route, but nobody took the snake into account. Not Eitan either. Here exactly is where he bit him. On the inside of the wrist. But that's not the picture I can't keep out of my head. Not the two fangs stuck in the flesh and not the squirt of the venom, what I keep seeing is Eitan running, hugging and carrying Neta in his arms, running and knowing it was hopeless.

ELEVEN

....

How did you meet?

Who?

You and Eitan.

Nice of you to ask. And also wise. The time has come for just talking, girl talk, fun stuff, not the downer of my disasters and not your boring history of the Yishuv.

We'll get back to both those topics. I'm counting on us both.

Is that a threat or a promise?

That depends upon you.

You will be surprised to hear, Varda, that Eitan and I were an arranged match. The matchmaker was my brother, Dovik. He came home one day all glowing and announced, "I met a guy who's perfect for us. I'll bring him here when I get the chance." And the chance was his wedding to Dalia. In the same breath that he announced that they had decided to get married, he also said he intended to invite his new friend to the wedding, so we could meet him.

"Never in my life have I heard you talking with such excitement about someone," I said to him.

"Because never in my life have I been so excited about anyone," he said.

"What did you invite him as?"

"What do you mean? As a friend."

"As a friend or as the bride? You seem to me slightly in love, Dovik."

"The bride? But he's a guy," Dovik said, with typical obtuseness.

"That's exactly what I'm talking about. Do we maybe have a *feygeleh* in our family?"

"Very funny," said Dovik.

"I don't understand the direction this conversation is taking," said Dalia. "We're announcing our engagement and all of a sudden all this talk about this guy?"

And Dovik said, "Dalia's right, you're talking nonsense, Ruta."

"Thank you, Dovik," said Dalia. "You're sweet. Can we move along now to truly important matters? I want to talk about the food we'll serve and the clothes we'll wear. I want every detail of the wedding to symbolize love and intimacy."

Dalia really loves symbolism. She finds it everywhere. She can be standing by the dairy section at the supermarket and say, "Wow, how symbolic, ten in the morning and already they ran out of three-percent cottage cheese." But Dovik paid no attention to the symbolism of the buffet, put on a sly look, and continued, "But if you're asking what I invited him for, then definitely not as a bride, but as a groom. I want you to make eye contact with him at the wedding, because it could be that one day he'll be the one for you."

At the time I was sixteen and a half and not interested in any matchmaking. But Dovik said it again: "Listen to what your big brother is telling you. Make eye contact with him, Ruta, you hear?" So then I was convinced I was right, that he was really in love with his new friend and that he decided to use me as bait to keep Eitan close to us or that this was the next best thing to getting into bed with him himself. Either way, it was very amusing to see him in such a state.

"Eye contact, Dovik?" I said to him when he nagged me about it the next day. "I'm all of sixteen years old, and if you hadn't noticed, I'm one of those sixteen-year-old girls who still has no tits at all. I don't deliver the goods."

As you've surely noticed, Varda, and I've noticed that you've noticed, even now I'm not outstanding in the boob department, but back then I was flat as the kitchen table.

Dovik laughed. "When you see him, it'll come to you naturally. As for your tits, we're all waiting for them patiently, so he can wait too."

To cut it short, Eitan came to the wedding, and I made the obligatory eye contact. It wasn't hard because I definitely found him attractive, and he definitely noticed me and smiled at me, and we also exchanged a few words, but that was it.

The truth? I was disappointed. He looked fine, not just a pretty boy, a nice inviting face, beautiful hands, graceful walk. What I liked best was his skin, which had a unique color, kind of golden. My diaphragm brain wondered if he glowed in the dark and I felt myself blushing.

It was obvious that he liked me too, but nothing happened. I mean something did happen, big time, but not with me. With me everything happened only much later, when Eitan kept coming to visit more and more, and it was quickly clear to me that he wasn't coming because of Dovik but because of me, and another thing, that although I was twenty and he was twenty-five, I was the one who would have to wait for him to grow up and not the other way around.

Whatever. Back to the wedding. Dovik and Dalia stood at the gate to the yard hand in hand, the same way Dalia symbolizes her happiness in public to this very day. They greeted the guests—hugs and backslapping, kisses on the cheek and big hellos, jokes about the gifts, who gave what and how much—until Eitan arrived. And then, the moment Dovik saw him approach, he said, "Here he is," and he left Dalia and went to him.

He took him by the hand and led him in with a look of "see what I found" and again whispered to me like an idiot, "Eye contact, Ruta. You hear?" But it was already clear that the last thing Eitan needed was eye contact with me, a girl of sixteen and a half who was too tall and too flat-chested, since all the well-developed women there were already looking at him. Even our mother, who deigned to come from the United States and got a new face-lift in honor of the wedding of her firstborn son, asked me, "Who is that *handsome* guy, the one Dovik likes so much?" And I said, "I have no clue, Mother"—it's so strange for me to say that word, to her then or to you now—"I have no idea, it's some friend of his from the army."

At the time, I didn't yet know all the details, but I later learned that they both had indeed served in the same army unit, but not at the same time or in the same job. Eitan was a combat soldier and Dovik an operations sergeant; that was the formal definition of his job, but in practice he was a jack-of-all-trades, a cross between a secretary, a quartermaster, a personnel manager, and an intelligence officer, a finger in every pie. He knew everything that was happening, took part in every mission briefing, designed and stitched together ammunition vests and customized carriers for special operations, pilfered equipment from other units, waited for the combat soldiers like a devoted doe-eyed company clerk, and to this day he is active in their veterans' organization and raises money and hires musicians for their get-togethers.

I'm sure one reason he fell in love with Eitan was that Eitan was a combat soldier, and he wasn't. Dovik has breathing problems, and from childhood he was wedded to his inhaler and exempt from gym class, despite which he turned into a fearless kid who never got tired. He climbed to the top of the tallest trees, leaped between rooftops, invaded the pens of horny young bulls, picked fights with dogs, stole cars, always with a plaster cast that migrated from limb to limb. When he was a teenager he would ramble in the hills and play make-believe: on a mission deep in the Syrian territory, en route to blow up the headquarters of Black September, to wipe out infiltrators, demolish bunkers, and sabotage missile launchers. And because Dovik is a romantic type, he also rescued girls from the harems of Saudi sheikhs and the prisons of the Arab Legion.

The draft notice came, and Dovik, with 45 out of 100 on the army fitness profile, moved heaven and earth to get into the best combat unit possible, in whatever job. He also succeeded, as you know, but he met Eitan outside the military and totally by chance, because Eitan is younger and got there only after Dovik got out, and it was a first meeting that was more random and charming and even more romantic than my first meeting with him.

Dovik knows all kinds of cool places. A really beautiful tree, a secret clearing in the woods, a natural spring or a well. "I've been all over this land on foot, in a car and a jeep," he loves to boast, and then doesn't understand why everyone's laughing at him. In short, not far from our moshava, past the ancient aqueduct, he had a place to be alone, which

I think I already mentioned, his hidden pond. In the shallow part there was always a lot of mud from cows who came to drink, but suddenly, all at once, it gets clear and deep and very cold, and there, they used to say when I was little, lived an old crocodile left over from the days when Nile crocodiles multiplied in the Land of Israel, young lions roared in the vineyards, and she-bears came out of the woods.

The older kids in the moshava told the younger kids that once a year the moshava has to sacrifice a boy or a girl to this crocodile so he won't hurt us. So watch out, Ruta, that they don't pick you, because the way you're behaving, it could happen. One day, incidentally, a little girl came to the moshava from the city, the type with golden curls and a short pink dress and red shoes, and went hiking in the area and got lost and drowned in the aqueduct, and when they found her they identified her only by the clothes she was wearing, and they said the old crocodile ate her, and some people were happy: We don't have to give him a child of our own; he already got one.

Okay. Back to the pond where they met. Totally hidden, surrounded by raspberry bushes, inula, reeds, and bulrushes, with a narrow path in the bush tunneled by wild boars, and always something slithering in the grass, something chirping and rustling. When Dovik grew up he used to take girls there; it was a melting place, that's what he called it, a place where girls melted. Dovik, as I told you, is not especially intelligent or elegant, and kind of clumsy, but he's great at closing in for the attack, an army term applicable to other situations as well.

He took me there too, when I was a little girl, to teach me how to swim. All the children of the moshava were taught to swim in the public pool by Shaikeh the gym teacher, and all the children knew that Shaikeh used this opportune occasion to touch all sorts of body parts, neglecting no one, boys and girls alike. In short, one day, after I had screamed "Don't touch me!" at him in the middle of a lesson and stuck a finger in his eye and bit his hand, Grandpa Ze'ev came to the school, beat him up in front of all the students, and made certain that he would leave the school and the moshava that very same day. As he phrased it: "Be glad you're leaving in an ambulance and not a hearse of the Hevra Kadisha." And he ordered Dovik, "Now you, and not that dog, will teach your sister to swim, because every child must know how to swim."

Dovik always did what Grandpa told him, but he discovered very quickly that I'm not all that coordinated and I get confused with the strokes and the breathing, and he had a brilliant idea: instead of swimming he would teach me to swim underwater, not in the pool at the moshava, but at his secret pond. I was six then, and he was fourteen, and at first he walked me into the water until it was up to my chest and told me to bend my head down into the water and exhale gently and then take my head out and breathe in, and do it again, and after I felt comfortable with my head in the water he told me to sink down to the bottom, all of me, and sit there and do nothing, just let air out very slowly and enjoy it. And if I felt like it I could take two stones and knock them together and listen to the nice noise they made, because everything sounds better underwater.

After I got used to sitting like that, he showed me how to do the breaststroke but told me to do it completely underwater, so the movements didn't need to be coordinated with breathing. And when I ran out of air, I should stand up, take my head out, fill my lungs with air, and go back under.

After a few lessons like these I started to lift my head from the water and inhale without standing, and that's how I still swim, like a seal. Most of the time underwater and taking my head out as little as possible. In general it's once every twenty or thirty meters, but if necessary or if I just feel like it, I can stay under for one hundred meters without stopping, and I can also hold my breath for four whole minutes. That's not a world record, but for ordinary people it's a lot. More than a lot, it's huge. Most people can't stay underwater more than thirty or forty seconds, and I became what they call a free diver without knowing I was one.

I don't know what I love more: diving itself or my ability to dive. Either way, it's good, and since the disaster it's had a soothing effect. It's like being weightless, like flying in slow motion. I'm not one of those deep divers. Two meters is plenty enough for me. I slide above the bottom of the pond, I glide like an underwater bird, and every time I dive I'm so happy I smile and also want to cry. Maybe I do cry, I don't know, inside the water it's hard to feel other wetnesses. Not sweat, if we actually perspire there, and not tears.

I remember: One day, when I was a young maiden, as the old ladies of the moshava would say, I was swimming in the moshava pool, and I picked up my head right next to Haim Maslina, who was sitting beside the diving board, trying to make an impression on someone I didn't know, some visitor from the city. I don't know if I've already told you about this pitiful loser, but he's the grandson of Yitzhak Maslina, a wimp in his own right, who was my grandfather's neighbor and likewise a founder of the moshava. To cut it short, as I took my head out of the water this moron says to me, "How can a girl with tits like nits have such enormous lungs?"

I wasn't angry or insulted. I love my little tits and they love me. And sometimes I'll say to them, How sweet it is that I got you, and not Dalia's, for example. And sometimes they'll say to me: How sweet that we got you and not her. They know how to talk, absolutely, but they're not into conversations with strangers, but only with me, and with each other, and with Eitan, when it was still possible to talk to him. Whatever. I said to Haim Maslina, "How does a family with a brain like a nit produce a genius like you?" And I dived back under and kept swimming.

By the way, ten years ago, on a school trip to the Jordan Valley, I took my students to the cemetery at Kevutzat Kinneret to show them the grave of the Hebrew poet Rachel, and I recited her words "I will wait for you till my days are done, as Rachel waited for her beloved," which is how I felt about my first husband. I also showed them the grave of Berl Katznelson, who lies there serenely between the grave of his wife and the grave of his other woman, and after these tidbits of Zionist education I permitted them to take a dip in the Sea of Galilee. A few of the girls joined in, and in their honor the boys decided to hold a contest of swimming underwater to a raft that floated fifty meters from the shore.

None of them reached the raft, and after they got out of the water I asked if it was okay for the teacher to enter the contest. They laughed, and somebody asked, "Hey, Teacher Ruta, we're finally gonna see you in a bathing suit?"

"Not really," I said, "I like swimming in shorts, and I bet you I can swim underwater even farther than the raft."

Somebody said, "And I bet you that you can't."

I asked, "What are we betting?"

He said, "Teacher Ruta, I'll give you a shekel for every meter you go beyond the raft and you give me a shekel for every meter you come up short."

I asked who else was betting, and ten hands went up.

Well, you can just imagine the rest. I got into the water up to my waist, waved goodbye, dived underwater, and after three and a half minutes that scared the shit out of them I came up twenty to thirty meters past the raft. I waved to them, took a gulp of air, and swam back to shore, under the water.

They were stunned. "What a Tarzan you are, Teacher Ruta, what else do you know how to do?" That's a good question. What, really? I know how to talk. A lot, as you have surely noticed. And I also know how to talk back to someone who deserves it, give a tongue lashing, like I gave Haim Maslina about his idiotic remark at the pool, and I know how to wait, a long time: twelve years I waited for my first husband to come back, and he was worth waiting for. I'm also not bad at crying, but the other three are my strongest suits.

And then, embarrassed and excited the way only teenagers can be, they tried diving in again, and the student I loved best, Ofer Maslina, the son of that same Haim Maslina, nearly drowned on me out there. This Ofer, you should know, was a very unusual boy. Not my best student and certainly not the hardest worker, but he was the most unique and interesting. He had something I really value and love—a completely different head. You could say he overcame the genetic baggage he got from his famously fucked-up family. I'll tell you something that once happened to me in class. You remember the Bible story about the prophet Elisha, the disciple of Elijah, how some kids laughed at him for being bald? They laughed at him, he cursed them, and when a prophet curses, there are consequences: "And there came forth two she-bears out of the woods, and tore apart forty-two of the children." Now as I tell you this I'm thinking, Too bad my grandmother couldn't also curse the kids who followed her and the tractor in the field and laughed at her.

Whatever. When I taught them that chapter, which because of Neta I have a really hard time with, I told them that Elijah the Prophet, Elisha's teacher, who in general was much more extreme and cruel, would never have done such a terrible thing to children, certainly not for ridiculing his baldness. And suddenly Ofer stopped drawing his little pictures, these little snails he always drew in his notebook, and raised his hand.

"Yes, Ofer, what would you like to ask?"

And in my heart: You sweet boy.

But I said, "Yes, Ofer, I'm waiting."

And in my heart: I am the grieving she-bear named Ruta. I would have come forth from the woods and devoured you.

"Teacher Ruta," he asked, "the Bible uses the feminine form of 'two,' but 'bears' is masculine, so how come you get mad at us when we say 'two shekel' or 'two boys' in the feminine?"

I looked at him. It wasn't clear if he was being a smart-ass or he just didn't understand, and I answered him, "You're right, Ofer, but 'two boys' in the feminine is an ugly mistake, but the 'two bears' is a lovely mistake. There are authors who would pay good money to make such a beautiful mistake."

And I felt more words rising from my diaphragm to my heart like bubbles from deep water: Like you, Ofer, a beautiful mistake like you. Lead me not into a big mistake.

Whatever. Back to the bet on the Galilee shore. Ofer took a deep breath, went under, disappeared, and after about half a minute I suddenly realized that was too much time and I got up and shouted, "Ofer! What's going on with Ofer? Anybody see Ofer?"

And then we saw his hands come out of the water, waving desperately, and then the top of his head, and he sank again, and it was lucky he was still fairly close to the shore. I ran in and swam to him, grabbed him, and pulled him out, and several students helped me get him from the shallow water to the shore.

We laid him down on the ground; he vomited a little and came to. The boys started laughing. "It's all an act. He wanted Teacher Ruta to give him mouth-to-mouth resuscitation."

He was confused and embarrassed, and I said, "Don't think this little drama made me forget about our bet." And I went around with my straw hat, Ruta-*mabsuta,* satisfied. "Put your shekels in here."

Somebody asked, "Teacher Ruta, what will you do with all that money?"

Another one said, "How about inviting us for a beer at the pub of the kibbutz?"

I said to them, "A teacher does not provide her students with alcohol." And I said to myself, Though here too I could easily outdrink them.

The next day I gave all the money to the school secretary, told her she should use it for new library books or test tubes for the lab, and I thought I was totally okay, but the students talked about it at home and parents complained: "What's a teacher doing betting money with students?" And Haim and Miri Maslina, our next-door neighbors, were alarmed: "Our son almost drowned with her!" And don't ask, all the problems that ensued. The principal summoned me for a disciplinary chat, the supervisor wrote a reprimand in my file, and in the end I got fucking sick of all of them, and in a parents' meeting I gave each parent the few shekels I won from their child in a performance they would never forget.

TWELVE

....

Dovik would usually drive to his pond alone. Grandpa let him take the pickup—this was our old pickup truck, the rickety Ford with the rounded fenders—from the age of fourteen, on condition that he not drive on the roads but only through the fields. At the pond he would undress and swim and then float naked on an inflated inner tube, which he called Dovik in the Basket, and imagine, so he told me, that if Pharaoh's daughter were to arrive, preferably with her handmaidens—as it is written in the Bible, so why change it—he would explain to them exactly how to pull him from the water and what to do with him after that.

As you surely understand, he would steal away and go there quite a lot, lying there and fantasizing about battling crocodiles like a king of the Zulu, and about our mother and what she was doing in America and whether she thought about us, and what it would be like to visit her there and pester her to buy him a Harley-Davidson as compensation for abandoning her son. And how on the one hand she handed us over to Grandpa, but on the other how good it was that she left us with him, and how could it be that everyone in the moshava was afraid of him but with us he was so good and gentle.

When he got a little older, he would escape to the pond from the chores Grandpa assigned him, hang out and dream how he would finally finish high school and go into the army and that he would kill himself if he wasn't accepted into an elite combat unit because of his asthma. And years later he began to escape to the pond from Dalia and her nagging and the symbolism she saw in everything, and once he also told me, "I realized that Pharaoh's daughters weren't coming there to pull me out, so sometimes I bring along a Pharaoh's daughter of my own."

Dalia, incidentally, is one of those women for whom it's terribly important to put on a display of happy marriage. She walks with Dovik in the street holding hands, and for this reason she also named their twins Dafna and Dorit—so all their names would start with the same letter—and when they were small, she would force him to come with her to the kindergarten every morning and afternoon, so that everyone would see that they brought them and picked them up together, and every so often she would hint at some special quality of lovemaking, and she would always speak about how much he loved her cooking, and don't misunderstand, she is a very good cook. I also love her meals. But food is food, and life doesn't center on that.

At first it slightly annoyed me: For whom are you making this show? But after a while I got it—she's not putting on a show for anyone; it's herself she's trying to convince, and at that point I began to feel a little sorry for her. Whatever. Today Dovik almost never goes to his secret pond, because despite its secrecy somebody told somebody who told someone else and in the end some journalist wrote about it in the paper. One of those journalists who recommends places worth visiting, so that swarms of kebab grillers and hookah smokers from all over the country will encamp there like families of locusts and leave behind empty potato chip and pretzel bags and piles of shit, pardon me, and toilet paper, and the noise they make remains even after they've gone. So one day Dovik saw a family there making a barbecue, which from his point of view is the greatest sacrilege possible. So distraught was he that he let the air out of their car tires and then began consorting with his Pharaoh's daughters in other secluded spots. "I discovered they could pull me even without the Nile or a basket," he once told me as he asked me to taste a fresh batch of *limoncello* and help him recalibrate the alcohol and lemon and water.

We did a lot of tasting back then, with different levels of strength, variations of sour and sweet, and at a certain stage we would begin laughing and talking nonsense. Dovik makes a beautiful *limoncello* and always says that it really depends not on the person who makes it but on the lemon tree, and something interesting happened with our old tree: ever since Grandpa Ze'ev died it has produced much better fruit. You could sense that it had an easier time of it when he was gone. The mulberry tree, on the other hand, mourned for him. It bore rotten fruit and lost its leaves in midsummer. That's how it is, trees have feelings and remember and don't know how to lie.

To make a long story short, one day Dovik came to his pond, and this time not in the pickup but riding lazily on the old bicycle, and saw an army jeep parked by the path. The jeep looked familiar. He took a look and saw that two of the modifications on it were his. Who drove my jeep? Who walked on my path? He crept quietly to the pond and heard someone swimming in the water. Who is that swimming in my pond? He discovered an army uniform hanging on a bush and underwear and a T-shirt and a worn pair of Balti trekking boots with socks stuffed inside. Who wears Balti and also wears them out like that? Only somebody from my unit.

Dovik hid in the foliage and waited. After a quarter of an hour this somebody stepped out totally naked and urinated on the ground. Dovik was elated. First of all this was not someone who pisses in a pond but comes out. Second, his looks, how handsome he was. Everything about him was handsome, he told me, a few years later: "If Pharaoh's daughter and her maids had shown up, they would have pulled him, not me."

The fellow finished pissing and went back in the water. And Dovik, without thinking twice, stripped and jumped in after him, splashing as loudly as possible, to indicate that the boss was present. That was it. That's how my brother and my man met: "Dovik, Eitan, nice to meet you, where're you from? Where are you from? Who told you about this place? And where are you in the army? I knew it. I was there a little before you and recognized your jeep."

"Really? What's your last name? Tavori? Ah . . . so you're Dovik Tavori? . . . They still talk about you, about all the mechanical tricks and upgrades you rigged up."

Dovik swelled with pride, and after the "Do you know him?" and

"Do you know that one?" and the "Get outa here!" and "No way!" he invited Eitan to have some mulberries from our tree that he had brought with him.

They sat naked till they dried and were not ashamed. Eitan made coffee; Dovik served mulberries; they ate and drank and got back in the water. Eitan suggested they dive to the bottom, and Dovik said he couldn't dive because of his asthma. But, he added, if you're into diving, you should meet my sister, she dives much better than I do.

That was that. Eitan finally had to go back to his base. Dovik accompanied him to the jeep and said, "I didn't only install this mount for the hi-lift jack, I invented it," and also "I have a feeling we'll meet again." And Eitan said, "I do too. Looking forward. See you."

And in fact, a few months later, after Eitan finished his army duty, they met again at a get-together of their unit. You should see the invitations to these get-togethers. Every invitation is just numbers, eighteen digits in a row. The first six digits are the date. Always six, because these cavemen include zeroes. The eighth of May 1967, for example, is zero eight zero five six seven. The next four digits are the hour, and the last eight are the coordinates of the location of the meeting. You should understand, Varda, with them every place is a waypoint and every get-together is a military operation. And even if it's a club in Tel Aviv, the address will not be a street and number but those asinine coordinates of theirs. Why? Because they don't simply go, they *navigate*. And anyone who can't find the waypoint doesn't deserve to be there.

They recognized each other right away, and Eitan, with his marvelous capacity for silliness, embarrassed Dovik in front of everyone. He pretended he didn't know who he was and finally said, "Ah, it's you, I just didn't recognize you with your clothes on," and everyone who heard started to laugh. And that was it, that was the beginning of their friendship, which unlike all the clichés about comrades-in-arms was a genuine friendship. Yes, Varda, clichés, idle chatter—all that army-buddy stuff is vanity of vanities, something they paste on like an actor's mustache, no more than a pose of men nostalgic for their youth and a pretext for another dose of action and experience. They will help one another, and they'll get together and tell stories, but it's not real friendship. Yes, rescues and fund-raising and loans when necessary, but they

simply don't know how to open up their hearts. And in truth, Eitan—
and I too, I'm the same way—never had real friends. Even those who
served and fought alongside him. It was Dovik, who didn't serve when
Eitan did and wasn't a combat soldier like he was, who turned out to be
his truly good friend.

And the reverse is also true: suddenly Dovik, who talked only about
glorious tales of the army and about girls he'd been involved with, began
to talk only about his new friend, and for the first time with love instead
of his usual bragging. And because of that he also fixed us up. I have no
doubt. He kept Eitan by his side. He told me how handsome and nice
and amusing Eitan was, and gave Eitan a briefing: "I have a sister much
smarter than I am," he told him, "and I want you to meet."

Eitan laughed. "The one who dives better than you do, or another
sister?"

"I have only one sister," Dovik said. "Come and I'll introduce you."

THIRTEEN

....

That's it. That's how I found myself making that eye contact. I knew the guy was called Eitan and that Dovik had met him at his secret pond and that he was crazy about him and wanted to fix me up with him, so I did as I was told. In other words, I made what at age sixteen and a half I thought was eye contact: I stared at him with calf's eyes. Funny. When I see my girl students today, with their craning necks and push-up bras and mascaraed eyes and glam makeup, mincing around the schoolyard, I remember that at their age I was basically a boy. But Dovik ordered me not merely to look at Eitan but to be sure that he noticed that I was looking.

Dovik is my older brother, and we are very close, and when he asks something of me I comply. I was, admittedly, always the more intelligent of us two, and because I am more intelligent I also know that I am and he sometimes forgets, but on the plus side, he is a good and concerned brother and top-notch businessman and manages the nursery with great success, and unlike me he also makes the most of what he has, and I, who am much more capable than he is, am satisfied with what I am and not with what I could have been.

Whatever. We were in the middle of eye contact, so let's go back there. At Dalia and Dovik's wedding I wore a white dress in order to annoy the bride, I put on flat shoes so as not to be taller than the groom,

I did my hair in a thick braid with a red band at the end—and I picked two sweet-smelling flowers from our plumeria tree and pinned them to my head—and looked in the mirror and said to myself, One day, when you stop being a wild tomboy and become a pretty woman, you'll be a very pretty woman. At sixteen and a half I didn't give myself stage directions as I do today, but I already had the brain in my belly, and I talked to myself quite a lot. Too bad I couldn't also prophesy the future.

By the way, you can still see that plumeria, here by the sidewalk. It's not at the same level of family importance as the carob in the wadi or the acacia in the desert or the mulberry tree in the yard, but it's mine. Grandpa Ze'ev planted it a few days after he brought Dovik and me here, and said, "This tree is called plumeria, Ruta. From now on, you are responsible for it and it will be your tree." And he told us, "When I was a boy in our moshava in the Galilee and my father would sometimes take me to Tiberias, I saw two plumeria trees there with flowers that smelled like perfume. Water it, take care of it, it will grow, and you will grow, and the two of you will be much more beautiful together than either one of you alone."

He stuck three poles around the sapling and tied its slender trunk to them with strips he tore from an old sheet.

"A sheet is better than a rope, it doesn't scratch the trunk," he explained, "and don't pull it too tight, so that the trunk will sway a little in the wind and develop muscles."

And Eitan? Eitan came to the wedding in a crisply ironed white shirt—Someone is ironing for him? He can iron that well himself? asked the pretty woman inside the wild boy—and golden skin, which took my breath away and filled me with a desperate urge to touch it and feel if it was warm and smooth to the hand as well as the eye, and gold-greenish eyes and brownish hair and khaki pants and sandals; I can't deny it, I liked what I saw. Really liked him. Not just as a guy but as a partner for playing ball and hide-and-seek. I immediately noticed that he was exactly my height, and that pleased me, because I knew he had already stopped growing and I hadn't, and given my inclination to asymmetry I like couples where the woman is slightly taller, and what I like even more is that the man likes it, and I even toyed with the notion that just as he decided to come to our first meeting in clothes and skin that I would find attractive, he also wore the height that I would love.

In short, it all looked very promising, but nothing happened. In other words, I made the eye contact that Dovik demanded I make, and Eitan looked back at me and even asked me if I was the groom's younger sister he had heard so much about and also smiled an undeniably nice smile, but I didn't smile back quickly or broadly enough or answer him in some unforgettable way. Basically, except for mazal tov wishes and another little smile he flashed at me half an hour later across the table—Dovik insisted that his new friend sit with us at the head table—we didn't get around to actual talking. Everything was potential, in an embryonic stage. The butterfly had not yet emerged from the cocoon.

We sat there, Dovik and Eitan and I and our mother and Grandpa Ze'ev and Dalia and her mother, who was called Alice. And you won't believe what happened. She also made eye contact with Eitan, a look that lasted half a second in all but was effective enough to take him home with her. The mother of the bride! You understand? Dalia rode off for a honeymoon with Dovik, and his friend rode off to Tel Aviv, to the bed of her mother.

The family was in an uproar. The whole moshava was talking. "Only in the Tavori family do such things happen, and now they are intermarrying with their own species." Good that for a change it was just a crazy story and not another horror from their cellar of horrors. But to me it was amusing, even exciting in a strange way, and I was also a little jealous, I must admit. Not that I entertained hopes of taking him to my bed—I was after all a boy without boobs, as I told you—but beneath the jealousy and beyond the inexperience and limited understanding was clear, sharp knowledge: Dovik would achieve his goal. One day Eitan and I would marry, and he would join the family.

And apart from that, it was all worth it just for the look on Dalia's face. I was Ruta-*mabsuta,* happy as a clam, when I saw her expression. Because her mother, this Alice, not only was much prettier and more elegant than she was but also stole her show. Walked out of there with a guy nearly thirty years her junior, more accomplished and better-looking than the bridegroom—and I say this as someone who loves

them both and knows them quite well—went off with him in front of
the whole crowd, before the wedding was over: "Bye-bye everyone, I'm
going home with my new toy. Ciao. Open the presents yourselves and
say goodbye to the guests for me."

Write it down, write it. You're always writing names anyway. Alice.
She was English. She also spoke English more than Hebrew. I think she
came from Manchester. Write that down too. Part of the history of the
Yishuv is where the Jews came to Israel from. What a character. With
style. The real thing. Sexy the way only a woman of fifty-one can be,
the way I will be in another few years, if I'll know what to do with the
brakes that stop me and the pain that contorts me and the weights that
sit upon my soul.

A lively divorcée, egocentric, well put together, savvy, took good care
of herself. She simply took Eitan by the hand—the hen that caught the
fox by the tail, like in the children's story by Bialik, which I read to Neta,
but not to his father—and waved goodbye to everyone with her other
hand, and I think she shot me a special look right then, as if she understood she was taking Eitan away not only from her daughter's wedding
but also from his first meeting with his future wife, and led him to her
car.

I remember: A few years later, when Eitan was already my husband
and I asked him why in fact he went with her, he said to me, "Because of
the car, Ruta. You didn't see what kind of car she had?"

"I didn't notice," I said.

"An old Mini Cooper," he said. "A woman with a Mini Cooper like
that has got to be something special herself. And besides going around
the block with her, I wanted to go around the block in that car."

"'Around the block'? You're disgusting."

And in the parking lot—pay attention, Varda, and learn!—she opened
his door and held it open the way a man opens a door for a woman, and
Eitan picked up on it and immediately got into the role. He pressed his
legs together, tucked an imaginary skirt under his butt, and sat down
like a female, and I understood what kind of party was about to happen
for both him and her.

She closed the door like a hunter on his quarry, walked around her
very special Mini Cooper—just a jalopy, if you ask me—to the driver's

door, and got in and started the engine and drove off, and everyone knew where and what for. And after they were gone, and people began whispering, it was clear how silent it had become when she took him and walked out.

And what did Dalia say about all this?

If that's what concerns you, Varda, if that's what is most important for you to know, then on that evening she said nothing at all. It began only after she recovered: "She ruined my wedding, she took all the attention away from me to herself, on my night, at my wedding. She's treated me that way ever since I was I little girl . . ." Until this day she hasn't forgiven her, and "until this day" means even after Alice died. You know those women who keep complaining about their mothers their whole lives? What she did to me, what she didn't do, at age three she forced me, at age ten she told me, at age fourteen she didn't let me . . . Grow up already, girls. You're big now. It's your life. Take responsibility. Our mother, mine and Dovik's, was worse. She left us when we were children, left us with her father-in-law and went off to America, so do I weep over it? The opposite. I look at it in a positive way: You have a shitty mother? Learn from her how not to be.

Okay, let's stop here. I have a lot to say about my mother and I've had it up to here with Dalia too. But it was Eitan, after I really mouthed off about her one time, who asked me to stop. He said it was unhelpful and unacceptable. It was hard to grow up with an Alice like that for a mother, sparkling, polished, an ambassador of classy Europe in the screwed-up Middle East.

And what did you feel when Eitan rode away with her?

I already told you, I was a little jealous. More precisely, I told myself that what I felt was what's commonly called jealousy. But my diaphragm brain kept deriving lessons and conclusions. I said it wasn't so bad. Not so bad, Dovik's friend Eitan or whatever your name is, I'm just the little sister who hasn't yet got the goods, but I'm a winner and getting better all the time, and I have time and patience. In the meantime she will pamper you with cakes and ale and teach you everything that later on will make me feel good.

So it was that the first worthwhile words of courtship that I uttered to my lover I spoke to myself and not to him. He, with her in the stupid

Mini Cooper that turned him on, didn't hear and didn't feel and didn't answer, but I, when I told him all this in my heart, felt hot all over my body. Good thing that back then I already had that dopey quality that protects me. I said to myself, Calm down, Ruta, wait, what is meant to be will be. And I did wait, and several years later, when he was mine, a few days before our wedding, when I was already pregnant with Neta, a first pregnancy that sweetened my whole body, he was like candy in my womb, I demanded that Eitan finally tell me what happened after they made their getaway from the wedding.

He asked if I really wanted to hear it, and we both laughed, because my first husband Eitan was the retro-jealous type. He doesn't agonize over what might happen and isn't bothered by what's likely to happen but gets irritated over what happened in the past. Even men who had walked past me on the sidewalk on my way to kindergarten irritated him.

"I really want to hear," I told him.

"Okay, for a month and a half we were '*the two of us* together *all day* in bed naked.' Those were her words."

Now it was my turn to be annoyed, because till then I thought that the English phrase 'the two of us naked' was something he had invented for us, and only the two of us said it about ourselves, he and I about each other. And suddenly it turns out that this was her invention. But it was okay, I restrained myself, because this wasn't the only good lesson he got from her.

A month and a half he was with her, and she barely let him go out. Not only out of her apartment, but out of her. She held him close with her arms and legs, and when they got hungry, she said, We'll crawl to the kitchen attached to each other; I'll show you how.

To make a long story short—she fed him delicacies to his heart's content, and just as a few years later I would read him poetry, she played him music, requiems and "Stabat Mater" hymns, Rossini and Hasse and Fauré.

"I also heard Egyptian and Turkish music at her place," he told me.

"Just like Ramona played for Saul Bellow's Herzog," I said.

He, of course, had no idea what I was talking about, but no problem. I see you don't either. She was also the one who taught him what and how to drink, and that's why besides Dovik's *limoncello* I also like to drink Pimm's and gin and tonic, sometimes I even treat myself to Hendrick's gin, like she did—who would believe it, the granddaughter of Grandpa Ze'ev—and a kir in the afternoon and Calvados at bedtime. Don't worry, I'm not getting drunk, just disconnecting a few synapses in my head. It's good.

So I see, Varda, that you are beginning to understand who benefited from all this in the end? I, Ruta. Thank you very much. He served all the customers and friends the *poikeh* he cooked under the mulberry tree, and to me he served in bed the delicacies he learned from his sister-in-law's mother. The whole deal about the *poikeh* is that whatever you throw in, everything but the kitchen sink, is considered a success. Eitan himself told me: a *poikeh* is a compost barbecue. That's planters' humor, a nursery joke. So all the putrid *poikehs* were eaten by friends and customers, and to me he served the meals she made for him: dinners where he and I were the first course, and suppers where he and I were the dessert. She only permitted him to cook one thing, the eggs at breakfast, because Eitan really knows how to fry an egg sunny-side up, with a soft yolk and crispy white. He always made two of those for me and him in the same pan and always gave me the one that turned out better, the one he would call the seeing eye, because always—and this is a principle of culinary history, Varda, and the history of mankind, and maybe even your history of the Yishuv—every time you fry two eggs in the same pan, one is always better than the other, and you give it to the one you delighteth to honor.

After two days he told her he had to hop home to change clothes; he would just change them and come back.

"No home, Ethan," she said, that's what she called him, in English. "No home, Ethan, no way, if you go out, with that smell on your fingers and cream on your face, someone will steal you away from me. Women can sense men that other women love."

She's right. They can feel it. Not just a man who is loved, that's no great trick, but also a man in love, and a man who will soon blossom, even if he is already a grown man, and a man who will soon wither, even if he's young, and a man about to die, even if he thinks he will live forever. Just like those dogs—I read about them in the newspaper—who can sniff cancer in a person. So too women can smell illness and health, strength and weakness, kindness and evil, potential, humor, intelligence, and stupidity. And it's not from studying the eyes or reading the palm of the hand; that's nonsense. It's from the angle of the lips, from getting up from a chair, from words that repeat themselves, from the pouring of water from the kettle to the cup.

In brief, she took him to a men's clothing shop, bought him everything he needed, and brought him back home with her for more love and more music and more meals, and everything was wonderful and also seemed wonderful to such a young guy, but after a month and a half she informed him, That's it, Ethan, it's over, now you have to go.

"What happened?" he asked. "You're sick of me? That's it? You've had your fill?"

It turned out that, no, she wasn't sick of him and would in fact have been happy for another serving and yet another. But her regular boyfriend, some rich old fart from England, and a distant cousin of hers to boot, was a ship's captain, on one of those supertankers that circles the globe, and was now done dispensing petroleum in the Philippines or Scotland or wherever the hell it was, and was arriving the very next day in the Israeli port of Ashdod.

"Why this surprise, why didn't you tell me ahead of time that it would be a month and a half and that's all?"

"Because I prefer a guillotine to an hourglass. A single blow instead of a slow burial. Come, let's do it one more time and say farewell."

She made him a festive and delicious last supper, fucked him, excuse me, in a final and festive and particularly pleasant fashion, slept beside him for the last time extremely close, and sent him away: "That's it. Get out!"

"If you think," he said to her at the door, "that you can throw me away now, and after your oil deliveryman sails off, you can call me back, you're mistaken, Alice."

"That's fine," she said, "you've already proved how young you are in very pleasant ways. You don't have to prove it further with foolish declarations."

When Eitan told me this he also said that, along with all the lamentations and angst and the "what a pity" and "what a waste" of hers, he found the whole situation really funny, because at the same time she was telling him he had to go, and it was clear to them both that they each wanted him to stay, all that went through his head was an image of her elderly English ship's captain, with hair white from age and a nose red from alcohol and sleeves with gold stripes almost to the elbow, sailing from port to port in his gigantic supertanker, and everywhere he went he dropped his anchor, tied up to the dock, stood on the bridge in a white jacket, ringing a big bell and shouting, "Oil . . . Oil . . ."

That's it. Ethan left, the sun was shining, and a Labrador puppy that stood on the sidewalk looked at him and smiled. Eitan said—to himself and to me years later—a Labrador puppy is a very good sign. He phoned Dovik and told him that he had just been thrown out of his mother-in-law's bed, that he would be traveling abroad for a while; he had gotten an offer to join the security detail of some Jewish millionaire in Miami and would be back in a few months and concluded with "How's your sister? Tell her hello."

FOURTEEN

....

INSOMNIA

(Draft)

Someone walking on our street at night, if he passes by the nursery at its eastern end, will see a strong, sturdy man, wearing blue work clothes and Australian work boots. Sometimes he sits at the entrance and sometimes he patrols the grounds. His gait is strange. His legs bespeak strength of thigh and ankle and weakness of knee and calf, and his hands are gathered at his chest as if hugging or carrying something that only he hugs and carries.

This is how he walks, looks, guards, and inspects. On his forehead he wears a hiker's flashlight, and in his hand is a small pickax, generally used for simple digging and uprooting onions and bulbs, but in the right hands it can be a lethal weapon. Between the fingers of his other hand is a cigarette, and he doesn't toss away the burning butt but stubs it against a wall or the sole of his shoe till the burning end falls off. He stamps that out with his foot and throws the extinguished butt in the trash.

The few passersby, a worker returning from his shift, girls laughing after a party, an early rising soldier en route to his base, a young man returning from a night of love, seekers of sleep—where did it wander to?—they all look at him. Some with a quick glance, some with a lingering gaze. A few recognize him and there are those who even greet him. But he does not return their look and does not greet them back.

It happened once that two youngsters, one from a local family and a friend on his first visit to the moshava, tried to make fun of him. One of them even thrust out his hand and tried to knock the flashlight off his head, and the man suddenly dropped the pickax, spread his arms with astonishing quickness, and seized him in a bear hug that stopped his breathing. Then he lifted him easily, like picking up a baby, and carried him across the road. When he let him go the young man fell, coughing and wailing, "You broke my rib, you son of a bitch," and vomited on the ground. His friend helped him get up, the two of them ran away, and the man returned to his post.

Who is the man? The young people and the new people believe that he is merely a watchman, a day laborer, or more correctly a night laborer, since by day he is nowhere to be seen. But the old-timers know that he is married to the granddaughter of the owner of the plant nursery, and he is the brother-in-law and friend of her brother, the manager of the nursery, and he works there at jobs assigned him by the grandfather. By day he lifts and carries and loads, whatever is necessary, and by night he stands guard, and he doesn't sleep at all. There are those who escape from their pain into sleep; what he escapes into is insomnia.

What do insomniacs do? There are those who bait traps for sleep, put up signposts to guide its way. They try various pills, warm milk, infusions of leaves that are reputedly effective, and infusions of grapes known as wine and cognac. That, for example, is what the man's wife does as she waits for him in their house and their bed and he doesn't arrive. She drinks, lies down, drinks some more, reads, waiting for him and for her sleep. And maybe this is better than lying awake together, sharing their insomnia, both of them knowing that they can't sleep because of their neighbor in the bed, and both close their eyes and pretend the other has drifted off.

And there are couples who need each other then, because orgasm, it is said, leads to sleep. And if they don't want each other, they make do alone, with their own bodies. But these two do not, and it has been years since this woman has slept with her husband.

Sometimes the man comes into the house, lies down in another bed, in a room that is not the bedroom, and sometimes thinks he has dozed off. But then he wakes up to the reality of being awake. In other words, he slowly shuts his eyes, lies there knowing he is asleep, and suddenly realizes he is awake. Not just his heart, like the sleeping woman in the Song of Songs, but all of him. His limbs are limp like a sleeper's limbs, his breathing is relaxed like a sleeper's breathing, his eyes are closed like a sleeper's eyes, and sometimes he even dreams a sleeper's dreams, but then he senses that his eyes are open, looking inside him, and his dream is not a dream but memory and thought.

He gets up and gets dressed and goes out to stand guard. So it goes, night after night. My man walks around outside. And I, in the empty bed, wait.

FIFTEEN

....

"Why did you wake up, Sarah?"

"Because of you. You're making a ton of noise."

"We're getting ready for a hike."

"What hike? You didn't say anything about it."

"A hike for guys. Me and Isaac."

"Just the two of you? It's not kind of dangerous?"

"We're not alone. We'll also take two boys and a donkey, and also God will come."

"Really?"

"That's what he said."

"If I know him, he'll show up only on the last day and say he forgot to bring food. You better bring some sacrifices."

Silence.

"And where are you going?"

"'To the place that I shall show thee.'"

"To the place that who shall show thee?"

"God. That's what he said."

"And what about me? I also want to come."

"This is a hike for guys. I told you. Isaac, the boys, God, the donkey, and me. Women, girls, mothers, she-asses—not invited. You sit in the tent, you don't go out hiking."

"Everything was nicer when I was called Sarai and you were called Abram. Ever since God changed our names something went wrong in this family."

Silence.

"And when are you getting back?"

"In a few days."

"A few days is a long time. What are you going to do?"

"What guys do. We'll walk, navigate to a place that he will show us. We'll get there. We'll sit on one of the mountains and look at the scenery. We'll talk, we'll be silent, we'll remember, we'll be nostalgic for things that happened five minutes before. We'll set fire to the wood on the first try, we'll learn to tie knots: tight sturdy bindings. We'll teach each other things that men have to learn."

I can recite them: to walk silently, track footprints, camouflage yourself, see and not be seen, and walk in darkness—and maybe "see a great light," like Isaiah says—and know which plants to make tea with, and how to feed hay to the cows, build a chicken coop, "tend the flora and dance the hora, just like the uncles do." Little bonus there for you, Varda, an old song from the Yishuv, after all you're not so interested in people, you deal with issues. A gender song for you—when the uncles do that stuff, what do the aunties do? To know the sounds of the night, to find the path, to fathom the eagle in the sky, the serpent on the rock, how a man has his way with a maiden. And how to dig wells, build an altar, kindle a fire, go barefoot, sharpen a butcher's knife, how to lead— the boy in the saddle, his hands gripping the reins, smiling with excitement that mothers do not understand.

Here are tracks of a rabbit, Isaac, and these of a hyena, its hind legs are smaller than the forelegs, and these of a ram, with a cloven hoof, here, he walked here. You can see his tracks from here to that thicket. See this stone, with the lichen facing down—that tells you he flipped it over with his hoof.

You're not that interested in these stories about rocks? A shame. Because stories about rocks are the most historical history of the Yishuv. Cornerstones, keystones, milestones, slingshot stones, smooth stones, rough stones, gravestones. Huge hailstones from the sky, stones you put under your head for a pillow, for dreaming dreams.

And here's the North Star, here's Ursa Major and beside her the Little Bear, Ursa Minor, we're all here—one God, two she-bears, four mothers, and a father and son. What's with the two she-bears, Abraham? *Shtayim dubim?* The Jewish people have just started speaking Hebrew and already you're making mistakes? Feminine masculine? We're in the Bible, Sarah, in case you've forgotten. Here in the Bible even the mistakes are holy.

That's it. They got up early, saddled the donkey, sallied forth. How words change. Today the word for "saddling" in biblical Hebrew means "bandaging a wound." Packed from head to hoof—water, food, tent, shade canopy, wood, butcher's knife, tools, and cooking implements— and went. "And the two walked off together." I believe I already told you that Eitan loved the sound of the biblical word "together," *yahdav,* and played with it all sorts of ways. "You're the teacher here, Ruta," he said on the eve of their departure for that hike, at dinner with Grandpa and Dovik and Dalia, "you're the teacher and I barely managed to finish the tenth grade, but I will explain something to you about grammar that I think you don't understand: just as *yeladav* means 'his children' and *begadav* means 'his clothing,' *yahdav* means 'his togethers.'"

Dovik laughed, Grandpa fixed his gaze, the patched eye and the good one, on Eitan, with affection and wonder: What else will this weird golden butterfly say or do at our family table? This fine-feathered bird who landed among us geese and chickens? I laughed, even Dalia managed a smile. The eve of the disaster, the last supper of its kind. We would have these loud and lively dinners, seasoned with stories and jokes and riddles, knocking salad off someone's fork, stealing their last bite or sip. Dovik is someone who really loves to eat. He eats a lot and chews a long time and sighs with pleasure and plans every last bite in great detail. Therefore it's great fun to ruin it for him. He would assemble on his fork a small sample of each salad vegetable, and a bit of yellow and a bit of white from the fried egg, a sliver of cheese and a hint of herring, and then, a second before it entered his mouth, I would stick out my fork and knock everything back onto his plate, and he would laugh and get angry.

We would report about the day just ended and make plans for the next, and Eitan, my man, my first husband, was always at the center:

speaking, imitating, making formal announcements. Dovik would look
at him with admiration, Grandpa Ze'ev with love and curiosity. His two
sons had left home, one of them, my father, was dead, and God had sent
him Eitan in their place.

I peeked in to make sure Neta was covered, and we went to bed.
Oddly enough I don't remember if I had sex with Eitan that night.
Probably yes, because we did it a lot then, at every opportunity, and if
so, it was the last time for many years. The twelve blighted years, the
evils were preparing to arise from the Nile and enter my bed—here we
are—like the sickly cows of Pharaoh's dream. And before dawn I heard
Eitan getting ready, and I got up and went to the kitchen to say goodbye.

And you didn't sense that something was about to happen?

No, Varda, no. I already told you. I didn't have any premonitions or
female intuitions, and I didn't feel that this was a final farewell, that this
would be the last time I would see my child alive and my husband as
he was. But like all mothers and wives, I worried a little for my son and
husband. I even gave them the concerned-mother speech:

"You decided where you're going?"

"More or less."

"Can you maybe tell me?"

"The Negev."

"You already said so. Where exactly in the Negev?"

"What's with the 'exactly,' Ruta? We're going hiking. Quality time
for father and son. We'll sit under a tree in one of the wadis."

"Because you yourself always say that if you go on a trip you have to
supply details of the route at home."

"You're right," he said, "but I told you, this time it's not a hike with
a route, but camping, and we don't know where yet. We'll decide when
we're out there. Someplace around Nahal Tzihor or Nahal Tznifim,
we'll find us a nice acacia, we'll pitch a tent in its shade, build a fire pit
with stones, make friends with birds, learn how to build a sand table.
Navigate in the hills with a map."

"Why does a six-year-old need to navigate with a map?"

"You prefer a six-year-old with a PlayStation?"

I got ornery. "I know that area. Nahal Tzihor and Nahal Tznifim are
half the Negev. You don't know where that beautiful acacia is exactly?"

"Wherever God planted it. When we get to it, we'll know it's the one, and if there's reception I'll send Dovik a text message with our coordinates and he'll show you on the map exactly."

"And if there won't be reception? Why is it so hard to tell me now where you'll be?"

"Wherever the steering wheel takes us, to the place God will tell us."

How did I not understand, I, the Bible teacher, what was happening? And Eitan kept talking: "Not everything has to be planned, where we're going, where we'll be. Not everything has to be known in advance. You can improvise and go with the flow."

As you see, he succeeded in upsetting me. On the other hand, Eitan was the best possible person to go on a hike with. He was an outstanding driver and a superb navigator. He never got stuck or lost. He was also a technical guy, knew how to fix the pickup if it broke down, a strong guy with a lot of experience, and underneath his levity and unworried pose he would plan every detail, as responsible and organized as a watchmaker. That's how he was when he put a pot on the fire, went to kill somebody, planned his wife's birthday, or took a hike.

He went out to the pickup, loaded and arranged the equipment, covered it, tied it down. In the nursery, he told me once, we have everything we need for a hike and also for ambushes and lookouts: ropes, boxes, jerricans and all kinds of containers, a pickax for digging or bashing someone's head if necessary, pruning shears, a shovel for hot coals and burying poop in the sand, hefty plastic bags for garbage, rakes and brooms to cover your tracks, and tarps for shade and camouflage and lying down on.

I saw him loading the pickup with quiet efficiency, and I relaxed a bit. I also remembered the last time they left me home and went to the desert without me, and I smiled to myself. That was a year earlier. They had announced on the radio that a meteor shower was expected that night, and Eitan said, "*Yalla*, Neta, let's drive down to the desert, we'll see them falling from the sky."

I asked, "What about me? I want to go too."

Eitan said, "No way! A zillion people will go to see them in the desert, because the nights there are totally dark, and who do they get? You! Shining as bright as the sun. Instead of watching the meteors they'll be looking at you, through grimy binoculars." I told you, Varda, my first husband was an irrepressible romantic, and also a very funny guy.

"It's all done. You want to get Neta or should I get him?"

I went upstairs; I picked him up wrapped in his blanket and laid him on the backseat. I hugged and kissed him on the cheeks and forehead, but he was fast asleep and didn't feel a thing, and Eitan gently lowered the front seatback to keep him from falling or flying off. I hugged Eitan and kissed him too, and that was it. They drove away and I made myself some coffee because it was almost my usual wake-up time. I wasn't worried, but I thought about them. Neta, as I knew, would sleep soundly the whole way down and wake up only when they got to the tree, and I imagined Eitan driving in the wadi and choosing that acacia out of all the others. I knew better than anyone how picky he was about the right shade tree to sit under, especially if the hike was in the desert and the tree was an acacia: it had to be symmetrical, it should have a beautiful silhouette, you needed to be able to stand under it without getting smacked in the head by a thorny branch, and there shouldn't be too many fallen branches under it because they can cause a flat tire or punch a hole in your shoe.

"The thing about an acacia," he once explained to me, "is that when it's a good tree it's also beautiful, and when it's beautiful it's also good. The pomegranate is also like that, and the cypress and the oak, but it's not that way with all trees. The fig, for instance, can be ugly as sin, but good, with wonderful fruit, and also the opposite, a beautiful fig tree with shitty fruit."

" 'Figs so bad they could not be eaten,' " I quoted him from Jeremiah.

He laughed. "Your Hebrew is a bit beyond me. But I'll write it down, so I won't forget."

I know: he picked them out a good and beautiful acacia, parked the pickup by the side of the creek bed, and together they covered it with the tarp so it wouldn't broil in the sun and to camouflage it—so nobody would see it who didn't need to see it.

I remember the principles: alter the shape, conceal colors and bulges, any glint of glass or metal. I'm guessing they also tossed twigs and dry branches on the tarp and a few fistfuls of sand and dirt. Then they pitched a small tent for the next two nights. Not just against the cold, but mainly against mosquitoes and snakes and scorpions.

And I can hear it: "We don't want guests, right, Neta? So go over to the dirt road, please, and when you get there look toward the pickup and the tent, tell me if you can see them."

Eitan fixed something to eat and said that at the hottest time of day you don't do anything, just chill out in the shade, which is what they did. They napped a little, woke up, talked, kept quiet, got into the atmosphere of the place.

"Drink some water, Neta."

"I don't want any."

"Drink, it's important."

"But I'm not thirsty."

"Drink even if you're not thirsty."

"But why?"

"Because it's hot and dry here, and you don't feel yourself sweating and drying out. You see those two rocks over there? One small and one big? Those were a father and son who traveled here before us and didn't drink enough."

Eitan took a few pictures with his old camera, of the tent and the tree, and Neta and him, together and separately. There were digital cameras available, and Eitan did like new gadgets, but stuck to his ancient Pentax. He said he liked the guillotine sound of the old cameras and didn't like being able to see the result right away in a digital camera and keep trying till you got it right.

Photography should be like sniper fire, he said. With all the planning and concentration and responsibility for the consequences. With old cameras, once the bullet is shot there are no regrets, no taking it back or shooting it again.

Then they looked at a field guide and together identified birds: warblers, rosefinches, and black-something, there is such a bird. I forget if it's a blacktail or blackback or blackbelly or blackhead.

"In a couple days he'll get used to us and eat from our hand," Eitan said to Neta, just like he said to me on one of our hikes, before we were parents and it was just the two of us. Lucky I wasn't there with them;

I would surely have upgraded his grammar, with that schoolteacher Hebrew I keep slipping into.

Toward evening, when the sun calmed down and no longer wanted to kill anyone, they went for a walk, to get to know the area and how it looked in this light, because "Tomorrow morning you won't recognize it, Neta, in the desert the landscape changes with the time of day.

"Come, I want to show you something," he said to him. I so loved that sentence of his. Always, when he said, "Come, Ruta, I want to show you something," there'd be something beautiful awaiting me, something funny, something good.

"Come, Neta, look. This is the hour when the sun is no longer strong and all kinds of animals start coming out to look for something to eat. Let's take water, and something to nosh, and the camera to take pictures of ourselves and the scenery, so we can show them to Mommy when we get back. Come, I'll lead us to the top of that hill over there, and you'll lead us back down here. So look around and remember how we go, because it'll get dark, and if you don't find the pickup and tent we'll have to stay in the desert forever."

How do I know all this? The truth is, I don't, but I know enough to guess. I'm sure that Eitan repeated and emphasized what he would also tell me on hikes, that you have to turn your head around every so often, to see and remember what the path looks like in the other direction. He preferred circular routes, not the back-and-forth kind, but sometimes there's no choice and we have to retrace our steps, and trails look completely different going and coming.

"That's another thing I love about you," he once said to me, "that I can take you twice on exactly the same walk, once in this direction and once in the other, and you think it's a new place you haven't been before. You're easy to please."

They went. The two of them *yahdav*. Together. First in the wadi, and at a certain point they climbed diagonally to the top of the ridge. "To get to the ridge we have to go diagonally, Neta, the way animals do, and it's best to walk on their trail and not leave a new line of footprints." I can recite that to you too, because I also hiked with him. "You climb at a diagonal, and you don't stand on the open ridge like a putz but a little lower down on the slope, because we don't want to be seen from kilometers away by someone who shouldn't see us."

They went up, they sat down to look at the grand expanse and the red sun beyond it, and Eitan took a few more pictures, and that's how they turned out: pictures of evening and sunset, a feeling of farewell, as if the camera knew something they and I didn't. He took pictures of the two of them too, last pictures, rather dim, teeth and eyes gleaming in dark faces. I'm not imagining or guessing. I saw them. But only a few years later. Maybe I'll tell you sometime.

"Come, Neta, it's already dark, take us back to the tent," and I figure that at that moment Neta placed his hand on the ground the way you put your hand when you get up from sitting on the ground, and on that very spot was the snake. This was the hour when they warm themselves on the rocks, which all day had been exposed to the sun, absorbing as much heat as possible before starting to hunt, and it bit him here, on the inside of his wrist, a place with big blood vessels close to the skin.

It was an adder. I know because adders live among the stones and rocks on the slopes, not like the ringed snakes and Persian vipers, which prefer the sand and pebbles of the wadi. All this I learned later, a little too late, I admit, but when they don't tell you anything you have to discover it for yourself, to research and to learn.

What a name, "adder," in Hebrew *ef'ah.* In Hebrew there are snake names that sound like hissing—*shfifon* and *tzefa* and *saraf* and *ef'ah.* The generic word for snake, *nahash,* is like that too. I remind you that this happened in springtime, and the adder had only lately awoken from its hibernation. It sounds like a children's story, right? But that one I will not write. The adder woke up from his sleep, yawned, and stretched: Whom will I bite today? With glands full of poison and a belly full of hunger.

That's it. It took a quarter of a second. That's all. Neta Tavori, age six, bitten by an adder. A boy whose father had warned him about every possible danger, who drank enough water not to be dehydrated, who camouflaged the pickup truck lest someone notice it who shouldn't notice, and who climbed to the ridge at an angle so as not to leave new tracks and didn't stand there like a putz but sat down so as not to be seen. You get it? If he had climbed in a straight line and stood up straight on the ridge, all those imaginary enemies would have seen him, but he'd have been a few meters away from the snake and would not have put his hand on it and would not be dead.

He screamed. A scream of shock and pain. Eitan leaned over to him: "What happened, Neta? Did something scare you? Something hurts? Did something sting you? Where?" A flashlight went on. "Show me." He saw the two fang marks, felt the trembling of the body, immediately understood, and immediately looked and found the snake. You understand? He wasted time finding and killing the snake and putting it in his pocket.

"You have to bring the snake to the hospital," he later explained to Dovik, "so they can identify it and know what antidote to give." But I don't buy it. Yes, it's standard procedure, but I know him too well. Forget the antidote. It was for revenge. It's stronger than he is, this automatic reaction, to kill anyone who harms a loved one, a family member, certainly his son. Not that I am arguing that the ten seconds it took to find the snake and smash its head with a rock would have saved Neta, but I can't not think about that possibility.

And so, with the dead snake in his pocket and the dying child in his arms, he ran down the slope and along the wadi back to the pickup. Neta at that time weighed twenty-seven kilos. I know that because I weighed and measured him every three months. I marked the height on the kitchen doorpost, and beside each mark I wrote the date and also his weight. Twenty-seven kilos for a boy of six and a half, a boy not especially tall and not at all fat—that's serious weight. A solid boy, Eitan used to say, a *shtarker*! And he would pat him the way you pat a calf, between the shoulder blades. That build, by the way, he inherited from my grandfather, but what difference does it make now? He's done enough damage. Rest in peace and please leave us alone, you and all the manly men in this family.

He ran. With the weight of Neta in his arms, in the darkness. But Eitan is Eitan: he does not stumble, does not get tired, does not lose his way, with those feet of his that can see in the dark. Running. Carrying and hugging. He got to the beautiful acacia he had chosen, lay Neta down on the ground, tore the tarp off the pickup, put the boy on the backseat. He then saw, by the inside light of the pickup, that blood was oozing from his nose and mouth and that the hand that was bitten was swollen and purple with blood under the skin. That's the bleeding you can see, but the worst bleeding is internal, in the heart and kidneys. He lowered the front seatback to hold him in place and took off like a madman, like only he knows how to drive, till he had phone reception and began making calls. Dovik, ambulance, police. Dovik, not me—that too I won't forgive. He reached the road, turned on the four emergency blinkers, poured out fuel from the jerrican, and lit a fire so that those who did need to see would indeed see.

He took Neta out of the pickup, and although he knew he was already dead, he set him down very slowly, protectively, on the ground. And then he collapsed alongside him because he had no more strength and he had nothing more to do and no reason to stand. Just to lie beside him and wait.

Meanwhile Dovik began to mobilize forces. They have these networks spread around the country, men who might not see one another for ten years, but when the network is activated it's high alert, phones are ringing, lights go on, maps and aerial photos are marked up, and the system is running, breathing, passing information, and giving orders. All this, by the way, comes under the heading of "Brothers-in-Arms," but don't be confused, Varda, I already told you and I say so again: there's no real brotherhood here. They will rescue, they will pitch in, they will lend a hand—but it's another one of their games, squeezing out another spermy droplet of action and adventure. This isn't friendship the way we understand it, and I say this as a woman who doesn't have and never had and apparently never will have a true friend. That's why I'm pouring it all out to you, a woman who's basically a stranger. You think this is easy for me? It's not.

Whatever. What's important is that within a few minutes Dovik organized a helicopter, and when the helicopter arrived an old reservist from their unit was already waiting there, having arrived in his car from Moshav Paran, with a boy of twelve, thin as a rail with big ears, I know what he looked like because he came to Neta's funeral the next day. They got out of the car, the old man ran over to Eitan, and the boy didn't say a word but immediately found a landing area and marked it with light sticks, those green glowing things that guys like that always have on hand, as if he'd been doing it every night before bedtime since he was three. And when the helicopter landed, Eitan wasn't able to do anything; he lay beside Neta like a shroud that slipped off a corpse, and they piled him too onto a stretcher because he couldn't stand up. He had carried the dead weight of Neta while running in the dark for several kilometers on sand and pebbles and stones, but his own body he couldn't lift from the ground, even take a single step. The friend phoned Dovik that the helicopter was flying to Soroka hospital in Beersheba, and he should drive there, and contacted another friend in Omer to get there right away because he was the closest. He then went back home in his car, and the skinny kid with the big ears drove our pickup to his house, by himself, off the road in total darkness, because he didn't have a license.

I, at home, slept peacefully that whole time. I already told you: not only did I not have a premonition, all those stories about the telepathic mother who wakes up suddenly with the feeling that something happened to her child and it turns out that at that very moment—are not told about me. Maybe I am not as good a mother as they are, or maybe they are better than I am at making up stories. And when I suddenly woke up, it wasn't from a sense that something terrible had happened but because there was noise coming from Dovik's house. Lights went on, phones, I heard Dalia shouting, "Wake up Ruta. You have to wake up Ruta. Why me? You wake her up!" And as I jumped out of bed Dovik came in and said, "Ruta, I have something really terrible to tell you. Neta is dead." And he added, "He was bitten by a snake."

And there, in the morgue at Soroka, after a dreadful ride with Dovik and Dalia, which I would have rather spent in the trunk of the car, I saw my only son and my first husband for the last time. I don't want to talk about how I saw Neta, but I saw Eitan being questioned by a policewoman, talking to her like a robot and saying not a word to me. He didn't speak to me and didn't dare look at me.

I don't understand: how can a man lose his courage like that? But luckily he gave all the details to the doctors and the police and also spoke a little with Dovik, because a few hours later he shut down and there was no one to talk to. You understand? He did everything he could do to save Neta; he failed; like a loyal soldier he reported everything there was to report, like they do after a failed military operation; and that was it. He shut down and was no more.

I yelled at him, shoved him. "What happened? Tell me what happened!"

I hugged him. I shook him. I hit him. "Tell me how this happened! How could a thing like this happen?"

I scratched his face with my fingernails. I cried on his shoulder. "Tell me, you hear?"

He did not budge. My brain did not understand. Our mouths did not speak. His body said to my body: I am dead. And my body answered his body: I can feel it. But to myself I didn't say and my self didn't say to me that this was it, that this dead man would be my second husband.

That's the story. And the next day was the funeral, Neta was buried in the cemetery, and Eitan was buried inside himself. And after the funeral, on the orders of Grandpa Ze'ev, he began hard labor at the nursery, did not speak anymore to anyone, also not to me, slept in what had been Neta's room, and it was clear that this was it, that life was over. So it went for twelve years, until one day, suddenly, right after Grandpa Ze'ev died, something happened and he began to come back to life.

I was surprised. I thought that Grandpa Ze'ev's death would finish him off for good, because they were strongly tied to each other, and Grandpa Ze'ev was the only one who knew how to treat him after the disaster—male treatment, simple, cruel, but treatment that succeeded. He worked him at the nursery at the hardest and most basic jobs, carrying and dragging and moving things and standing guard at night, and that was what kept him going in life—if you can call it that—my grandfather's therapy and the connection with him. Not the friendship with Dovik and not the army buddies, and it pains me to say so but also not love and life with me. Twelve years of silence and hard labor, and then Grandpa died and Eitan returned. Not a hundred percent, I'm also not the same Ruta I was before Neta died, but he returned. To me and to himself.

SIXTEEN

....

The first thing I thought, after my shouting and screaming that the whole moshava could hear, was: God, I do not want any more children by this man. And later I thought: And if by chance I am pregnant now, please make it a girl.

God did not answer, but I knew he was listening. I urged and prodded him: You can, God, you can. And I also translated it into his language, so he would understand better: "Shall anything be beyond the Lord's power?" In third-person honorific, so he'd be pleased. And apparently I convinced him, because one week later, Aunt Ruby came to visit. I think I'm smiling, and if so it's because of you. You don't need to write down the name Aunt Ruby. She's not a relative of ours and she's not a character in the history of the Yishuv. "Aunt Ruby" was one of the many nicknames for my period. And this one was a period the likes of which I never had, a flood. And with pains and symptoms that till then I'd only heard about from other women. As if God were explaining to me that the world as he designed it was still functioning, that the sun was rising and setting and the moon waxing and waning, and so too my body, which informed me that even with all the anguish over one child who died, it was thinking about the next children. But for the next children I needed a guy. Aunt Ruby arrived, left, returned, left, and I stayed here with my dead son and my living-dead man, who from then on did not talk to me or smile at me or cook for me or touch me or make me laugh. He did only what my grandfather told him to do—he loaded and moved and stacked and unloaded, and everything was heavy and everything was slow—but I, every time I saw him, I saw a person running. It was clear to me that inside his body he was running. Running with the child in his arms, hugging and carrying, from Neta's scream to his last breath. One step and another, one year and another, twelve death anniversaries he didn't take part in, twelve birthdays which I marked alone, twelve Passover seders without Neta and without his father, who sat by himself in the nursery and smoked, ignoring the matzo balls and gefilte fish that I brought out to him the way you bring leftovers to a dog tied outside, and hundreds of my visits, without him, to the cemetery, and one long wait, not for Neta, I knew Neta would not come back. I waited for Eitan to return.

Look at me—I watched him from the window—I'm here. Smile at me, come back to me. Come back and we'll come back, comely man of mine. I already told you I prefer the word *ishi,* "my man," and I also told you the reasons, but there's one more reason, you'll laugh, and it's the sound and look, which Eitan loved so much, of the letter *shin* coming from my lips. I never imagined that someone would want to know how a certain consonant emerged from the mouth of his beloved, and never thought that my *shin* was different from other women's. But Eitan was a meticulous guy and got down to details in every area that interested him.

I remember: One day, I was in my eighth month, a Friday afternoon, a sweet moment, we were sitting in bed, Eitan and I and Neta in my belly. And suddenly he said, "Soon he'll come out and we won't ever be just the two of us naked in bed. We'll be father and mother and baby, so I want to take advantage of still being just us and do something important."

"Whatever you say," I said, because after sentences like that very nice things would always happen.

"I want you to go over the letters with me one by one because I want to see how each one changes your face when you say it. Say *alef,* and *bet—ah, bah—*and *dalet, dah, di, doh . . .*"

He didn't ask for *gimel* or *het,* because they do nothing to the face, and *nun* is ugly and makes you ugly, so he said. Then we got to *shin,* almost at the end of the alphabet, and he started to test it out with all kinds of words and sounds: "Say 'shalom,' and say 'Shimshon,' and say *ashasheet,* say the number *shishim v'shesh,* and the hour three thirty-eight, *shalosh shloshim u'shmoneh.*" I did whatever he asked, and he looked at me but wasn't satisfied until I said, "Just a second, Eitan, I have to sneeze, *ani mit'ateshet.*" And he said, "That's it! The *shin* of *mit'ateshet* makes you the most beautiful and the most *you.* From now on, say the word *mit'ateshet* whenever possible. And do it in front of the mirror."

It was a summer day. There was a popping sound outside—the pods of the lupine plants that Grandpa had spread out in the sunlight on the concrete floor. He did this every year, explaining that lupine seeds needed a decent dose of summer sunshine so they could sprout fully later on. I remember those sounds well, the popping of the pods, the pinging of the seeds flying out, the soft and hard noises of their cracking open.

I said, "So this is love? Sneezing all day long?"

He laughed. "You just have to say it, not do it. That's the lovely thing about language, a word can be more beautiful and true than what it describes."

I was taken aback. I had no idea that he had thoughts like this in his head.

"You're funny," I told him.

And let me tell you, he really was funny. One day, a new guy from Tel Aviv came into the nursery, one of those city types who move here and right away want to plant a vegetable garden and raise chickens. He wanted to buy seeds and saplings, tomatoes, peppers, lettuce, and so on, and asked if they were organic. Eitan told him that it's not the seeds that are organic but the way you raise the vegetables afterward.

"What does that mean?" asked the customer. "What do I have to do?"

"It's very simple," Eitan told him. "Ordinary vegetables are sprayed during the day and organic vegetables are sprayed at night."

Dovik said, "Our Eitan is so funny that you can't always tell when he's joking and when he's clowning." Sometimes even my blockhead of a brother comes up with a good one. And he would always say, "our Eitan," and not just "Eitan" or "your Eitan."

Let's go back to the *shin*. Eitan took out his camera, and over and over I had to say the word he liked so he could take my picture saying it again and again, and as a result I am the only woman in the world who has naked pictures of herself, with an eight-month belly, saying "sneeze" and bursting with laughter. And all this because, as I told you before, I am a mother without premonitions. I did not know then that the child I had in my belly would die at the age of six and a bit. Six, *shesh,* two *shins* of my lips and teeth and tongue.

It was also written up in the newspaper, but not six and a bit and not six and a half but six exactly. And not the word but the number, "Neta Tavori" with 6 in parentheses, "bitten to death by a snake." And below, in smaller letters: "Tragedy in the Desert. A boy found his death on a hike with his father." What a strange expression, "found his death." Because it's death that finds the victim and not the other way around. That's the expertise of the Angel of Death, no? Learn the map coordinates, routes, navigation; getting there, finding the place, remembering addresses. But no, insists the Hebrew language. Death walks behind us for our whole lives. Follows and seeks and draws near, and now, we found it. This is a language that knows and remembers things that we don't want to know or that we forgot long ago. Okay, let's drop it, Varda, before I cry so much I'll start laughing.

SEVENTEEN

....

THE SHOT

1

The birds fell silent all at once, as if clearing the air for the thunderous gunshot. The blast echoed in the wadi and quickly died out. Despite the proximity of the target and the speed of the bullet, the avenger could sense the interval between the bang of the percussion cap and the hitting of the target.

The tall, beefy young man screamed and staggered, circling in place. The tail of his jacket fluttered for a moment as he fell. From the way he collapsed, the avenger concluded that he had hit him precisely where he had wanted, in his right knee, to render him helpless, racked with fear and agonizing pain but fully conscious.

For a moment the wounded man lay on his back, then dragged himself sideways, trying to wriggle behind a thornbush that was not big enough to hide him and whose name he did not know. He took a pistol from his pack and peeked out, looking around. There was no one to be seen. He waited a bit, terrified and hesitant, immobile.

Open skies and the rising sun washed over him. A pleasant, sweetish odor of fading flowers assaulted his nostrils. Fear filled his heart. The rocks, the bushes, the landscape were all foreign to him. He knew how to function in the city and the street, among houses and cars, not in the wadi, the woods, the open field—places whose rules he did not know and whose signs he could not read and whose language he did not speak. He now surveyed the slope across the wadi with sun-blinded eyes, aware that someone was watching him through the same gunsight he used to shoot him, knowing what was in store and awaiting it with dread.

A few minutes went by, and then the wounded man saw a man of medium height, holding a rifle waist high, heading toward him. The sun rising behind the man sketched a muscular, faceless silhouette.

When he was thirty meters away the man stopped and shouted, "Put the gun in the pack."

In his condition, at this range, with that weapon, he had no chance of effectively returning fire, certainly not at an enemy armed with a rifle who had already proved his sharpshooting ability.

He put the pistol back in the pack and waited, groaning with fear and pain.

"Close the pack," the man said.

The wounded man closed the pack.

"Throw it toward me."

The wounded man clutched the pack. The man drew closer and moved sideways, so that the sun was no longer behind him. The silhouette turned into a man with chestnut hair that shone in the sunlight, his face empty of expression and his eyes bright, his skin astonishingly, eerily white. He was dressed in old work clothes: a blue cotton shirt and worn-out khaki pants. His shoes were wrapped in strange coverings, like thick towels.

He came closer, leaned over, and picked up the pack. The wounded man held tight to the strap. The man said nothing, and as the wounded man pulled the pack toward him, he slammed the rifle barrel into his shredded knee.

The wounded man screamed, let go of the pack, and rolled over.

The man said, "Don't scream. You don't want anyone to hear and come over."

And added, "Remember you're here because of a murder. I'm not yet."

He took the pack and asked, "What were you looking for under the tree? What were you sent to find?"

"Nothing. I'm just taking a hike," moaned the wounded man.

"With those shoes and clothes and that pack you don't look to me like a hiker. What are you looking for at this hour?"

"Just hiking. I told you."

"Maybe this?" the man asked, and took out a gold cigarette lighter from his pocket.

The wounded man did not reply.

The man sat down on a big chairlike rock, near the trunk of the carob tree, and flicked on the lighter.

"It even works," he said. "Is it yours?"

The wounded man did not reply.

"I cleaned it up a bit. It was all muddy. Then I saw the initials on the back."

The wounded man did not reply.

The man opened the pack he had taken from him, took out a wallet, examined the driver's license.

"No. These aren't your initials. These are someone else's initials. Someone else forgot the lighter here and sent you to get it."

The wounded man said, "I'm just hiking. I don't know nothing about a lighter."

"You don't know nothing about double negatives, you moron. You're just a punk who can't even speak properly."

He got up from the rock. "So whose lighter is it?" he asked again. "And for whom is it so important that it not be found here?"

"I don't know what you're talking about."

The man drew closer and said, "This time scream quietly. For your own good. Remember what I told you before. You are here because of a murder and I am not yet."

Again he hit his knee with the rifle barrel. The wounded man screamed into the palm of his hand. His screams ended in sobbing. His whole body shook. Sweat flooded his forehead and dripped onto his face.

"Whose lighter is it?"

"You don't know who you're dealing with. You won't see the sun come up tomorrow."

He tried crawling backward, twisting and wheezing, spraying saliva with grunts of rage and terror. The avenger picked up his cell phone, which had fallen when he was shot, and examined the names on the speed-dialing list.

"Here he is," he said, "who else could come before mother and dad and before Adi? And what's a girl with a nice name like Adi doing with a piece of crap like you?"

The wounded man said nothing.

"So who killed the old man who was here yesterday? You or he?"

The wounded man did not reply.

"I'll describe him, to refresh your memory. An old man, white hair, wearing work clothes exactly like mine. He didn't carry a gun, just a walking stick and a backpack, and had a hearing aid in his ear and a patch over one eye."

"Nobody killed him. He slipped here and fell and broke his head on a rock. I swear by all that's holy."

"Three mistakes," said the avenger. "First, you have no idea what's holy. Second, he didn't fall and break his head on a rock. Somebody picked up the stone from the ground and hit him on the head. Third, how do you even know he died from a blow to the head and not from something else?"

"He fell," whispered the wounded man. "It was an old man with a stick, with no sense of balance, can't hear, and can't see in one eye. He fell and broke his head on a rock. We were here and right away we took off. We were just hiking. We didn't want to get in trouble."

"Yesterday you went hiking here and today too? A lover of nature and the land, very nice."

The avenger bent down, picked up a rock the size of a large grapefruit, stood tall over the wounded man. "You are wrong," he said, "he came here when you were here, and you killed him with a rock just like this," he said, and hit the wounded man on the side of his head, a light and painful blow, "but a lot harder. And then you put the rock under his head as if he had fallen on it, but you are idiots and put it upside down. This way, you piece of shit," and raised his hand.

The wounded man tried to get up, his face contorted with pain and supplication, his mouth widened for a scream, but the avenger smashed his temple with the rock, this time with his full strength. He knelt alongside the body, lifted it into a sitting position, stripped it of the coat, and wrapped the head with it, lest he be stained by the blood. He clutched the dead body, and despite its size and weight he stood up as easily as someone carrying a baby.

He carried the body to the wadi below the carob tree, took it into an adjacent cave, threw it and the rock into an ancient cistern in the bowels of the cave, then climbed down into it. The carcass of a goat lay there. The man dragged it aside, covered the body with rocks from the cistern floor, laid the goat on top, climbed out of the hole, took a last look at the cistern, and exited the cave, returning to the carob tree. He sat down on a rock that resembled a large chair and waited.

2

A few minutes later the dead man's cell phone rang.

The avenger put the phone to his ear and said nothing.

"You're making me wait," said the voice on the phone. "I told you, I don't like waiting."

"Sorry."

"You found it?"

"No."

"Who is this? You sound different."

"It's me."

"Very good. You have learned not to mention names. You looked carefully?"

"Yes."

"Who is this? Why are you talking like that?"

"Because I'm dead."

"You're in a mood for jokes?"

"You won't believe what happened. Somebody came here, found it before I did, waited for me here, and killed me. Bashed my head with a rock."

"What's going on? Who are you?"

"A rock to the head. Exactly like we killed the old man yesterday. He killed me and threw me beside our goat in the pit."

"You found it or you didn't? This is no time for jokes."

"I am lying here in the pit covered with stones, my brains are pouring out and my mouth is full of dirt and blood, our goat is on top of me and it's starting to stink, so what do I have left? Only jokes."

"I see. Who killed you?"

"Some guy. I don't know his name."

"Did the two of you talk before he killed you?"

"Sure. We had a lovely conversation."

"What did you say, bottom line?"

"Bottom line, he left you what you forgot here."

"What do you mean 'here'? Where exactly?"

"You'll have to look for it. He also found the rock we hit the old man with."

"How did he find it?"

"He also said that we were idiots, that we put it upside down, I didn't exactly understand what he meant. I think you better get over here quickly before he tells the police and they'll come and find my phone and your lighter."

The avenger hung up, hoisted the dead man's pack on his shoulder, went back, and hid in the hideout in the mastic tree, ate the two remaining granola bars, crossed them off the list in his pocket, drank water, and rested. Half an hour later he drank more coffee from the thermos, looked at the wadi, at the big carob, at the big thronelike rock beside its trunk, at the dark mouth of the cave in the adjacent gully. He had time. He had plans and an objective. He waited.

EIGHTEEN

....

How would you describe your family in relation to this moshava?

An abnormal family.

That's interesting. Other people here also define their families as unusual and different.

That's because they're bored. They tell stories, make things up, want to be special. Not me. I would just as soon not be abnormal. This also proves I'm telling the truth. People don't make up stories like these about themselves. Someone who tells them is apparently telling the truth.

But not the whole truth.

No. Not the whole truth.

Especially about your grandfather. You're not telling me everything about him.

No. Or about Eitan. I told you, I write. The terrible stories about the terrible things that were done by the terrible men I love, and in fact, the terrible things that I would do if I were a hundred percent male.

And what did you mean by the word "abnormal"?

Most of the families here are clans of cyclamens. That's how my grandfather described families where the children stay close to their parents, as opposed to our family, which is a family of ragworts, flying off to distant places. Grandpa Ze'ev and his brothers left the family home in the Lower Galilee. My father and his brother fled this house as fast as they could. Our mother left Dovik and me with Grandpa and moved to the United States. Eitan left me and the world, but he came back; Neta died before his time and won't come back. I'm not into the World to Come and the Immortality of the Soul, and you won't hear me saying "he went up to heaven," "watching over us from on high," and all that garbage. Death is earth and dirt, not sky. Neta is buried in the earth, and after twelve years there's nothing left of him. There's nothing left of anyone. Nothing of a little boy, just little tiny bones, like a bird's.

Neta's room, by the way, was not turned into a museum. I don't keep his bed the way it was and the little clothes in the closet and the teddy bear on the pillow. A short time after he died it became Eitan's room, and not because Eitan wanted to sleep in his dead son's bed but because he didn't want to, or was afraid to, sleep with me. Whatever. I'm not big on memorials. I keep only a few small mementos, mainly his drawings from kindergarten and his unfinished notebook from first grade with the first few letters of the alphabet and a few of his costumes. All of which, by the way, I would have saved even if Neta were still alive.

I remember: He had all sorts of costumes. I don't call it masquerading because it wasn't only that. It was a blend of my talent for mimicry and Eitan's for camouflage, and his own creativity. Here was this child-man, solid, simple, strong, good hands. But every so often he would start to wrap himself in scarves and rags, even hold them together with safety pins, with a real and surprising flair for design. Sometimes he would explain: I'm a magician, I'm a king, I'm a daddy. One day he announced, "I'm dressing up as someone not from here." And once he asked us to give him black cloth for his birthday because he wanted to dress up as the Angel of Death. That scared me. I admit it. I said to Eitan, "That's enough. I will not go along with this game." I was alarmed: He's not that kind of child. Where does he get ideas like that?

Whatever. I kept some of these costumes, and I gave his everyday clothes to the social welfare department of the regional council and to two friends with sons his age. Dalia said to me at the time, she makes me crazy, that woman, "Why don't you give me Neta's clothes? Maybe I'll have a son someday?"

"For that very reason," I told her. "Precisely because you might have a son one day."

"I don't understand," she said.

And I, in my diaphragm brain, answered her, It's okay, I didn't expect you to understand. And out loud I added, "Believe me, Dalia, you don't need sons. You started out with daughters, keep it that way. It's better." And I smiled at her. "Girls are also much more symbolic."

Again I sense that I'm smiling. Sometimes I smile but don't feel the smile. Sometimes I feel a smile, but I'm not smiling. Whatever. Let's go back to Neta's clothes that I gave to the social welfare department. One day, two years after he died, I saw a little Russian boy on our street wearing his pants. I recognized them immediately because there were two colorful patches on the knees, one shaped like a heart and the other like an eye, which I had sewn on by hand. He and his mother were standing in the street by the notice board and speaking Russian. I saw them, and you know what, Varda, I didn't faint or run away, nor did I go over to them. I just stood and looked at them, at the mother and son, and suddenly she gave me a look, took his hand, and the two of them walked off, away from me, and disappeared around the corner. Maybe she picked up something from my look; maybe she'd heard stories and knew who I was or just looked at me the way women sometimes look at me. I think I already told you that women look at me no less than men do. Not because I'm any great beauty, I'm not, but apparently they see that I'm very pleased with the way I look. That's one of my weapons. The drink that puts me to sleep at night is my secret weapon, and my looks are my unconventional weapon. That's just fine and it gives me strength, all the more so at my age. If I were really beautiful, it would be even better, but I can also make do with what I have. Every year I teach the story of David and Goliath, and every year I tell the students that David's beauty was his weapon no less than his brains and courage and his sling and stone. Goliath, that ugly idiot, showed up with armor, shield, sword, and spear. The biblical word for shield, *tsinah,* also means "coldness." Nice word. As if people's coldness defends them against others. And David came with his beauty—his face, the beautiful eyes, like a woman who goes into the street armed with her beauty: "A thousand shall fall at her left, ten thousand at her right." Male enemies turn to stone; female enemies melt.

That's what defeated Goliath: that he suddenly realized that this boy didn't have the strength or courage of a man, which he could have overcome without any problem, but rather the frightening confidence of a beautiful woman, like the radiance of the angels who came to Sodom and struck everyone there with blindness. And I remember, I don't know why, that prior to our wedding Eitan and I drove to Ben-Gurion Airport to fetch my mother, who had deigned to attend. There were automatic doors at the entrance to the terminal, and we were from the least-automated moshava you can imagine, so I said to him, "You see these innovations, Eitan? No need to go to America; America is already here. In the moshava people don't open doors for one another because of things that happened back in the British Mandate, and here doors open on their own for everyone—come on in."

"No innovations, Ruta," he said, "these are totally ordinary doors. But when *you* arrive they open by themselves. When you arrive—all doors open."

He was a romantic, I already told you, and I was then newly pregnant with Neta, with all the beauty of a first pregnancy—I had filled out a bit, I no longer looked so skinny. I remember: Once he said to me, "Twenty minutes after fertilization you put on seven hundred grams. Ten grams the weight of the embryo, ten grams weight you gained, and the other six hundred eighty are your added beauty."

He exaggerated slightly, of course, but I really did have the radiance of a first pregnancy. If only Neta could have stayed inside me forever. Nothing would have happened to him, and I would have stayed radiant forever.

Whatever. The doors opened; Eitan picked me up in his arms and groaned—"You're so heavy, who knew your beauty weighed so much"—and carried me into the terminal and said, "How do you like the new house I built you? In a minute everyone will fly away and we'll be alone."

NINETEEN

....

How did he die?

Neta? I already told you. What kind of question is that?

Not Neta. Your grandfather.

My grandfather died in a fitting way.

Meaning what?

He died the way men like him used to die. "Moshe, Shlomo, every man *bimkomo*," each in his own way. Some in the pasture or the field, surrounded by their fruit trees or their wheat. Some on the battlefield in wartime, among dear comrades and enemies. Some at sea, surrounded by waves that swallowed their friends and their ship. Or at their workbench, surrounded by pliers or test tubes or words or paintbrushes. In the orchard or the garden, surrounded by vegetables or trees that they planted, like in *The Godfather*—the most biblical film I've ever seen—when Don Corleone dies in the garden beside his little grandson, amid his tomato plants. How I cried during that scene. Terrible. Till now I don't understand why. Who died there, anyway? A mafioso, a murderer, a piece of shit, but the fact is I cried. That's what happened. I can hide feelings even from myself, but not facts.

And your grandfather?

Grandpa Ze'ev died in his wadi, next to his big carob tree, in the place he collected seeds and took Dovik and me for educational walks.

But how?

Not entirely clear. He apparently tripped on the path, which can happen if you're ninety-two and insist on hiking alone. He fell and broke his head on a rock. That's how Dovik found him.

Awful.

Why awful? Ninety-two years old, suddenly, and in a place you know and love so well. Luckily Dovik got to the body before the birds and beasts did. I have here in the drawer something I read at his funeral. You want to hear it?

Yes.

Very well. I tried to describe the misery of old age that he was spared. It's a bit flowery, so I apologize in advance. That's how it turned out. I'll just drink a little water first. Okay. A little cough and we're on our way: "Slowly shall the men of valor bend down, slowly shall the guards of the house become shaky, shall the joints weaken, the eye grow dim. Here a strap will become undone, here a pipe will drip, plaster will peel, ears go deaf, and the sound of the mill grow faint. But not for you, Grandpa Ze'ev. For you all at once. The jar is broken at the fountain, and the wheel smashed at the cistern, and the dust shall return to the earth as it was and the spirit shall return unto God who gave it."

That's beautiful. Very special.

I agree with you. I can compliment this text wholeheartedly because I didn't write it. I lifted almost all of it from Ecclesiastes, and people who heard it at the funeral also gave me compliments I didn't deserve but the Bible did. But what's important is that it worked out well for Grandpa Ze'ev. He didn't deserve it, but he succeeded. He lived a long life, died with sound mind and body, and, as I told you, surrounded by his landscape and plants. In a certain respect he died at home, because, like the house and the nursery, the wadi was his territory, and that's what he was—a man of the land and borders and fences and declarations of ownership. As Caleb the son of Jephunneh said at age eighty-five, "as my strength was then, even so is my strength now, to go out and come in," to rise up and inherit the land. The house and nursery were his, and the body of Grandma Ruth was his, and this wadi also belonged to him.

From the day he died, by the way, we went back there only twice.

Once with the police, right after Dovik found the body, and another time the next winter. But when Dovik and I were children, we drove out there with him many times, to mark plants and collect some seeds and mostly to learn to identify them by name. Those were pleasant trips, full of love and patience. The small amount of good in him he invested in us. I, the younger granddaughter, sat in the back, and Dovik, the older grandson, in the seat beside him, provoking me incessantly: "I'm sitting up front, I can see better, I was in Grandpa's wadi before you, he took me there even when we lived with Mom in Tel Aviv, and he showed me the cave and told me about the caveman before you were even born."

And then he began to annoy Grandpa: how could he drive with only one eye?

"I can," said Grandpa. "It's a fact. I'm driving, aren't I?"

I'm wondering inside: If we had also asked him about all the other things he did. How could you have done them, Grandpa? Would he have answered the same way: I did them, no? That answer—"It's a fact!"—answers many questions: How could you? How did you? How did it happen? How could it happen? And how could you, Ruta, have lived with this grandfather and also loved him? It's a fact. I hated him, I was afraid of him, I loved him, and I lived with him. It was good to live with him and it was good for him too, not only for us. The cases are vastly different, but maybe raising us and taking care of us, so alien to his character, were for him what the hard labor, years later, was for Eitan.

Whatever. It's complicated. Let's go back to traveling with him. He drove the way he always drove. Slowly, poorly, and confidently. He derived no pleasure from driving and didn't quite understand how his vehicle related to other vehicles, and like various other laws, various traffic laws made no sense to him. And despite that and his one eye, he wasn't involved in any accidents until his first one, years later, when he was almost eighty. You want to hear about it? He was driving on an old dirt road in the vineyards and got on the main road without looking to either side and without stopping and without giving the right-of-way to a woman driving there. Nothing happened to her or to him, but the bumper of his pickup truck sent her fancy-assed Audi to the body shop for a week. She was one of the city people who had come to live here, built a villa the size of a community center, and planted old olive trees so she could spend weekends with friends playing at "I own an estate and this is Tuscany." There was shouting. I mean, she shouted: "You came from the field onto the road! You have to give me the right-of-way!" And he didn't shout at all. He answered her calmly: "Madam, here I have the right-of-way."

"How? You went from a dirt road to the main road!"

"This is the road I traveled on my horse to the vineyard when we established the moshava, and then neither this road nor you were yet here."

She screamed, "What does that have to do with it?"

He said, "It has to do with the fact that the right-of-way is the right of the one who got here first."

"You're not only stupid, you're half blind. How do they let you drive with one eye?"

"When I see you," he said to her, "I'm sorry I didn't lose my other eye. And now calm down, because I can leave you here and you can keep yelling at the trees and rocks, or I can take you home and send my grandson to tow your car to a garage and pay for the repair. So what's your decision?"

On the way she tried to conduct a slightly more civilized conversation, but Grandpa Ze'ev told her to shut up because she had already used up her right to speak to him. Dovik, by the way, met her later at the garage and described her as a most worthwhile daughter of Pharaoh and hinted that she had provided him an opportunity to correct the bad impression she had perhaps gotten about the men in our family. But Dovik's tales need to be taken with a grain of salt, and even without this addendum the whole story was very charming and we all laughed a lot about this city woman who didn't even realize she had been saved from troubles far worse than a week in the body shop. But in the evening, at home, when no outsider could hear, Grandpa Ze'ev told us that in truth he simply hadn't seen her, and that a man needs to be responsible and draw conclusions. That same week he sent his license to the motor vehicle department and informed them that in honor of his eightieth birthday he was suspending himself from driving.

From that day onward one of us would drive him to his wadi and let him off by the small bridge on the road. From there he walked up to his flowers and bushes and seeds, and at midday he rested under his big carob tree and always ate the same meal: bread, cheese, cucumber, garlic, a hard-boiled egg, a slice of salami, hot green pepper, olives he had pickled himself, and a few swigs of red wine from a flask. Then he napped awhile on the royal throne, as we called one of the rocks, which resembled a giant's chair and was easier on the buttocks than it appeared, and then got up and continued to leave markers or collect seeds, depending on the season. And in late afternoon he went back down to the road, where one of us was waiting to take him home.

But back when I was a little girl, he still drove there himself and often took Dovik and me with him. We would leave the pickup truck in the shade of the oaks at the side of the road and follow him up the gully. He taught us how to identify and how to find and how to gather the seeds of his wildflowers. In their flowering season he stuck thin, tall marking sticks beside them, because later on, when the seeds were ready, the plant was completely dried up and hard to find among the other dry plants. Sometimes he would attach a label to the stick noting some special quality, like a cyclamen of a richer color or an anemone with unusually large flowers, a hollyhock that was darker than normal or a squill that year after year flowered early.

We went from marker to marker, stick to stick, we collected seeds in paper bags—not plastic, so the seeds would not get moldy—and in each bag put a note with the name. Grandpa Ze'ev could identify every seed and every fruit of every plant as easily as he identified their flowers, but he did this so we would learn and also know. Sometimes he would give us a quiz—he put seeds on the table and asked us to name the plants they came from: the brownish-purple seeds of the cyclamen, which retained a sweetish scent even when dry, and seeds of anemones, in the fluff that carries them in the wind, and buttercup seeds, like golden flakes you had to rub between your hands to free them from the stalk, and seeds of the blue thistle, smooth and yellowy, that jump out of the dry berry when you squeeze it, and seeds of flax, also smooth and oily, but smaller and darker and barely sprouting, and seeds of squill, like thin dark flakes. And how to tell the difference between poppy seeds and snapdragon seeds, crocus and gladiolus, and the common corn cockle and slender corn cockles, whose seeds are almost identical.

At the end of every collection and marking we returned to his big carob tree, which surprised us anew every time, how big and thick and green it was, and we would sit in its shade and eat. Grandpa Ze'ev explained to us that in nature luck and chance are very important. The layer of soil in the hills is very thin, sometimes only a few centimeters deep, and under it is chalky rock. But this carob got lucky—that's what he said—and took root in a good place, in deep soil, and the creek provided plenty of water and every winter swept in some new soil.

The big rocks under the carob kept away the cows and nettles that tend to gather under big carob trees and leave stinking turds on the ground and burning blisters on the skin. Grandpa Ze'ev said that only people from kibbutzim think that cow dung has a good smell and even sing songs in its praise: our moshava had real farmers who knew the truth—all shit stinks, even if it's the dung of socialist calves and Zionist cows.

We often found cigarette butts there, the remnants of a campfire, the footprints of visitors.

Dovik got annoyed. "Who gave them permission to sit under our carob?"

Grandpa Ze'ev displayed remarkable tolerance. "They apparently don't know it's ours," he said, and even complimented the campfire of the anonymous visitors, which was small and neat and built precisely on the remains of a previous fire. That means they're completely okay, he declared, adding that the tree belonged not only to us and them but to the birds who live in it and to the beetles and lizards who climb on it and the ants and goats who eat its fruit and the snakes who live in its shade among the rocks.

He gathered a few twigs, taught us how to set them on fire, built a small campfire on the same spot that others had lit similar campfires. Dovik sat on the throne, and Grandpa told him to move over a bit so I could sit beside him.

"There's enough room for Ruta too," he said, and took out the cucumber and cheese from his backpack, and the bread and salami and olives and garlic and hot green pepper. He put up a small kettle and made us tea and told us about the nearby cave, which was once the home of the caveman.

Go have a look in the cave, he told Dovik, maybe he's home and we can invite him to have lunch with us.

Dovik hurried over there, peeked in, shouted—"He's not here!"—and came back.

"That's really too bad," said Grandpa Ze'ev, "we could have learned from him how to light a fire with flint rock, not with a match or lighter." There was genuine longing in his smile, not that of an archaeologist or a historian but of a man looking for a worthy friend.

Grandma Ruth was still alive in those days, but he was the one who raised us. She was there in the house but not present in our lives, which we could sense even in the sandwiches she would make us for school. All the necessary components were there, the fresh tomato and cheese omelet, but his cracked olives and hard cheese and garlic and cucumber and hot pepper were much tastier and fresher. Sometimes I tried to engage her in conversation. In general I didn't succeed, but I once saw her sitting motionless on the steps of the kitchen porch and asked her what she was doing.

"I am longing," she said.

"For whom?"

"For my children, who flew the coop as soon as they were able to fly." And then she said, "Away from him and because of him, which I also tried to do."

She explained to me that here, in the moshava, there are big extended families that stay together, on the same plot of land, and never stop arguing, and there are some like us, where the children run away, and who knows which is better.

Grandpa also spoke with us on the very same topic, about offspring who go far away from home and offspring who stay, but he did so by means of clever parables about plants that scatter their seeds versus plants that leave their progeny, as he put it with unexpected tenderness, "at home near Mommy and Daddy."

He showed us that the plants that scatter their children to the winds equip the seeds with all sorts of tufts and wings to help them fly with the wind, and with thorns and hooks to stick to the fur of animals that would carry them away, and produce fruit that would be eaten to spread the seeds someplace else. But those who want the children at home, close to them, plant them nearby. Actually plant them, he explained and demonstrated: the cyclamen, for example, bends its stalk to the ground and drops its seeds right beside it. The lupine has a kind of spring mechanism in its pod, so when it dries it bursts open and casts the seeds a meter or two away. And the poppy holds its little seeds inside a fruit that resembles a saltshaker, with holes in it, and when the wind blows they drop to the ground like salt into a salad. But the ragwort lets its seeds fly off without knowing where, far, far away.

The cyclamen says to herself—that's what he said, "says to herself"—If I've succeeded in sprouting here, growing, producing a bulb, leaves, flowers, and seeds, it's a sign that this is a good place, and my children should grow up here. But the ragworts have their logic: It's fine here, kids, totally fine, but there, over the hill, maybe there's a much better place. And they send their children there: Enough clinging to Daddy and Mommy. Go, try your fortune. Know new places and new people, struggle, adapt, and, besides, how many offspring and generations can one plot of land support, even if it's very good land?

A jaybird screeched from the tree. Grandpa Ze'ev got up and threw a stone into the foliage, and the jay flew off and disappeared. He couldn't stand jaybirds. I believe I told you that he used to shoot them with his old Mauser. At first I didn't understand what he had against them. Maybe their screeching during siesta time between two and four, maybe their irresponsibility and recklessness, the stealing and mimicry and mischief, or maybe what annoyed him was the arrogant little crest they have on their heads. The crest, and that blue patch in the middle of the wing—what's that all about?

That idiot Haim Maslina, the neighbors' son who was then a classmate of mine, told me something he heard from his grandfather, the equally idiotic Yitzhak Maslina: "When they were young, your grandpa shot all the jaybirds in the moshava and killed them. This was known to all their friends and relatives in the hills and other villages, and this is why until today there are no jaybirds in our moshava." And he added, "Maybe they'll come back to us after your grandpa is dead."

The truth is that Grandpa Ze'ev was a pretty good shot. When Eitan came to us he invited him to a shooting contest and was fairly surprised when Eitan shot better than he did. Not only with the M16 he had brought from the army—that he could accept—but also with his old Mauser, which had a recoil that knocked the shooter backward and is made in Germany and weighs what a rifle should weigh, "not like your plastic toy from America."

But Eitan said that Grandpa was also a real sharpshooter. His firing speed needed a little work, he pointed out, but every bullet hit the bull's-eye, because in his day you would be given two bullets for practice and seven for battle and ten to establish the State, and you didn't pull the trigger without being a hundred percent sure of hitting the target.

When Eitan came to us Grandpa Ze'ev already had colorful eye patches with flowers I embroidered for him, and he liked them very much. But before that he had only two black, frightening patches: one on his eye and the other in a bathroom drawer.

"Watch out," Dovik told all the kids who sized him up when he entered a new grade at school. "Watch out! My grandfather is a pirate!"

Grandpa Ze'ev's black eye patches filled Dovik with pride. Once he even wore one of them and went outside, but Yitzhak Maslina saw him and yelled at him, "For shame! This is not a game! I'll tell your grandfather and he'll let you have it!"

Dovik ran home, where Grandpa surprised him three times over—he was in the house and saw him, he didn't let him have it, and he also burst out laughing. "I'll give it to you for Purim, you'll put it on, and everyone will know that you dressed up as your grandpa."

"What's under it?" asked Dovik.

"Nothing," said Grandpa.

"Just a hole?"

"No. No hole. There's an eye, but it's dead. I can show you."

Dovik was frightened. No, he didn't want to see it. But after a few days of restlessness he asked, "Show us, but not just me, also Ruta."

I was four at the time, and the blob that had been Grandpa Ze'ev's eye became one of the first images engraved in my memory. He slid the patch to his forehead, and we saw sort of a tiny shriveled egg, chilling, grayish white, lacking the expression that an iris and a pupil give a seeing eye. I didn't phrase it like this at the time, but I felt it: here was the first touch of death in a body that was still alive and warm.

"What is that, Grandpa?" I asked fearfully.

"I already told you, this was once my eye."

"Why is it like that?"

"It got hit and it died."

"How?"

"By what?"

"By the branch of a tree. I was galloping on a horse in the woods, and a branch hit me in the eye."

"Were you chasing robbers?"

"No."

"Then who were you chasing?"

"Nobody. I was just galloping. That's all."

"Did it hurt?"

"Not so much. The branch only scratched my eye, and I didn't go to the doctor right away. Grandma Ruth put a bandage on it, and the neighbor put on some cow sulfa. By the time I got to a real doctor, the eye couldn't see a thing."

And he smiled. "Now you two put patches on one eye and try pouring water from a kettle into a glass."

We did as he said and couldn't do it. The water spilled on the table.

"You see?" he said. "I had to learn to do many things with one eye. To make tea, lace my shoes, but shooting a rifle was no problem."

A number of years later, approaching my bat mitzvah, I sewed and embroidered him a present—a new patch, light blue, with tiny yellow flowers. "I want you to wear it at my party," I said, "and not this old black one."

"Sure," he said, and because he was a man of his word he came wearing it, arousing new amazement among some guests and old fear among others. From then on he wore it on ordinary days, and I embroidered more patches for him, with a flower he loved on each of them: blue thistle, pink flax, chrysanthemum, poppy, cyclamen. When he died, by the way, we put them all in his coffin. I don't believe in the afterlife, but Dovik said, "He's starting a new life there now, so he should go there showing his good side. Not the murderer with the black eye patch but the grandpa who loved flowers and whose grandchildren loved him."

TWENTY

....

A WOMAN AND A RIFLE
AND A TREE AND A COW

(Draft)

1

At first Ze'ev saw only the treetop poking above the distant mound of earth. The tip of a small tree, which had not been there yesterday and should not be there now.

He clutched his stick and waited, and the tree, to his amazement, moved. It moved, drew closer, emerged from the hillside, and revealed itself. It was sitting in a wagon, the wagon was drawn by an ox, and a cow walked behind, tied to the wagon by a rope.

On the driver's seat was the figure of a man, and in the wagon, in the shade of the tree, sat another figure. Ze'ev knew who these two were even though they were far away and their faces not yet visible. Under the driver's seat, he knew, a rifle awaited him too, cold and silent and ready to strike.

He smiled to himself. A month ago he had informed his parents that he'd found a new place and purchased a plot of land in a new moshava, and now they were sending him everything a man needed to get started.

The wagon drew closer. The figures grew sharper and now had names: the wagon driver became his big brother Dov, and the tree became the young mulberry from his parents' yard, and the woman became Ruth Blum, the neighbor's daughter he had desired from the time he was a youth and she just a girl; he wanted her and had written his parents to ask her and ask her parents.

The wagon came nearer and arrived. His brother halted the magnificent ox with a shout. Ruth jumped out and came and stood before him and said:

"Do you remember me, Ze'ev?"

That is actually what she said: "Do you remember me, Ze'ev?" Which meant, in the language of those days: I have not forgotten you, Ze'ev, I have never stopped thinking about you from the day you left.

He said, "Yes, Ruth, I remember you. The youngest daughter of the Blum family." Which meant: I love you.

And she said, "If so, I am happy." Because that's how one would say: And I you.

And he said, "You grew up." As if to say: Before you filled only my memory and my dreams and now you also fill my eyes and my heart.

And she asked, "And you're happy I grew up, Ze'ev?" That's what she actually said: "And you're happy I grew up, Ze'ev?" Which meant: All this is yours.

He answered her: "Yes, I am very happy you grew up." And she heard and understood every word: I lust for you, big and beautiful girl that you are. I want to touch you, touch you and everything that grew and became beautiful in you.

"And you're happy that I agreed and came, Ze'ev?"

And he was slightly abashed and his fingers tightened around his stick, and his mouth uttered, "Yes, I am happy that you agreed and came."

And Ruth translated to herself: Don't go, stay with me, please.

His big brother Dov, who all the while had kept a respectful distance, checking the axles and reins and pouring water into a pail, first for the ox and then the cow, stood up straight and looked at them and understood what they were saying by the tilt of their necks and their hand motions and angles of their bodies, and finally shouted, "Enough, Ze'ev, let her be for now. Look, I also brought you the mulberry tree from home, and the cow, and most important"—and from under the driver's seat he pulled out and lifted up something elongated, wrapped in a flowered blanket and tied at both ends—"also the rifle you were promised! Everything a man needs to get started!"

He approached them, the bundled rifle in his hand, and continued, "And Father also put seeds and a harness in the wagon for you, and a *taburetka* stool to sit on while milking, and a pickax and two hoes, and an extra blade for the plow, and the blanket on the rifle is from Mother, a blanket with flowers she embroidered. I told them that they were giving you too much, more than what's left for me and Arieh, but that's what he decided. Come and look, it's all in the wagon."

Ze'ev drew close. The ox extended his mighty neck toward him and stuck out his tongue to lick him. Ze'ev stroked his nose affectionately and rubbed his forehead with his knuckles and looked in the wagon and saw the tools and sacks and also a black basalt stone, about forty centimeters long. From the basalt of the Lower Galilee, lichen stains on its upper side, bits of earth and spiderweb on the other, smoother side.

He held it and lifted it and hugged it. Its weight—it was heavy—felt good in his strong arms. Its heat—the heat of the lava that spawned it and the heat of the sun it had absorbed in its life—flooded his chest and his eyes.

"Father said you should put this stone into the wall of the house that Ruth and you will build," said Dov. "Place it about a meter and a half high, and do not cover it with plaster. One black side of it should face the street and another black side face into the house. That way you will remember who you are and where you came from, and the neighbors will know: here lives someone who comes from the Galilee, and no one messes with him."

He untied the blanket, his mother's embroidered flowers fluttered, and the rifle was revealed.

"This is your rifle, Dov," said Ze'ev with great surprise.

"I know it's my rifle, but Father decided to give it to you."

2

Dov had taken his German Mauser from a retreating Turkish soldier at the end of the First World War. He was just a youth, and his father had ordered him to plow a portion of the field. He rose early in the morning, took provisions, hitched the wagon to a mule and loaded the plow on it, and went. When he neared the field he saw a figure lying in the shade of a big jujube tree. He carefully came closer and saw a Turkish soldier sleeping with a gun in his hands.

He was scared for a moment but not surprised. The British had already advanced northward, and retreating Turkish soldiers, alone or in small groups, were to be seen here and there, hungry, worn out, frightened, thirsty, some of them sick and wounded.

The soldier awoke and sat up. Dov saw the trembling hands, the cracked lips, the weary, imploring eyes, but his own eyes were fixed, with desire and trepidation, upon the rifle. He stopped the mule at a safe distance, smiled at the soldier, made a calming gesture with his hand, and then took from his pouch a quarter of a loaf of bread and waved it in his direction.

The sight of the bread had an immediate, wondrous effect on the man: he dropped the rifle and began crawling toward Dov on all fours, like a tired but determined animal. Dov, atop the wagon, tore off a piece of bread and tossed it to him. The soldier seized it and chewed and swallowed in haste, with muffled grunts of joy, and Dov jumped from the wagon and ran to the tree and took the rifle and pointed it at him.

The soldier did not panic. He extended a pleading hand, and Dov hoisted the rifle on his shoulder and returned to the wagon and tore off and threw another piece of bread and also took from his pouch a tin of olives, came close and began tossing him one olive after another.

The soldier could not summon the strength to catch them in flight. He crawled on all fours, gathered the olives from the ground, and put them in his mouth with the dirt and stubble of the field that stuck to them. His eyes sparkled with happiness and gratitude. Dov approached him cautiously, put his water jug on the ground and took a few steps back, gesturing to the soldier to take it.

When the soldier had drunk all the water, he ordered him to strip off his ammunition belt and throw it on the ground and then shouted at him in Arabic to go away, and to drive the point home made a slaughtering gesture across his neck with a finger and pointed in the direction he should go.

The soldier, somewhat revived and encouraged, stood up straight.

Dov was frightened. Never had he seen so tall or broad a man. Again he pointed the rifle at him, but the giant clasped his hands to his heart in a gesture of thanks intelligible to any human being and common to all languages and bowed down. His damaged lips smiled. His staggering legs carried him, step by step, away from Dov and the tree. He did not even try to take back his weapon. He seemed glad to be rid of it—of what it could do, of the temptation loaded within it, of its weight.

Dov waited until the soldier became a dot in the distance, then hung the rifle and ammunition belt on branches of the tree, so that someone possibly watching from afar could not see them. All day he plowed, and at nightfall he hid the rifle in the wagon, returned home, and told his father what had happened.

"You did well," his father praised him, adding that he did not want the village council to know about the rifle lest they take away the rifle that had been given to him for guard duty.

They removed a few boards from the floor of the shed in the yard, dug a pit in the earth, wrapped the rifle in rags soaked in engine oil, buried it, and replaced the floor above its grave. At the first opportunity the father obtained a tin box, and they put the rifle in that and again buried it in the ground, and when Ze'ev went to live in a different place, Dov brought him the rifle in the wagon.

"This rifle is part of our history," Ze'ev told his sons and later his grandson and granddaughter.

The eyes of the children, generation by generation, sparkled, and Ruth, first a mother and then a grandmother, said nothing. Only once did she remark: "It is not part of our history; it determines and writes it. You are in its hands, not it in yours."

TWENTY-ONE

"So what did they send me from home in the wagon?" Grandpa Ze'ev would quiz me and Dovik when we were little. And we were supposed to answer him in rhymes that he composed: "A rifle and cow / A stone and a plow / A mulberry tree / And Grandma for me." The mulberry tree, by the way, he loved no less than he loved Grandma, and out of love he didn't plant it in the ground but left it in the barrel it came in and on the same wagon, and everywhere he rode, so he told us, he rode with his tree.

And the mulberry grew and grew, and grew and grew, until what happened? "What happened, Dovik? Ruta? What happened, Neta?"

The roots of the mulberry tree burst through the barrel, and Grandpa Ze'ev filled the whole wagon with earth, and so the wagon became a giant flowerpot on wheels, and Grandpa Ze'ev and his tree continued to go out to work together. The magnificent ox pulled the wagon, and when they got to the field it was harnessed to the plow, and Grandpa plowed and planted and seeded, and at lunchtime he lay in the shade of his tree and ate and rested: "I ate what Grandma Ruth prepared for me, and for dessert I had berries from the tree, I cut grass for the ox and piled it up for him, I gave his poop to the tree, and the ox pulled it and me in the wagon. That's how families are."

Ultimately the mulberry grew so big that even two pairs of oxen couldn't pull the wagon, and the wagon itself began to fall apart from the pressure of the roots and weight of the tree and wetness of the soil.

"And what happened then, Dovik? And what happened then, Ruta? And what happened then, Neta?"

"Grandpa dug a long deep hole at the edge of the yard, the oxen pulled, he pushed, the wagon went into the hole."

"And what happened then, Dovik, Ruta, Neta?"

Grandpa Ze'ev released the oxen, and they climbed out with their harnesses; he removed the wagon shafts and covered the wagon with a lot of dirt. That's it, that's how he planted the mulberry tree in the yard and how it became our big mulberry tree today, which looks as if it was there forever, as if it hadn't come to Grandpa Ze'ev and been planted in his yard, but instead that Grandpa Ze'ev came to it and decided to build a house in its shade. But we knew it came in a wagon, which was buried beneath it, and Dovik—who was a very active child and wanted to make an impression on other children and also to make money, so he said, to buy plane tickets and visit our mother in America—kept nagging Grandpa to dig out the wagon and attach it to a tractor instead of an ox so we could ride in the shade of the tree as he had in his younger years and maybe sell tickets to people who wanted a ride. But Grandpa Ze'ev said that the wagon was already completely rotted away, and even if it wasn't, the roots of the tree had already pushed through the bottom and stuck way deep into planet Earth. That's what he said—"stuck deep into planet Earth"—not into our yard or the land of the moshava.

Eventually, when Eitan showed up and joined the family and heard the story about the mulberry tree that rode in the wagon, he went to the carpentry shop of an old army buddy and came back with a small wagon, about eighty centimeters long, a precise model of an old farmer's wagon, with rubber wheels and tall sides. He filled it with dirt, planted a lemon sapling, and said we should manufacture and sell these in all sizes with different kinds of trees.

The idea was that one could move the trees from place to place in a garden and change its appearance every day, but Dovik said, "It won't work. People don't like it when their trees move from place to place. It gives them a bad feeling."

He was right. It's enough that we move, we are shaken, pulled, shoved. Trees must stay in place and bestow confidence and calm. And I tell you all this, Varda, because our family can be described not only by the seeds and flowers from Grandpa Ze'ev's wadi but also through its trees. Not the tens of thousands of poor little saplings at the Tavori Nursery, with roots yearning to break free from their black bags, wondering, Who will buy and raise me? Who will eat my fruit? Who will sit in my shade? I don't mean the trees we sell, but the three truly important trees: Grandpa's big carob in his wadi, in whose shade he taught us about plants and under which he died. The good and beautiful acacia in the Negev, in whose shade my man and my son camped on the trip from which they did not return. And the big mulberry, under which nobody has died as yet, except for Eitan's cold *poikehs,* which sat on the chilly ground for twelve years and came back to life after Grandpa Ze'ev died.

Three big trees. Size matters. Big trees help people relax. It's the thickness and strength of the trunk, the shade and security and serenity of the scene, the whisper of the wind in the branches, which even in a storm sway slowly—such is the calm and beauty of the natural landscape. I won't take you to the carob and the acacia, but you can see the mulberry through the window. Turn around and look. You see?

By the way, you can also see it clearly in the aerial photograph on the wall behind you. Get up a moment, Varda, come, I want to show you something. Here, you see the dedication on the photo? "To Teacher Ruta, who taught me everything, I want you to teach me more." This is a present from Ofer, the son of the neighbors, Haim and Miri Maslina. My beloved student, who almost drowned from that bet about swimming underwater in the Kinneret. He started taking pictures when he was about bar mitzvah age, and when he finished high school he put together a wonderful exhibit that counted toward his matriculation exam. Everyone called it "the exhibit of aerial photographs of the moshava," but Ofer called it "God Looking at Our Moshava and Thinking Thoughts." I remember how he took those pictures. A friend of Haim's took him up in a motorized paraglider every day for a week, and all day long he took pictures from different heights and at different angles of the sun, street by street, house by house, plot by plot of land, yard by yard, and the noise of the motor overhead drove the whole moshava crazy.

"Maybe shoot him the way you used to shoot the jaybirds?" Dovik suggested to Grandpa Ze'ev. But Grandpa for some reason surprised us all and didn't shoot him, and Ofer kept taking pictures. He had the prints made in the city and had them framed with captions that also annoyed everyone concerned, in other words the whole moshava without exception.

About us, in case you're interested, he wrote: "The Tavori Family. Vast floods cannot quench, the earth cannot cover up, memory will not be swallowed in the abyss." I asked him, "How do you know that? Where did you get that language?" And he said: "From you, Teacher Ruta," and he made me this print and gave it to me with that dedication. What a boy he was, so different from that family of his, wretched people generation after generation. So you see? This house, the one you and I are sitting in right now, was Grandpa Ze'ev's house, and that one is Dovik and Dalia's house, and that one is the house that was mine and Eitan's. Dalia wanted to rent out Grandpa's house, but Dovik and I refused. We don't want strangers wandering around on our property. One day it'll belong to one of Dovik and Dalia's twins, Dafna or Dorit, whichever of them gets married first. The husband has yet to appear, no one knows his name or his face, but Dovik hates him already, because he, unlike Eitan, will not change his family name to ours, and the House of Tavori will become the house of who the hell knows.

And here's Grandpa Ze'ev's old storage shed, which Ofer wrote was the "subconscious" of the other houses of the Tavori family and perhaps the whole moshava, and not long ago, after Grandpa Ze'ev died, we tore it down, and Eitan poured a new concrete floor and built a new storage shed, which isn't the subconscious of anything, just as a shed should be. And this is the area of the hedges and vines of the nursery, and there the spices and medicinal plants, and there are the seedlings of the vegetables and all the equipment you need to create a flowerbed.

Do we also have orchids? You want to buy some? I knew it. I knew that not only the Tavori family but also your family is hiding a terrible secret, and now, in a moment of indiscretion, it comes out. Just as we've begun to develop a kind of intimacy, it suddenly turns out, Varda, that you love orchids. So you should know that from the perspective of the Tavori family and the Tavori Nursery this amounts to a declaration of war. This is our red line. If there is one plant that we all agree is unbearable, it's orchids. Even Dalia can't stand orchids, though it would be just like her to love them. I'm not talking about Grandpa Ze'ev's cute little wild orchids, which no one wants to buy anyway, but orchid-orchids. The most plastic, kitschy, pampered, nouveau-riche, pretentious, arrogant, show-offy, love-me, alien plant there is.

I remember what Grandpa Ze'ev said to Eitan after we told him we were getting married, and he began giving him instructions in advance of his joining us. Among other things he said, "Three types of dreck will not enter our nursery—orchids, bonsai, and the people who grow them." He also couldn't stand cactuses but didn't make a big deal about it. Bonsai are those Japanese dwarf trees. I told you before that trees need to be big? So these are the littlest trees possible. They take a seedling, plant it in a pot that's too small, like they used to bind the feet of Chinese women, and the pot doesn't let it develop and makes it look like an old distorted dwarf, and I'm sure that it's not just the pot, that they abuse it in other ways. So because of the suffering of these trees and the sadists who grow them, we don't want plants and people like these around here. It's true that a fair number of customers are interested in them, but we don't want in our nursery a tree that some Dr. Mengele of botany experimented on. Not here.

Here's the domain of Dovik, the office of the nursery. Nothing grows there, but it's the most important place. My being able to chat with you about wildflowers and mulberries and big versus little trees is all because of the office. Dovik, despite Grandpa's teaching, isn't really interested in flowers and plants or nature in general. But he's the one who does our big business, and big business is not Grandpa Ze'ev's cyclamens and squills and poppies and not Eitan's *poikeh* club and not the petunias and periwinkles and vegetables we sell to private customers. It's the decorative trees and landscaping of the squares and boulevards of the cities and regional councils—and Dovik handles all this skillfully and successfully.

In this corner behind the office, you can see a shower and toilet for the staff and another for customers and the tool and equipment shed of the nursery. Here's the outdoor storage: flagstones, patio stones, tufa, gravel, flowerpots and planters, poles and netting. And what are those? Are those people? From high up it's not immediately clear. Most of them are customers, but that one I think is Dalia, coming back from work and going to the office to make sure that no daughter of Pharaoh is pulling her husband, and this strange creature, hard to make out at this angle, is Eitan, hugging a barrel with a seedling and carrying it to this truck. That is what Grandpa Ze'ev sentenced him to do and that is what Eitan wanted: punishment. Prison with hard labor, with no time off for good behavior and no reduction in sentence or granting himself a pardon. That's what he looked like then and that's what he did for twelve years. At most he would sometimes take it easy by weeding or, to be exact, eradicating. For hours. He would get down on all fours and start to crawl through the whole nursery, crawling and uprooting every evil weed, eradicating without mercy. Making very slow progress, and the ground, which had been dressed up and dotted in green, was left brown and bloodied, naked and bare.

That is what he did until my grandfather died. And then something happened, as if someone blew on the dirt and an old ember suddenly came to life, glowing red, a tongue of flame, a tiny finger, flickering, catching fire.

TWENTY-TWO

....

At Neta's funeral I screamed only once. That was when the old man from Eitan and Dovik's unit arrived, the one with the skinny kid with the big ears who guided the helicopter landing on the road and drove our pickup truck to their house in Paran. Now they brought us the pickup. The old friend went over to Dovik, a brief ritual of hugs and backslaps, and gave him the keys.

I'd never seen this man before in my life. I hadn't seen him and never heard of him before the disaster; he also wasn't one of Eitan's or Dovik's buddies, but much older. But he drove the whole way up from the Arava to return the pickup and attend the funeral. And his wife, with this strange kid—a son? grandson? maybe he too, like Dovik and me, was raised by his grandparents?—drove behind him in their car all the way from their home in the Arava to take him back down south afterward, and they also brought two cartons of vegetables to eat during the shiva. But I, when I saw him handing the pickup keys to Dovik, attacked him without realizing what I was doing. It was awful. You have no idea how sorry I am over that. I screamed at him in front of everyone, "How can you be so organized? How come you're so efficient, and find your way everywhere in the dark without getting lost, and you bring and organize and help, so how is it that by you everything is so hunky-dory, but it was by you that my son happened to die? You should all go to hell! How does a thing like this happen?"

The skinny boy came over immediately, stood, and stared at me with his cold pale eyes, and the man, who was about sixty, sixty-five, with tiny little sapphire eyes, thick gray hair as curly as steel wool, a small wiry body, sunburned and tough as an old work boot, who had not known of me previously and saw Neta for the first time only as a dead child, gave me a good look and said nothing, and Dovik, who felt a need to help out, went over and said to him, "Niso, I'd like you to meet my sister, Ruta, who is also Eitan's wife." And to me he said, "Ruta, this is Niso, an officer from the unit." In other words—Know before whom you stand. Here was another of their Lords of Hosts, a rider through the deserts.

But this Niso, as if we had known each other for years, simply took me aside and said, "Ruta, for heaven's sake, I'm a friend, I'm just trying to help . . ." And I stopped yelling and cursing and I started to cry: "So why didn't you help before? Why didn't you make sure to warn them there was a snake like that over there, why didn't you kill it? You live there, you know every wadi and stone, you must also know all the animals."

I saw Dovik gesturing to him to let me be, that I would soon calm down, but what he did was hug me, which was pretty funny because I was a head taller than him. Whatever. At the cemetery I behaved just fine. I exploited my talent for holding my breath underwater, and also a technique I developed when our mother handed Dovik and me to Grandpa Ze'ev and went off to America: I gave myself secret stage directions, clear, curt instructions. At first in the imperative—Stand, Sit—and then the wording of a professional dramatist writing about herself: She smiles, She sighs, She waves goodbye, She wipes a tear. And just as I didn't fall apart then, when my mother left her children, I didn't fall apart at the funeral of my child, who left his mother. In this family we don't fall apart.

It so happened that one of the first directions I gave myself was not to walk beside Eitan. To be precise, I didn't direct myself to walk beside him, and so it went. We walked separately. People noticed, how could they not? Whoever heard of such a thing, that a couple who had lost a child, a young couple, a small child, an only child, would not walk together behind the coffin? We were spaced out, literally and figuratively, distant and apart. Not only that, but Grandpa and Dovik walked with Eitan, and Dalia, dripping with symbolism, walked beside me. I noticed that people noticed, and whispered, and I knew it would be discussed in the moshava well into the future, the Tavori family supplying them all with yet another story.

And later, at the grave, the clods of earth knocking like clichés on the coffin, I gave myself additional direction: not to fall on the ground, not to collapse, not to scream the way you always see at funerals in Israel. But Eitan, apparently, did not give himself direction and did fall. He didn't scream, that he did later; but he did collapse.

They picked him up, sat him down on a chair. They expected me to take care of him. But I didn't give myself that direction. Instead I directed myself to go over to that Niso and apologize to him and I even smiled: "This won't happen at the next funeral. I promise you." That's how it is in our family. We are also able to smile. Even to laugh and make others laugh.

So, alone and spaced apart, Eitan and I heard the clods of earth falling onto the lid of the coffin, and the strangled sound of Neta's blood crying out from inside it, and the weeping of so many people, and the eulogy of his first-grade teacher, who spoke about what was "folded up within him"—the butterfly wings that would never open, never spread, those were her words, and we would never know what might have been.

I found myself silently correcting her Hebrew grammar, the word "wings" being feminine not masculine. What's become of you, Ruta, you teacher you, unable to restrain yourself. But that, after all, is what will be imagined and pondered for years to come: the wings that will never be spread. Where would they have carried him? On what winds would he glide? To what heights would he soar? Where would he land? Put down roots and blossom? Years later I had an odd habit—I would see around me the girlfriends he might have had, in the schoolyard, at the bus stop, in the library, at the beach. Once I even saw his wife crossing my field of vision for a moment: tall like me, with low-waisted pants and a shocking belly shirt, so revealing that I could see the faint glow of the hundreds of thousands of eggs that gilded her lower abdomen, some of which—four? three?—would become grandsons and granddaughters of other grandmothers.

But at the time I heard only the hoe in the mound of earth, the raking sound, the falling and knocking, which I heard as if I were lying with him in the coffin; I heard it and gave myself direction: Stand up straight, lips sealed, don't look behind you. Not even when Eitan, who stood a few steps behind me and didn't give himself direction, suddenly fell like a toppled tree.

As I told you: everyone expected that his wife would go over and take care of him, but I didn't even look at him. Not there, beside the grave, and not on the way back home, and not under the tarp that friends had already put up to shade our front lawn. The plastic chairs were arranged, refreshments placed on the tables, and the comforters approached the mother, namely me, who sat under the big mulberry tree—Too bad this happened at Passover and not later in the spring when we could've served you all buckets of mulberries, it occurred to me, in between my brain spasms and clenched throat—and then they wanted to approach the father too, but he was not to be found, because he went off to a far corner of the nursery and paced around until he disappeared in a maze of vines, where he started to scream, more precisely to bellow, a hideous, horrible bellowing.

No one dared approach him, as if a wounded ox or bereaved bear were hidden in the foliage. Everyone kept looking at the mother, waiting for her to say or do something, and she just smiled with exhaustion. "Let him yell, it can only help." And when I said that he reappeared, crawling out from under the bushes.

Everyone was frightened, but Grandpa Ze'ev stood up and went to him and held out a hand and said, "Get up from the ground, Eitan. Get up." And in a whisper that only I heard, because I knew what he would say and my ears were already attuned for the exact words, he added, "A man must not fall like that and scream like that in front of everyone. You hear? Not in our family. Get up!"

That night I wrote down that scene in one of my notebooks. I still remember a few lines by heart: "The father rose heavily. Gone was the spring in his step. Gone were his lightheartedness, his carelessness, his quickness to act. From now on the body will burden the spirit, and the spirit the body. The weight of sin, the weight of disaster, the weight of his dead son—how heavy are the dead—he will carry on his back forever."

In normal language, Varda, Eitan gave his hand to Grandpa Ze'ev and walked after him like a toddler, straight to the shower I showed you in Ofer's aerial photos. Eitan had built the shower a few years earlier and screened it off with bamboo and installed hot and cold water faucets and hooks for clothes and towels and equipped it with sponges and brushes—a small brush to remove mud from under fingernails and a brush with a long handle for the back—and a laundry basket and a small bench to sit on together, the togetherness of naked men after a day of work, how good and pleasant to curl and spread their toes, to drink cold beer and dry off in the breeze.

"And the grandfather," I wrote, "without turning his head, ordered his granddaughter to bring clean work clothes. Whether it was because she was accustomed to obeying him, and maybe out of curiosity, and maybe because she didn't want to argue in front of the crowd of comforters, which kept growing and swarming, a storming monster of goodwill—she did as he said. And when she brought the clothes he had requested, she saw that he had already gone with her husband behind the bamboo partition and she quickly followed them."

Eitan stood with his back bent and head drooping, one hand on the shoulder of Grandpa Ze'ev, who sat beside him on the milking stool, which till today, years after Grandpa sold off the last cow, we still call the *taburetka* in Russian like the day it arrived in the wagon with the woman and the tree and the cow and the rifle, and which in recent years he would sit on to wash his feet without fear of falling. That was one of the first signs he was getting old. A sign that was belatedly understood, but from then onward it touched the heart and was never forgotten.

Grandpa Ze'ev began undressing Eitan. First he untied his shoelaces, then he tapped him on his legs, one calf and then the other, the way you tap a horse when shoeing it, and Eitan picked up one foot and then the other, and then his arms like Neta used to do when he undressed him for a bath before bedtime.

I remember: "One handie," he used to say to him, or sometimes "hando" or "handle," and "Now a leggie" or "leggers" or "legeleh" and other cute names that were very funny to a boy of three and four and five and six. Before three he didn't yet understand, and after six he was dead.

Shoe after shoe, button by button, one sleeve and the other, left pant leg and right. And all these with precise, gentle pats and pulls, and she quickly realized she was dreaming a waking dream and would never forget the sight she saw: the old man tapping, removing the clothes caked in the mud in which the young man had wallowed, and the latter cooperating with quiet trust and obedience, his eyes closed, his shoes side by side under the bench, his clothes thrown in the basket, until he was completely naked and ready to be washed, purified, prepared for the rest of his life.

Eitan didn't say a word. Didn't give me a look. But Grandpa Ze'ev suddenly turned his head and stared at me.

"What is this, Ruta? How long have you been in here?"

"Since his second shoe, Grandpa. Just joking. Since you went in, from the beginning."

" 'Joking'?"

"Is there any other way?"

"You brought his clean clothes? Very good. Put them here and go back to the guests. They came for you."

"These are not guests, Grandpa, they're here to console us at the shiva."

"These are guests, but let's not argue now. Go to them, please."

But I couldn't go. Even though he said "please," a rare word in his vocabulary. My feet were stuck to the ground and my eyes stuck on them, the two men left to me, the clothed old man, who would stay with us till the day he died, and the naked young man, who would be here but switch off and disappear and would return to us on the day Grandpa Ze'ev died, the day of redemption—his redemption, our redemption, payback time.

I was filled with curiosity, but also concern, because Grandpa Ze'ev was not a normal person and had done unexpected and even horrible things in the past. And also, I admit, I stayed because I was curious. I felt that if I stayed I would see something that women don't usually see.

That famous male bonding that few men experience, and fewer women have witnessed.

You know, Rudyard Kipling has a short story about an Indian boy named Tuma, who learns how to be a mahout, which is an elephant trainer or elephant driver or something like that, I don't recall exactly. Not training for the circus, God forbid, but training for serious things: working together in the forest, carrying tree trunks and other loads. In short, the oldest of the elephants, I forget his name, but don't worry, it'll pop up in a moment the way other things do. Whatever. This elephant, which the boy would wash every day in the river, took him one night to the forest, to see the meeting of the wild elephants, an event that no human eye had ever seen. I'm telling you this because that's how I felt then. I felt that if I wasn't afraid and I stayed, I would see something that a female eye had never seen, or at least the eyes of this female.

Grandpa Ze'ev glanced at me with his typical glance, which on an ordinary day would mean: This is not for you! But the corners of his lips expressed agreement, and his one eye suddenly turned warm and good, so I should understand that it was for me, that I should stay. I was surprised. Sometimes I think that he did this since there was no choice, because I took advantage of my new status. You understand what I'm taking about? Neta had just died, and I was already exploiting the status of bereaved mother, who cannot be refused or insulted, and she and her wishes must be respected.

In any case, I stood my ground, and Grandpa Ze'ev said, "I see you're staying, so hold him a minute so he won't fall because I have to get up."

I held Eitan's left hand with my right one, and I leaned my left hand gently on his chest. A woman's hand in the middle of her man's chest, especially with the fingers spread apart, says only one thing: I am here. I am with you. Sometimes, when he would lie on his back and I would ride him, we would put our hands like that. His palm on my flat chest and my palm on his flat chest. But now I did it so he wouldn't fall. I didn't actually hold him up. That's not always necessary. Sometimes just a touch like that is enough—clear, exact. Instilling confidence: It's me. I'm here.

I remember: Once, when Neta was three, we were walking with him in the street, and he wanted to walk on top of a garden wall that was a few centimeters wide. He was crazy back then about balancing and walking like that, and it made us crazy too, because we couldn't pass by a fence without his wanting to walk on it, and he would ask over and over and promise: Just this time and no more.

Eitan picked him up and put him on the concrete fence, held his hand, and walked alongside him, and I saw that he was smiling.

"Now Mommy will give you a hand," he told him after a few steps, and whispered to me, "Just feel it, what great balance he has. He doesn't need support, he just needs the touch of a hand." What was his name, Kipling's elephant? It's making me nuts.

I put my hand on Eitan's chest, and he leaned on it only a bit, but I could feel how cold he was. Only after a few weeks I understood that this coldness foreshadowed the dying of the flame and fading of the gold and the creeping iciness that would turn his skin to white.

And then, when it seemed that Eitan was standing steady, Grandpa also began to undress. I was shocked. He had never been naked in front of me. He used to berate me if I went around undressed at home in front of Neta.

"He's all of four years old," I told him then.

"It's not right," he argued, "a son should not see his mother without clothes."

And now he was disrobing, right in front of me, and I am not four years old, not a little girl, and he's undressing in a calm and natural way, like a woman taking out a breast and nursing her baby in front of strangers, men she would never expose herself to in other circumstances.

I looked at him, our elderly male. I didn't stare, God forbid, but I looked. I definitely looked. This was the first and only time I saw him naked, and I was sorry I hadn't seen him like that when he was young, and I knew that Neta would have looked like him if he reached that age.

I will read, with your permission, what I wrote in my notebook about that day: "I explored his flesh with my eyes. I studied it. This terra incognita with its ridges and plains, its dead zones and forbidden cities. In his old body one could see small islands of youth, clear and defined and alluring: a smooth strong back beneath a wrinkled neck and crooked shoulders, big lively calf muscles below gaunt bony thighs that had lost their shape, a surprisingly solid curve of the buttocks."

It's funny. Usually with men the butt is the first to go. Not that I've seen a representative sample of butts, but you know how it is, women tell each other. I heard somebody say that from her point of view a man with a dead butt was dead overall. Another one said, "My husband would sit shiva over his butt, if he had one to sit on."

Eitan once said to me, when the subject came up, "What difference does it make? In daily life the owner of a butt doesn't make eye contact with it anyway." I would be happy to keep telling you funny stories about backsides, but we are in the middle of a funeral so I will resume the proper tone.

I surveyed my grandfather's body and thought that, for me, the opposite was surely true by now—little islands of aging in a body still young. I was twenty-nine years old then, but I already had the start of little wrinkles here and there, and two strands of gray in my black hair. When they appeared I thought it was too bad my mother wasn't here with me to see them. And today I think how I won't see white hairs on Neta's head or on the head of my other child, who will never be born.

It's interesting, no? Interesting what a person thinks when he sees the first gray hairs on the head of his son or daughter, like the first quiet mourners at his own funeral, or little warning flags that foretell his death? Or maybe I didn't exactly think it, and these weren't thoughts but little particles of light and understanding that passed extremely quickly through my mind. Don't be alarmed. I pounded the table because I remembered. Kala Nag, that was the name of the elephant from the Kipling story. Kala Nag means "black snake" in Indian or Hindu, whatever you call that language. I told you it would pop up and here it is.

And then, when Grandpa Ze'ev was completely naked, he gently removed the patch from his blind eye and handed it to me. "Hang it there, please." And the pale ugly awful mass that had once been an eye looked at me, like the day he took off the patch and showed it to Dovik and me.

Now, totally naked, concealing nothing, he adjusted the water temperature, stood under the shower, and said, "Bring him to me and please step aside."

I hope you are attentive to these subtleties, Varda. To the fact that he said "step aside" and not "get out of here" or "leave us alone," as he said to me on many other occasions, and again he said "please"—for the third time that day if I'm not mistaken.

And I walked Eitan the two steps into the shower and I stayed there because I wanted to see more. I watched. Of course I watched. I stared. I didn't even dare to blink, so as not to miss a thing. You wouldn't have stayed to see something like that? It was a onetime opportunity that only my guys, Neta in his death and Eitan in his disappearance and Grandpa Ze'ev in his wisdom, could give me.

I see. I hear. I remember every detail: Grandpa Ze'ev put his arms around Eitan and held him tight to his body and said, "It's all right now, Eitan." Yes. And then: "It's already better now, right?" And Eitan suddenly answered. He spoke. He said a small weak yes.

I didn't say anything. But I remembered the teacher I had in the third grade who would ask us every morning, "Have you prepared your homework?" We would all say, "Yes!" And she would say, "That was a truly insipid yes." I liked the teacher very much, her name was Batya, I liked that she didn't say "Did you do" but "Have you prepared," which I also say today, maybe in her memory, and I especially liked that expression of hers: "a truly insipid yes." There were years when I used that too in the classroom, until I realized that most of my students didn't understand the word "insipid" and thought it was a medical term.

TWENTY-THREE

A few days later, I wrote: "Silence suddenly fell. The clatter of the water in the shower was the only sound in the ear, the nursery, the moshava, the whole world."

I realized that the hundreds of men, women, and children who had come to Neta's funeral and shiva were stone silent. They stood and listened behind fences and walls. No one came close, but the ears were perked and the mouths were sealed and the hearts heard and understood.

The two stood under the water, joined in their nakedness. My grandpa supported, my man leaned, their lips moved, but the voices were unheard.

I know what they said:

Grandpa Ze'ev asked: "Are you standing, Eitan? Standing well?"

And Eitan said: "Yes. I am standing."

Grandpa Ze'ev said: "I have to sit down now so I'm letting go. Don't fall."

And Eitan said: "It's fine. When you're with me I won't fall."

Grandpa Ze'ev said: "I let go. I'm not holding you now. Stand up."

And Eitan said: "I'm standing. But stay here near me."

Grandpa Ze'ev pulled the milking stool closer and sat down next to Eitan and again tapped his leg, and Eitan again picked up one leg and then the other with the same obedience and the same closed eyes that expressed total trust, and again placed a limp hand on Grandpa Ze'ev's shoulder, not for support, just to touch it. And Grandpa Ze'ev washed and soaped him, first his left foot and leg, then his right foot and leg. Soaped, washed, tapped him to turn around.

I could not fail to notice that Eitan's penis was really close to his face, nearly touching it, as Grandpa Ze'ev matter-of-factly washed it too and I realized this was how it would be, that Eitan and I would not shower here together anymore, and this organ would always remain limp, and I wouldn't get him off anymore in that very same shower with my soapy hands, fastening our lips to muffle the moans from before and the laughter of just after, because more than once we did it during business hours, with customers present at the nursery.

Grandpa Ze'ev also washed him behind his knees and between his legs, buttocks, and toes, the way you bathe a child, and Eitan understood every tap and tug and lifted and lowered as necessary and turned this way and that, and Grandpa Ze'ev got up from the milking stool and continued on to the chest and shoulders and back, and lifted his arms one by one to soap and rinse his armpits, and finally tapped him on the back of his neck so he would sit on the stool for a thorough shampoo, behind the ears included.

And that was that. He rinsed off the shampoo and soap and Eitan stayed seated, hunched and dripping and apathetic, as Grandpa Ze'ev finished soaping and rinsing himself too, and closed the faucets and dried Eitan and dressed him in the clean work clothes I brought, tapping him with the same orderly efficiency—Pick up, put on, turn around, come here. And then he dried and dressed himself and extended a hand to me.

"The eye patch, please," he said. "Give me the eye patch. We're leaving."

And so, clean and clothed, they came out. The crowd parted. Grandpa Ze'ev crossed on dry land, like the Israelites at the Red Sea. He led Eitan to the outdoor storage area and said, "You see the sacks of compost and the flowerpots and the sod all arranged here? They all have to be moved to the other side of the storage. So do it, Eitan, now, please."

That was it. That's how it started. Each sack like that weighed thirty kilos, and there were a hundred sacks, none of which really needed to be moved. But Eitan did what Grandpa Ze'ev told him to do, and we all saw him: crouching, clutching, lifting, carrying, stacking neatly in an enormous new pile.

The next day, when he was done, he came and said, "I'm done, Grandpa Ze'ev."

He could barely walk, his knees were like butter, his whole body trembled weakly. But Grandpa Ze'ev said to him, "Very nice. Now the flagstones, move them from here to there and arrange them again."

You know what flagstones are, Varda? Those flat stones for paving paths and other areas in gardens. Each one weighs a couple of dozen kilos, sometimes more. "Move them to the right side of the parking lot and stack them in piles of five," said Grandpa Ze'ev, and Eitan began to move the stones one by one. Bending, lifting, clutching, carrying, bending, laying, and over again.

No one who had come to console approached him, not even his so-called army buddies. And a lot of people were there at the shiva. They sat, chatted, kept quiet, cried. A shiva is also an event, a reunion, we talked about that before. People who haven't seen each other for many years meet again, and despite the grief and mourning, they also chat about other things, argue, and even laugh. The shiva for Grandpa Ze'ev, twelve years later, was like that too. Dovik even said at the time, "Lucky he's dead. If he were sitting here with us he wouldn't like what's going on." But at Neta's shiva that didn't happen. People talked, told stories, but they didn't laugh. When a boy of six dies and it's his father's fault, you don't laugh. And when that father doesn't say a word to anyone, only shows up every few hours and repeats, "I'm done," and asks, "What should I do now?" that's also not funny. You understand? The guy that ran half the nursery business and attracted customers like moths to a flame and kept track of every item, from flowers to funnels, from fertilizer to drip irrigation, and now he's carrying stones and sacks like a beast of burden.

Grandpa Ze'ev always had strong-minded principles and clear-cut solutions. He gave orders, Eitan obeyed, Dovik watched them, and I could see he was about to burst out crying. But Dovik is Dovik and got hold of himself. "Mazal tov," he announced a few days later, "we have a new forklift. Thanks, Grandpa." And we all smiled together with him, except for Grandpa Ze'ev, who said, "Eitan, a truck will soon arrive with flowerpots and window boxes, unload them."

That's what Eitan did during the shiva, and in the weeks thereafter, moving and hauling everything from everywhere to everywhere else in the nursery. I went to Grandpa Ze'ev and told him, "Maybe tell him to stop all this?"

Grandpa Ze'ev said, "He can stop whenever he wants. Nobody is forcing him. If he keeps doing it, it's a sign that it's good for him." And he added, "We won't be able to save your child, but we can and must save your husband."

At the time I still didn't realize that Grandpa Ze'ev would save Eitan in another way. I kept silent and said to him in my heart, If this is what you call saving, enjoy yourself. And under my diaphragm I said, But this is your business, the business of the men in the family. So go save one another, kill one another, kill your women, their lovers, their children. Just leave me out of it.

TWENTY-FOUR

After the shiva Dovik announced that he had to drive Dafna and Dorit down south to Sde Boker. That was the year they started to study there, and if you ask me, Dalia sent them there because she had already felt my connection with them getting stronger, and maybe feared that now, after my son had died, I would take control of her daughters. In any case they loved hanging out with their cool aunt Ruta next door, somebody they could talk to and do things with that were forbidden or weren't fun to do with their mother. But apart from all that, it was clear to me that Dovik would take advantage of the trip to continue farther south, to Nahal Tzihor, to find and bring home the equipment Eitan had left under the acacia and to see the place where the disaster happened.

And in fact, I saw him talking to Eitan and Eitan handing him some sort of note, and when I questioned him he said that he wrote him the coordinates of the place. He didn't say them in words but wrote them down. He silently wrote him the numbers on a piece of paper, handed it to him silently, and silently returned to that awful work of his. And only after a few days did I realize that this was not just work but a punishment, he was serving a sentence of hard labor, and the silence was no ordinary silence but his great silence, and no one, not even I, had any idea how long it would last.

Dovik marked the place on the map and proudly declared that he would have no problem finding his way there and then took me aside and asked if I wanted to come with him. I told him no, that I couldn't bear it, and asked, "And why are you going there, anyway? For a tarp and a ratty old tent? It's not worth the time or the gas. And besides, someone probably stole the stuff by now. You yourself always say that's how it goes on trips to the Negev, that you can't leave a vehicle for more than ten minutes without thieves showing up and stripping it bare, not to mention the times when the vehicle vanishes into thin air."

"It's not just the equipment," he said. "I need to check it out and understand what happened. And besides, Ruta, it's not just the tarp and the tent. I'm going to find and bring back the camera that Eitan took. I bet it's where the biting happened."

"Snakebite."

"Okay, Ruta, snakebite."

"That's why you're going? For that old camera?"

"Ruta," he said, "Ruta, you're supposedly the smartest person in the Tavori family, certainly smarter than me, so how do you not understand something so simple: I'm going because there might be pictures in the camera. Eitan must have taken pictures of Neta and the scenery. These are the last pictures of your son. Have you thought of that?"

"I did, and I can't bear the thought. I don't even want to know if you find it or not."

Dovik loved Neta very much and was a wonderful uncle. "Because he is a male child," he used to say, "he's my son too," adding more than once: "Because with my twin daughters, I don't sleep at night, worrying that sons-in-law will take control of our family's land."

As I already told you, Dovik is a very good big brother, but he's no great genius. He often talks foolishness, but luckily in our family we have stories and problems that are much worse than my big brother being a bit of a moron sometimes. Whatever. That wasn't the first time he talked that way about future sons-in-law. Dalia and Dafna and Dorit didn't like that at all, and one time Eitan remarked to him, "And what about me? I'm also a son-in-law." That was before the disaster, of course. After the disaster Eitan didn't do any remarking.

"You're something different," Dovik said at the time, and said to the twins, "I'm just kidding, you guys. Where's your sense of humor?"

Dafna and Dorit corrected his language. "We're not guys, we're girls."

Whatever. He took them down to Sde Boker—"We know where you're heading from here, Abba, and we want to go too," they said—and continued farther south by himself. Mitzpeh Ramon, the Crater, past Nahal Meshar, across the Paran, finally arriving at Tzihor. There he turned right onto a dirt road marked in red—I saw it all on a map, in case you're wondering how I know the details—reset his odometer, and drove to the tree. There are guys like that who only need coordinates and a reset button and everything is clear and good. On the other hand, if you take away their coordinates, they're worthless.

He reached the acacia, which was standing there among other acacias exactly where it was supposed to be. It wasn't hard to identify it, he told me when he got back, because it really was the most beautiful acacia in the area. And when he got closer he saw that all the equipment was still there. Nobody had touched it, as if the thieves also knew what had happened and didn't touch a thing: the tent still stood there, waiting, and the gas burner, cold and waiting, and the tarp still tossed to the side, and the two mattresses they never got to sleep on, and the bird handbook that I read and studied later on, to know which birds my little boy saw and identified before he died and which birds saw and identified him.

Dovik put it all in the pickup, spread the tarp over it, found Eitan and Neta's footprints, and followed them. The footprints of a father and son on a leisurely hike were mixed with the footprints of a father who ran back on exactly the same path. The footprints of a running man look completely different from those of a walking man, especially if he is carrying a child in his arms, and especially if this child is dying, and especially if this dying child is his and he is to blame for his death. Things like this have a great effect on the footprints. You can learn a lot from footprints, even about the state of mind of the person who left them.

Dovik followed the footprints, climbing to the top of the ridge on a diagonal, as one should, and reached the place where the snake bit Neta and Eitan killed it. There he also found the camera, which in the commotion had slipped a bit down the slope, where it was blocked by a rock that luckily shaded it from the sun during most of the day.

He also found the stone that Eitan used to smash the snake, and also the bare spot of ground where the stone had originally lain. I know all this because a few weeks later I changed my mind and asked him to take me there, and he, my dear big brother, suddenly objected: "Why do it, Ruta? What for? You yourself said you couldn't bear it." It was a good imitation of me, by the way, and he also tried to tell me that there was nothing at all to see there. There had surely been flooding since then and everything was erased.

He told me all that, and I put on a performance of a mother and sister that he would never forget. Even Bialik never imagined a mother and sister like that. An imitation of a bitterly grieving she-bear from the woods, roaring loud enough for the whole moshava to hear her. Don't be alarmed, Varda, I'm just imitating myself screaming at him: "What kind of flooding in your dreams, Dovik? Where'd you pull that one from? It's the dry season and you're going to take me there. Otherwise I'll go by myself to look for your coordinates and you'll be responsible if anything happens to me!"

Sorry, I apologize. I already told you. Sometimes screams and shouts emanating from our property provide raw material for all the ears and mouths of the moshava, and this was one of those times.

Whatever. We drove down there, and on the way we didn't talk much, but there were nice songs on the radio and we joined in, he singing the melody and I the harmony, and we arrived at the acacia that Eitan had picked out, which was indeed good and beautiful, and we walked to the spot where Neta was bitten, and Dovik said, "This is it, Ruta, here's where it was." And I actually held up well, and on the way back we stopped at Sde Boker to visit Dafna and Dorit, who were surprised by the visit but not by its cause. I was very happy to see them, because after Neta died and they went off to Sde Boker, we were left without children, and it was terrible. The yard was empty. Yes, I had more than enough children whom I taught at school, but that's not the same. I'm not one of those teachers who calls them "my" children. They're not.

"Abba took you to see the place where Neta died?" asked the girls, both asking and declaring, and I said yes, of course, it's the duty of a brother and the right of a mother.

A few weeks later we went down there one more time, because

Grandpa Ze'ev suddenly wanted to visit the place where his great-grandson had died. He was eighty by then, and it was easy to see that he wasn't comfortable in the desert, it wasn't a place that suited him, the plants were unfamiliar, it was all too yellow and dry, stony and bare, but the footprints were still there and Dovik showed them to him, and he walked along the wadi without a problem, and he looked and examined and asked questions. And a few months later, during the Sukkoth holiday, there was a sudden rainstorm there with flash flooding. A huge rainfall, the likes of which the Negev hadn't seen for many years. Flooding in Tznifim, Tzihor, Paran, Karkum, I look at the map from time to time and know the roads and the names of all the wadis.

It was the first rain after Neta died, and the first rain of that year, which fell not in the Galilee or Golan or in our moshava, which gets a lot of rain, but in the desert. There of all places, in that shitty wasteland.

The rain came down, and there was a flood, and everything was washed out. God took time off from his other activities and for a few hours did not kill or bring to life, did not make marriages or break them, did not uplift or bring low, did not bring forth cows from the Nile or she-bears from the woods, did not visit the iniquity of fathers upon children or the iniquity of children upon fathers. No. He only returned to the scene of the crime and destroyed all the evidence.

....

TWENTY-FIVE

THE CAVEMAN AND THE FIRE

Another Story for Neta Tavori Also by His Mother

1

Many, many years ago, in the wadi of Grandpa Ze'ev, there lived the Caveman. That's what they called him because in those days people didn't have names.

Grandpa Ze'ev wasn't there yet, and neither was his carob tree. But the wadi was there, and on the other side of it was a cave, and that was the Caveman's home.

The Caveman loved the cave very much. In summer it was nice and shady and cool, and in winter it protected him from the rain. But in winter there were also clouds, and the sun disappeared, and there was not only rain but snow and hail, and the wind blew in the wadi, whistled through the rocks and reached the top of the hill.

The Caveman sat in the entrance to the cave, looked out, and felt cold.

Really cold.

Terribly cold.

He hid very deep inside the cave—but that didn't help.

He wore a bearskin—but that didn't help either.

He cuddled with his wife, the Cavewoman, inside the

bearskin—and that was very pleasant and it did help, but only a little and for a short while.

2

One day the Cavewoman said to the Caveman, "We're out of food, you need to go out and bring us more."

"In this cold?" he asked. "It's raining outside, the winds are blowing, there's a storm."

"There's no choice," she said, and made a joke: "Otherwise you'll have to eat me and I'll have to eat you."

The Caveman loved the Cavewoman. He didn't want to eat her and didn't want her to eat him.

He went out, and walked and walked and looked and looked and walked, the rain whipping his face and the wind freezing his body, but he kept looking and walking and didn't rest for a minute.

And all of a sudden, right above him, there was a flash of lightning and a huge clap of thunder, and the tree beside him caught fire and burned in a big yellow-red blaze.

The Caveman had never seen fire before. He was scared and fell to the ground, and quickly got up and shouted, "A monster . . . a yellow monster . . . no . . . a red monster . . ."

The Caveman had also never seen a monster before, but that seemed a very appropriate word.

3

He was so scared that he ran away from there, back home to the cave.

"Come quick!" he said to his wife. "I want to show you something."

The Cavewoman loved hearing those words. Every time the Caveman told her he wanted to show her something— something nice happened.

"What?" she asked.

"Something really terrible."

"What?"

"There's a monster over there," said the Caveman. "It's enormous. It's going wild. It's red and yellow. It's eating a tree on the other side of the hill."

"What is a monster? We don't have a word like that," said the Cavewoman.

"I just invented it. Now there's a monster and also a word for it."

"What does it look like, this monster of yours?"

"It doesn't look like anything at all."

"Like a bear? Like a rhinoceros?"

"No."

"Does it have wings? Claws? Scales? A tail?"

"Yes! A whole lot of tails and a wing and another wing and another wing."

"Is it skinny? Is it fat? Does it have a trunk? Or just a nose?"

"What do you mean? It has no shape at all. Actually, it has many shapes. Every minute a new shape. Come on, I want to show it to you."

4

The Caveman and the Cavewoman ran together in the rain and the wind and the cold and the storm, went around the hill, and reached the burning tree.

"Look," said the Caveman, "have you ever seen a monster like this?"

The Cavewoman drew closer. Raindrops hit the burning tree and made whispering sounds.

"Be careful," the Caveman called out. "It's very dangerous."

"It's nice," said the Cavewoman, "it makes me warm. You should come closer too."

The Caveman came closer slowly. He felt nice and warm. He stuck out his hand and touched it. All he wanted to do was pet the monster, but it hurt really bad.

He jumped and shouted, "It bit me! The monster bit me!" And he ran back to the cave.

5

The Cavewoman stayed near the fire and enjoyed being warm.

After a few minutes a big bear showed up. He stood up on his hind legs and growled at her, but he didn't dare come close because he was afraid of the fire—and he ran away.

A few minutes later a tiger came near. He crept toward her and roared but didn't dare come closer because he was afraid of the fire—and he ran away.

A few minutes later, a pack of wolves appeared. They ran around her and bared their teeth, but they didn't dare come close because they were afraid of the fire—and they ran away.

A few minutes after that, the Caveman returned and she told him what had happened.

"You know," she said, "if we had a yellow monster like this inside the cave, we could keep warm and it would also protect us from wild beasts."

"True," said the Caveman, after thinking it over. "But only if it's a small yellow monster."

"So let's take home a branch like this with the yellow monster on it, and when it finishes eating we'll give it another branch, and then another, and that way we'll have a yellow monster like this in the cave."

And that's what they did. They took a branch with a little monster, brought it to the cave, gave the little monster branch after branch, and called it a fire.

And at night they slept beside it, and they felt nice and warm, and no bear or lion dared to come inside.

And the fire also gave them light, and shadows danced on the walls and ceiling.

The Caveman asked, "What are these black things? They're really scary."

And the Cavewoman answered, "They are me and you." And she made him shadows that looked like animals—a bear and a she-bear, and a tiger and tigress.

The Caveman looked at his wife and said, "Outside it's raining and cold and stormy, and here it's nice and warm and you are so smart and capable and beautiful."

"Really? What do I look like?" she asked. "Like an anteater? A fox? A lizard? An egret?"

"What's an anteater? There's no such animal here."

"But there surely is someplace else."

The Caveman laughed. "You're so sweet, you little monster Cavewoman. You don't look like anything. Every minute you have a new shape."

6

The winter came to an end. Spring arrived and then summer, and one day, when the Caveman returned from hunting, the Cavewoman said to him, "Come quick, I want to show you something."

The Caveman loved to hear that sentence. Every time his wife told him she wanted to show him something—something good and pleasant happened.

He came to her and she showed him a little tiny Caveman, wrapped in an animal skin.

"What's that?" he asked.

"This is the Cave Baby," she said. "He's mine and yours."

....

TWENTY-SIX

THE WEDDING NIGHT

1

The journey was over. Dov drove the wagon to his brother's yard. Ze'ev and Ruth followed him on foot. When they got to the house the brothers hid the rifle and unharnessed, fed, and watered the cow and the ox, which like a man at the end of a mission collapsed with exhaustion to the ground. Ze'ev petted the ox on the head and asked Dov what was happening back home, and he whispered that their father had sent the message—that's what he said, "sent the message"—that he needed to begin rubbing his hands with olive oil twice a day.

"What for?" grumbled Ze'ev, who viewed such things as wimpy and feminine.

"That's what he said I should tell you and that's what you have to do."

That night, as Dov slept a deep sleep, Ze'ev and Ruth sat and talked. Ze'ev told Ruth about his father's orders and she smiled to herself. The next night they also talked, and the following morning Dov and Ruth went back to the moshava in the Galilee. Ruth told her parents that she had met Ze'ev and that they wanted to get married, and she gave Ze'ev's parents a letter from their son.

The wedding was set for just after the Shavuot holiday, on Ze'ev's twenty-third birthday. He came to his parents' home three days ahead of time and first of all he and his father went walking through the orchard and the yard. Then he walked around in the village, met friends, told them about the new moshava where he lived, and at night, as he lay in bed, he smelled the aroma of pipe tobacco and knew his father was waiting for him in the yard.

The father cleared his throat and asked if he knew what happens on the wedding night.

"Don't worry, Abba," said Ze'ev. "I know very well."

"And what, for example, do you know?"

Ze'ev was embarrassed. "I know."

The father said, "It's good that you have gained experience. And good that the bride is still a virgin and the groom is not, but that's not what I'm talking about, but rather that you have to understand and remember that this is the woman who from now on, for the rest of your life, will be with you. You will be her one and only and she will be your one and only. And therefore, Ze'ev, on this important and special night, the wedding night, you must not make her angry or hurt her or insult her or leave her a bad memory for whatever reason. You need to be gentle and patient and pleasant and polite, and everything you do to her and with her you must do with affection and tenderness."

Ze'ev was not surprised. He father was a tough, aggressive man, but with his wife, Ze'ev's mother, he was always patient and faithful. He said nothing, and his father continued: "On all other nights we have to be tough and strong, inside and out, in body and soul, because there's not only a wife, there's also land to be farmed and livestock to tend and thieves to catch and enemies to chase away. But on this night the groom belongs only to his wife, with a good heart and soft hands and hard only in the place he needs to be."

Ze'ev kept quiet. He had never heard his father, a man of few words, make a speech like this.

"Do you understand me, Ze'ev?"

"I understand, Abba, thank you."

"Even the little details are important," the father went on. "You need to be closely shaved, washed, and clean and sweet smelling in every part of your body, your nails clipped and filed, because you might touch a delicate place and you mustn't scratch it. That's why I told Dov to tell you to rub your hands with olive oil, every day, so they will be nice and soft and smooth."

The mother of the bride had a similar talk with her daughter, but her talk was much more practical than the father of the groom's to his son. Along with similar recommendations about patience and thoughtfulness, cleanliness and fragrance, the mother gave clear technical instructions. "And if he doesn't find it, you have to take it in your hand and put it in the right place," and made a biblical joke: "'Come in, thou blessed of the Lord, why are you standing out there?'" And Ruth burst out laughing.

Everything was thus in order. The neighbors baked bread, brought homemade cheeses; men carried boxes of fruit and vegetables. Meat was not served; several bottles of wine and schnapps were opened but were consumed at a separate table, so as not to offend the Muslim guests who came from adjacent villages bearing figs and cakes. Members of Hashomer, the Jewish militia, raced the Arab horsemen, galloping and waving sticks as if they were swords.

The wedding ended late at night. The guests who came from nearby went home. Those who came from afar took turns guarding the horses and wagons and getting some sleep, in various corners of the family home or at the neighbors', in storehouses, granaries, milking sheds. "From the firstborn according to his birthright, and the youngest according to his youth," the elders on beds and mattresses, the latter on jute sacks filled with straw.

Neighbors and relatives came to the bride with good-night wishes, woman to woman. Two of them whispered in her ear that a baby conceived on the wedding night would be big and healthy and good. But the bride paid them no mind. The neighbors could say what they wanted, her body had already spoken the truth: in the hopeful excitement of her loins, the expectant dryness in her throat, the pleasant uneasiness of her diaphragm. She had not yet known a man and was fearful, but her fears were overcome by emotion and desire and curiosity.

She remembered: When she was about eleven and Ze'ev was fifteen, she saw him at a spring down in the wadi, bare from the waist up. The magnificent ox of the Tavori family was also there with him. Ze'ev first washed the ox with pails of water and a hard brush and combed the end of his tail, and then stripped completely naked. Ruth saw his arms and the back of his neck, bronzed by the sun, and his thighs and back, completely white. He bent over and stood straight and poured water from the pail over his body and apparently sensed that she was looking at him, even from afar, and turned around.

For a moment she saw his sparkling eyes and the dark patch of his loins. Did he smile at her? Did he get angry? He ducked into the bushes and shouted, "Go home, Ruth!" And when she didn't leave, he continued, "You already saw me, you saw. Now please go, because I'm washing up." Then she went, but the words "you saw me" mixed love into her desire, and though she was only eleven, she knew that love and lust were mingled for him too.

The couple rose from their chairs. The invited guests looked at them with affection. They were a handsome and loving couple. Neither of them was especially beautiful, but together they were strikingly attractive. This was perhaps because they looked alike: they were both tall and broad-shouldered, their teeth were straight and white and their necks thick and strong, and both radiated the dumb luck of healthy young people. They smiled at each other, and because of their height their smiles sailed over the heads of the guests. They wanted to repair to their room, but they knew they had to play by the rules, and were also a bit abashed, because everyone would know why they were going.

The yard emptied out very slowly, and finally the bride's mother called her into the kitchen and said, "Well, we had a big long day, and you probably want to rest now." Ze'ev and his parents and Ruth's father also entered the room, and the father said, "The guests have gone to sleep, let's also go to sleep."

The four parents exited the kitchen. The couple was left alone.

"Ruth"—Ze'ev smiled—"I am very happy you agreed to marry me. Thank you."

"I'm happy too," said Ruth. "I hoped you would want me and I knew I would say yes. I knew it even when we were children and you would come to our yard, riding on your ox."

She came closer to him and, in a gesture of the moment that would remain in their family in future generations, she extended her right hand and placed it in the center of his chest, spreading her fingers as a sign of love and faith, and he leaned a little forward to sense her soothing strength.

They entered their room, locked the door, did not turn on a light, and went to the opposite sides of the bed. A new sheet was spread upon it, and a new lightweight blanket. As a wedding gift, the mothers of the bride and groom had sewn them each a new nightshirt. Together they had bought the cloth and together had sewn the shirts, broad, white, and long, identical in pattern and different in size—the mother of the groom sewed the bride's shirt, and the mother of the bride sewed the groom's. That was the custom then.

The nightshirts were ironed and folded and placed on the conjugal bed, which also had been built—assembled—for the wedding. Most of the beds in the moshava were single beds, built by the same carpenter and therefore of uniform shape and size. And when a couple got married, the two fathers would take the groom's bed from his house and the bride's from hers and attach them one to the other with three wooden boards and large screws, at the head and middle and foot. And here in the center of the room stood the bed that Ze'ev's father and Ruth's father had put together, and on it were the nightshirts sewn by the mothers-in-law, hers on the left and his on the right.

The two of them took off their clothes and put on the shirts in the dark and immediately the bride heard the groom grumble that his shirt was too small and wouldn't fit across his shoulders. She understood that the mothers had mistakenly laid her shirt on his side and his on her side.

She laughed softly, a laugh he didn't appreciate, since she had already taken off his shirt while he was still wrestling with hers, and he knew she was totally naked, waiting in the dark, but he was afraid of tearing the stitches of her shirt. He finally worked free of it, and as they tried to exchange shirts, their hands touched. Although the darkness engulfed their blurry nakedness, they were suddenly frightened and withdrew, tossing the nightshirts to each other. White and silent, like two giant barn owls, the shirts floated past each other, landing on the correct sides of the bed. The two felt around and picked them up and put on the shirts that had been given to him and to her, sat down on the bed, the man on his side and the woman on hers, then lay down on their backs.

They lay side by side. Only the woven linen covered the skin, and the skin the flesh, and the flesh the ribs that enclosed the two hearts. They had already stolen kisses in the vineyard, as the old saying went, and the groom had once even stroked the bride's right breast over her blouse, and they had also hugged and squeezed and felt the rising heat of their loins through his clothes and hers, and his hardness and her softness, but they had not yet become one flesh, as a woman and her man.

They lay there in the darkness, until Ruth felt Ze'ev's hand looking for hers, finding it, lifting it to his lips. He sat up and leaned on his left elbow and kissed her fingers one by one, and she was pleased by his unexpected gentleness, so different from his rough conduct in the fields and on guard duty, and was happy that the words of one of her married friends—"all the disgusting stuff that awaits you"—had not materialized. "And if he attacks you like an animal," her friend had continued, "lie there quietly. It's over quickly, in general. And if necessary, I'll explain what to do to get it over with even quicker."

His other hand joined in, rested on her cheek and nudged her face toward him. She leaned over to him and they embraced, and kissed, lovingly taking their time, in the confident knowledge of what was to come, as if wishing to postpone it a bit, to enjoy a few more minutes of curiosity and longing.

After kissing the fingers of her other hand the groom leaned over to his bride and put his hand on her hip and pulled her a bit toward him, and she responded and drew closer, and when their bodies were pressed together he again kissed her lips and she could sense that he was smiling in the dark and hoped that he could feel her smile. The groom pulled up the bottom of his nightshirt almost to his chest, and the bride pulled hers up to her hips and lay motionless on her back, as her mother had instructed, quoting a verse from the biblical book of her namesake Ruth: "And lay thee down, and he will tell thee what thou shalt do."

His weight was strange and new to her body. She tried to anticipate the feeling she was about to have, when he would be inside her. She held him, moved her body a bit so that their knees and ankles touched, and her breasts were pressed to his, nipple to nipple, and this was very pleasing to her body and her heart, and when she spread her thighs for him and moved her body under his, she let out a deep sigh, so loud it surprised them both, and she suddenly felt that his flesh had gone limp and soft, and a shock ran through him and through her.

She, despite her lack of experience and perhaps because of it, tried to draw him closer, to embrace him with her thighs, and he pressed his flesh to hers, but he already understood, though this had never happened to him before, that on this night his flesh would not comply. The feeling was so clear and simple that he imagined that his organ had fallen off his body, like a fruit dropping from its tree to the ground.

For a moment he touched himself, as if seeking verification, and when his fingers confirmed the feeling he slid off her, lay beside her on his back, pulled the nightshirt down to his knees, and covered up with the blanket. Very quietly, very slowly, he again sent a stealthy hand to reconnoiter the territory, to assess if it was strong or weak, small or big, and the organ was in fact there, in its usual place, but the hand felt that same strange feeling, that it wasn't part of the body but detached from it.

He was young. So young that quite often his organ would get hard all by itself, from ideas and images that went not through its owner's head but through its own. So young he didn't yet know the potential consequences of an odd glance, a teasing word, an inappropriate smile, an unpleasant body odor, a stupid remark, a lingering grudge, an uninvited memory, one drink too many—the reasons are plentiful and the result is the same.

His hand was still there, as if defending his loins, and he again gave a little squeeze—was there anything solid inside the limpness? Something to build and be rebuilt? And with horror he sensed another strange thing: that only the hand felt the squeeze, not the organ. And now he felt his hand was not alone, that his wife's hand was there too, stroking him.

There was something clinical in her touch, chilling. He recoiled.

"What are you doing?" he whispered furiously.

"I just wanted to take your hand in mine," she said. "To lie hand in hand. What's the matter?"

Confused, she tried awkwardly to embrace him. He froze and pulled away.

"Leave me alone," he said. "You don't need to hold my hand like I'm a little boy."

And after a minute or two he said, "Go to sleep now."

"And you?"

"I have to check the water by the cowshed. My father drank too many *l'chaims* and undoubtedly forgot, and the cows are not to blame that there was a wedding."

"Don't go. Your father didn't forget, and Arieh and Dov are here too. Stay with me, we'll doze off and sleep together. You also had quite a bit to drink. It will pass. It's nothing."

Ze'ev did not reply. Ruth sat up in bed and again put her palm to his chest with her fingers spread out, but he shrank from her and her touch. She lay down on her back and closed her eyes. After a short while, without checking if she was asleep or awake, he got up and took off the wedding nightshirt, dropped it on the floor, put on his pants, and opened the door.

The moon had already moved to the west and shone so brightly that his body in the doorway was a huge, masculine silhouette. She saw him walk out and close the door after him. His feet felt the dirt of the yard, his bare chest felt the wind, its warmth and chill interwoven, typical of the spring month of Sivan.

For a moment he felt good, but then he smelled his father's pipe and followed the scent and saw him sitting on a chair and smoking beside the grape arbor, a bottle of schnapps in his hand.

He tried to withdraw into the shadows, but his father felt his presence.

"Why aren't you sleeping?" he asked him.

"I couldn't fall asleep."

"Usually you fall asleep afterward, but sometimes all that love and excitement can keep you awake," the father said and gave his son a look that invited an exchange of manly smiles, but quickly realized that this was not the case.

"Was everything all right?" he asked worriedly.

"It wasn't."

"What wasn't?"

"It wasn't."

"What wasn't? You weren't together?"

"We almost were. But suddenly not."

"What happened?"

Silence.

"She rejected you? She was scared? Wouldn't open?"

"It was me. Suddenly I didn't want to."

"What do you mean you didn't want to? You're a young guy. At your age it's not you who does or doesn't want. Your body does the wanting. At your age it always wants."

"At first my body wanted and suddenly didn't want."

The father puffed on his pipe and fell silent. Then he said, "These things happen to everyone once in a while."

And after a moment, which seemed very long to the son and short to him, he took a swig from his bottle and probed. "She said something to you? She did something that wasn't right?"

"No. She didn't say or do. She lay there and waited."

"Go back to her," said the father. "You hear? Now go back to bed. If you don't do it tonight, that's very bad."

He took apart his pipe and blew into the mouthpiece to remove the tobacco juice that was burning his tongue.

"Tonight it won't happen, Abba. We'll do it tomorrow. Tomorrow night."

"Go to her now. Get into bed and lie next to her."

"I already lay next to her."

"Touch her the way you dreamed of touching a woman."

Ze'ev was silent.

"Think of a different woman and the things she did to you."

"How can you talk that way, Abba. This is my wife. I love her."

"Love? Love is a luxury. Only a small part of the life of a man and woman. You need to think about your whole lives now. If you don't do it tonight, she will think that you're not a man. Then she will consult with her mother and her sisters and their friends, and they will tell their mothers and sisters and friends. This story must not start to go around here in the moshava."

"She already went to sleep, Abba. Tomorrow will be fine. Maybe I drank a little too much, I'm not used to it like you are."

The father sighed.

"I'll go check if there's water for the cows," said Ze'ev.

"I already checked," said the father.

"Just to be sure," said Ze'ev and went and checked, and when he got back his father was no longer on his chair, but someone else was on guard duty, who flashed him a gap-toothed smile.

He went back to Ruth, worried she was still awake and afraid she had fallen asleep. He lay beside her, listened to her breathing, hoping she would touch him and hoping she wouldn't, and eventually fell asleep and did not dream.

In the morning they awoke. At first they lay side by side in silence and then got up and put on their clothes with a mixture of embarrassment and hostility. Ze'ev joined his father and brothers in the vineyard. Ruth, to his dismay, joined the women in the yard and kitchen.

The next night was reminiscent of the first, and the third was reminiscent of the previous two, and on the fourth night, when Ruth didn't put on the nightshirt in total darkness but instead lit a candle and got into bed as naked as the day she was born and caressed his genitals first with one hand and then with two and then also with her tongue, he was shocked: Where did she get this expertise? Had she been with another man before him? Or maybe she had spoken about his failure and gotten advice from one of the women in her family, and even now the story was going around with winks and whispers? His father was right. The whole moshava would know, and so terrified was he that his whole body shriveled.

2

A few days went by, and Ze'ev told his father that he wanted to take his wife and return to his new home in the new moshava. The father asked that he stay two more days, because he wanted him to come with him to Tiberias and help him with something.

They rode to Tiberias, chatted a bit on the way, mainly about horses and farming and pruning and grafting, and the British attitude toward Jewish settlement versus their attitude toward the Arabs. On the way they stopped at a Bedouin encampment, where they were served coffee and the father conversed with a few male acquaintances. Ze'ev sat on the side and listened. He was proud of his father, who spoke good Arabic and knew how to behave according to local custom. They then bade farewell to their hosts and traveled northeast along the mountain ridge.

The Sea of Galilee, languid and milky, lay before them, with Tiberias on its shore. Most of its houses were then built of black basalt, and only a few sat on the slopes west of the lake. They drove down toward the town and turned north onto a spit of land with several handsome homes. In one of these dwelt a wealthy Arab, a friend of the father. They sat in his garden, the older men ate and drank and talked, and Ze'ev ate a little and drank a little and kept quiet. More people came, some sort of contract was signed, paper money changed hands, and then the father whispered something into the ear of the host, who whispered something back and signaled with his fingers.

A little boy darted from the shade of a tree, ran off at great speed, his heels raising dust. A few minutes later he returned, beaming proudly, seated beside the driver of a carriage drawn by two horses. Ze'ev and his father left their horses in the host's garden and got into the carriage and rode to a filthy alley near the lakeshore, south of the fishermen's pier.

The driver came to a halt beside a house with pink window curtains and two large flowering pinta trees in its yard, and opened the carriage door. Ze'ev had never been to such a place, but understood at once what it was. The father told him to wait a moment in the carriage, went to the mistress of the house, and gravely explained to her that his son had gotten married a few days ago and there were problems.

"How many days?" inquired the lady.

"One week exactly."

"You should have come the very next day," said the proprietor, a fat Jewess, a speaker of German and Arabic and French and English and the sign language of the deaf and Yiddish and Ladino and Hebrew, "but not to worry. I have just the girl for him."

"I would like a clean and healthy lady for him, good and patient," said the father, adding: "Not too young and not too old, not too beautiful and not too ugly." And he explained that everything about her should be middling and average, so that she would not later reappear to his son as either nightmare or the object of longing, haunt his nights or suddenly shimmer before him in the heat of the day, and must not leave marks on his body or his soul and should be experienced without flaunting it.

The madam smiled and said that he was not the first father ever to bring her his son, "and you, sir, I can see from your hands, the wrinkles near your eyes, and the way you walk, that you are a *fellah,* a man who works the land, so you need to know that my girls know a lot about agriculture, how to plant and water, to grind and pluck, to pick grape after grape or eat the whole cluster, and most important, sir, the virginity that young men lose here will never again be found, even if hunted with a lantern."

"All well and good," said the father, "but planting is enough, and only in the hole, and everything should be normal, as God made us. She shouldn't scare him with special things, which your girls, I have heard, do with their eyelids and fingers."

On the wall behind the madam, four tassels, yellow and blue and red and green, dangled at the ends of ropes that disappeared into the ceiling. She nodded with understanding and asked if he would like an Arab lady or a Jew.

"I have heard," said the father, "about a Circassian woman you have here."

"The Circassian isn't appropriate," said the proprietress. "She is exactly what you said not to give him. But I have already decided who will take him."

"Who?" asked the father.

"If you like, you can see her first."

The father was shocked. "See her? Certainly not! I rely on you."

"And in the meantime?" asked the madam. "Perhaps the gentleman would also like some small service?"

Absolutely not. The gentleman will wait at the café next door. He turned around, heading for the street, then paused on the third stair and turned back to the madam and asked if she happened to know how to use her fingers to whistle too.

Most men do not take their sons to whorehouses, and such a question would seem odd to them, but the madam nodded: Of course she knows how. She will pay attention and keep an open ear and eye, and if something happens, she will whistle at once, loud and clear.

"You can hear me from here to Damascus and from here to Jaffa," she promised him, "and not just you—all the fathers who worry about all the sons will hear, from the Nile to the Euphrates. There's just one more small matter: I generally get paid in advance."

The father paid her and summoned his son. Ze'ev came from the carriage, fairly embarrassed. The madam looked him up and down the way a man looks at a woman, reached out to the wall, and tugged the blue tassel.

The joyful ding-dong of a distant bell descended from the upper floor, and the madam told Ze'ev to climb the stairs, where he would see a yellow door and blue door and red door and green door, and knock on the blue one and wait for it to open.

Ze'ev glanced at his father, who indicated with his chin and eyebrows that he should go upstairs, and he did. The landlady listened, counted silently till four, the number of seconds that young men like him hesitate at the blue door, and then heard him knocking and it being opened and heard his steps—confident steps, she privately noted.

The prostitute who was there, not young and not old, not ugly and not beautiful, not skinny and not fat, greeted Ze'ev by taking his two hands in hers and stepped backward toward the bed. She lay down on her back, leaned against the wall on a big round pillow, and undid the belt of her robe. Ze'ev feared she would expose herself completely, that her nakedness would instantly eclipse his imagination. To his relief she was not naked but wearing a flimsy shirt, and when she stretched backward the fabric oscillated in breaking waves that augured excitement.

"All yours," she said, and instructed him to get undressed behind a screen while she got up and closed the heavy drapes, leaving the room almost totally dark, for she knew that he would likely be abashed by his naked arousal. He emerged and sat beside her, and she stroked his head and hugged him a bit, and after a moment removed his hand from atop his loins, gave a good look, and said, "They said a little bird was coming for its first time and they sent a warhorse."

About half an hour later, as he left there and went downstairs to the café, Ze'ev saw his father studying his walk and facial expression, trying to determine what happened. The two got into the carriage, returned to the home of the Arab where their horses were tied, and on the way said nothing to each other. When they rode up to the ridge from Tiberias and saw the valley below, the father asked, "So what do you say, Ze'ev?"

And Ze'ev smiled and lied. "Everything is fine now."

Another day went by, and the father asked him again, and Ze'ev again lied, and on the third day he and Ruth traveled to their home in the new moshava and apart from necessary banalities did not converse the entire way. They entered the house, Ruth began organizing her new kingdom, Ze'ev went out to the field, and at night they went into their new bedroom and found that changing their place was not enough to change their luck.

3

How does a man know that his wife has slept with another man? Sometimes she herself tells him, sometimes someone else does, sometimes she looks at him with new disdain, and sometimes with unprecedented fear. Sometimes she denies herself to him, or the opposite: desires and demands him in a way she had not desired and demanded him before.

If our man is endowed with brains and sensitivity, he will understand that all of these are evidence that testifies to nothing. Not to her loyalty or her betrayal, her indifference or her lust, old impatience or new patience, not to anything else or its total opposite. And if he is not endowed with brains and sensitivity, he will understand the very same thing. These things are elusive. One moment someone looks you in the eye and the next moment their eyes are averted, one moment you pierce them with your gaze and the next moment you're knocking on shuttered eyelids, and the truth doesn't shine out but sinks inward, where the worm of suspicion crumbles the soul and burrows tunnels in the body.

Night after night, day after day. There are those who do nothing, but there are those who investigate and clarify: surveillance, searches, sniffing clothes, emptying pockets, cross-examination, digging through the trash bin, and inspecting the bedsheets. I haven't included phones and computers, since these didn't exist in those days, but then as now, all the troops are lined up: ears are attuned, eyes alert, trackers pick up the scent—commandos of memory, platoons of logic, battalions of deduction.

As for Ze'ev Tavori, he was exempt from all that, for he did not suspect his wife until the truth hit him full force in the face. At first he observed that she made a greater effort than usual to cuddle close to him and initiate intercourse, but he didn't understand the real reason. Then he noticed a new habit: she would get up suddenly and leave the house, sometimes in a great hurry, and when he followed her one day, he saw her heading for the cowshed, or beyond it to the vineyard, and when he drew nearer he saw her bending over and vomiting between the grapevines. He almost hurried after her to ask if she needed help, but withdrew and went away. And then, one day, one of the local women approached him, her face bright and happy, and congratulated him on his wife's pregnancy.

He was shocked. His anxiety now had a name and a meaning. But he quickly recovered and thanked the woman, who gave him a strange look and said, "Your wife is young, this is a first pregnancy, it's possible she hasn't told you yet, but other women don't need to be told. They know what they see."

Indeed, Ruth's figure had not yet thickened, but her eyes glowed with the beautiful glow of a first pregnancy, something that few men notice but was apparent to the women of the moshava. In the ensuing days other women congratulated him and extended their good wishes. He did not know if they approached her too or what they said or what she answered, but his heart was heavy and dark and his gut convulsed with terror, for only she and he knew that she was not pregnant by him. How long could they pretend? And how could he watch her belly swelling beside him? An alien sperm had invaded her womb and his home, a fetus not his was growing inside her, multiplying cell upon cell, declaring its existence to others.

Ruth said nothing to him, and he was afraid to question her and considered the possibility of pretending he was the father and responded to well-wishers with an odd mixture of smiles and gloom. They attributed this to the fact that not all men adjust quickly to a first pregnancy, and there are those who are upset by second and third pregnancies too; and he feared the truth would come out and therefore did not confide his agony to anyone. He merely looked at every man in the moshava, trying to find the answer in a gaze or downcast eyes, laughter or fear. He imagined a crushed neck in his hands, a pulverized chin under his fist, gurgling lungs, and the snap of broken bones.

And he saw her that way too, beaten, strangled, stoned to death as an adulteress, buried alive. He pictured the foreign, fleshy battering ram pounding within her, spilling its seed at the lip of her womb, the tiny bastard growing in there, floating in its fluids. What would he do at the moment of the birth? And afterward? As he pondered this, all he could see was a curtain with nothing behind it.

A few weeks passed, and Ruth began to sense that the fetus was female. Another womb, small and pure, she felt, was growing within her, in that perfidious, lustful womb of hers, as she described it in her heart. If she could kill this fetus by the sheer power of her mind, she would do it. If she could, she would rip it out with her fingernails, but the mind does not always control the body. A little daughter grew inside her, very slowly, with the calm confidence of someone who knows nothing about her mother. A little daughter. A baby. A girl.

She did not yet have good friends in the new moshava to talk with about her worries and fears, and she was afraid to write a letter to her mother, because in every moshava there are eyes that read letters even in sealed envelopes. As for Ze'ev, he was never inclined to candid conversations with others. And though he searched the eyes of neighbors and relatives for sparks of derision, or at least of suspicion, he did not find them, but reality has its own ways of showing itself, and when his wife's belly began to protrude under her clothing, men too began smiling at him and congratulating him on the pregnancy, which was the first pregnancy of the moshava, and Ze'ev responded with gloomy smiles and nods of greeting. His father, who came for a visit, said, "Well, well, I knew everything would be all right," and then, as if unable to contain his joy, clenched his fists and declared, "Now here's a real man. Hands of iron, brow of basalt, *shvantz* of copper!"

But Ruth, who knew her husband, realized that something terrible was going to happen. Unlike Ze'ev, who had not understood the signs of her pregnancy until he was congratulated by the local women, she understood his pregnancy: the revenge and the rage swelling in the placenta of his fury, joined umbilically to his soul and nourished by its dark arteries, and she knew that this birth would come sooner than the birth of the fetus in her womb.

TWENTY-SEVEN

....

Every time Eitan came to visit Dovik he would come alone, never with a girlfriend, and he would always ask me how I was and make conversation. And when I went into the army—I didn't want to join their unit, which was how it went with them, guys bringing in their sisters—and I came home in uniform, he suddenly looked at me differently, like I was no longer his friend's little sister but someone interesting in her own right. Mainly when I came in my work uniform, which was short on me and too wide, but suited me fine. It aroused a desire to touch me, he told me years later, "to check if you were actually real."

We began to talk, and even before we became a couple we made each other laugh, and we had looks that we exchanged when Dovik and Dalia didn't get what was funny, and there were little discoveries of our similar tastes in movies and food. Not books, by the way, for the simple reason that Eitan doesn't read. And I saw how Grandpa Ze'ev trained his eye on us the way he didn't look at others, and I picked up that not only Dovik but he too was interested in this match and that Eitan would stay.

That was it. Every encounter added more layers and desires and reasons, and we fell in love. It didn't happen as quickly as I'm making it sound, but when we fell in love we understood that we had already been in love for a long time. When I say "a long time" I mean I was already out of the army and had gone to university and gotten my teaching certificate.

That really is a long time.

Correct. But it makes no difference. Things have to happen at their own pace. We understood. We fell in love. And finally I got pregnant and then we got married. I hope you have no problem with that. Eitan joined the Tavori nursery business and Neta was born, spitting image of his father as a child. There are women who don't like the expression "spitting image." These are women with two family names, and instead of common sense they have emotional intelligence. I, by the way, have not an ounce of emotional intelligence. I have tons of emotion and I also have intelligence but, alas, with me they don't mix.

I remember: Our first time was beautiful. That's important, because it's not like that for everyone. Sometimes it's so tense and clumsy that it's awful. From time to time my female students come and tell me that it happened and how it was and what happened and what they felt, and want to know if what they felt was okay or not, and if in the future it'll be better, as if I were some sort of authority. They sit with me under the mulberry tree and ask for advice—what if he, what if she, what if people will know with whom, and what if they tell. God, how pathetic is that. Ruta the teacher, the pal, the wild woman, the strong one who over-came her disaster, who smiles, who bravely looks to the future. Ruta-*tuta,* who hasn't had sex with her husband for years but overflows with advice for her female students: It's important that the first time be with love, and important in general that it be with love, and how you know that it's love, and at what age to start, blah blah blah . . .

Twice, by the way, male students came to me with similar questions. There was a period when I hoped that Ofer would come to tell me that it also happened to him. Ofer, yes, my former student, who almost drowned on me in the Sea of Galilee, the one who takes pictures, and I would tell him, Very nice, Ofer, tell me how it was but not with whom, so I won't stomp out of the woods and tear apart the girl who stole you.

Whatever. For Eitan and me the first time was during my second year at university when I came home for a holiday, and he came to visit Dovik and Dalia. He brought fish and barbecued them, and Dalia, who is a good cook, prepared fabulous rice in her special rice pot, and her marvelous spicy tomato-garlic-pepper salad, and potatoes for Dovik, for whom a meal isn't a meal without a kilo of potatoes. We drank white-wine spritzers the way Grandpa likes them, and after the meal everyone went to take a nap, Grandpa under his mulberry tree, with the big fan and the extension cord, Dovik and Dalia under the air conditioner in their bedroom, while Eitan rocked in my hammock with his eyes closed.

I sought to clarify the meaning of this takeover.

"Eitan," I said.

He didn't reply.

"Eitan," I said, "this is my hammock. I haven't been home in two weeks and I want it."

He didn't answer, and I grabbed the edge of the hammock with both hands and yanked it upward. Eitan toppled over, landed on the ground, but managed to break his fall with his hands and got up quickly.

"You see? I got out for you. You just have to ask nicely," he said.

I lay down in the hammock, he went in the house for a few minutes, came back, took a chair, and sat down next to me and rocked me gently.

"You have plans?"

"To study art in Italy."

"I mean now."

"To nap undisturbed in my hammock."

"Want to take a little trip?"

"To Altamira in Spain, to see the cave paintings."

"Not a honeymoon, Ruta. Now."

"If you hook up the hammock on the back of the pickup and drive slowly so I won't fall, yes. A little trip now."

"Want to go to Dovik's pond?"

"You have a bathing suit?"

"Already wearing it."

"And you'll bring a treat for later?"

"Already in the cooler."

"And if I didn't want to come?"

"I'd go alone and eat alone and swim naked."

That was that. We went. We talked on the way. It felt good, like a breeze was moving back and forth between us with the tempo of the words and sentences and glances. We were at that dangerous phase where if we didn't do something we would turn into just friends and condemn ourselves to the fate of friends: permanent longing. Not to eat or be eaten. Not to drink or be drunk. Not to be satisfied or slaked. I later wrote myself a note: "We are both Tantalus, the pure water below, the tasty fruit above."

We arrived at the pond. We lay down on the bank, Eitan in his bathing suit, I in a bikini top and shorts; that was always my style. Eitan told me how he and Dovik first met here, and I was surprised. In general everything that becomes a story has several versions, but the story Eitan told me was absolutely identical to the story Dovik told about the very same meeting. Then we got in the water to swim. In the middle of the pond I smiled at him and said, "Let's see if I can dive down to the bottom," and I disappeared.

I dived to the bottom, hid behind a big rock, and stayed there the way I know how, my full four minutes. After thirty seconds he began to worry. He dived, came up, looked for me, called my name. I saw his silhouette, swimming and looking for me, I heard his legs beating the water, worried and scared. His voice reached my ears: "Ruta! . . . Ruta! . . . Where are you?" And again he dived down, came close, but didn't see me. Every few seconds I exhaled a few tiny bubbles, so as not to form a cluster that would give away my location.

I was filled with desire, which did its thing. Even in the water my loins were burning. Even in the water I was totally wet. You remember I told you that I cry underwater and don't feel the wetness of the tears? Well, that I felt clearly. I touched myself, I told him long after that day, when he asked if I didn't get bored there—it was four minutes, after all—I touched myself and I felt the body's tears of joy and love and lust. And that was that. I finally ran out of breath and had to come up for air.

I floated slowly to the surface. The body was still, the arms outstretched. Eitan pounced on me and began to pull me toward shore. I hugged him and laughed. "Eitan, you love me!"

"Love you? I was just worried. You're my friend's sister. What would I tell him if something happened to you?"

"Don't give me that 'friend's sister,'" I teased him, "you love me. You're allowed to admit it."

I put my face close to his and we kissed. Kind of a quick peck, but tender. Closed lips but firmly pressed together, like sealing a deed of ownership.

His hand slid over my left hip, massaged it gently under the water.

"So nice to touch you," he said.

"That's because I put on weight in the army," I said, "I got soft. I have to lose weight."

And I remember putting my right hand on his chest with the fingers spread out.

"That's nice," he said, "and you don't need to lose any weight."

"Maybe you don't see it because I'm tall but I need to lose three kilos."

We got out of the pond. Eitan spread a blanket on the rough grass.

"This is going to be our first time," he said, "I don't want it to be stickly and prickly," and got undressed like a married man—I mean like someone accustomed to getting undressed in front of his woman—and lay down naked on his side.

I got undressed too, lay beside him, and we looked at each other up close. Things were suddenly very clear.

He said, "Ruta."

"What?"

"I want to ask you something."

And he brought his face so near that his golden skin shone warmly on my face.

"Ask me," I said.

"It's something important."

"I'm listening."

"Those three kilos you're going to lose . . ."

"Yes?"

"Can I have them?"

For a moment I didn't understand. I looked at him and he looked at me. His face was serious and focused. I burst out laughing.

"I love it so much that you're laughing at something I said," he said. "Your laugh makes me feel good all over."

"Me too," I said. "All over my body. And not just my body. Your body too. I can feel it."

"So what do you say?"

"About the three kilos or the laughing?"

"About the seventy kilos that are left."

"They're also yours."

"When?"

"Is now okay?"

"Now is very okay."

He stroked my hip again and said, "Remember we started here, at your hippy, and that'll be the first word in our dictionary, and there will be more."

We hugged with eyes open and kissed with eyes open, and it was our first time, beside the "clear, calm, silent pond, where everything is seen and foreseen"—that's what I wrote to him afterward as a memento. I quoted, actually. As much as I love Alterman's poetry, when Bialik is good, he's better than anyone. I wrote: "With eyes that didn't blink once, not to miss the sight of the other's face. With a full heart. With the knowledge of doing what is right, the hunger to be sated and the thirst to be quenched. With the ceremony of a first time and the hope of the times to come, and in the strange lovely knowledge, so true yet untrue, that I am sleeping for the first time with a man I have slept with many times before."

TWENTY-EIGHT

....

I've already told you, if I'm not mistaken, that Eitan had been waiting for me to turn forty and said it many times. Well, that day arrived. I remember: I got up early, I'm forty, good morning to me, alone in bed. I waited awhile. Nothing happened. Then I got dressed, went down to the nursery, and stood before him.

"Eitan," I said, "I'm forty. Congratulations!"

He didn't react. He kept on dragging, carrying, working. Did what Grandpa Ze'ev told him to do. There are situations and there are men that require hard work and not psychotherapy.

"Eitan," I called out, "this is me. Just like you always wanted me. I'm exactly forty, today."

He didn't look at me or answer me, and I wasn't surprised. I would often come to tell him about something and he wouldn't react.

"It's a shame, no?" I stood in his way, blocking him. "Isn't it a shame I'm forty and you're no longer with us?"

He didn't say a word, set down the heavy sack in his arms, and did what he had done on a few prior occasions: grabbed me, hugged me, and lifted me like a feather. For the first second it felt good, and then I couldn't breathe. All that work had made him so strong. Like a bear. He was able to crouch, wrap his arms around a pot with, say, an eight-year-old olive sapling, stand up, and carry it to another spot in the nursery.

Crouch again, very slowly, so as not to harm the sapling, and lay it gently on the ground, then get up and go back and take another one. And every time a truck arrived with merchandise he was the one who unloaded it and arranged the goods in the storehouses or yard.

Incidentally, we also sell old railroad ties, for garden paths and stairs, and he would move them too, from where they were to wherever Grandpa Ze'ev said, and then back again, sometimes just a day later. I saw him once carrying a railroad tie on his back, with the end dragging behind him leaving a trail in the dirt. You can imagine what kind of thoughts that brings to the mind.

In the beginning I would yell at him, get angry, cry: "Look at yourself, Eitan. See what you look like. Smell yourself. You stink from compost and sweat." And once I went over and blocked his path. "Maybe it's enough, Eitan? Maybe you've worked like this enough?" And suddenly, involuntarily, I screamed, "Enough! Wash up already! Change your clothes! I can't look at you. Don't let yourself go like this!" And then too—he crouched, set down whatever it was he was carrying, picked me up, and put me aside like a mannequin. It was frightening. Look at me, I'm a fairly big woman, not a lightweight in any sense. He put me on the side and returned to his work.

He did a similar thing to Dovik once. Dovik is a friend, and a brother-in-law, and a man, and on top of these he's an imbecile, so one day he pounced on him and shook him hard and shouted, "Enough already, Eitan! Even if he told you to do that, it's enough! How long will you punish yourself and us this way?" And he picked him up too, and carried him aside, but judging from the color of Dovik's face he squeezed him harder than he squeezed me, and when he let him go, Dovik collapsed, and coughed and spit and groaned.

"You okay?" I asked.

"Yeah, right." He moaned. "I couldn't breathe. He could kill somebody like that, he's gotten so strong."

Later on I found a method. I grabbed a garden hose in the nursery and sprayed him with cold water, and then he had no choice: he changed his clothes, and the occasion also constituted an overdue bath. He also had the awful smell of the cigarettes that he started smoking again after the funeral. This disaster provided us both bad habits. He started smoking and I started drinking, so that the alcohol would help me fall asleep and drive away bad dreams. Before the disaster, Eitan would come to our bed like Ruth came to Boaz. Festive and fragrant and clean, the whole biblical routine—"Wash, anoint yourself, put thy raiment upon thee, and go and lie down"—is that gendered enough for you, Varda? He had golden skin then, skin that glowed in the dark, and we would make love and then fall asleep together. And now, every night I can't fall asleep without drinking and I think I'm slightly addicted.

You started to tell me about your fortieth birthday, Ruta.

Yes. Thank you for putting me back on track. I informed him that I had reached forty, and he removed me from his path and placed me on the side. That's how he celebrated the day he had long awaited.

And what happened then?

I got up. I went back home, and then a teacher from the school called me. I thought she wanted me to substitute for her somewhere, but no. She and a few other women friends had decided to take me out for my birthday, she said. You understand? Let's take Ruta out, the poor thing. For years she's been without her son, and that situation with Eitan, and now a big birthday, let's do something nice for her.

I said thank you, I went to work, came home, drank a little, ate a little—in the evening there's a meal waiting for me—napped a little, woke up, took a shower, got dressed, went out with my friends to a restaurant.

The food was very good. I enjoyed the women rather less. I think I already told you that I've never had a real close woman friend, a soul mate to confide in, a female shoulder to cry on. Maybe because I'm not only a girl but also a guy, and maybe because, due to my family, I don't talk about everything, and also because not all the rules and codes are clear to me, especially not the rules and codes customary among women. But it's okay with me to go out with women friends for a good time and since the disaster it's mainly to restaurants. It's fine, because bereaved mothers also have to eat sometimes, and it's also fun because I truly enjoy good food. I celebrate. I enjoy it like thirty pigs. That's also a line from my first husband. "Like thirty pigs" was for us the most fun possible. Eitan would ask, not just about food, about many things: "So, Ruta, like how many pigs did you enjoy it this time?" And I would answer, sometimes ten, sometimes twelve, even twenty-seven. You don't need to lick caviar from a silver spoon. Sometimes seeing a beautiful landscape is enough, or a good movie, like Fellini's *Amarcord* or *The Straight Story* by David Lynch.

Or to be one flesh, Eitan in me, I in him. Sometimes mashed potatoes that only I know how to make but had no one to make them for. Then I would eat them alone and enjoy them, without thinking, You should be ashamed of yourself, Ruta, Eitan and Neta are dead and you are filling your belly, rebelling and defiling and defying. And playing word games.

The truth is, I'm not a glutton, I actually prefer small portions, and I also enjoy reading restaurant reviews and recipes. Sometimes I clip them from the papers. I loved the ones by the cardiologist Eli Landau, the finest gourmet in Israel. So we women went out and ate and talked and made dirty jokes and laughed a lot, and nobody flaunted what ailed them or dumped their burden on the table and we didn't compare troubles, because the idea was to cheer me up and not to show me that others were suffering too. I also got a few nice gifts, but my enjoyment amounted to maybe nine pigs' worth at most. All evening long I had this pang in my heart. "Pang" is an understatement, my heart was mashed inside a fist with my gut wrapped around it.

It started even before they came to pick me up, because while I was getting dressed and organized I again saw Eitan through the window. It was starting to get dark outside and I simply started to cry. I remembered how he had invented the word "fortyward" about this special day, the word that should have been my invention and by chance was his, and I cried even more.

Excuse me for just a moment. I have to take a breath now, a little breath, and walk around. Don't be alarmed, it'll pass quickly. I am a big strong woman, I am the granddaughter of Grandpa Ze'ev, and I am the best thing that ever happened to me. If I were a different woman in the same situation, it would be very bad. But sometimes, behind that bigness and those genes, I am really little. An empty peel. I'm like the passion fruit we used to poke a hole in when we were kids and suck out the insides and throw away. Funny, it's been a long time since I ate a passion fruit that way. Today people cut them open and eat them with a spoon, even with ice cream. Whatever. I saw Eitan and I decided to give my fortieth birthday another chance. I wiped my face, opened the window, and called out to him.

He didn't answer. He didn't even turn his head toward me.

"Eitan, look at me. I'm forty. Just like you always wanted. Let's get into bed, the two of us naked."

He didn't respond. Dovik and Dalia's kitchen window opened for a moment, then slammed shut. A car horn sounded. The friends who came to get me were in front of the house, waiting. I wiped off my makeup. In general I don't use makeup, and if I do it's sparingly, but even the little bit I had put on was smeared by the tears. I quickly reapplied it, and went out to the street.

When I got back, very late, a bit drunk from the gin and tonics I overdid and stinking from cigarettes that someone else smoked, he was already lying in bed in the room that had been Neta's, camouflaged according to his classic rules: not budging, because the eye notices movement, and blending into his surroundings, the whiteness of the sheet enveloping his own whiteness.

I got undressed, lay down beside him, drew close.

"Congratulations, Eitan, I'm forty," I said to him for the umpteenth time that day.

His eyes opened. I lay my hand on his belly and said, "We've waited a long time for this birthday, no?"

I thought, And now what? Leave my hand on the sheet or slip it underneath? And where to go from there? Higher up and spread my fingers? Lower down and grasp? To the right and stroke his left hippy? To the left and stroke his right hippy? I withdrew my hand, climbed on top of him, lay my whole self on him, embraced him, buried my face in his neck, pressed the mound of my *tuta* on his body, my overripe mound that drove my first husband crazy and is the reason I swim in shorts and not a bathing suit, and, suddenly, a miracle: I felt he was returning my hug. For a moment I was left breathless, but quickly realized it was not from joy or love but simply from pressure. And again he did the one thing he knew how to do: he sat up and carried me into the next room, which had once been ours, and put me in the bed where we had once both slept, and returned to the bed that had been Neta's and became his.

I coughed, regained my breath, got up. I smiled to myself, for seven times I rise and smile, as it is written of the righteous, and despite the level of gin in my system I headed for the freezer and poured myself an ample glass of my brother's homemade *limoncello*. I drank with great pleasure and then stood up and looked at the mirror and the drunken woman in it. Because if not me and Eitan, then here we were, the two of us: tall and thin, broad skinny shoulders, strong prominent collarbones, too strong, I might add. Long neck, eyes far apart. The two of us naked and drunk. Ribs protruding in the space between her small breasts, just like mine. Her feet are as big as a man's, her thighs are long, and where they meet is that domed space which only a chosen few, she and I, have. We both have muscular calves and, surprise: round ankles, almost chubby, like a baby's. Luckily I didn't inherit my mother's legs and boobs. I inherited my legs from Grandma Ruth and the boobs from Grandpa Ze'ev, and I am very happy with that. All my busty friends, who always laughed at my doelike buds, ultimately discovered that Newton was right: there is gravity and it is very strong. Now their fabulous mammaries are on the floor and my little titties are still in their original place—"Moshe, Shlomo, every man *bimkomo*," just where God and I intended and wanted them to be, all in order. This, by the way, is one of the few things about which God and I agree: that I may be on the ropes, but my tits will rejoice on high.

"That's that, Eitan," I told him, "we're forty years old and you're not here. I hereby announce that the party's over."

TWENTY-NINE

....

Varda: What are you doing, Ruta?

Ruta: I'm putting my face close to yours. Don't be afraid. I don't bite and I won't plant a kiss on your lips. I just want you to see. I don't have many wrinkles, and still only the two white hairs. You see? No new ones, though a disaster like mine could wrinkle a woman and turn her white in a heartbeat.

One day, at a parents' meeting, one of the mothers told me that she and her daughter had been saying, en route to the school, how good Teacher Ruta looked, despite the disaster and all, and I told her, Thanks, how nice of you. And I remarked that maybe this was God's way to compensate victims. And she said, "We never know what God wants. I go to a kabbalah class and they told us this is the way things are and even proved it by the numerology of gematria."

Suddenly I felt extremely tired. Idiocy wears me out, and when I see and hear an idiot of either gender I can recognize them with ease. Any number of them grow in my classroom, and I know what will become of them before they know themselves. Also absolute justice tires me out, a lot. Almost as much as the people who believe in it.

I'm smiling, right? Sometimes, if I don't tell myself to smile, I don't do it. Or I smile, but don't feel it. That's because there are days when

I'm just an actress. I got the lead part in a play about a woman who lost him and his son, her two guys, in a single day. But apart from that, Varda, my life isn't bad. I have work that I love, I do it well, and I have songwriters who write songs for me, so I can sing the harmony, and writers who write books for me, to read and edit as necessary. And I also know how to be alone, and I like it, and most of all—I know how to keep myself busy.

It's not nice to say this, but sometimes I enjoyed life even after the disaster. Here and there I even heard myself suddenly laughing. And sometimes some man would try to catch my eye, not that anything came of it, because I had become a kind of Penelope, waiting for her husband to return from his travels, and his travails, his and mine. A great deal was destroyed, but not everything. And life wasn't really over. I would say to myself: "Be happy, Ruta, that you're alive. Be happy that you look good. Be happy you're not an idiot like that mother."

Well, Dr. Canetti, Yishuv historian, we've strayed again from the topic, so let's go back. It's a method Eitan taught me once, when we were young and out hiking and he tried to teach me to navigate and what to do in case of error: first we have to admit the error. That's hard, but important and necessary. We need to admit we're wrong and not try to redraw the map or the reality, not to raise up mountains or level the hills. And so, with a sense of optimistic failure, as he would say, we have to return to the last place we could confidently find on the map and in the field, and there start over.

So that's what I'm doing now—returning to the last clear point in our conversation: I am Ruth Tavori, everyone calls me Ruta, I am the granddaughter of Ze'ev Tavori of blessed memory who raised me and my brother, Dovik. I am the wife of Eitan, who disappeared on me for twelve years and came back, and I am the mother of Neta, who died of a snakebite at the age of six, and I am a secular teacher of Hebrew Bible and eleventh-grade homeroom teacher at the high school in the moshava. It's interesting how we define ourselves, no? According to family and work and not one's loves, wishes, disappointments, inner qualities. So besides being the "granddaughter of" and "sister of" and "mother of" and "teacher of," I also love and know how to sing, and if

need be I am able to dive underwater and hold my breath for four minutes. That's it. We went a long way back so I could sum myself up. Now
you know everything.

Apropos of singing, I don't mean, God forbid, organized folksing-
ing with someone playing the accordion. That I leave to my neighbors,
Haim and Miri Maslina, and to my sister-in-law, Dalia. I mean real singing. I sang in the choir of the regional council, and we performed all
over, we even sang once at the Abu-Gosh choral festival. But singers
in a choir, you should know, sometimes shed a few tears, and with me,
after the disaster, there were moments in the music where I would suddenly get choked up, and after this happened twice, when I had just
been given a solo—"out of pity," as one woman muttered at the time—
I stopped performing and later stopped going to rehearsals.

And not just the choir. Many things dwindled or came to a halt:
friends, having fun, making love, the long, deep sleep that came afterward. I used to touch and be touched, love and be loved, lull and be
lulled to sleep, in one sweet sequence. We were the kings of sleep, Eitan
and me, falling asleep joined together, but not like spoons, we fell asleep
like a windmill. Whatever. A few years ago one of the women friends
who wanted to help me invited me to join her travel group: a regular
guide, history, nature, archaeology, culture. Mostly in our country, but
sometimes also at the neighbors—Egypt, Jordan, Turkey. The farthest
we got was Italy. It was a nice group, mostly from this area, but once
somebody brought a friend from Kfar Saba, and it turned out that this
friend was also a bereaved mother, but not like me, an ordinary mother
whose ordinary child died, she was the bereaved mother of a fallen soldier, which here in the ancestral homeland means true bereavement,
the real thing. With Memorial Day and the siren and ceremonies and
all that.

The truth? She was perfectly fine. Didn't make a big deal of it, like
those bereaved parents you run into for whom it's not just their situation but also their title and even their profession. But the woman who
brought her kept mentioning it to everyone, as if some of the majesty
might rub off on her, and she apparently made sure to tell her about my
disaster, in case we might want to sit together and talk, and she could tell
the other women how she had helped us both.

Don't misunderstand. At first I really did want to talk to her. It's true that it's different for everyone, even between parents it's very different, look at me and Eitan, what happened to him and what happened to me, but a child is a child, it doesn't matter how old he was and how he died, and a mother is a mother, right? So we started to talk, and after two minutes I got the picture: even if she really is okay, and believe me, I had nothing against her, in this country, when it comes to us two and our sons and bereavement—she's number one. And even if she behaves nicely, politely, empathetically, as they say, she's looking down on me. And what's worse, I also obeyed these rules. I suddenly found myself looking up to her, a rare phenomenon for me both physically and psychologically. I then decided I couldn't handle it anymore. The ceremonious gravity, the right and the left together bereft, and this unfortunate woman with her radiant, precious, heroic son. You know what irritated me most? That she, on top of all that glory, also had someone to blame, from the petty officer to the prime minister, and I have nobody except Eitan and myself. I even stopped complaining to God, because I doubt his ears can hear the frequency of my voice after getting used to the frequency of prayers and rams' horns.

To make a long story short, that's why I stopped going on those trips, which in any case I was sick of—the crowded bus, everyone singing the same songs and chatting the same chat and telling the same stories, and there was always the idiot who took the microphone from the guide to tell bad jokes. And on top of all that, the constant sense of being checked out and tested and judged. And I also felt that regardless of where we were going, I always missed my home and wanted to go back. Missed it in the dumbest, vaguest sense, being homesick without knowing why or for what or whom exactly, and I also worried that while I was away from home something else terrible would happen to Eitan or because of Eitan or with Eitan. After all, when the disaster happened, I also wasn't there, it was just the two of them alone.

Varda: Sorry for the interruption, Ruta, but what does falling asleep joined like a windmill mean?

Ruta: You poor, sweet thing, this is all you thought about this whole time? I'm pouring my guts out to you and bleeding on the floor, and you're not listening and not thinking about your history of the Yishuv either, because sleeping like spoons you know, but you tried to imagine what "like a windmill" means, and to come home this evening and tell Yossi, or whatever his name is, your happy husband, your partner, excuse me, how could I forget, your partner—not Yossi? For some reason I thought that most husbands of women named Varda are named Yossi. Whatever. So, Yossi, listen what I learned today, something new and charming, falling asleep like a windmill, the one on top is still on the one on the bottom, but with the bodies at a slight angle like an X, all four arms and four legs spread out, and whoever is watching from above— God, usually—says to himself: What a lovely windmill, why not turn it? Come, wind, and blow, blow those dry wings, so they may fly.

....

THIRTY

TRAVELS WITH A GOAT

1

About an hour before the death of Grandpa Ze'ev a big jaybird flew along the length of the low ridge between the two wadis. It flew from west to east, flew and shrieked.

Shrieking is not merely the language of the jays, it is their very nature, and this jay shrieked and didn't quit. He announced to the entire world that in the two wadis, where human beings are rarely to be seen, several people were walking, and to the walkers he announced that they had been discovered, that a brave and alert jaybird had spotted them and was not afraid of them as he watched them from his lofty flight.

In the wadi to the south the jay saw three men walking in single file: a tall young beefy man, clad in a leather jacket, was the first. Now and then his soles slipped on a stone and his lips expelled a curse. At the rear walked a man of about fifty, short and chubby, eyeglasses on his nose, a small knapsack on his back, and a light-colored hat on his head. And in between, a tall thin man, his mouth sealed by a wide swath of tape, his nose dripping, knees struggling not to buckle, and on his shoulders—the curious jaybird wheeled downward, to be sure of this point—he carried a dead goat.

The three walked up the wadi, made a sharp turn, and arrived at the big carob tree beyond. It was an especially big carob tree. It was one of those hillside trees that got lucky and did not have to settle for a thin layer of soil below which lay limestone, deprivation, and hunger. Here the soil was rich and deep, and here the carob struck its roots.

Somebody or something, perhaps the hands of shepherds or the jaws of cattle, took the trouble to prune the lower branches, creating a shelterlike structure in place of the bushy sprawl that carobs tend to become. One could stand beneath it, and the thick treetop kept out the rain in winter and cast a full, cool shade during heat waves. A few rocks sat at its feet like petrified oxen, chewing a cud of lime and time, and the chilly remnants of a campfire spoke of previous, rare visits by people: little piles of ash, ancient cigarette butts, charred stones. The jaybird knew that these men would also sit in the shade of the tree and hoped that they too, like their predecessors, would leave scraps of uneaten food.

In the parallel gully to the north, the jaybird saw an old man making his way slowly, a small pack over his shoulder, his hand gripping a thick walking stick, one eye covered with a patch and the other scanning the ground. From time to time the old man put down the stick and got down on all fours to inspect an object of his desire.

The jay landed on a rock not far from the man—something jays are not wont to do—and cawed at him softly. Jays know how to shriek, shout, mimic, usually a baby's cry and the yowling of a cat, but a caw like this one they produce only rarely. The old man looked with his one good eye at the bird, stood up straight, and walked past it, and the jay flew off and landed about two hundred meters away, on the shallow ridge between the two wadis, conspicuous in a way that on any other day it would avoid.

The old man noticed the bird and headed toward it, strolling up the slope. The wisdom of his step, his knowledge of the path, made up for the frailty of his body. He knew that in the parallel wadi, a bit to his south and east, stood the big carob he would always visit, to rest in its shade and eat. What he did not know was that in one hour he would die, for his murderers were already sitting under that very same tree.

And they too, the three men sitting under the big carob, did not know all this—that the elderly, one-eyed collector of seeds was approaching them and that they were going to kill him. On any nice day, people move among people, attentively or not—on the street, in the fields, on foot, in cars—each along his way and wadi and path, each toward his destination, with his baggage and his purpose and his grudges and his memories, and nothing happens, certainly not what is about to happen here, in this wadi.

In the shade of the carob, the men were doing what they came to do. The one in the hat—a panama hat with a loud pink band—took a gun from his coat pocket and ordered the carrier of the goat carcass to drop it on the ground. But this man, quick and agile and stronger than he looked, threw the goat at him and tried to attack him. The young man in the leather jacket jumped on him with all his weight, forced him to the ground, and beat his head with his fists, and the man in the hat aimed his gun at him and did not speak. The man gave up. He put his wrists together and let the young man tie them behind his back.

In the meantime the old man reached the top of the ridge and began walking down into the parallel wadi, and the jaybird took off and flew a few dozen meters, landed on another rock, turned its head, again cawed, and looked at the old man as if to confirm that he was following. A few hundred meters away, under the carob tree, the man in the hat laid the gun down, took a gas burner and teapot from his pack, and stood them between the rocks in a spot sheltered from the wind. He removed his hat, mopped his sweaty brow, put the hat back on, lit the gas burner with a gold cigarette lighter he took from his pocket, and sat down on a rock that resembled a big armchair.

He was short, with thick eyeglasses, but a sharp-eyed person could tell from his neck and wrists that he was very strong, and from the way he walked and talked that he was the leader of this group and familiar with this location.

Two living people, then, were present, plus one dead goat, and a man who was tied up and taken there to be killed as well. His legs were gathered to his belly, his sideways body was spent, a rag poked out from under the tape that sealed his mouth. When he blinked, his eyelids moved very slowly, as if trying to prolong the barrier between him and what was about to transpire. He had gone, in the past, on other travels with a goat, but this time he bore it on his own shoulders.

The young man in the leather jacket sat a few meters away, near the edge of the carob's shadow. His beady eyes, set close to each other, studied the tree. His potbelly, small and recently acquired, strained the buttons of his shirt. The man in the hat rose from the rocky throne, looked into the teapot, and turned off the gas. There fell a great silence, the silent sound of an opening curtain, pleasing to the ear and boding evil. The old man did not hear any of this. He walked up the gully, past the bend, and when he neared the jaybird, it flew off again and landed on another rock, higher up.

Now the man in the hat took out two glasses, checked their cleanliness in the sunlight, poured tea into each, and declared, "A nature hike, in the Land of Israel. Like the hikes in the youth movement, when we were young and beautiful and filled with values and hope."

"We weren't in the movement," commented the young man in the leather jacket, taking one of the glasses.

The man in the hat pointed a stern finger at him, like a schoolteacher: "Don't take before I do, you hear?!"

The young man replaced the glass, his boss took the other one, again sat in the stony throne, sipped a small sip from the steaming tea, sighed contentedly, and poured the remaining tea on the face of the man who was tied.

"Now you may drink too," he said to the young man. "And you," he turned to the tied-up man, "will not drink, because your mouth that spoke about us is sealed with a rag, and your hands that pointed at us are tied."

And he refilled his glass and drank and continued, "So here we are, the two of us, there's a book by that name, a book I would read to my son when he was small, but I would recommend to adults as well. The two of us are more than just you and I, and the two of us have been together long enough for you to understand why the goat has joined the hike."

And he stooped over the man who was tied and recited:

"Out for a hike on a glorious day
Peretz and Zerah—hello and hooray!
Up on the hill, down in the vale
And suddenly, whoa! Here lies a tale—

Almost a miracle, a moment of note:
There in the road lay a very dead goat."

And he stood up. "And we will now remove the rag from your mouth, for I have questions and you have the right of reply. We will chat a bit, quietly, in a civilized fashion. And if you scream, we will strangle you along with your scream."

The young man in the leather jacket drew near, pulled the tape from the face of the man who was tied and the rag from his mouth, and the man spat, coughed, and let out a loud long scream that echoed down the entire wadi.

The jaybird flew off in panic from the rock, flew and hid among the branches of an oak that stood on the opposite slope, beside a tangled mastic tree. The old man walking behind it did not react at all. Beside the carob tree the young man seized the screaming throat in his left hand and thrust his right hand at the open mouth to silence it. But the man who was tied quickly turned his head and dug his teeth into the young man's hand and would not let go.

The young man groaned in pain and pounded the man's head, but the latter's jaws held tight. The man in the hat took the gold lighter with which he had lit the gas fire, placed it against the man's earlobe, and flicked on the flame. A scorching smell filled the air. A choking wail, not human, escaped the fastened jaws.

"Enough!" said the man in the hat. "Mad dog that you are. Open your mouth or I'll kill you this way, I'll burn you bit by bit with this lighter."

The man who was tied opened his jaws and lowered his head as if waiting for a blow. The young man inspected the tooth marks on his hand.

"What's wrong with you?" demanded the man in the hat, setting the lighter beside the gas burner. "Why weren't you more careful?"

The screeching of the jaybird could be heard from the opposite slope—brief, hoarse, surprising.

"Go see what's going on there, why is that bird shrieking like that?" said the man in the hat.

The young man went over and had a look at the wadi.

"Somebody's walking in the wadi," he said, keeping his voice low. "But pretty far away."

The man in the hat grew tense. "Shut his mouth, now."

The young man put the rag back into the mouth of the man who was tied, sealed it again with tape, and returned to his lookout position.

"The somebody walking there, what kind of somebody is it?" asked the man in the hat, handing the young man a small pair of binoculars from his knapsack.

"Somebody old. White hair, walking with a stick and wearing work clothes like from a kibbutz. I should go down to have a look?"

"What's this 'I should go down'? Speak Hebrew like a normal person! 'I will go and look.'"

"You'll go?"

"No, you idiot."

"So I should go?"

"It's no use," said the man in the hat to the man who was tied. "A lost cause." And to the young man he said, "We'll wait a bit. Maybe he'll go away. What kind of stick does he have?"

"A stick stick. Like an old Arab's stick."

"Salt of the earth. Kibbutznik in work clothes and also an old Arab with a stick."

"Now, when he picked up his head," said the young man, his eyes glued to the binoculars, "you wouldn't believe what he has on his eye. Like a pirate thing. How do you call it, kinda Moshe Dayan."

"'Kinda Moshe Dayan'?"

"Exactly."

"It's called an eye patch. 'Kinda Moshe Dayan.'"

"Eye patch. Now I should remember."

"Lost cause. So what do we have so far? Arab, also kibbutznik; pirate and also old. How old?"

"Old. White head. Walks slow and bent over."

"Bent over looking for something or bent over because standing up is hard?"

"Bent over looking. Really old, without one eye and with a stick."

"Don't make fun," said the man in the hat. "There are some kick-ass old men in this country like you wouldn't believe." And he laughed.

"If he's alive and kicking, think about whoever took out his eye—what happened to him."

And added: "You see white hair, a walking stick, bending over. But there are things even the best binoculars don't reveal. Look at our friend here, who bites like a dog but lies on the ground, bound like a sheep. He saw me, a short older guy, a bit of a weight problem as the doctor put it, Coke-bottle glasses, a lovely bald spot growing under my hat, and he thought he could do whatever he wanted. But 'many are the thoughts in the heart of man, yet the Lord's plan will prevail': I am drinking herbal tea and he is lying in the dirt beside a dead goat knowing that soon he will lie beneath it in the pit.

"It has no shepherd and has no master
It stands and chews on leaves in a pasture.
They took the goat and went on their way
Perah and Zerah are done for the day."

"A very nice poem," said the young man. "Did you write it?"

"Lost cause. What's going on down in the wadi? Where's that old man now?"

"He disappeared on me. Suddenly I don't see him," said the young man.

He walked past the tree and urinated. But he didn't look at the stream he emitted nor at the spot it hit the ground, as men always do when urinating, but into the distance, to the point where he lost sight of the old man. When he was done he zipped up his trousers, absentmindedly sniffed his fingertips, smiled a little smile to himself, and returned to his place.

The man who was tied began convulsing on the ground. His eyes were wide open and his lips produced a strangled moan.

"Again you're starting? You want the lighter in your other ear too?"

But the man kept twisting and bending and groaning. He stared at something behind the young man's back, his eyes filled with suffering and supplication. His two captors turned and saw an old man, very near them. First the white-haired head came into view amid the rocks, then the big bent-over body, an elderly man dressed in old blue work clothes.

A pack over his shoulder, the heavy walking stick in his hand, and a colorful patch over his left eye—a whimsical patch that seemed to belong to someone else—sky blue with a red poppy embroidered at the center.

"So. The friend you saw before has come to visit," said the man in the hat to the young man. "You didn't take him seriously and now he got to us without our knowing."

"I watched him till he disappeared, like you told me, and you also said maybe he would go away on his own, and suddenly he's here and I don't know from where."

The old man drew near and stood still. His one eye stared at the man who was tied up, twitching and moaning. He shifted his gaze to the dead goat and the young man in the leather jacket, who massaged his right hand and distorted his face in pain, then glanced at the gun without pausing and stopped at the man in the hat, who looked back at him and smiled politely. The jaybird, which had watched them the whole time from the branches of the oak tree, flew away.

2

"Good morning," said the old man.

"Top of the morning to you," the man responded, doffing his hat with a theatrical flourish.

"Excuse me a second," said the old man. "I don't hear so good."

He took a tiny pouch from his shirt pocket, pulled out a hearing aid, and stuck it in his ear.

"What did you say?"

"I answered you, good morning."

"Good morning. I usually don't meet people here. You hiking?"

"A nature hike. You're also hiking?"

"I collect seeds here."

His good eye again scanned the three men, but his facial expression remained unchanged and he asked no questions.

"What kind of seeds?"

"You interested in flowers?"

"Interested in flowers? Did you hear him? Am I interested in flowers . . ." And the man in the hat laughed loudly. "Tell him which flowers.

I have a big hothouse of orchids. Orchids from Thailand and Costa Rica and Ecuador. A hothouse plenty of people would be more than happy to inhabit. With timers, sensors, humidity and acidity gauges, mist generators, and irrigation with purified water."

"Those are plants that don't belong here," said the old man, sitting down on a rock. "Like you, in this wadi."

"So you heard us here and decided to come and see what's happening?"

"I didn't hear a thing. As you saw. My hearing aid wasn't in my ear but in my pocket. I always come here, rest awhile in the shade, and continue collecting."

"That's allowed, collecting seeds?"

"You don't tell on me and I won't tell on you."

The man in the hat chuckled. "That's a good one. Drink some tea with us?"

"No, thank you, I'll go on my way. I haven't yet managed to collect much. I won't bother you. Have a nice day."

"How will you get back from here? You want us to take you?"

"No need. They'll come get me from the road later."

The man who wore the hat nodded at the young man in the leather jacket, who replaced the binoculars in the knapsack.

"Sit with us awhile, let's talk," said the man in the hat to the old man. "I'm bored with these two. This one doesn't talk to me because he has nothing to say, and this one doesn't talk to me because, as you see, his mouth is closed."

The old man did not respond.

"What happened to your eye, if I may ask? The wars of Israel?"

"No. My wife did it."

The man in the hat burst out laughing. "What kind of story is that?"

"The truth."

"How did it happen?"

"She hit me with a piece of a branch."

"A man like you?"

"If you hit the right spot you don't need your gun or my stick. A simple thin dry branch is enough."

"What did you do to her?"

"We did many things to each other. I deserved it. She cheated on me and I killed her lover."

"Listen, all I wanted to do was chat a bit. You don't have to tell me everything."

"I always wanted to tell somebody that story. It's too bad that it's a shit like you who gets to hear it."

"You know how it goes. If you tell me things like that, in the end you'll have to kill me."

"Not a bad idea."

"Based on what you've told me till now, there's not much difference between us."

"You're right. I should have been killed too. Everybody would have been better off."

"Could you show me a few of the seeds you've already collected?"

"They're in my pack. You can see them afterward yourself."

"I want to see them now, if you don't mind," said the man in the hat.

The old man's eye surveyed the three men and suddenly narrowed, and his fingers gripped his stick tighter, and his jaw tightened too. But the man in the hat, taking notice of all this, thrust his hand with surprising speed and force, seized the end of the hefty stick as the old man raised it, pulled it, and flung it away.

"There was a time," said the old man calmly, "when no man could do a thing like that to me. But after I turned ninety I got a bit weaker."

"The seeds, please. I don't like waiting."

"They're in the pack, in paper bags. You can open it and look. If you intend to take them for yourself, don't put them in plastic bags or a closed box, or they'll rot."

He took the pack from his shoulder and handed it to his interlocutor: "Take it, you worthless bum. What're you afraid of?"

Behind him, the young man in the leather jacket bent down, picked up a rock the size of a grapefruit. The old man sensed this and turned but could not withstand him, and the young man swung his arm and hit him. The rock smashed his temple. The big, heavy body fell sideways to the ground.

"Leave him just as he is," said the man in the hat, "and put the rock in your hand under his head. Make sure the side with the blood is exactly under the fracture."

The young man did as he said. "What do we do now?" he asked. "He said they were coming to get him."

"Exactly so. They'll come, they won't find him on the road, they'll go looking, they'll come up here. He said this was his regular place. They'll get here, Oy-oy-oy, what happened? Grandpa is lying here dead, they'll call the police, the police will say an old man a hundred years old went for a hike, fell, and broke his head. What kind of family are you, that you allow a man as old as that to hike here alone? And here's the rock with all his blood, right under his head."

"It was me put it there to look like that," said the young man with satisfaction.

"But you forgot something."

"What?"

"His hearing aid. Luckily it's in his other ear, not the side where you hit him. Take it out, wipe it clean, and put it back in the pouch and his shirt pocket. And quickly, please. We have to get out of here."

The young man did as he was told. The man in the hat said to the man who was tied, "You left me no choice." And to the young man he said, "Hold his legs. He'll go wild and kick."

He seized the neck of the man who was tied and strangled him, not stopping even after he went limp. After a minute more he let go and said to the young man, "Into the pit."

The two carried the corpse to a small cave at the edge of the wadi. At its bottom was an ancient water cistern, half full of stones and sediment. They threw the dead man in, the young man climbed down and covered him with stones, climbed back up, took the dead goat, and threw it in too.

"Check that you can see the goat from the top without going into the pit," said the man in the hat.

"I can see it," said the young man.

"And him?"

"No."

"Final check. That we didn't forget anything."

"I did it already."

"You call that 'I did it'? Where's his stick?"

"Where you threw it before."

"What will they say later on, when they find him? That a man throws his stick five meters away when he falls and dies? Put it by his hand and let's move, we'll go out through the other wadi."

They climbed to the shallow ridge, the man in the hat first, the young man after him, slipping on stones and cursing.

"Why did you wear those shoes?" said the man in the hat. "You knew we were hiking in nature. You could have come with the appropriate shoes."

THIRTY-ONE

On that morning Dovik took Grandpa Ze'ev to his wadi, said goodbye, but after a few seconds ran after him and said, "I'll walk with you a little, Grandpa."

"No need," said Grandpa Ze'ev. "You have to get back to work. We'll meet here at three."

"I have time," said Dovik and joined him. I think he wanted a taste of our sweet childhood hikes with him.

"You weren't afraid to leave him there?" I asked him the next day. "You didn't have a sense that something might happen to him?"

"No. I did this so many times before. And you also took him there sometimes and left him there without any concern. Why worry about a man like him, in a place that's like his second home?"

The two walked together, talked a bit, Grandpa asked Dovik if he remembered all the plants he had taught him about.

"No. Only some of them. Ruta remembers them better."

At a certain point they parted. Dovik left him there with his stick and pack and as always went back in the afternoon to pick him up at the appointed place and time: three p.m., on the road by the little bridge. But Grandpa Ze'ev, a very punctual person, wasn't waiting there. Dovik got worried. He didn't know what to do. He wanted to go to the carob tree to look for him, but what would happen if Grandpa Ze'ev would show up and not find him at the meeting place?

He shouted "Grandpa! Grandpa!" a few times, and finally went and found him lying there with his head in a puddle of blood.

He called me immediately, and along with the shock of the news that our grandfather was dead, I was frightened by the way he said it. He used the same words with which he informed me twelve years earlier about Neta's death: "Ruta," he said, "I have something really terrible to tell you, Grandpa is dead." And continued: "He apparently fell, cracked his head open on a rock, right under his carob tree. We'll talk more later, I want to call the police."

After two minutes the phone rang again: "The police said they're coming, I should wait by the road and bring them here, but I told them that I'm not going to leave the body, that you would meet them."

I ran to Dalia, told her, asked that she come too and that we go in her car because I was in no shape to drive, and suddenly Eitan turned up and asked me what was going on. In that first moment I didn't even realize that these were the first words he had spoken to me after twelve years of silence and hard labor and I simply answered him. I said that Dovik found Grandpa dead in the wadi, that I was going there with Dalia.

"I'll come too," he said, and only then did I realize. I didn't just realize, I was shaken: not just the first words, but going somewhere for the first time since Neta died.

He sat in the backseat. Dalia said, "Eitan, how come you started to talk? What happened that you decided to come?"

He didn't answer.

We rode. Involuntarily, maybe because Eitan was sitting in back, I remembered drives we used to make, the two couples, going out together. Dovik driving, Dalia next to him, Eitan and I in the back. Dovik would say to him, "You don't know that in our moshava the men sit in the front and the women in back? The whole moshava will talk about this girly husband we brought."

Those were fun trips. Mostly to get ice cream at the junction or see a movie in the city. I remembered that once a young soldier hitchhiking on the main road came over at the traffic light and asked where we were going. Eitan said to him, "We're going to Alice to return the scarf she forgot at our place on Friday and then for coffee at a cousin of Dalia's. Does that work for you?" The poor soldier was so confused that Eitan had to get out of the car and usher him in. "Come, we were only kidding, we'll take you all the way home. We were also in the army once. Just get in and tell us where."

At the entrance to the wadi stood a van, and a constable and police inspector were getting out. I told them, "Yes, it's here, but we have to walk a bit into the wadi on this trail."

They looked at us suspiciously.

"I'm the sister of the man who called you," I said, "and the dead man is our grandfather."

"And who are these?"

"These are my husband and sister-in-law. My brother informed us and we know the area and know exactly where he is, so come with us. Here, this is the trail."

The inspector asked, "You said this is your husband?"

"Yes."

"Then why are you talking instead of him?"

I told the inspector that my husband doesn't talk much. What could I tell him, about our disaster?

The inspector looked at him. "Where do you work?"

I said, "He works at our family's plant nursery."

The inspector shrugged his shoulders. "Okay, we'll discuss it later. Who's showing us the way, also you?"

"Yes."

He told the constable to stay on the road and when the forensics team arrived to show them the trail. And to me he said, "Lead the way. I'm right behind you."

We started walking. No one spoke. We heard only the heavy smoker's breathing of the inspector and the shoes on the stones.

After ten minutes he asked if it was far.

I said, "At this pace, another fifteen minutes."

He asked, "How do you know this trail? It's not marked."

I told him that in our childhood we would hike here a lot with our grandfather.

"The one who just died?"

"Yes."

"So what was Grandpa doing here alone?"

I wanted to throw up. Not only from the ache in my gut, which had so far succeeded in blocking my tears, but also because I can't stand it when someone calls someone else's family member "Grandpa" or "Abba" instead of "your grandfather" or "your father." What's going on? You're also his grandson all of a sudden? And how does he know that my grandpa was here alone? Maybe he wasn't here alone? Maybe there was someone else here? Maybe that someone saw something or even attacked him? The last thing we needed was a stupid investigator.

"Don't worry," said the inspector, who was apparently as intelligent as I feared. "We take all possibilities into consideration." And he asked, "And how did you know to come exactly here?"

"Because my brother told me on the phone that he found him beside the big carob, and I already told you that this is a place we went to a lot and we know the tree well."

And in my heart I felt how the words "wadi" and "carob tree" sum everything up, as if I knew that one day this would happen and he would die at his place, as befits men like him to die.

I walked first, the inspector behind me, followed by Dalia, with Eitan at the rear. After a few hundred meters Eitan suddenly went up the north slope of the wadi and walked there, parallel to us.

"What's he doing there? Tell him to come back and walk with us," said the inspector angrily.

"Eitan," I called, "come back, please. Walk with us."

He scurried down the slope toward us. He step seemed lighter to me, as if my first husband had suddenly popped out of him, but only slightly, for a brief moment. He didn't stumble or slip like Dalia and the inspector but neither did he have those old "Come my beloved" Song of Songs moves of his, skipping in the hills and valleys.

Too bad we didn't force him earlier to come out to places like this, I thought, without Grandpa Ze'ev having to die. Maybe we were afraid that whatever he would remember on the hike would be bad for him, and besides, he didn't ask, and anyway, who could talk to him? Only Grandpa told him what to do.

"Here," I said. "You can already see the carob, and the man over there is my brother, who called you."

I saw him pacing there restlessly, sitting on the throne and getting up and sitting down again. We got closer and then we saw Grandpa lying on the ground beside him. Dovik got up and said to the inspector, "Shalom. I called. My name is Dovik Tavori. I am his grandson."

The inspector looked at the body.

"How old was he?"

"Ninety-two," I said.

"And the eye patch, what is it?"

"It's an eye patch. What exactly is your question?"

"How long has he had it?"

"A very long time. Before anyone here was born."

"An eye patch with a flower? Why not black?"

"He loved flowers. I embroidered it for him."

The inspector bent down, looked again, said that the picture was pretty clear. "A very old man, blind in one eye, walks around here in the middle of nowhere. He must have stumbled, fallen, hit his head on a rock. Here, this rock, look. With all the blood, right under his head."

We all looked, and Eitan even got down on all fours and leaned his head to the ground and examined the rock from close up, like a dog sniffing something.

The inspector asked him what he was doing and he didn't answer. The inspector told him not to touch anything and added that elderly people also fall at home, a safe and familiar place, on a level floor, so why wouldn't they fall on some godforsaken goat trail with stones and rocks and uphills and downhills?

"How could you have let him go around like that?" he wondered aloud, so we would understand that a family that allows a man that old to hike alone in some obstacle-course wadi—that's what he called Grandpa Ze'ev's wadi in a burst of eloquence—is an irresponsible family, as he declared.

"A person of this age is like a child," he announced, "like a baby. And if it had actually been a child, I would arrest you right now for negligence."

I felt my anger rising but decided to keep quiet for the moment. Fortunately Eitan had kept his distance, looking around among the rocks, not hearing any of it. But Dovik blew up. He didn't tell the inspector that we had a child who died on a hike but said that this was not the time to give us a lesson in the care and feeding of old people, and if he thought we had broken the law, he was welcome to arrest us but without sermonizing.

"And I ask that you remember that apart from your investigations we are in mourning now," said Dalia.

The inspector said, "I understand your pain, but I have a job to do and I am doing it and you are not allowed to be disrespectful to a police officer. It's against the law."

"Fine," said Dalia.

"And what's he doing?" The inspector pointed at Eitan, who bent over and examined something near the tree trunk. "Get away from there, sir, you hear? You're contaminating the scene." And again he grew suspicious and added: "So I gather you know this place, that you were all here in the past."

Dovik said, "We were here many times, several times a year, over many years. This is a place where our grandpa loved to hike and collect seeds of flowers and he knew the place like the palm of his hand. We even called this wadi Grandpa's Wadi and this carob his carob."

And I said, "I already told you. He took us here from the time we were little children."

Dalia said her "how symbolic" thing, and because stupidity is a slightly contagious disease, Dovik, whose prolonged proximity to her had made him even dumber than he actually was, said, "You're right. And maybe this was the symbolism with which Grandpa wanted to die."

"What's symbolic here?" asked the police inspector.

"So maybe not symbolic," she said, "but definitely the closing of a circle, no?"

I suddenly felt that I was there alone, with Grandpa's body and his big carob tree, and that one minute I saw everything from above, myself included, and the next minute I saw it from ground level. I was a bird in the sky and an ant on the ground. I shed a tear, but didn't cry. Nobody cried. We weren't brought up to cry, especially not in front of strangers.

"Here come the *mazap* guys," said the inspector, as if we were friends of those guys and supposed to know that the acronym *mazap* means "forensics unit."

The cop who had waited by the road arrived with two men in civilian clothes, who opened a small suitcase and began taking photographs and examining things the way they do in movies. The inspector put on gloves that they gave him, took Grandpa's wallet from his pants pocket, examined it.

"There's three hundred fifty shekels here," he said. "Is that a normal amount in his wallet?"

"A reasonable amount," said Dovik.

The inspector fished into Grandpa's shirt pocket and removed a small pouch that we knew well.

"And this?"

"That is his hearing aid," I said.

"He didn't keep it in his ear when he walked?"

"Not always," I said. "Even at home he didn't always use it."

"Did you look in his pack?" he asked Dovik.

"I didn't touch anything."

The inspector opened the pack. "There's wine in here," he said, with an odd look.

"He always drank red wine with his lunch," I said.

"It's even healthy," said Dalia, "one glass a day."

"Wine in the middle of the day?" grumbled the inspector. "No wonder he fell afterward on the rocks. Believe me that it's only because of protocol that I don't tell these guys to pack their stuff and go. We have plenty of other cases to investigate."

The forensics people worked for a solid hour, looking among the rocks, and finally said it was okay to "turn it over."

" 'Turn it over' means to the pathology lab," said the inspector. "Now is the time to tell us if you object to an autopsy."

"We don't," I said.

With my extra brain I wondered, What else would the pathologist discover in this dead body? What other secrets?

"Where's your husband?" asked the inspector. "Where'd he disappear to?"

"He went down to the wadi," Dovik said.

"What's he doing there?"

"He went down there to take a piss," Dovik said.

I was thinking how similar and how different this was from my trip to the desert with Dovik to see the place where the snake and Neta met: acacia there and carob here, yellow there and green here, there a son and here a grandfather, there a snakebite and here who knows what, maybe in fact a fall. And rocks here and there, the one Grandpa fell on, the one that Eitan used to smash the head of the snake.

"I don't see him," said the inspector.

"Maybe he went into the cave," I told him. "There's a cave there we call the Cave of the Prehistoric Man."

The inspector briskly walked down to the wadi, entered the cave, looked around. "He's not here," he announced. "But some goat fell in here. Lying dead on the rocks inside."

Dovik went over too. "Poor thing," he said. "Probably wanted to drink from the cistern. There are herds in the area. Good thing it happened recently, or it would really stink."

Eitan suddenly surfaced from another point in the wadi. His heavy steps had grown lighter, as if his legs remembered an old forgotten dance. I could tell that something was happening at that very moment. In general, when you go for a hike with people, you quickly see who is accustomed to walking and who isn't. Those who aren't are always looking at the ground, checking where they plant their foot and walking too closely to others. And there are those like my first husband, who live in harmony with the trail and the rock and the earth and can walk at night as if they had eyes in their toes.

He approached the inspector and asked, "You'll also be sending a tracker?"

"So you do talk? Very nice."

"You'll also be sending a tracker?" Eitan asked again.

"Why a tracker?"

"Because you also need someone who knows how to read the ground."

"You're teaching us how to do our job?"

"Perish the thought," said Eitan, and he turned to me and said, "I'm going back to the road."

I was stunned, and Dovik told the police inspector that at this stage we had no more questions, and if he didn't either, we would like to leave because we had to arrange the funeral and the shiva.

The inspector ordered the constable to wait by the body for the ambulance crew, and I hurried after Eitan because I started to worry: where was he rushing and what would stop him and where, because his body was still the thick sturdy body of my second husband, but his walking had become that of my first husband. Twelve years from the time Neta died, twelve years that he didn't leave the nursery, and only walked along its paved paths with fifty kilos on his back, and now he was walking like then, on our hikes, with Neta on him.

The inspector went with the forensics people, who spoke with him in hushed tones, and then he joined us and expressed sorrow about the accident and even apologized for a few things he had said before.

"You realize," he said, "that until the professionals say it's an accident and not murder, everyone is a suspect, including, and sometimes especially, family members. But here it's clear as day what happened."

I told him that was okay and he explained how and when we would receive the body after the autopsy for burial.

When we got to the main road we found Eitan waiting by the car. We said goodbye to the inspector and headed home. After we drove off, Dovik asked Eitan what he was looking for and if he found something, and to our great surprise Eitan gave him an answer. Though all he said was "nothing," any answer in his case was quite an accomplishment.

Dizzy with our success, I asked him again what he was looking for, and this was apparently a special day, because Eitan the chatterbox answered my question too, in the very same way.

I gasped. I felt that my name, Ruta, was poised to be spoken at the end of the answer: Nothing, Ruta. But he did not speak my name.

We understood not to expect further benevolence from him and moved on to other, more urgent topics. We phoned various relatives and people at the regional council, and when we got home there was already a voicemail message: the daughter-in-law of the deceased, in other words Dovik's and my mother, said not to wait on her for the funeral, she would try to get to the shiva.

"She won't come," said Dovik.

"Has she no shame?" Dalia said. "Then again, since when is anyone in your family ever ashamed?"

Dovik remarked, "It's okay. We haven't yet reached the level of your mother at our wedding, so we have something to strive for," and all distraught he went to his office at the nursery, to make more phone calls.

Dalia and I began talking about the refreshments we would serve the guests at the shiva, which she formally referred to as "collation for the consolers," because collation is more respectable than mere refreshments, and the similarity of "collation" and "consolation" well suited her sense of symbolism.

I said that in my opinion some crackers and pretzels and cut-up vegetables and cookies and soft drinks would do just fine, and we'd also have hot water and paper cups for coffee and tea. But she said that a shiva was indeed a shiva and not, God forbid, a party, but many people were expected and this was also a family and social occasion. That's how she put it, "a family and social occasion," and also, listen to this, Varda, here's a perfect Dalia-ism you can feel free to use: "Paper cups are fitting for a shiva, so we should remember that life is also a onetime thing." And she also said it wouldn't hurt for Eitan to cook up something in his *poikehs*.

"Where is he, anyway? Where did he disappear to again?" she wondered.

"Twelve years have passed," I said. "Not only Eitan, but his *poikehs* too have probably forgotten how to cook."

But Dalia didn't think that was funny. "Where is he, anyway?" she asked again.

I didn't answer. I sat down with Ecclesiastes to write something for the funeral, and the next day at dusk we buried Grandpa Ze'ev beside Grandma Ruth, woman of valor, wife, and mother, as the headstone said. Many people came. But later on a small group remained, closer friends and various distant cousins, old-timers from the Galilee, who spoke about Grandpa and told stories about the moshava, and Dovik, who was a little drunk, suddenly said, "Watch out for Ruta, she's been writing stories lately and she might be writing about you or steal your ideas." And Eitan smiled suddenly and said, "Why don't you read us something, Ruta?" And I was astounded: He also speaks like he once did, with a style and tone reminiscent of my first husband.

I brought my notebook and read them the story I wrote for Neta about the prehistoric man, and they got all enthusiastic and said, "You have to publish this!" And then I also read them, with small changes, a story about some young man from the moshava whose father took him to a whorehouse, and Eitan spoke again, as if relishing an ability that had been restored to him, and said, "Ruta, you have to keep writing."

THIRTY-TWO

....

THE PROOF

1

Ze'ev Tavori did not stalk his wife. He did not investigate or probe. And when the truth was revealed to him, it was revealed without his intention. He just happened by chance upon his wife and her lover, but chance need not affect the quality of proof. He went into the woods to inspect a dead oak tree and determine its suitability for firewood. After he completed his examination he heard a loud screeching of jaybirds, the screeching with which the jays alert one another to a gathering or celebration or riot. His curiosity aroused, he went deeper into the woods, and after walking two hundred meters or so, he heard human voices, a man and a woman.

He crept up silently and saw a couple making love on a blanket they had spread on the grass. The man lay on his back and the woman—from where he stood, he saw her from the back—on top, her thighs straddling his grinding hips, her loins fastened to his, her nape concealing his face. But Ze'ev recognized the blanket at once, for this was the embroidered blanket his mother had sent him in the wagon, and also the man's boots nearby, the boots from Istanbul, unique in the moshava. They stood beside the blanket waiting patiently like a pair of servants who see nothing but know everything.

Ze'ev was surprised not only by what he saw but by his reaction—

namely, the lack thereof. Precisely because he was so bold and violent
and strong, so quick to wave a fist and wield a club, he couldn't understand how he of all people was flooded by a frightening weakness. He
stepped back a bit, stood for a moment behind a tree, and then began
to tiptoe stealthily in a wide circle, to see if this was indeed his wife.
The moment he saw the profile of her face and could no longer protect himself with uncertainty or doubt, Ruth leaned forward, buried
her face in Nahum's neck, and embraced him, and when she sat up to
take a breath he extended a gentle hand and fondled her breast with
love, a love that had grown over time and created its own language and
world.

The scene shook Ze'ev to the depths of his soul, but it was also beautiful and fascinating, because the two looked like a woman and child
playing in a field, she, his tall wife, with her broad hips and shoulders,
and her belly that was already a bit swollen, and he, Nahum Natan, his
neighbor and friend, with his thin arms, smooth skin, a body without
blemish. A body that had not endured a life of manual labor, had not
grown rough or scarred, had neither dealt blows nor absorbed them.

At that moment something even more terrible happened. Ruth
turned toward him, toward Ze'ev, and seemed to be staring at him. A
few seconds went by until he realized that she had not noticed him and
was only looking in his direction, but before those seconds had elapsed
he was certain she saw him and knew that he saw her, and his body
froze with dread. He of all people, who had performed hard work since
childhood and had given and gotten beatings and knew how to kick a
wild dog and seize the neck of a burglar and slap the cheek of someone
who dared insult his pride, did not know what to do now. His bones and
muscles, pleading for a command, could not comprehend the weakness
of his spirit, whose strength was depleted like water from a cracked barrel. He closed his eyes, shuttered the awful sight inside them, hoping
it would not migrate into his memory, from which it could never be
uprooted.

He stood still for a moment, and then Ruth turned back to Nahum,
and Ze'ev managed to get away from the scene. His legs carried him
a fair distance, but before the trees concealed the pair he turned his
head back and gave them another look. He was shocked to realize that

the image unexpectedly gave rise to feelings of love and longing for his wife, whom he had never seen in this way, and Nahum's body, strangely enough, also aroused a tender stirring he had never felt before, and this angered him so much that he realized he had been mistaken: that he had suspected the two of them for a while, that his peaceful nights had been sleepless, that his dreams were not dreams, that for months he had been agonizing in his bed and seeing exactly these images, not in his heart or his mind or his churning gut or clenching fingers, but inside his eyeballs, whose frazzled nerves had plastered pictures on his retina that came not from without but from within. Pictures that returned again and again until they were projected outward and became real.

He picked up his pace. His heart was hard and pounding and his body so limp that he almost floated over the stones and almost plunged into the potholes. He remembered what his father had told him through-out his childhood and youth and told him on his wedding night, when he went out and saw him sitting in the yard, smoking his pipe and drink-ing schnapps: A man who lets others trespass on his territory, a man on whose mare other men ride without asking permission, and whose weapons they play with and touch, a man whose family members start to eat before he does, about whom people speak behind his back, whom strangers treat as if they were his friends—a man like that must fight back and lay down rules and facts. All the more so a man whose wife sleeps with another man. He must take revenge, teach a lesson, inflict pain, punish. But not now, he said to himself. Not at this moment. First his strength would return and grow.

2

In the fall of 1930, the year when two farmers here committed suicide, Ze'ev went to the cabin that housed our first synagogue, to celebrate the holiday of Simhat Torah. He saw Nahum Natan dancing vigorously and entertaining everyone with traditional Sephardic melodies, stamping his feet in his Turkish boots, and could not contain his mood.

He escaped from the synagogue and when he got home headed directly to the toolshed in the yard, took out a large saw, and went into the house. Ruth left the women's section as she saw him exit. She rushed home from the synagogue, arriving a few seconds before him, and began fussing with something in the kitchen. She saw him enter and head for the bedroom and she was afraid. His demeanor and step, and the saw in his hand, prompted her to hurry after him.

Ze'ev pulled off the two mattresses that lay upon their bed, the double bed in which were joined the two beds, hers and his, from their parents' homes. He leaned his left knee on it, inserted the sharp blade of the saw into the crack between the halves, and with gritted teeth and several precise and powerful strokes, he severed the first connective plank. He quickly slid the saw along the crack to the next plank and sawed that one too.

"What are you doing? What are you doing, Ze'ev?"

"What should have been done already on that night."

With a few more strokes he sawed the third board and separated the beds one from the other. He pushed one half against the wall and threw one mattress on it; the other half and other mattress he picked up in his arms and carried outside, shoving and overturning chairs, tripping and knocking things down from shelves and tables, tearing a picture from a wall and a curtain from its window.

He went into the yard, straight to the shed, set down the bed and its mattress, returned to the house, put his face close to hers, and whispered: "From now on I will sleep in the shed! Not with you."

"Why, Ze'ev, why?"

"You know why, and so do I."

And so it was. Every evening he went into the shed after dark and returned to the house before sunrise, so no one would know. But he knew, and Ruth knew, and also Nahum Natan, who sneaked and eavesdropped and peeked—he knew. He knew and understood that he too had to act, before something terrible happened.

Ten days later, on the night of the first rain of that year, he peeked from the window of his house, waited till the oil lamp in Ze'ev's shed went out, crept into their yard, stepped between the puddles and the rivulets that the rain had already carved in the ground, and knocked on the shutter of Ruth's window. She opened the door and he took one step inside, stood in the entrance, and tried to persuade her to leave her husband and marry him and give birth to their child.

Ruth replied that she could not do that. "He'll murder us both," she said.

"We won't stay here," suggested Nahum, "we'll run away."

"He will pursue and catch us and kill me and you," said Ruth. "You don't know him and his family. They are not the kind of people we have here, certainly not people like you."

"The seaport is not far," said Nahum, "and there we'll get on a ship. We'll go to my father. Istanbul is a beautiful city."

But Ruth again refused.

"Then what shall we do?" he asked. "In a few months the baby will be born."

"I don't know. He will probably kill me, and you might have to run away with the baby girl."

"Girl?" asked Nahum. His heart filled with tenderness and love. "How do you know it's a girl?"

"It's a girl," said Ruth. "A girl who is better than her mother."

He again tried to convince her, but his wish was unfulfilled. Finally he despaired and left. He stood a few minutes in the rain, trying to decide whether to knock again on her window and implore her till she understood and gave in, but then the light in the house went out, the rain grew stronger, and a storm drew near from the sea, with thunder and lightning.

He decided to return to his house, wondering what his father would say if he suddenly appeared in Istanbul with the pregnant Ruth. A son who slept with a married woman? Pregnant with a bastard child? Could he ask him for help?

As he passed the fence a large figure appeared before him. It emerged from the blackness and rain with a rifle in its hand.

"What were you doing in my house?" asked Ze'ev.

"I spoke with Ruth," said Nahum, quivering.

"About what?"

"About us," said Nahum. "About the two of us. I asked her to leave you and marry me."

"No one leaves me," said Ze'ev.

"It would be better for you too," said Nahum. "You'll get another

wife. A woman who will love you, and you won't have to sleep alone in
the shed."

"You're telling me who to sleep with?" snarled Ze'ev with suppressed rage. "You're telling me what's good for me?"

He pointed the rifle barrel at him. Nahum shouted "No!" and again
shouted "No!" and then noticed the light of an oil lamp coming toward
them from the adjacent yard and cried, "Help, he's going to kill me!"

Ze'ev punched him with his fist. He sank to the ground unconscious
and Ze'ev leaned over and fired one bullet into his mouth. Ruth, inside
the house, did not hear a thing. The thunder and lightning that shattered the darkness, the sheets of rain and tearful wailing and the gunshot,
blended into a single noise. Although the murder took place beside her
house—and the victim was her lover and his killer her husband—she
was the last to know about it.

Even at dawn, as the rumor traveled from house to house, and the
terrified residents arose and congregated where the body had lain, and
cows left in midmilking began to loudly moo—she was asleep in her
bed. She was always a good sleeper and her plight deepened her sleep.
The running around and shouting of people who had been summoned
to the scene did not wake her. She got up on her own, and when she
woke she saw the gray wintry light outside, and because a hard rain was
drumming on the roof she decided to do some cooking and wait till later
to do the yard work.

Only after a few minutes did she sense the bustle near her house,
the unusual traffic of people, the agitated whispers that broke into syllables and recombined into words, and when she went out, she also
saw the British policeman arriving in his black automobile, and before
she understood what she saw, a wave of nausea rose from her belly
and gagged her. Before she could rush back inside she vomited on the
ground and realized this was not just the nausea of a pregnant woman.

She rinsed her face and mouth and walked hesitantly to the crowd.
She was surprised by the slowness of her steps, by the fear apparent in
them. What am I afraid of? she wondered. What makes me so weak?

Her ears heard the people talking among themselves, the words
"unfortunate" and "broken" and "betrayal" and "revenge." They stared

at her, and she heard the words "because of her," and more whispering whose content was inaudible but whose overtones were obvious, and then everything became clear at once. She made up her mind to get away from there, to find someplace where she could scream with her hand clamped on her mouth. But then her husband appeared.

"Our neighbor has committed suicide," he whispered, his eyes hard and inquisitive, his body near to hers.

She was silent.

"You don't want to know which neighbor?"

"I know," she said.

"Very true," said Ze'ev. "He shot himself. One bullet in the mouth." Ruth was silent.

"With my rifle," added Ze'ev. "He stole it from me. Yitzhak Maslina saw what happened."

Ruth began to retreat and Ze'ev advanced, his steps driving her backward.

"With my rifle," he repeated quietly. "How could a man dare to touch the rifle of another man?"

His eyes continued to study her face, cold and alert as the eyes of a snake assessing the best time to strike. He continued: "How could a man dare to take what belongs to another man?" And whispered: "Cowardly dog. Perhaps you know why he did such a terrible thing?"

Her legs, stepping backward, failed her. She sensed the weight in her belly and the sour taste of vomit in her throat and knew that more disasters would befall her, even greater than the one that had just occurred.

"Get in the house," said Ze'ev. "People are watching. Now they're still talking in whispers, but soon they'll be talking out loud."

She withdrew into the house. Ze'ev escorted her with his gaze and then returned to the crowd. Some of them theorized new theories and some talked more talk and some were gathered in worried silence, recognizing that this was not over.

With the remains of her strength Ruth walked up the three front stairs, and at the moment she entered the house she began to wail, trying and failing to choke her screams, flinging herself on the bed, burying her face in the pillow, dearly wishing to fall asleep as deeply as she had last night, at the very moment her husband shot her lover.

Too many things became clear in such a short time: she got pregnant, the man who got her pregnant died, he did not kill himself but was murdered, and the murderer was her husband. She stood up, began walking aimlessly in the house, wondering, asking and answering, and predicting the worst. What would be her fate? And the fate of the fetus growing in her belly?

In the afternoon the British policeman got into his car and drove away. A few hours later Nahum Natan was buried at a ceremony attended by very few people, and several days later the head of the committee was summoned to the police station, where he was informed that the investigation had confirmed the fact of suicide. Ruth, confused and crazed with fear, realized she had to flee, to save her life and that of her unborn daughter. Several days later she packed a small bag, hid it, and waited for a window of opportunity, the hour of escape.

3

On that day, at 5:30 in the morning, Ze'ev came out of the shed, put on his boots, walked across the yard, took off the boots, and went into the house. He fixed himself a glass of sweet tea and two thick slices of bread with salty cheese. He drank and ate, put his boots back on, and went out to the field. A few minutes later Ruth also came outside, the bag over her shoulder and the baby in her womb, and hurried to the vineyard. She ran hunched over between the vines, crossed the muddy stream in the wadi, climbed its opposite bank on all fours, and disappeared into the oak forest.

Half an hour after she set out, she heard Ze'ev's shouts drawing closer and closer, and the sound of hoofbeats, stamping on solid ground or splashing in mud. Fear stricken, she tried to hide behind a bush. She lay there, her face pressed to the ground, feeling her belly tighten beneath her, trembling all over. The pounding of the hoofbeats grew nearer and stronger from second to second.

Her hand, as if acting on its own, groped around. Her fingers found a fallen branch and seized it, trying to summon strength and confidence. Her forehead rested on her arm. She noticed a small black beetle inching among the blades of glass, so near it was blurry. She followed it with her eyes. Sister of mine, she thought, what are you doing outdoors? Spring has not yet come.

She heard the horse approach, the voice of Ze'ev ordering it to halt, and his feet landing on the ground, walking three steps, stopping beside her.

He leaned over and said, "Get up."

She didn't move.

"Get up and come home."

She didn't budge.

"Nobody leaves me. Get up and come home, or I will kill you too."

She didn't answer. Floating on high she saw the forest where she lay. They alone were there, she, Ze'ev, and the horse, who lowered his head and munched some grass. Her body filled with silence. Lines and points of light danced behind her eyelids. His hand grabbed the back of her neck. She held the branch tighter, suddenly wheeled back, opened her eyes, and whipped him with all her might.

THIRTY-THREE

....

A few days ago you told me about the camera that Dovik brought back from the desert. What happened to it?

Good, Varda, you already know and use our names. Pretty soon we'll add you to the family.

You also said that Dovik said there was film in it.

Correct.

So what did you do with it?

At first, nothing. It sat in my house for four years, and I didn't have the nerve to touch it, then suddenly I felt brave and gave it to Ofer to develop the film inside.

Ofer? Who is that?

Ofer, I told you about him. My student. The one who almost drowned on me in the Sea of Galilee. The one who took pictures and made an exhibit about the moshava. Here's that picture of our house that he took from the air, as I already explained to you.

Correct. The student you loved. I remember now. So you simply asked him to develop the film without your knowing what's on it?

More or less. It was at a parents' meeting. He came with his father, that moron Haim Maslina. I remember telling him, "Good for you, you're the only father who came with a child, in general only the mothers come."

"It's because of you, Ruta." He grinned. Those very words, without shame, and Ofer was mortified. "If it were another teacher I wouldn't have come."

Whatever. I restrained myself, got down to business, told him that his son Ofer was a smart boy and a good student, not always one hundred percent plugged in to what went on in the classroom, but who stood out for his understanding and originality, just barely resisting the impulse to add that as such he also stood out in his family.

Ofer said, "Thank you, Teacher Ruta. It's nice of you to say this in front of my father, because he doesn't think of me that way."

You want to thank me? Take off your clothes! I turned deep inside into an animal, and the proud father smiled and said, "That's not so. Ofer is absolutely okay at home too, helping out and working, and he also has a hobby."

He turned to his son. "Tell her."

"Drop it, Dad."

"Tell, tell her," he insisted. "Tell her about your hobby."

"No need, Dad. It has nothing to do with school."

"Ofer has set up a darkroom," announced Haim. "He develops and prints and spends the whole day there."

"Now you do this?" I asked. "With everybody going to digital?"

Ofer beamed with excitement. "We have a ton of old film and negatives that my father's grandfather left us, and I've already developed a few and printed a few. And my mother convinced my father to give me the old shed as a darkroom and money to buy all the chemicals and paper and trays and enlarger. And I cleared out all the junk from the shed, and look what I found there, Teacher Ruta"—and he stretched out his legs—"you ever seen boots like these? Nice, right?"

"Very nice," I said, "but kind of old, no?"

"I like them. All I had to do was clean and oil them, just that one stain refused to come out."

"I told him," said Haim. "It's a bloodstain."

"My father says they belonged to his grandfather," continued Ofer, "but later on, when I printed the old negatives"—he turned to his father—"I saw them on the feet of someone else in one of the pictures."

He took a photo from his shirt pocket. "You see these three guys?

This is Grandpa Yitzhak, my father's grandpa, on the right. And on the left is Ze'ev Tavori, your grandpa, still with two eyes, you see? And here, the boots I'm wearing. On the feet of the third guy, the short one standing between them. I brought this picture so you could help me. Maybe you know who that guy is?"

"No," I said, my blood turning cold and thick in my veins. "Why don't you ask your father?"

"He asked, but I don't know," said Haim.

"Could you ask your grandfather?" asked Ofer.

"Leave me the picture and I'll ask him."

I showed the picture to Grandpa Ze'ev.

"You look a little strange with two eyes," I told him.

He didn't react. He looked at the photo for a long time and didn't say a word.

"I recognize you and Yitzhak Maslina, but who's this?" I asked, indicating the short guy in the boots.

He asked where I got this photo, and when I said my "whatever," he said, "I bet those Maslina bastards gave it to you. Where else could it come from?"

"So who is this guy?" I asked again.

Grandpa Ze'ev was silent. He didn't like talking too much about certain events and certain periods.

"So who is it?" I asked again.

"He was a neighbor of ours in the first years here."

"And what happened to him?"

"He committed suicide, we had three suicides in one year. It was very bad."

"I know the suicide version, Grandpa," I said.

"If you know, why are you asking questions?"

"What was his name?"

"Who?"

"The guy who committed suicide. The one in the middle. Stop pretending."

"Nahum. Nahum Natan or Natan Nahum, I don't remember."

"So how did his boots get to my student Ofer, the great-grandson of Yitzhak Maslina?"

Grandpa Ze'ev stood up. "I'm in charge of shoes? There was a British policeman here and he also determined it was suicide."

I told Ofer that he was wearing the boots of someone named Nahum Natan who committed suicide many years ago, and I said I now had a request of him.

"Whatever you want, Teacher Ruta."

"If among your negatives you find other pictures of my family, I would like copies, especially if there's something with my grandmother Ruth."

"Okay."

And then I decided.

"And another small thing," I said. "I have an old camera at home that nobody uses, but it might have film inside. Could you take it out and develop it for me?"

"Sure. I can try."

"I'll pay you."

"Forget it." He smiled. "We'll make a trade, Teacher Ruta."

My cheeks burned. I felt I was blushing.

"You said no one uses that old camera anymore. So let me have it."

"It's yours. No problem."

"So we have a deal?"

"I have one more condition," I said. "I want to be with you in the darkroom when you do it. I want to watch."

"Totally okay. Saturday?"

On Saturday, when I went to their house with the camera in hand, there were two cars parked across the street, of the type we call city-people cars. Miri and Haim sat under their pecan tree with two couples eating pecans, which is what visitors here are generally served. "Eat, eat, they're from our tree," which in our language means: Eat, eat as many as humanly possible, because these pecans are coming out of our ears, but we don't want to throw them out.

Incidentally, Varda, as an expert on the history of the Yishuv you ought to know that this is why we came to the Land of Israel and drained the swamps, fought battles, plowed, built, and established—so that at the end of the day the Jewish people would sit, everyone under his vine and fig tree, and eat pecans.

I somehow get the feeling you're trying to make fun of me, Ruta, but continue, it's completely fine.

I entered the Maslinas' yard with Eitan's camera in my hand. Miri Maslina gave me a sour look, but Haim Maslina stood up with that unctuous family smile dripping from his lips: "What did we do to deserve such a guest?" Saying to the visitors, "This is Ruth Tavori, Ofer's teacher. She lives next door but never comes to visit the neighbors. Just look at her. In all the schools of Tel Aviv there's no teacher like this."

And he yelled out, "Ofer, come quick! You have an important visitor!"

Ofer came out of their old shed, a wise and good-natured boy, who will never forget my crazy outburst of a few minutes later. It didn't happen at the very start, when I went with him into the shed, and not when he turned on the red light and opened the camera and carefully removed the film, nor when he developed it, but only afterward, when he inserted the photo paper into the chemicals and it was covered in blotches that became rocks and stones and acacia trees and a white wadi and a solid little six-year-old boy with a serious expression. Here you are. Neta. Where were you these last four years? Where were you? Where did you go?

He looked at me from the deep and I—champion diver, not just four minutes but four years underwater now—did not pull him out.

My knees buckled. I felt almost like that evening when Dovik came and told me, "Ruta, I have something really terrible to tell you." I was so weak I had to lean on someone, and that's what I did. I leaned on the closest person beside me. I grabbed him tight. Held on like I was drowning. Not like a life preserver or crutch, but as a living creature, warm, breathing, flowing with strength and blood.

I held on to him, this sweet embarrassed boy, hugged him, and started to shout and scream. My screams came not from my throat but from my innards, my guts, my womb. I shouted, I cried, and I hugged and kissed him and screamed again and again. Terrible, it was terrible. A student should not see and hear a teacher in such a state. A child should not see and hear an adult in such a state. A person should not see and hear another person in such a state. Believe me, Varda, the whole thing took no more than ten seconds. The blink of an eye for a historian like you, but ten seconds can be very long, and I cried and screamed everything I didn't cry and scream for the four years that Neta was inside the camera, because in general I'm not much of a crier, not at all. For ten seconds I shouted and cried and hugged him and then I let go of him and I fell silent and found the door and escaped. I didn't go out into the street, I ran from their yard straight into ours.

I remember: I ran like a madwoman. The light and the tears blinded my eyes, but I could see. Miri and Haim Maslina still sat by the garden table with their city guests and pecans, their faces shocked and scared. My screams had preceded me. Left the shed before I did, hard not to hear.

I said and explained nothing. I ran. Those poor guests surely had no idea what had happened. Guests from the city always think that in the moshava, with what my first husband used to call its chirping flowers and flowering birds, the local people are happy and serene, with garden tables, garden chairs, the garden itself, mown grass, visitors, pecans, crackers, and a ball of cheese. You remember that ritual, serving a ball of cheese? Here in our moshava we still do it. If there's one thing worse than pecans, it's a ball of cheese, and even worse are several cheese balls—one pepper and one garlic and one paprika and one, the worst, basil. Casus belli, Varda, this means war.

The next day Haim came, like a slimy snake, holding a brown envelope.

"We were pleased that Ofer helped you with the pictures," he whispered.

"I'm sorry," I said.

"No harm done. These things happen," he said.

"I must have embarrassed you in front of your guests from the city."

"We were a bit surprised by your screaming, even frightened, but afterward, when we saw that the pictures were of Neta, we understood. We phoned and explained to our friends, who, by the way, got up and left a few minutes later."

"What did you explain?"

"That Ofer's teacher had a child, and the tragedy that happened, and that Ofer developed his pictures. The truth, Ruta."

He handed me the envelope. "Here they are, Ofer printed them for you. And here are the negatives too. All yours, we kept nothing. And Ofer is sorry too and asked to tell you that he apologizes and will give you back the camera you gave him. Something in it needs fixing and it should be cleaned inside. He'll do all that and give it back. And we apologize if for a moment we had the wrong idea."

"Why give it back? Apologize for what?" I said. "He has no reason to apologize. I need to. And the camera is his, I promised it to him. He helped me and I apologize for what happened."

But Haim did not give in. There's a point in the life of every shithead when he realizes that's what he is, and decides to act that way.

"When we heard your screams from his lab, we didn't know what to think," he said, "but Ofer explained it to us later, and we understood, so from our point of view everything is all right now, really, it's all right, Ruta."

I didn't answer him, and he, uninvited to do so, suddenly sat down.

"Ruta," he said, "our two families go back a long way. Neighbors in good and bad times for seventy, eighty years. I know all kinds of stories and you know all kinds of stories, and they aren't necessarily the same exactly, but I was simply shocked that maybe God forbid another terrible story was beginning here."

I didn't understand what he was getting at. "I'm telling you again," I said, "that I'm sorry for what happened. And the truth is, I knew that maybe I would see Neta in those pictures, and I prepared myself. Four years that camera waited in my house with the film inside. I didn't dare throw it away and didn't dare touch it. It was like another grave of his, you understand? How can you open the grave of a son? He's inside of it. But at the parent meeting, when you told me Ofer has this hobby and a darkroom, I decided to ask him to open it. And then, when I saw Neta's face emerging on the paper, an illusion of lifelike movement, of return—for a moment he's alive and then dies again, becomes a picture. And because it was happening in water, and in the dark, it was like the netherworld. I lost it."

"But Ofer said you hugged him, you kissed him."

"Haim, really. It's not the way it sounds. I had to lean on someone, and Ofer was the only person there with me. I needed sturdy support, I needed closeness."

"Too bad it wasn't me standing there." He chuckled.

I didn't understand. Apparently I didn't want to.

"I know it's not okay," I said. "I know I'm his teacher and he's my student, I'm a grown woman and he's a youngster, but believe me, it was nothing. I hugged him, it's true, the way a drowning person hugs the one who saves him."

"Funny you should mention drowning and saving, like on that class trip you took to the Sea of Galilee."

My body tensed at once. I felt myself getting angry. "What are you saying, Haim, where are you going with this?"

"Not going anywhere. You think I'm going somewhere? I'm only asking. This is my son, I'm not allowed to ask?"

"What are you saying, I shouldn't have saved him then?"

"No, no," he said, backing off, "we already thanked you for that, but parents talked, and other teachers too, the whole thing was strange from the beginning, the underwater swimming contest you organized, and the bet."

"Yes," I said, "very strange. That contest, and that bet, and Teacher Ruta in general, if you ask me, a strange woman, very strange. And now, if you'll excuse me, I have exams to correct, including your son's. Please convey my thanks for the pictures and tell him that the camera I promised him will remain his. And if he has any further questions about old pictures he finds, my grandfather will be glad to help him. I spoke with him."

But Ofer's father gave no sign of leaving. He even leaned back and got comfortable in his chair.

"How do you hold up?" he asked. "In such a situation?"

"What situation?" I stiffened.

"The situation that Eitan piles up sacks and rocks all day at the nursery, and at night walks around on guard duty, so you have no husband, in effect. A beautiful girl like you, we're the same age and you look so good, and all these years without a man, or so it seems."

"I think, Haim, you're getting into topics outside your field," I said.

"Look," he said, "this is a small place, and people see things and say things and hear rumors."

"You can talk with whomever you like. This conversation with me is over."

"If you feel lonely, that's no disgrace. Just give me a sign. I'm very near, over the fence, you know."

"Listen," I told him, "you know what happened in the past with my grandfather and your grandfather."

"Of course," he said, "who in the old families doesn't know?"

"My grandfather," I said, "was once a violent man, cruel, primitive. He became a human being only after he brought me and Dovik here. We were his tikkun, his correction, atonement, metamorphosis, if your limited mind can understand what I'm talking about. But your grandfather was a louse and remained one till his dying day. A worthless coward. You and I both know the truth, how the boots of Nahum Natan ended up on the feet of your son, and that your wonderful dairy began with the cow that Yitzhak Maslina got from Ze'ev Tavori in return for his false testimony."

"Why do you talk like that?" he said. "And why are you putting the blame on the men? Everyone knows what your grandmother did, and she deserved what she got. My grandfather told me that. Ruth Tavori earned what she got."

"Your grandfather was and remains a worm," I said, "and I now see that his traits are hereditary."

Silence. Sometimes I can be scary.

"And watch out," I added, "because traits are also handed down in our family from generation to generation, and my grandfather's Mauser is still in the house, and he's still here too, and I can call him. One shout and he'll come."

He was dumbfounded. "You're threatening me?"

"I'm saying that just as you resemble your grandfather, I can resemble mine. And apropos genetics," I went on, "I don't understand how a good-for-nothing like you could produce such a successful boy as Ofer. And I say this not merely as your neighbor but as his teacher. How do you explain it, Haim? Maybe in your family too women get pregnant by some neighbor? You know how it is here. It's a small place, and people see things and say things and hear rumors."

He stood up, his brow darkly furrowed, his lower lip protruding. He looked at me and said, "You'll be hearing from me," and left.

For a moment it seemed that his grandfather had come back to life. Hunched and gaunt, walking like a mongoose. You ever drive on a back road and suddenly see a mongoose? Slinking, bent over, like it has no legs, like a snake, crossing the road and disappearing into the bushes? That's the way he walked.

THIRTY-FOUR

....

Ofer, Ofer, Ofer, Ofer. The time has come to talk about Ofer. I've already disbursed a few tidbits of information, dropped a few hints, come close, gotten cold feet and retreated, but that's it, there's no choice.

Ofer. The student I waited for, till he would grow up and be my lover after my first husband died and the second one didn't want me. He wasn't as good-looking or funny as Eitan or as masculine, but he did resemble him a bit, in some ways a lot, and worst of all, he resembled Neta too. Could it be? Anything can be. Ofer was only a few years older than Neta, but Eitan also used to visit here before he and I fell in love and got married. Do I know what he did and with whom during those years? Does anyone ever know everything about their partner? About their own children? About their father and mother? Miri Maslina was already here in those years, right on the other side of the fence, and who knows, Varda, maybe she also had her eye on Eitan at Dovik and Dalia's wedding?

You can stop here, Ruta. It's not connected to my research, and I'm not interested in knowing everything about you.

Don't worry. I won't make you an accomplice to a crime, because it wasn't a crime. I was a teacher and he was a student and I'm not stupid. I coveted him, I admit it. The tenth commandment is a law that no one can obey, including me, but my covetous musings were merely in princi-

ple, not in practice. And enough already, Varda, enough with that critical, judgmental look of yours. I was and remained a law-abiding teacher.
I coveted, I restrained myself, and I waited. For time to pass, for him to
finish high school and no longer be my student. And in the meantime
I developed and printed pictures in my head: how one day I would see
him in the dappled light of our street, which is the prettiest street in the
moshava, with the most character, with the biggest trees and memories,
and I would come out of the gate and take him like I already told you,
like a she-bear coming out of the woods and snatching a boy. I would've
preferred to take him the way Alice took Eitan from her daughter's wedding, but the she-bear fit me better.

Whatever. You go around this moshava interviewing people, so you
realize that people tell plenty of stories about me and my family, and
rightly so. But one thing I ask of you, Varda, that regardless of what
they tell you, you should know that from the first day I was with Eitan,
I was only his. I was the woman of one man, and had it not been for the
disaster I would have stayed only his. But this Eitan went away, disappeared, and my second husband appeared, who didn't speak to me or
sleep with me or make love with me. He sentenced me to the asceticism
he had imposed on himself. He wasn't the man I dreamed of; he wasn't
the one I married. I didn't owe him anything.

In short, Varda, after a few years in that situation I decided I deserved
to love and be loved a little. Not the "be mine" I once had, but a little skin
against skin and lips on lips and eyes locking and smiles exchanged, and
becoming one flesh. And also, how to put this politely, I really needed
it. I've heard there are women who can live a long time without it, but
I'm a bit of a man, as you already know, and I felt it in my whole body,
especially the point where pain and pleasure coincide. I have no doubt
that my grandmother, whose blood flows in my veins and for whom I
am named, felt exactly the same thing. She too was with another man
only after her husband didn't sleep with her. But with her it was different. With her it was that way from the beginning, and she waited much
less time than I waited, and she was a young and inexperienced girl
who wasn't careful, in every sense of the word, and you have no idea
what a mess it turned into. A classic episode of gender, nowhere in the
settlements of the Baron was there such a gendered episode. I've written

about it, but I won't tell you about it. Certainly not at this stage. At this stage you'll hear what I want to tell, and maybe later on I'll tell you what you want to hear.

So that was that. One day I decided it would happen, that I was permitted. Because whom was I betraying, really? If it was Eitan my first husband, he was no longer with us. And if it was my second husband Eitan, then the fact that he had sentenced himself to life imprisonment at hard labor and put his penis into retirement, excuse me, didn't mean I also had to take his vows of celibacy.

Whatever. Even after Ofer graduated I didn't initiate anything. I waited patiently. One day he would appear, maybe after he got out of the army or maybe while still in uniform, and walk in the shady light of our street until we were facing each other. I would charmingly ask, Ofer, where've you been? And he would answer with a smile, Hi, Teacher Ruta, here I am, I've come. And that's how it happened in the end, except for one detail, important though not really, that he did national service instead of the army.

I actually liked that, but in the moshava people were unanimously critical. I already told you that our moshava is proud of being known for providing industrial quantities of boys for all sorts of elite combat units, the air force pilots' course and various commandos, and every year the head of the regional council issues an announcement, and a photo of him with the new recruits appears in the newspaper, with some of their faces blurred for security reasons. It's like we already have boys in the tenth grade that nobody can recognize because their faces are full of pixels instead of acne.

Whatever. It was obvious to me that Ofer wouldn't become one of those fighters. I thought he might be a photographer in the air force or in the army spokesman's office, but he didn't do that either. Ofer decided he wanted to do national service instead of the army, the option usually offered to religious women. So get this: One of those army officers who go around to the schools to scout new blood for their units gave a lecture one day in my classroom. He talked on and on, in that army Hebrew that mangles proper pronunciation, and Ofer suddenly raised his hand and declared that working in a home for children in distress was much more important than serving in his commando unit.

Pandemonium. Several students started yelling at him, and the officer calmed them down, and then said to Ofer, "You're wrong." And Ofer replied, "It's not enough to say 'You're wrong.' Explain to me why, in your humble opinion, I'm wrong."

Not only the officer but also most of the students didn't catch the sarcasm, but I cracked up over that hysterical "in your humble opinion" line, and like with Eitan's "fortyward" thing I even chided myself: How come I hadn't thought of it first? In short, it became an issue, and one day, when his friends who were competing for acceptance to combat units sneered at him that army was army and national service was draft dodging—that's what they said: "For us you're like a draft dodger"—he just smiled at them and said, "It's not nice to talk that way to a religious girl."

I heard that and realized that his head was even more different than what I'd thought till then. I like heads that are different. I too have a different head; the first Eitan had a different head; my grandfather, for good and bad, especially bad, had a different head. Dovik and Dalia, by contrast, do not have a different head. Most people don't have a different head. They all have the same head, and they also lend it to one another when necessary.

And what finally happened?

What happened was that it happened. I'm smiling, right? That's because of that scene, which every time I think of it makes the corners of my mouth rise. I had just come back from visiting Neta in the cemetery, and I walked home and got to our street, and on the other side of the nursery fence I saw my second husband carrying his sacks and rocks from here to there and from there to here and I felt I'd had enough. I simply couldn't watch him that way anymore, couldn't go in there and tell him again about visiting the grave of our son and ask him when he would pardon himself already and when he would come too, and couldn't hear him be silent the way he was silent on previous occasions.

My eyes filled with tears. I feel it's happening to me now too. Look— a second ago I felt I was smiling and now I feel my eyes are damp. It's nice, the way the body reports to its owner on its condition: I'm cold, I'm hot, I'm hungry, I'm excited, I'm bored, I'm filled with passion, I'm sad, I'm tired. But I ordered myself to continue. Like a director in a play. I said to myself: Ruta passes the gate and keeps walking a bit farther. And like an obedient actress I kept going a bit farther, and then, by Haim and Miri's house, I saw Ofer coming toward me, walking on the sun-dappled sidewalk, his long hair in a ponytail, carrying a plump Labrador puppy that augured good things.

We began to smile at each other even at a distance. And when I smiled I felt one of the tears flow from my left eye and trickle to the side, into a wrinkle produced by the smile. In retrospect I think that's how I realized I was smiling, by the direction of the tears. Whatever. There's something wonderful in people's smiles, and two of those smiles are especially wonderful. One is a baby's first smile at a few weeks old, such a small investment—a tiny twist of the lips—which ropes its parents into permanent servitude: I love my son, my daughter, I will never be free. And the second is the smile of a man and woman walking toward each other as they had seen in her hope and his dream, in a street they know so well, where their steps are the only thing that's new. That's nice— "had seen in her hope and his dream," no?—I don't remember if that's a line I read somewhere or if I just made it up. Whatever. That's how the smiling ones walk. Toward each other, and at first each smiler feels only his own smile and then the smile of the other one too, and then they stop.

"Ofer, you disappeared on me. What's going on with you? What's with the puppy?"

"Hello, Teacher Ruta. Great to see you."

I liked that he called me Teacher Ruta; I told him so and he said, "Because that's who you are," and we chatted a bit. He told me about the children he took care of at a facility in Haifa and said, "You should know, Teacher Ruta, even though they are difficult children with problems and you teach nerds like me, a lot of what I do with them I learned from you."

I asked what exactly he did with them. He told me a little. Mainly how he used animals. They had an old donkey there who had fallen on hard times and the kids took care of him, and they had a partly trained crow and a few hedgehogs and turtles, and "Now I'll bring them this puppy," he said, and added: "A Labrador puppy brings out the best in people."

It was nice talking with him. He was more serious and interesting than all the combat soldiers who came out of my class and arrived at school during recess on Fridays to make an impression with their uniforms and insignias and weapons and berets. We talked, and after a few minutes I suggested he come into my house instead of continuing to talk on the street. We sat here in the kitchen where you and I are sitting. I squeezed some lemons and made us fresh lemonade with ice, and I don't remember anymore who touched whom first, but five minutes after we went inside we were kissing; it's always interesting, how a first kiss happens, what led up to it, and immediately after that I was lying on my bed in a dress hiked up to my chest and that was it. Eitan moved his sacks and rocks in the nursery, Dovik did his business in the office, Dalia did her work at the regional council, Neta lay in his grave at the cemetery, Grandpa Ze'ev, the only man I was afraid of, was gathering seeds in his wadi in the Carmel range, I was under Ofer, and Ofer was inside me with his hand on my mouth so no one could hear me crying. But the little puppy wailed freely and, as it turned out, also left a puddle.

That's how it started. I didn't take him to a love nest in Tel Aviv, because I don't have such an apartment, and I didn't pick out and buy him clothes, because I prefer that everyone chooses what they like. And I didn't play him any music or make and serve him pastries and sweets, and I didn't prevent him from leaving or lock him in my home or in my flesh and also didn't throw him out after a month and a half, because I didn't have a ship's captain who was returning. It was he who parted from me in the end. And only when that happened was I thinking that I'd never said to him "I love you," nor he to me. It's like someone once told me, the parents of premature babies don't give them names until they're sure they are out of danger, that they'll live, so you also don't call love by its name until it breathes of its own accord.

What's that look you're giving me, Varda? You're disappointed we split up? You're judgmental that I started up with him? I'm sorry. But this isn't Tel Aviv, that glorious anonymous Gomorrah, full of people who don't know and don't want to know one another. This is an old moshava and an established family and well-known mouths and eyes and names and pointing fingers. And besides, I don't have Alice's class. What can you do. Class like hers is something you drink with mother's

milk, and in my family, we drink blood and poison, wormwood and hemlock. She had what it took, which is why I was glad every time she came
to visit here. On each of those visits I enjoyed looking at her: always in
beautiful, subdued clothes, without makeup, one small piece of jewelry
at most, no splashy colors or extraneous accessories. At first she would
come once a month to visit Dalia and Dovik, then once a week to visit
Dafna and Dorit, who were identical twins until their grandma showed
up, and then you could see that one of them looked like her and the
other not at all.

She always smiled at me affectionately and struck up a conversation, and was of course invited to Eitan's and my wedding. Dalia said,
"I hope that from this wedding she won't take him home." But Alice
behaved perfectly and also brought us a wonderful gift: a large mosquito
netting attached to a carved hardwood frame from India, which her old
friend had brought her from some Far Eastern port. He was also at our
wedding, by the way, with his white hair and red nose but without the
bell from his oil tanker. He didn't know anybody here but smiled at
everyone and walked around and wobbled from an excess of alcohol
and the waves that had accumulated in his body.

Alice didn't come to all family events and get-togethers, but when
she did deign to come, I always enjoyed seeing and talking to her. She
aged well and continued to look good after her English captain died,
ever elegant and thin but with good meat on her, not one of those skinny
emaciated old ladies or the fat flabby type, but a sort of gladiola. But
then, at Eitan's and my wedding, when she congratulated me and said
"Good choice" and air-kissed my cheeks, I unthinkingly put my hand
on her hip, like Eitan would put his hand on my "hippy" and say, "How
good to touch you, my love."

So, absentmindedly, I put my hand on Alice's hip, and maybe absentmindedly on purpose, because I wanted to feel the flesh that my husband liked so much and see if it still had some of that magic. I touched
her, and apparently without thinking I also massaged her gently, and
before I realized what I was doing and feeling, she smiled: "I know that
touch. It's good that a woman resembles her man." And joked: "Watch
out, Ruta, don't you be the guy I take home from this wedding." And
I joked too: "I'm not sure I would object," and I felt so polished and

mature and so much like her, no longer the unwanted youth but the woman who waited inside and now, at last, emerges from the cocoon. You know, with many people, not all but many, there's someone like that inside, but not everyone gets to come out and spread her wings.

And then I saw Dalia staring at us. I'm sure she didn't hear anything, but she hated what she saw. She weighed twenty kilos more than Alice and never stopped getting angry and blaming her for everything. I've never in my life seen a woman so jealous of her mother, of how she takes care of herself, of her self-confidence, of her not giving a fig what anyone else thinks. One day she even said, "She couldn't give me a few of her genes? That bitch that I call Mommy?"

"She did offer them to you," said Dovik, "but you didn't want them. You panicked."

"My mother looks really good," she went on, "well preserved, but it's her evil egotism that preserves her." And she took another careful sip of *limoncello* and added: "She's pickled in hemlock."

Nice expression, "pickled in hemlock," bully for Dalia. It annoyed me that she came up with it and not me. Bad enough that Eitan instead of me said "fortyward" and Ofer "in your humble opinion," but Dalia? How does she even know the word "hemlock"? Annoying. Whatever. A few years ago Alice died and we went, Dalia and Dovik and I, to her funeral. Not that I'm crazy about funerals, as you can understand, but I wanted to see if there'd be any other Ethans there whom she collected at other weddings. Maybe I'll take one as an inheritance. There weren't, and her Ethan and mine wasn't there either. He didn't come, nor had he shown any interest the previous day when I told him she had died.

I remember every detail: I went down to the nursery, stood before him. He stopped, a fifty-kilo sack of gravel resting in his arms like a fat tired child.

I said, "You remember Alice, Dalia's mother?"

He didn't reply. Hugged the sack in silence.

"She died."

He didn't respond. Moved aside, walked right past me.

I followed him. "Alice, who took you home from Dalia and Dovik's wedding."

He said nothing. So much strength built up in those embracing arms, carrying such a load with such ease.

"So she's dead, you hear me?"

He didn't answer.

I said, "Ethan, we're going to her funeral. Why don't you wash up and get dressed and come with us? I think she's entitled to that."

He laid down the sack next to the sacks he had already moved and went back to get another. I looked at him and didn't see the slightest hint of change in his expression. He wore the same look he'd worn since the disaster. Not angry, not worried, definitely not happy, but not sad. A face like a curtain. Not opaque, not transparent. So that was that, he kept serving out his sentence, his hard labor, and I represented him at her funeral. She was entitled. She really was good to him and taught him things that were good for me later on: to cook for me, to serve me, to keep me interested, to make me laugh, to touch me, where and when and how. There are those who will tell you that every woman is different, it takes all kinds, this one with butterfly kisses and the other with vigorous squeezes, that one with "don't stop" and the other with "wait a second" every half minute, and everyone with her own "here" and "there." But overall we're also pretty similar, Varda; let me put it this way: nobody ever had an orgasm from someone stroking her knee.

Did I see right? You smiled? You're even laughing. Very good. Now I have recorded proof that I can still make someone laugh. I myself have no trouble laughing, but only if I'm surprised. For a moment I forget that I'm sad, and then, a second after I laugh, it hurts. Like the joke about the guy in the forest, everyone around him lying there dead, and he's the only one alive but with a knife stuck in his belly. Okay, let's drop it before I start crying from too much laughter.

THIRTY-FIVE

NETA AND THE ANGEL OF DEATH

A Story for Neta Tavori from His Mother After His Death

1

Once there was a boy and his name was Neta.

When Neta was four he started to ask me questions:

"Why is there darkness only at night, and where does it go in the daytime?"

And "What's the difference between 'not a thing' and 'nothing'?"

And "When will I have a little sister already?"

And "Who will look more like her: me or you or Abba?"

And "Why doesn't Grandpa Ze'ev have a wife like Abba has you and Uncle Dovik has Dalia?"

2

I answered all his questions with the greatest of ease.

But I thought a little more about the last question, and I thought a little more, and some more.

And finally I answered: "Grandpa Ze'ev once had a wife. She was called Grandma Ruth."

3

Neta went to Grandpa Ze'ev: "Grandpa?"

"Yes, Neta?"

"Where's your wife called Grandma Ruth?"

"Angelofdeath took her," said Grandpa Ze'ev.

Neta asked, "So now she's his wife?"

"Enough, Neta," said Grandpa Ze'ev. "There are things we shouldn't talk about and you ask too many questions."

4

The next day, on the way to school, Neta asked his father who Angelofdeath was.

"Angelo who?" asked Abba.

"Angelofdeath," said Neta.

"I have no idea," said Abba. "And I don't know that name."

"Grandpa Ze'ev said that Angelofdeath took Grandma Ruth," said Neta.

"Ah . . . ," said Abba, "he meant the Angel of Death. That's the angel who takes people when it's the time for them to die."

Neta was pleased. "An angel? With big white wings? He takes them to fly with him?"

"No," said Abba. "The Angel of Death has no wings, for sure not white ones. He has a great big scythe and a black robe and a big black cowl that hides his face."

"If he has no wings, then how does he fly?"

"He doesn't fly," said Abba. "He appears. Suddenly he appears, and no one sees and no one knows, only the one that he takes."

"I wish he would appear here too," said Neta. "I really want to see his robe and cowl and scythe."

5

"Enough of that talk!" I got angry. "There are things we don't talk about and you ask too many questions."

"So what should we talk about?" asked Neta.

"Soon it will be your birthday," I said. "Maybe tell us what presents you would like?"

"Will you give me what I ask for?" asked Neta.

"If you ask for an elephant, no," said Abba.

"Good," said Neta. "I want a great big scythe, a long black robe, and a big black cowl."

I was not happy with his request, but Abba said, "I promised, and a man has to keep his promises."

He bought black cloth and sewed him a cowl and robe.

And Grandpa Ze'ev took the old rusty scythe from the shed and cleaned it up. And on Saturday we had a birthday party for Neta and gave him the present.

6

Neta put on the robe,
    Covered his head with the cowl,
    Looked in the mirror and said to himself:
    "Wow, the Angel of Death!"
    He took the scythe in his hand,
    And went out into the street,
    And when he saw people
    He began to run and chase them.
    They were all afraid
    They all ran away
    They all shouted:
    "Mommy . . ." and "Angelofdeath . . ."
    "He's going to take us . . ."
    And "We're all going to die!"

7

Neta laid the scythe on the ground, took off the cowl and the robe:

"Sorry, folks,
It was only a joke.
Please relax, dear madam,
And sir, you may breathe free,
I'm not the Angel of Death, I'm only me."

And he went out like that the next day and the day after that.

And the day after that and the next day too.

And on the fifth day the people no longer ran away.

And by the sixth day they were smiling, and on the seventh—

Because the Angel of Death also works on Shabbat—
They all laughed:
"He's not the Angel of Death at all, he's only he."

8

But on Sunday when Neta went out,
Hooded and scythed and totally robed,
Whom did he meet in a robe and a hood?
Absolutely right—
The actual Angel of Death!
"Come here, little boy," he said to Neta, in a whisper.
Because that is the voice of the Angel of Death—
Like the whisper of a snake.
"A little closer, don't be afraid,
Closer . . . closer . . .
Enough, now stop.
And explain—what's going on here?"
"It's just a game," Neta said.
"I'm just playing now,

It's great that you came,
We can play together."

9

"Play together?" whispered the Angel of Death. "You and me? You're dying to play, I can see."

"For sure," said Neta, "we'll play, we'll dress up, it's really fun."

"I don't play games," said the Angel of Death, "not together and not alone."

And he got angry: "And now, because of you, people don't take me seriously."

And he complained: "They think I'm only a boy who masqueraded as me without permission.

"And now excuse me, Neta, I have a lot of work to do."

10

"Hey," said Neta,
     "You know my name?"
     "Of course," said the Angel of Death.
     "I know names,
     And I know dates,
     And I know addresses,
     This address too."
     "How come?" asked Neta.
     "I have been here before and I am a very organized angel.

     So don't do anything else foolish, and till next time, goodbye and see you again."
     And he disappeared,
     As if he were never there,
     And would never be again.

And only the words remained:
"Next time,"
And "been here before,"
And "Neta,"
And "see you again."

THIRTY-SIX
....

THE BIRTH

1

A few days before the birth two women came to the moshava, got down from the wagon that had slowly made its way through the swamps, and continued on foot through the fields.

At first they looked like a large dot and a small dot, and then like two human figures, an adult and a child, to judge from their size, or two adults, to judge from their pace, and finally turned out to be two middle-aged women, one tall and skinny and broad-shouldered and the other small and chubby, and despite their very different clothes, skin tone, walk, and bodies—the bigger one was the mother of the woman giving birth, and the smaller was a Bedouin midwife from Wadi al-Tamasih— they resembled each other: both were jolly and talkative, both had thick hands and eyes spaced widely apart. Clearly the trip and its purpose had drawn the two women close, and they exchanged looks and gestures and burst into shared laughter that an outside observer would find inexplicable and secretive.

Neither of them, as it turned out, was needed. For although this was a first child, the birth went easily and quickly, as if the mother had known that the real suffering would come only later. She didn't even scream. She only moaned from the labor, and sweat poured from her forehead. Perhaps she wanted no one to hear her and realize what was happening. And perhaps she didn't feel pain because she, like her husband, knew the child wasn't his, and she was filled with a deathly fear that suppressed all other feeling.

She didn't think about the sex of the newborn, because she was sure it would be female, or about its health and weight or about becoming a mother but only about him, her husband, and what he would do now.

With a final moan the baby slid into the hands of the midwife, and the new grandmother smiled and said, "Mazal tov, Ruth. You were right, it's a girl. You have to pick a name for her." And Ruth, the mother, said, "I haven't thought about a name yet, Mama," and suddenly whispered, "No, not yet, the name can wait," and called out, "She shouldn't cry yet, Mama, she shouldn't scream! The midwife shouldn't slap her!"

But the midwife's experienced hand had already landed, automatically, on the tiny buttocks, and the baby girl burst into the first cry of a newborn, which nothing can stop or weaken, and a moment after her voice was heard came a mighty blow, and the door was nearly knocked off its hinges from the weight and force of the woman's husband, who broke into the room.

The light of day broke in as well, outlining his dark body in the bright rectangle of the doorway, shining between his sturdy legs. His long shadow quivered on the wall above the bed.

"You don't have to barge in like that," said Ruth's alarmed mother. "In a few minutes we'd have invited you in."

And even as her heart told her it wasn't so, her mouth spoke the words that are always spoken: "Mazal tov, Ze'ev, you have a new daughter."

Ze'ev—that was the name of Ruth's husband—strode forward, and Ruth let out a terrible cry: "Give her to me! Give her to me!" and despite her pain sat on the bed and extended her arms. The midwife, who had already prepared a bowl of hot water and a wet diaper and a dry diaper, intending to clean and wipe and wrap, was frightened and handed her the baby as she was, dripping blood and birth fluids. But Ze'ev strode onward, grabbed the baby's tiny thigh and snatched her away. And the little one, dangling upside down from his hand, fell silent at once, and a moment later burst out crying.

With the baby in his hand, Ze'ev turned and went out into the yard. His mother-in-law, who knew nothing and did not understand what was happening, hurried after him, calling out: "What are you doing? You don't hold a baby that way." She raised her voice to a shout: "The baby has to nurse, give her back to her mother!"

She was big and quick. In three paces she caught up with him and grabbed the edge of his coat, but Ze'ev whirled backward and shoved her to the ground and screamed one terrible scream: "No!"

He went to the shed at the edge of the yard, the shed where for months he had slept alone, and placed the shrieking baby on his bed. He didn't throw or drop her, but set her down softly and gently, the way a father sets down his baby. But he didn't set her down that way out of fatherly love, but so she would not be harmed or injured, for he had designed a different fate for her during the long nights when he lay on that same bed, awake and hateful and planning revenge.

2

The baby shrieked. Ze'ev covered her and opened a tin box he had prepared before the birth, taking out bread and olives, a tomato and hard salty cheese, the long-lasting kind that is soaked in water, and set them on a wooden board.

He also had two jugs filled with drinking water, some pita bread, vegetables, cans of sardines and meat, a jar of tahini, and a bottle of olive oil. All these he had prepared in advance, so he would not have to leave that place, and would have enough to eat.

He picked up his rifle and wooden club, came out of the shed, locked the door, and sat down on a large wooden chest he had put there a few days earlier. No one at the time had understood its significance and no one knew what was inside, but now Ze'ev took out a big embroidered pillow and placed it on the chest, a pillow festooned with embroidered birds and flowers. Colorful and eye-catching, a pillow prepared for long and comfortable sitting.

It was a day in spring. Ze'ev leaned the rifle and the club beside him, placed the wooden board on his lap, sat and ate and drank. The sun warmed his face, the air was aromatic with seasonal blooming, and the baby, inside the shed, shrieked and cried. The wooden walls of the shed did not muffle her voice, because the sound of a shrieking baby, hungry for food and human touch, is a piercing sound that can be heard even from afar.

Ruth's mother, back on her feet, paced around in the yard, helplessly wringing her hands, accosting him again: "What are you doing, Ze'ev? What's going on? These are your baby and your wife, what's going on?" She fell silent for a moment, and then went on: "The baby needs to nurse. She needs her mother . . ." And suddenly she grabbed his hand and pulled it and shouted: "Get up! Open up that shed now! I want to take her to her mother, this is my granddaughter. Do you hear me?!"

Ze'ev took the wooden board from his lap, put it aside, stood up, again threw his mother-in-law to the ground, and sat down on the embroidered pillow.

"That's right! This is your granddaughter!" he shouted. "But she's not my daughter! She's the daughter of another man! The child of adultery! A bastard!"

"She's only a baby, she's not to blame. What did a newborn baby do to you? First let her nurse and eat, and then we'll work out all the problems."

"She's the child of a whore. She will scream and cry here. And you, and your daughter, and the whole moshava, will all know why and wherefore."

He filled his mouth with bread and cheese, took bites of olive and hot pepper, and chewed, and the mother got up, rushed out into the street, ran up and down, and shouted, "Help! Help me! He kidnapped the baby!"

She was answered by Ruth's screaming from inside the house, and several people hurried over and came with her into the yard. But when they saw Ze'ev Tavori sitting in front of the shed with his rifle, they went back to their homes. She again went into the street, ran shouting all the way down and back, and no one came to her aid. Here and there a face could be seen peeking from drawn curtains, here and there a door was shut, a back was turned. She hurried to the neighbor and found him in the cowshed, feeding and stroking a lovely Dutch calf born to a cow he had purchased at a bargain price, so he said, a few months earlier, arousing the envy of the entire moshava.

"Come quick!" she cried, "Ruth gave birth to a girl and Ze'ev took her. He went crazy. He locked her in the shed and won't let her nurse from her mother."

But the neighbor said to her, "Mazal tov. But we don't stick the nose of one family into the affairs of another family."

"I beg of you! He hit me and he is killing his daughter," she shouted. "She has to nurse. This way she'll die."

"Are you so sure it's his daughter?" asked the neighbor.

Her mouth went mute. Her knees buckled. With difficulty she managed to retrace her steps, and Ze'ev grabbed her by the arm, led her to the house, pushed her inside at her daughter, dragged the midwife outside, and banished her in Arabic: "Fly home!" And she fled.

Ze'ev locked the two doors of the house and all the windows and returned to the shed. He sat on the chest, his rifle in his hand and his club beside him, he sat by the door and waited.

3

That crying, which no one imagined would last a full week, was heard by the whole moshava. It heard, and hushed. People thought she would cry for a day or two until Ze'ev came to his senses and returned her to her mother. But the baby cried and cried, day after day, one day and two days and four and five, and the moshava heard and hushed, kept quiet and did not forget.

And also saw: the man sitting on the big chest, the embroidered pillow, the rifle and the club, the locked door. Saw, heard, kept quiet, and did not forget. From inside the shed came the screams of the hungry baby, in desperate need of its mother's milk and arms and warmth, and from the house came the crying and shouting of the young mother. At one point she burst out of the house, ran to her husband to attack him, and hit him, but he stood up and grabbed her by the back of the neck and dragged her to the house, weakened and pained by the birth and the fear and the guilt. No one from the moshava came to help her. She went into the house and sank into a deep sleep.

The baby—she was unnamed—screamed and screamed. The moshava—which had a name and has one to this day—heard and hushed. But the cries of hunger and dying attracted the attention of the jaybirds living there.

These birds, denizens of the nearby woods, had long since discovered the benefits of proximity to humans and, being bold and impudent, began visiting the new moshava, on the lookout for leftover food and fruit to steal, and as the trees planted by people's homes grew taller, the birds built nests in them and raised a new generation. In no time they stopped fearing anyone and behaved like they owned the place: they shrieked, stole, bothered dogs and people, and learned as jaybirds do to imitate human screams, the wailing of cats, barking and whistling, and enjoyed the tumult they wrought.

Now several of them arrived, perched in a nearby tree, listened to the screams of the baby, and after about half an hour began mimicking her voice. First, as if testing their strength, and then with complete accuracy. A few children threw stones at them, but they flitted from tree to tree, dodging every throw, shrieking the shrieks of the baby, so there was no escaping them. It seemed like she was screaming from every rooftop and treetop—and the moshava heard and hushed.

On the third day, when the jaybirds came back and shrieked, Ze'ev shouldered his rifle and picked off two of them with two quick, precise shots. All their comrades flew off in a panic, and when they calmed down and returned he shot two more, and the rest of the jaybirds went away and did not return. From then on, all that could be heard were the screams of the dying baby in the shed, becoming ever weaker. On Shabbat afternoon, five days after the birth, they were replaced by a constant, feeble wailing, and when this too was heard no longer, the people of the moshava gathered near the fence and waited for new developments. Until that moment they had avoided the house and the street, and only one person had been there all along, that same neighbor, owner of the superb Dutch milk cow and the tender calf, who brought Ze'ev pots of hot tea and even pieces of cake, sat beside him like a dog beside his master, and kept watch while he dozed off for a few minutes or answered nature's call.

4

The screams came to an end very slowly, and the moshava gradually fell silent. Ze'ev, his rifle on his lap, sat on his embroidered pillow with his eyes closed, the neighbor by his side, surveying the scene, the people in the street, some of them slowing their pace and some stopping and looking and waiting. A week had gone by, and it was clear to them that the horror would be over at any moment.

The sun came up, shortening the shadow of the house on the wall of the shed, and when its rays struck his eyelids Ze'ev rose, went to the animals' trough, and washed his face. He sat back down, and after half an hour had passed with no sound from the baby, he stood, took out the key, and unlocked the door and opened it. Before he could enter, one big final scream was heard. The jaybirds answered it from the woods in a terrible chorus of infant voices, screams came too from among the crowd, people shifted in place, but no one stepped forward and no one said a word.

For a moment Ze'ev lurched backward as if he had been struck, but then recovered and walked in. After a few minutes he came out, carrying a sack in his right hand and in his left a shovel. He got on his horse and disappeared. After an hour he returned, went into his house while ignoring the crowd, seized Ruth's mother by the arm and removed her from the house.

"Go home," he told her. "And you'd best keep quiet, so they won't know back there too what kind of daughter you raised."

Ruth sat on the bed, didn't budge and didn't speak. After eating, Ze'ev went out to work and that night moved his bed from the shed to the house, set it in the kitchen, lay down, and waited.

For a whole year the two lived in the same house, slept there night after night, and didn't say a word to each other. Twelve months, day after day, Ze'ev rose before Ruth, prepared her breakfast of sliced vegetables, a piece of bread, olives and cheese, a hard-boiled egg, sometimes he even opened a can of sardines, left it on the table, and went to work. And every evening, when he finished his work, he came home, cleaned the kitchen, tidied the house, and once a week washed the floor. And every day Ruth left the house, and wherever someone was plowing or digging or boring a hole, she stopped and looked. Perhaps this was where her husband had buried her daughter.

A year went by, until one night Ze'ev got out of his bed, entered Ruth's room and her bed, took off his nightshirt and hers. She did not move a muscle or say a word. That same night she became pregnant with their elder son, and two years later with another, two boys who grew up and hurried to leave home as soon as they were old enough to do so. One of them was my father, who died young, when I was a little girl.

To those who wonder how I could write such a horrible story, let me say this: If I had made it all up you could ask me that question. If this horrible story had been the product of my imagination, it would have been easier to write it. But this horrible story is a true story; Ze'ev is my grandfather and Ruth my grandmother; that's the answer.

THIRTY-SEVEN

On Neta's fifth birthday we invited children from his kindergarten and their parents, and even managed to persuade Grandpa Ze'ev to wear, one time only, an eye patch on which I had embroidered Mickey Mouse. The present that Neta requested was a long black robe with a cowl that hid his face; that was his specification. I didn't understand how a five-year-old knew the word "cowl," but in any case we didn't get him what he asked for but a toolbox like his father's and grandfather's, with real tools inside. Not children's plastic toys, but actual work tools, as befit the grandson of Grandpa Ze'ev and the son of Eitan: small pliers, small vise, real hammer—also small—and Allen wrenches of various sizes and lots of nuts and bolts. Nothing that could cut or stab, of course, because Eitan said—how ironic and tragic it now sounds—"You have to be careful with kids because anything near them could be dangerous."

I remember how happy Neta was to get this present. For a moment he even forgot the black costume he wanted, and he built and assembled and bolted and connected and dismantled and filled up with joy. I could see how patient and serious he was, and how he trusted the way the world worked. It wasn't trust that derived from innocence but rather from confidence. He had confidence that he got from the two of us, but in every child there's also something completely new, not inherited from his father and mother, and Neta's confidence was quieter and more serious than ours.

I didn't know Eitan as a child—which makes me very curious. And I won't know Neta as a teenager or an adult—which tears me apart. Naturally I imagine him looking like Eitan on the day I first saw him, at Dovik and Dalia's wedding. Not just because of genetics, but because he wanted to be like him, and I'm sure that's a factor. I saw it in the way he walked, and how he smiled, and how he had the family knack for mimicry, and how they played together with the new tool kit.

Neta looked at Eitan, studied him, practiced being like him, in almost every way. I remember: Eitan taught him how to light a fire, which was very important for us in the cave. I don't know if I told you, and if I did, maybe not as categorically, but my first husband was the Prometheus of the Tavori family, the man who brought us fire every morning. I remember: On every winter day the yard would awaken to the sound of his ax, chopping the wood for the stoves that heated our houses— Grandpa's, Dovik and Dalia's, and ours. Dalia would get annoyed by the noise, Dovik said it was the nicest alarm clock, and Grandpa Ze'ev declared: "For a real man, work is also morning exercise." My grandfather, by the way, couldn't stand pure exercise. Such as the bicycle riders who turn up here every Saturday in their ridiculous outfits, or the gym that two women, one local and one from Tel Aviv, set up here: "*Tfoo,* a real man doesn't need that nonsense."

I loved watching Eitan from the bedroom window, his graceful precision, the blade that rose from behind his back in a perfect circle and landed with amazing speed. I would stand in the window half naked with my breasts exposed and he would yell, "Put something on, I can see how chilly you are."

After he split the wood he built a fire in the *poikeh* pit and after about half an hour he had enough coals to bring to all of our stoves. He would appear, balancing the red, whispering pile on a shovel: "Good morning, pretty woman, I have brought you fire. So you will be warm and cozy even when I'm not here."

He put the coals into the stove, and over them a couple of wooden sticks, pinecones, two branches, and a log, shut the iron door, and stood up: "When the fire catches, close the vents halfway."

He brought another shovelful of hot coals to Dovik and Dalia's house, and a third one to Grandpa Ze'ev, who was waiting for him with Turkish coffee, a slice of bread, salty cheese, and Neta, who had sped over there to sit with his father and grandfather and watch the flame that burst from the coals at the first contact with the wood.

"*Nu,* what do you say, Eitan?" asked Grandpa Ze'ev. "It's time to teach Neta how to make a fire too, no?"

"He's still too little," said Eitan, in a tone that said—You're right, but let's have a little fun with him first.

"I'm not too little," said Neta, very serious and a little worried.

"I'll teach you, but not here. We'll do it at the fire pit by the mulberry tree.

"Most important of all," he told him, "everything has to be ready before you light the match." And together they prepared—that damned togetherness of theirs—the paper and slivers of kindling and twigs and thin and medium branches and the thicker logs, organized and ready to be added to the fire in proper order, each at its time and turn.

Best to start with slivers of pine, which catch fire easily, he explained to him, and then some slightly thicker twigs, and pinecones, which also catch easily and burn at a very high temperature, and then the thicker logs. "If we were in the desert now, we'd also put on some branches from a broom bush. One day I'll take you to the desert and show it to you. The broom burns at the highest temperature of all, and afterward we'll come home and you can tell Mommy what we did."

He crumpled newspaper into balls, put a few wood slivers on them and then twigs, and over the twigs a structure of slats taken from old loading pallets.

"You can build it like a little tent, or the way I just did, you see? This is called an altar, and you have to leave spaces for air. Fire needs air. It breathes, like we do."

Neta gazed at his father. With wonder, it's safe to say.

"Touch your skin, Neta, you feel how warm it is? And touch me too, you feel how we're both warm? That's from the fire burning inside us. That's why we breathe. So the fire will have air and not suddenly go out. Don't be afraid. Our fire isn't like a campfire. It's not as hot and also we don't see it. A campfire burns quickly and dies quickly, and we burn slowly and we'll live for many years."

Eyes filled with wonder—serious, trusting, with a trust greater than any other, a boy trusting his father. I remember: "Come, Neta, I'll take you to the top of that hill over there, and you'll take us back here." I write: "Come, Neta, we'll walk up at an angle, and sit where we won't be seen by anyone who shouldn't see us."

"Now we'll light our campfire, but on one condition—you promise me you'll never light a fire by yourself without telling me and asking my permission first. You promise?"

"Yes."

"Not in the house and not in the yard and not anywhere else. Yes?"

"Yes."

Eitan lit the match, touched it to a corner of newspaper. A tongue of flame, a thin curl of smoke, blackening and wrinkling the paper, swirling through the kindling, flaring upward into the thicker twigs.

"It always goes up, you see how it moves? From the skinny ones to the fatter ones."

Neta's eyes, like the eyes of so many children before him, from the prehistoric children in the cave in the wadi down to Neta in our cave, were glued to the little flames. He took a stick and moved one of the burning branches, so its flame would reach the other side of the "altar," and Eitan smiled—another boy snared in the old male trap.

"Pretty soon the whole thing will fall down," he told him. "And if we've built the fire well, it'll fall into a little pile of coals, and then everything will catch and burn without a problem, even oak, and all you need is to feed it some more wood. The fire doesn't stop eating."

"Like Dovik," said Neta, and Eitan laughed.

That particular custom, of bringing us hot coals every morning in winter, continued even after the disaster, but without words. I once went over to Grandpa's place to see if he was silent there too, like with me. Eitan came, with the burning shovel, with his awful whiteness and mute lips, failed to react to my presence, stuck the coals in the stove, and was about to leave.

"You won't light them for me?" asked Grandpa Ze'ev.

Eitan didn't answer, but Grandpa Ze'ev said to me, and Eitan heard him, "He still has the fire inside. The coals under his ashes are still alive. You'll see, Ruta, something will light them. Someone just needs to breathe on them."

He fell quiet. After a moment, he said, "Somebody or something. Something blowing on them."

Eitan said nothing.

"Thank you, Eitan, for the fire," said Grandpa Ze'ev. "Go to the nursery and get to work. I'll come see you later."

He stood up and opened the door and Eitan walked out to serve his sentence: to carry and lift and pile and move and weed and clean. Okay, enough. All that is over, belongs to the past, I don't feel like talking about it anymore. I'll go back to that birthday of Neta's, a nice birthday, and in the evening, when everyone had gone home, we went through all the gifts and I told Eitan I was glad we had bought him the toolbox, not because of the gender thing, boy presents versus girl presents, because at this age it was still possible to combine work and fun and vice versa, and this led to a conversation that went from toolboxes to toy boxes, and from there to ammo boxes and having guns at home and from there to domestic accidents and disasters, and finally I asked Eitan, "Of all the fears and anxieties that parents have over a little boy, what do you most fear could happen to him?"

Eitan said, "Why even think like that?"

I said, "Because it's normal, and surely you have fears like that in your head."

"The usual things," he said, "road accidents, the house burning down, a child molester, I would kill the guy, and disease, playing with guns as we said, some lowlife going wild in a dune buggy on a beach, whom I would also kill, and drowning in the sea, falling from a tree. Did I leave anything out?"

I said, "You forgot to say you would chop down that tree."

He laughed.

"You have no imagination, Eitan," I said. "You only think about external factors that could hurt your son. What about internal things? What's the story with his masquerading as the Angel of Death? Maybe it's something inside of him, something internal that will bring the Angel of Death, send him a sign—I'm here, I'm here—like the homing devices that you and your buddies would attach to a target. I'm very glad we didn't buy him the robe and scythe he asked for."

A little over a year later, when our son died in a way that neither I nor Eitan had imagined, I remembered that conversation. There was no one then to remember it with, but I'd already perfected the ability to talk to myself: Maybe he reached out to the snake, as if tempting it to come? Maybe he compelled him to bite? And I remembered how a few months earlier a snake had turned up in the nursery, and it all came back to me. Somebody saw a viper among the flowerpots, someone else started to scream, "A snake, a snake . . . ," and they immediately called for Eitan, who else would you call. Eitan came, stood over the snake which had already tensed and cocked its head, and told me to bring Neta, because here was a chance to show him how you approach a snake and how you kill it.

I didn't even say no. I didn't say, Why does a little boy need to see an act like this? I brought him. "Come, Neta, Daddy wants to show you something," I told him.

"What?"

"How he's going to kill a very dangerous snake in the nursery."

"Really?"

"Come."

Eitan stood over the snake, Neta slightly behind and to the side, and I saw that he wanted to learn from him, to please him, but he was shaking all over. He was wearing, now I remember, the pants I patched at the knees with one patch like an eye and the other like a heart, which I had no way of knowing I would see someday on a cute little Russian boy on our street with his mother.

I wasn't afraid, because I had seen Eitan killing snakes in the yard. One or two every year. He always said that out in nature there was no need to kill any animal, not even a poisonous snake, but that in the yard and at home it was different. I wasn't afraid, but suddenly I panicked. I said to him, "Maybe that's enough, Eitan? I don't like it that Neta's so close."

And Eitan said, "It's easy to kill this snake. It's poisonous, but fat and slow, not like a black snake, which is very quick and a person can't outrun it. With this snake only the strike is quick, so all you have to do is keep a proper distance."

And he turned to Neta. "So, how far should you stand from a snake, Neta? A distance greater than its length. Pay attention. My arm goes from here to here, the hoe from here to here, together they're longer than the snake is. All you need is two hits, the first one anywhere, you see? Now it can't run away, and the second one in the neck. As close as possible to the head.

"Don't be scared, Neta, snakes still coil up a bit even after they're dead. Here, one more to be on the safe side. And now let's pick it up and I'll show you how the fangs with the poison open and close. Like a pocketknife, you see that? Let's go scare Mommy a little."

After dinner, when the crows had eaten the snake and Neta was asleep, I asked Eitan, "What was that good for, that whole business?"

"What business, Ruta?"

"The business with the snake in the nursery today. What are you teaching him that stuff for? What do you want, that he'll go near the next snake without fear? He's all of five years old."

"He won't go near any snake without me," he said, "not at age five and not at age ten. But at a certain stage, yes. He'll grow up and he'll go near, for sure. And without any fear. You have to dare."

"To dare," I said. "I'm tired of all your macho mantras."

He grinned. "We're men. Not nice to laugh at the handicapped."

"You want to hear something interesting?" I said. "A few months ago I read in the paper about some new research. Most animals that get run over on the road—jackals, foxes, cats—have something in common. Can you guess?"

"That they're dead."

"Bravo, Eitan. Two points. Something more interesting? Perhaps something significant?"

"I don't know, Teacher."

"What they have in common is that almost all the animals that get run over are male."

"Really?" he said. "So I also did some research, and discovered that it's because the animals on the other side of the road are female."

"That's not why. It's because they also think they have to dare. All these darers that their father taught them to dare before he himself was run over from an excess of daring. The females are careful. They always have a child, in their belly or at home or in their heart or mind. So they don't dare."

"That's very interesting research," he said, finally serious.

"A responsible parent," I continued, "a parent who really cares about his child, doesn't teach him to kill snakes or build fires. A responsible parent teaches table manners, Chinese and English, and also arranges him a second passport, a credit card, a flash drive with pictures of the family, and wings to fly like ragwort, as far away as possible."

Eitan brought his face close to mine and I felt the warmth of his skin. "A poisonous snake is a poisonous snake. If it comes to your house like this one did, you're going to talk to it in Chinese? A poisonous snake that comes to your house or gets near your family, you have to kill it. Like you kill a mad dog or weed the grass."

You know, Varda, there are men who every once in a while need to kill something, and sometimes even someone. Otherwise they simply go crazy. It's very simple.

THIRTY-EIGHT

....

THIS IS REVENGE

1

At first a head appeared, peeking cautiously from behind a rock on the ridge. Then a rifle barrel, then the rest of the figure. A young, slender man, armed with an M16 with a telescopic sight, darted down the slope and crouched behind a bush.

A few minutes later he stood and went down to the carob tree. He checked the surroundings and climbed straight toward the mastic tree beside the oak on the opposite slope. Eitan, hiding in the mastic, watched as the man drew closer. His easy step, so unlike the steps of the guy who had come in the morning to look for the cigarette lighter, was the walk of someone who feels at home in the outdoors. The man's choice of the mastic tree was as logical as Eitan's had been. It was clear that he meant to hide behind it and provide cover for whoever would soon arrive at the carob. Eitan sat in the hiding place he had made among the branches, the Mauser in his hand.

The sniper arrived, lay on his belly behind the mastic tree, very close to Eitan, who was motionless inside it. He aimed his rifle at the carob, and as he adjusted his position Eitan said, "Don't move, I'm aiming a rifle at your head."

The man didn't move.

"Nod your head yes, that you understand."

The man nodded.

"Throw the rifle to the side."

The man did as he was told.

"Put your forehead on the ground and your hands behind your back."

He emerged from his hideout and hit the man in the back of the neck with the butt of the Mauser, tied his wrists to his ankles behind his back, and pulled the rope tight. He sealed his mouth with the duct tape, sliced and removed his shirt, wrapped it around his head and eyes, and tied the sleeves around his neck. Then he lifted him up and put him behind the oak tree, and returned to his hiding place.

2

The man in the hat arrived fifteen minutes later. He sat down in the shade of the carob tree, removed his shoulder bag, drank water from a bottle, and looked around, trying to imagine where his adversary would come from and where his helper was hiding. Eitan looked at him for two minutes or so, climbed out of the mastic tree, and approached the man, pointing the Mauser at him.

The man didn't budge, just followed him with his eyes. When Eitan reached the carob, the man said, "Put down the gun. I have a sniper here. You're in his sights."

"We already met," said Eitan. "Your sniper and I."

"Did you bring it?" asked the man.

"What?"

"What you found here."

"What exactly do you mean?"

"A gold lighter."

Eitan took the lighter from his pocket. "Here it is."

"What do you want?" asked the man.

Eitan said, "For the lighter or for your life?"

The man said, "Don't answer me with questions."

"You're in no position to tell me what and what not to do," said Eitan. "Now get up and put up your hands. I have to search you."

The man hesitated for a moment, and rose. Eitan held the rifle in his right hand, one finger on the trigger guard, the others around the butt, with the end of the barrel at the man's throat, and his left hand frisking his body.

"Your pistol is in the bag?"

"What do you want," said the man, "that I go around with a gun in my belt like an idiot?" And added: "This is ridiculous. You don't intend to shoot me. The shot will be heard all over the area."

"This is not Tel Aviv," said Eitan. "I already shot the guy you sent this morning and nobody came to check."

"A second shot will attract more attention. Even here."

"Okay," said Eitan. "You convinced me. We'll do it quietly, with no second shots."

He dropped the rifle, wrapped his outstretched arms around the man, and tightened his grip around his chest. The man responded with greater force and alacrity than his physique had suggested. He pummeled Eitan's back, kicked his legs, tried to head-butt his eyebrows, but Eitan increased the pressure, and the man realized that his grip was more dangerous than a standard wrestling move. He thrashed like a madman. From inside his body, a snapping sound. Two of his ribs, now broken. Eitan too felt the same snap and loosened his grip a little.

"You see," he said, "all quiet. No shooting. No one hears a thing, and if someone sees us from afar, he will think I love you very much."

The man inhaled a chestful of air. His broken ribs pierced his lungs and he wanted to scream, but Eitan grabbed him again, this time with his full strength.

"I'm letting you have a little air," he said, "so you can hear a few important things before you die."

The man's face reddened and his eyes bulged. He understood what was coming and was gripped by a deathly fear. Not a fear of losing blood or a fear of thirst and hunger, but the primal fear of strangulation.

"This is revenge," Eitan told him, his mouth against the man's ear. "I am killing you because of the old man you killed here yesterday."

Again he loosened the pressure. The man, twisted in agony, took a gulp of air and groaned. "Let's talk. Tell me what you want."

His red face had by now turned purple and his eyes popped some more, for Eitan's arms had again tightened around him.

"I want you to die with the knowledge that you deserve it, to die with the knowledge that you're an idiot."

He again relaxed his arms a bit and the man moaned. "He fell and broke his head."

Eitan tightened his grip again. "This is revenge," he repeated. His chin pressed the man's throat, and his lips whispered in his ear, "You come here, scum like you, and think you know everything. But this place has its own logic and laws. A different kind of people live here and every stone has its side of darkness and side of light. And if idiots like you lay a stone upside down, the police might not notice, but we notice it right away."

And tightened some more. With the full power that twelve years of hard labor had implanted in him.

The man tried to beg, to scream, but he couldn't breathe again or produce a sound in his throat. His face went almost black, blood dripped from his nose. His brain wondered one last thing: How had a man acquired so much loyalty and strength?

His lungs emptied of air. His hands were too weak to hit back. Urine drenched his trousers and his legs fluttered and twisted and then went limp and still. Eitan kept squeezing for a minute more, and carried him that way, pressed to his chest with his legs in the air, to the cave in the wadi. When he unlocked his arms the corpse plummeted into the pit, straight onto the dead goat that was flung there the day before.

He returned to the carob tree, took the man's hat and shoulder bag, went back to the cave, and climbed down into the pit. There he smashed his cell phone, scattered the fragments on the dead man, placed his hat and bag on his chest, and took his wallet. He covered him with stones, pulled out the goat and laid it on top, climbed the carob for an additional scan of the area, and then went up to the mastic tree on the slope.

The sniper jerked and twitched, trying to work free of the ropes and the shirt that covered his head.

Eitan told him, "Calm down. You're better off not seeing me. It would not be good for you." He leaned over and tapped his shoulder. "Your boss is dead. I'm counting on you to get to the road somehow, and on the way you can think of a good story to tell whoever finds you."

He went through the man's pockets, took his key ring, and removed the bolt assembly from the M16. Then he gathered his tools, checking off item after item on his written list. He removed the pieces of green duct tape from the branches and put them in his pack, wrapped the Mauser in the blanket and tied it, shouldered it, and headed for the pickup truck.

It stood where he had left it the night before, by the oak trees. He took off the tarp and put it in the rear, backed up the truck onto the dirt road, took the rake, erased tracks and footprints he couldn't see in last night's darkness, got behind the wheel, removed the sheepskins from his shoes, and drove across the main road, toward a garbage dump.

There he stopped, picked up a rag from the ground, and wiped the bolt assembly of the M16. He flung it and the keys into the distance, tossed the wallet and tarp and pieces of tape and sheepskin shoes onto a burning pile of trash, and carefully added a little diesel fuel from a reserve jerrican in the pickup. There were bloodstains on his shirt, and he stripped it off and burned it too. He put on a T-shirt he had in the pickup and drove off.

He went from the other side of the dump onto a road that led to the banana and avocado plantations of a nearby kibbutz. He drove slowly, not to attract attention or raise dust. He suddenly felt himself whistling. With difficulty at first, as he had not puckered his lips like that in twelve years, not for whistling or kissing or pronouncing certain syllables, but after a few minutes his whistling became more even and melodic. He drove along the fence of the plantations, then a few kilometers through the fields, and then got back on a paved road and accelerated.

He broke out in a smile. The third smile in the past twenty-four hours. Slightly distorted, the smile of lips that had forgotten this task too, but nevertheless a smile. He had done what he had to do. Maybe now it would be a little better.

The twelve years have passed and come to an end, and another day awaits him, the day of the burial of Grandpa Ze'ev. A day when he will say goodbye to his old and good friend whose blood he has just avenged. A day when for the first time he will enter the cemetery of the moshava and see the gravestone of his son.

THIRTY-NINE

....

THE SHED

1

One evening, a few months later, Dovik and Dalia and Eitan and I were sitting, eating Dalia's salad and Eitan's fried eggs and olives that Grandpa Ze'ev had pickled and bequeathed us—and Dalia, of all people, suddenly said, "Maybe now that he's dead, and it's clear he won't come back, maybe now we can finally tear down that old shed of his that's such an eyesore in the yard?"

"You're right," I said to her, for the first time, I think, since I'd known her. And I said to Dovik too: "Your wife is right. It should have been torn down a long time ago."

"Why tear it down?" asked Dovik, who had prematurely become as stingy as a stuffy old farmer and begun to resemble people whom he ridiculed in his youth. "What's wrong with it?"

"Everything's wrong with it," I said, "it's moldy and damp, has no floor, water leaks into it, and memories leak out of it. We should throw out everything in it. Tear it down, pour a concrete floor instead of the wooden one that disintegrated, and put up a new shed. Today there are plastic ones, which do the job and also look very good."

"How symbolic," said Dalia. And for the second time since we met I told her she was right.

"You finally found symbolism where it actually exists."

"I meant, how symbolic to go from a wooden shed to a plastic shed," said Dalia.

"Of course," I said, "I apologize for briefly suspecting you of a different symbolism."

"But why throw out what's in there?" insisted Dovik.

"I give you permission to inspect it and take what you want before we throw things out."

"Okay," said Dovik. "I'll bring a worker from Chinatown."

"Chinatown" is what people here call a small building at the periphery of the apartment blocks in the moshava. About a dozen Chinese workers live there, raising ducks and growing vegetables in the yard, and apart from their regular construction work, they hire themselves out to whoever needs them for whatever job. All-seeing but invisible, they go about in our streets, and though they've learned a few words of Hebrew, they talk to no one. But the owner of our mini-market spotted them wandering among the shelves of his store and began stocking the noodles they needed and various black and red sauces and strange canned goods and cheap strong beer. It was he who helped them find daywork, and whoever needs a worker asks him.

"Chinese or not Chinese, a worker is not a good idea," said Dalia. "Someone has to supervise him. Who knows what your amazing Grandpa hid there—documents, hand grenades, gold coins."

"All right," said Eitan, "I'll supervise him."

He phoned a friend who owned a building-supply business—another synapse in their network—and ordered iron webbing and wire, sacks of cement, limestone, sand, and gravel.

The next day he got up early and put a pot on the fire, and Dovik drove to Chinatown and brought back a short, thin worker with the hands of a much-bigger man, and together they emptied the shed of its contents: old paint cans, rags, rusty iron bars, and wires.

On the same day I began teaching at eleven, and instead of grading papers and exams I found myself in the yard, observing the clearing out and demolition from up close. Eitan poked around and found a folding shovel, apparently from the British army, which they resurrected with rust remover and steel wool. And Dovik found and took a hammer and a big wooden chest that to his great disappointment did not contain either hand grenades or gold coins but only a very dusty pillow. He beat it against a tree and a suffocating cloud arose. The pillow blossomed with embroidery: all kinds of flowers and birds, buttons and buds.

"You want this pillow, Ruta?"

"I really don't. Thanks."

"That's it," said Eitan, "there's nothing else here. He can work without supervision."

Tearing down the shed was very easy. From the moment the worker ripped out the doorposts, its pieces no longer supported one another and crumbled with a few light blows and kicks. It seemed like the shed was happy to come apart, disgusted by what it contained and what had happened within it.

I went into the house to get ready to leave for school. When I looked out the window I saw that Eitan was using stakes and string to mark the perimeter of the hole that would be dug and the cement floor that would be poured for the new shed. After he was done he gave the worker a hoe and shovel and a wooden board about twenty centimeters wide to mark the depth of the digging. Honking its horn, a fancy car entered the yard, towing a large load. The building-supply friend brought everything Eitan had ordered and included a soil compactor and a small cement mixer.

He got out of his car, sniffed the air, sat down under the mulberry tree, and waited for the *poikeh* to be uncovered. Dovik and Eitan joined him, sat with him by the fire. I watched them through the window—who am I and what's my name? Jezebel? Michal? Sisera's mother?—and I saw my man, my first husband, talking and smiling, his hands gesticulating, moving coals and logs in the firepit.

He showed his friend the old military shovel that he found, and the three of them, happy as puppies, opened and closed its blade and took turns sticking it in the ground. After they ate they unloaded the machinery from the trailer; the friend explained a few things about their use and drove off.

2

Dovik and Eitan went about their business in the nursery, the Chinese worker kept on working, and I, instead of hurrying to school, kept on watching him. He had the crisp, efficient movements of an experienced laborer, pleasing to the eye, but I sensed that I was staring at the shovel, sticking into the soft ground, collecting and tossing clumps of earth.

The worker finished digging and removing the dirt and began to smooth the bottom of the hole with the hoe to prepare for laying the foundation. I remember: The phone suddenly rang, presumably the school secretary, but I didn't answer. I looked at the blade of the hoe, smoothing and leveling the bottom of the hole, and I suddenly heard a strange sound: a cry from the top of the mulberry tree, the cry of a baby.

The worker stood up, looked curiously at the treetop, then turned and looked at the ficus in the street, for a similar cry had come from there too, and then another from the neighbor's pecan tree. He didn't know, of course, that he was seeing and hearing the first jaybirds to return to the moshava after many years of exile. And it's doubtful that he knew that they were jaybirds, because the jays in China are very different from here. A few days later I looked it up and found that their tails are long and their bodies are black and white and the Chinese call them "the happy bird," whereas our jaybirds have a crest and a blue spot on the wing and are not happy but quarrelsome and insolent. But both of them, the jays of China and the jays of Israel, are good mimics, and the crying of babies is similar in both countries.

The worker shrugged his shoulders, took hold of the hoe, and continued his work, but then came more shrieks and cries from the jaybirds, who by now filled all the trees on the street, each one producing the piercing, soul-searing sounds that only the throat of a baby can make.

I opened the window and leaned outside. Now the jaybirds were visible, flying from tree to tree and filling the air with blue flashes and shrieks. The worker looked at them again with trepidation and curiosity, and went back to his work. The blade of the hoe slid along the bottom of the hole, and more shrieks were heard; he raked a thin layer of dirt, and more jaybirds arrived, congregating from faraway orchards, from the oak forest, from the hills and wadis, perching in the trees of our pretty, quiet street and joining the choir.

Dovik shouted from the nursery, "Ruta, what's going on? What do those goddamn birds want?" But I paid no attention to them or to him but rather to the workman, who suddenly dropped his hoe, knelt on the ground, got on all fours in the hole he had dug, and inspected something closely.

He turned and looked at me, standing in the window looking at him. I hurried outside, bent over, and saw that he was examining something, like a piece of a tiny dome, that stuck out of the ground.

I knelt down and had a closer look. The jaybirds shrieked like madmen; my body understood and froze even before my mind caught on.

"What's going on there?" Dovik shouted again. "Why doesn't Eitan shoot them?"

The workman scraped with his strong fingers, brushed away and gently blew off the dirt. The piece he discovered seemed to be a fragment of pottery, maybe a bowl, but when he dug deeper, two big round holes appeared, which looked at me and at him.

"Stop! Stop!" I shouted in English. But the workman kept digging carefully until the tiny skull was completely exposed. He picked it up. The eyeholes gazed at him with a penetrating human gaze, and when he put it down it rolled over and the holes disappeared and reappeared like the eyes of a doll that open and close. Here I am, the dead baby girl of Nahum Natan and Grandma Ruth. Here you are, the baby girl that her mother searched for everywhere else—in ditches and furrows, foundation pits and planting holes—but not in the shed where she was killed, on our land, near us.

"Dovik!" I screamed. "Dovik!"

"What happened?" he shouted from the nursery office.

"Come here! Quick!"

The workman, quiet and focused, kept at it. He scraped and burrowed and exposed a few more small, delicate bones. Were it not for the skull and the story, one might have mistaken them for the bones of a bird. He spread out a sack on the ground and arranged them one by one, and since the mind always looks for patterns, and wants and

seeks and finds meaning, the pieces turned into a little arm and hip
and chest and tiny hands. A jaw whose teeth had not yet grown joined
the skull and the eyes and together became a face. Here you are. The
dead baby girl of Nahum Natan and Grandma Ruth. Is this what Neta
looks like too, after twelve and a half years in the ground?

Dovik came, looked, understood at once. "He buried her inside the
shed, then went out and got on the horse with a sack and the shovel we
found here." That's what he said, with quiet logic, and then raised his
voice a bit: "He put on a show for everyone, as if he were going to bury
her someplace else."

And suddenly he began stamping his feet and screaming horrible
screams: "What you did wasn't enough for you? You also wanted to
see Grandma searching for her all her life? Searching and not finding,
searching without knowing she was here in the shed, right by us, two
meters away from her mother!"

Dovik simply fell apart. He either knelt down or fell, crouched on all
fours over the remains of the skeleton, shouted more than Eitan had at
Neta's funeral, cried like I didn't dare cry then: "How could you raise
us, you piece of shit, in this house? How could we all walk on this land,
with Grandma's baby under our feet?"

He kicked the wheelbarrow and knocked it over. "Look at these
seeds and plants and flowers of his! Look at what he really sowed and
planted here!"

I never saw him in such a state. For a moment I was glad Grandpa
was dead, because if he were alive Dovik would have attacked and
beaten him.

People gathered near the fence. They did not see the bones, but they
did hear the screams. The Tavori family, as usual, raised a ruckus, and
the moshava, as usual, heard and hushed.

"Get out of here!" shouted Dovik. Spittle sprayed from his mouth.
He leaned over, looking for a stone, a piece of wood, something to throw
at them. "Get out of here, this isn't a theater!"

The confused workman moved aside, and I bent over and snatched
the tiny figure he'd arranged on the sack, to turn it back from a week-old
baby into a small random pile of unidentified pieces. Eitan, for his part,
said nothing. He bent over beside me, gathered them up, and put them

in a small cardboard box, set it aside, and immediately started up the compactor and noisily packed the dirt, grabbed the hoe, quickly spread and smoothed the pulverized limestone, and packed it down too.

He was fast and efficient, the way only my first husband could be. Compacted the dirt. Spread nylon sheets. Laid down some stones and over them the webbing. Switched on the mixer, put in cement, added water from the hose, and when it was ready began pouring the concrete.

"Faster!" he ordered the workman. "Faster!" And the man took the hoe and spread and smoothed the concrete with long broad strokes.

Only a few minutes had passed and a new floor was in place that would soon harden and dry, a new floor of a new shed, where no one would be able to starve or bury or find another baby. The workman smoothed the concrete with a few more strokes of the hoe and finished it with another tool, whose name I don't know, a kind of wooden plank with a handle.

"That's it," said Eitan. "Now we just have to wait." And he paid the workman his wages and sent him home.

3

The sun went down, and a few hours later, when total darkness had fallen, Eitan and Dovik and I took the little cardboard box and a plastic bag containing four large bulbs of white squill and walked to the cemetery. Dalia didn't come along. She said, "I'm not ready to be part of this thing," adding: "Just be happy I'm not going to the police, which should have been done in this family a long time ago."

We were unafraid. The Tavori family is not afraid of phenomena like Dovik's Dalia. Dovik, who by now had calmed down, smiled as he told her, "We overcame him, we'll overcome you too."

We arrived at the cemetery. Eitan dug a narrow trench in the small space between the graves of Neta and Grandma Ruth, to bury the bones there.

He dug quietly, with his small pickax and the shovel he found in the shed before it was destroyed, and when he got to a depth of about sixty centimeters he set down the box, added a layer of earth, then two of the squill bulbs, and covered them. On the other side of Neta's grave he planted the other two bulbs, all of them sprouting the first green leaves of autumn—in case someone might see signs of digging and wonder why.

Dovik watered them and we went home. When we arrived Eitan said he had to check on the new floor, to see if it had started to harden. He looked and touched and said that if anyone wanted to leave their handprint, this was the last chance. Dovik called Dalia, and that's what we did: Dovik set down his hand, Dalia hurried over, imprinted her hand so their pinkies were touching, then Eitan and I, our hands identical and close.

"Nice floor, Eitan," I said. "You just poured it, and I already forgot that terrible shed that stood here."

"It's for you," he said. "To please you."

"You have."

"I'll give it a little water," said Dovik, now completely calm, "so the concrete won't crack."

"No need," said Eitan. "I just felt a raindrop on my head."

"So did I," I said.

A raindrop, and then another, and all of a sudden the clouds opened and the first rain of the season came down on schedule. Pounding rain, as ever at our moshava.

The windows of heaven opened—like in the Bible—fat drops struck, lightning slashed the darkness, distant thunder rumbled and roared, the skies became a cage filled with animals.

Dovik and Dalia fled home; Eitan and I went to our house. We stood together in the window and looked outside. Eitan put his hand on my hippy, rested his head on my shoulder. The rain grew stronger, arousing memories and seeds, digging new channels, destroying evidence.

Eitan said, "It's funny, Ruta. Somebody had to come all the way from China to find that poor baby."

I said, "It's not funny, but it's very true."

4

That winter was a very rainy winter. Thunders thundered, lightning streaked, chilly winds blew. The wagtail heralded the rain, the redbreast danced between the drops.

Rain fell in sheets and formed little ponds, hail pummeled the roofs. It was a winter that earned the name "that winter."

And when that winter ended and we went on our first spring hike without Grandpa Ze'ev to his wadi, we were greeted by a surprise he would have appreciated: under the carob tree, in a spot where nothing had ever grown, a little family had flowered, a riot of poppies and lupines and blue thistles, and little leaves of buttercups and cyclamens.

Dalia said, "How symbolic, this is his true gravestone."

"One more line like that, Dalia," I told her, "and I'll bash your head with a rock."

Dovik laughed and Dalia said, "So how do you explain that in the very place he died the flowers he loved are now blooming? What is that, if not symbolism?"

Dovik said, "It's because he fell here, and when he fell so did the seeds he gathered, and that's how they planted themselves here."

"I love it, Dovik, how you explain things to me," said Dalia, and took his hand.

FORTY

THE SUMMER THAT CAME
AFTER THAT WINTER

(Draft)

I write:

That summer was very hot. Burning winds blew. Days dragged on, months dried out, like an empty reservoir.

Cicadas and jaybirds sang along, one by one and in noisy bands: came when summer came, stayed when it stayed, went when it went. That summer ended slowly.

Only a few words were spoken. Not about the time that had passed, not about that snake, not about what I imagined that Eitan did in the wadi, near the big carob tree. Words that could make things better, not to explain and cover up.

I tell:

In that summer my first husband came back to me. Returned as a baby born of itself. Born, and grew, and as with babies, every day another good thing: a first smile, first word, already sitting, standing, walking, talking. Lighting a fire. Trying to be funny. Smiling. Did he remember all these? Did he invent them from scratch? Whatever. He is with me, here.

I see:

He lost weight, soon he'll be back to his old shape. One day I took him to Dovik's pond, not so secret anymore. We got undressed in front of each other. From a certain angle of the eye and the sun I saw his skin was getting golden. This is good. When we got back we went together to the cemetery.

I sleep:
    With him.
    Only him.

I talk:
    With my brother. His name is Dovik. Named for Uncle Dov, who in his wagon brought us a rifle and a cow and a black rock, and the mulberry tree and Grandma Ruth.

    "Nothing has changed in this family," I said to him. "We were and still are like the basalt in the wall of Grandpa Ze'ev's house. He and Eitan and you, and I'm that way too. But we won't take it out the way we demolished the shed because if we take it out the whole house will crumble."

    Dovik didn't answer. He stuck a spoon in the stewpot where he mixed his *limoncello,* tasted it, and offered it to me for a taste and an opinion.

    I shook my head no.

    "But what do I care?" I went on. "The main thing is that Eitan is back. Back home to me. At least him, if not our son."

    Dovik didn't answer.

    "And what's funny in this whole unfunny story," I said, "is that he wasn't saved by my love or healed by my patience, but by virtue of Grandpa Ze'ev. By virtue of the work he made him do, by virtue of his last will—to avenge his blood."

    Dovik didn't answer. Like Grandpa Ze'ev, he also doesn't like it when people talk too much about certain acts and certain times. I shut up. I remembered: I'm also that way.

One of Israel's most celebrated novelists, Meir Shalev was born in 1948 on Nahalal, Israel's first moshav. His books have been translated into more than twenty-five languages and have been best sellers in Israel, Holland, and Germany. His honors include the National Jewish Book Award and the Brenner Prize, one of Israel's top literary awards, for *A Pigeon and a Boy*. He has been named a Chevalier de l'Ordre des Art et des Lettres by the French government. Shalev lives in Jerusalem and in the north of Israel.

About the Translator

Stuart Schoffman worked as a journalist at *Time* and a screen-writer in Hollywood before moving to Israel in 1988. He has written about Jewish and Israeli culture and politics for many publications including the *Jerusalem Report* and the *Jewish Review of Books*. His translations from Hebrew include *Beginnings* by Meir Shalev, *Lion's Honey* by David Grossman, and three novels by A. B. Yehoshua: *Friendly Fire, The Retrospective,* and *The Extra.*

A Note on the Type

This book was set in a typeface named Bulmer. This distinguished letter is a replica of a type long famous in the history of English printing that was designed and cut by William Martin in about 1790 for William Bulmer of the Shakespeare Press. In design, it is all but a modern face, with vertical stress, sharp differentiation between the thick and thin strokes, and nearly flat serifs. The decorative italic shows the influence of Baskerville, as Martin was a pupil of John Baskerville's.

Typeset by Scribe, Philadelphia, Pennsylvania

Printed and bound by Berryville Graphics,
Berryville, Virginia

Designed by Betty Lew